About the Author

Stuart Campbell has been practicing and teaching martial arts for over 40 years, the last 29, under Grandmaster Masaaki Hatsumi, head of the Bujinkan Dojo, Noda, Japan. He holds a teachers license in the Bujinkan and has trained under Hatsumi and various high-ranking Shihan in his home country of New Zealand and abroad, including the birth place of *Ninjutsu*, Japan. During his many years of training, Stuart has gained valuable insights into Martial Arts and in particular, the shrouded arts and history of Japan's legendary shadow warriors.

This is his second novel in which he endeavours to give the reader a glimpse into the true nature and philosophy of these arts and how they were used to shape Japanese history, ultimately for the better.

Yamakiri
Warrior of the mist

Printed in New Zealand

First Printing, 2014

ISBN 978-0-473-29249-2

Books by S.J. Campbell

Black Dove Series
Black Dove
Yamakiri-Warrior of the Mist
Sleeping Giants

Authors Notes

This novel is based on factual events and places that took place in Japan in the 14th Century. Accounts of this period and historical information are hard to verify as a lot of the historical documents were destroyed by various leaders.

The motivation and actions behind the various factions vying for power are at best sketchy and in the small number of historical texts such as the *Taihekei*, definitely biased by circumspect and romanticism. However, what is known from this period, are the outcomes and subsequent flow on effects of various individuals and their desires.

Searching historical records in the course of my own martial arts studies, there is as little account around this as the *Samurai's*, but it is well known that the *Ninja* and the *Sohei* were very active in this period and in these specific regions.

Therefore it would be fair to conclude that their unique skills and methods would have been in high demand against the highly skilled *Samurai*. Furthermore, the information provided by my teacher Masaaki Hatsumi and historians within the Bujinkan, attest to the evolvement of such skills to meet the needs of these warriors.

Speculative at best, it does provide some context around this period and the use of these arts to assist in maintaining some semblance of order. Go-Daigo, Takauji Ashikaga, Masashige Kusunoki and Ryushin Yakushimaru were real figures who not only existed in this period, but they were also well noted as key figures in history and the shaping of Japan.

Dedication

This book is dedicated to my late parents,
my loving family and my infinitely inspiring teacher - Masaaki
Hatsumi.

And to my students and teachers, past and present, who continue
to inspire, question and motivate my search for enlightenment
through the warrior way.

Also I give thanks to the following people who helped bring this
story to life;
<u>Editors</u>
Tahnee Campbell
Phil Burkett
Eugene de Bruyn

And the on-going encouragement of my family and the Taumarunui
Writers group.

Foreword

Feudal Japan – September 1335. As part of the *Kenmu* restoration emperor Go-Daigo, with the help of loyal *Samurai* Masashige Kusunoki had successfully liberated the country from the stranglehold of the Minamoto Shoguns; restoring relative peace to the provinces and replacing the oppressive regime with a more democratic and fair system of governance.

Go-Daigo had based himself in the capitol of Japan, Kyoto, from there he was able to maintain stability, thereby ensuring the support of the common people, who had assisted him in the uprising some years earlier.

However, the tide was once again turning and some of the rulers of the ousted *Shogunate* were not going to accept his governance or be subservient to him. One powerful *Samurai* was Takauji Ashikaga; who after being sent to topple Go-Daigo by the previous *Shogun* in the earlier *Genki* rebellion ended up siding with him and serving his cause.

But soon after, the ousted *Samurai* clans became disillusioned with the re-established imperial court and tried to rise up; led by *Hojo* Tokiyuki in what was to be later known as the *Nakasendai* rebellion. This was an attempt to re-establish the *Shogunate* in Kamakura. However, Takauji, who on the orders of his new master Go-Daigo quashed the uprising, quickly turned this around and instead of remaining loyal to Go-Daigo, he took Kamakura for himself and attempted to secure support of the disaffected *Samurai*, by allocating land to them.

This period in history saw families and friends pitted against one another, as each side jostled for control. Even the temples and mainstream religions were not immune to attack; especially as they were often used as safe havens in times of such upheaval.

This required the once peaceful monks to train in the martial arts, to provide a defensive barrier to any would be attacker. This meant seeking out teachers with these skills to train them.

So when one such person arrived at Enryaku-Ji temple, atop Mt. Hiei in Shiga province, he was coerced into training the *Sohei* – its warrior monks, in such skills. Although reluctant to support any type of action that would see more blood spilled, he was offered training in return in *Shugendo*, the way of the *Yamabushi*. This he believed would free him from his inner demons and help him to find the inner peace that he so disparately longed for.

Prologue

The young girl merrily danced before her parents, as she skipped and twirled they clapped and laughed loudly, her elaborate silk *Kimono* gracefully tracing her movements in the air. The sound of melodic music played by a group of skilled musicians provided the up-tempo rhythm in the background. The girl danced over to the young man on the other side of the courtyard and held out her tiny hands, urging him to join her in the dance. He reluctantly responded, holding on to her and following her lead. They spun around together, going faster and faster, the girl laughing so loud it nearly drowned out the music in the background. She looked into his eyes, the sparkle a reflection of her innocence and lust for life. Her smile lit up her face, accentuating her light brown eyes, enveloping him in a swathe of pure love.

Suddenly everything stopped, first the music then the dancing and in that moment the energy changed completely. The sky turned dark, as her eyes filled with fear. The smile on her face changed and as her mouth opened; deep red blood ran out of the corner of it, rolling down her chin, staining her *Kimono*. She gasped in the several times as her body tried to hold on to life, as if drowning in the very life force she embodied and exuded so lavishly. Then her body went limp and the young man shook her to try to revive her. Spotting the arrow embedded in her back, he realised it was fruitless. The little girl's face was pale, her previously sparkling eyes glassy. She was dead.

He woke in a cold sweat, the image of the dying girl fresh in his mind. Every night he had the same nightmare, haunted by his past and a fatal mistake, which had caused the death of the little girl. He had been taught that in war, there will always be casualties. But as far as Yamakiri was concerned, nothing justified the death of this innocent soul; what's more, he believed his training should have prevented such a tragedy, but of course, what had happened could not be undone.

His life seemed to be a continual battle with the inner demons that haunted him. His only respite; a hard and relentless training regime that in some way attempted to prepare him for any such occurrence, should it happen again. But this wasn't enough; he knew he needed to confront his past and to face the truth, before he could move on. Reluctantly he set out on a *Musha Shugyo*– a warrior quest, ironically to find the inner peace that he so desperately desired. This journey would take him far beyond his expectations and into a world that he could not escape from.

Chapter 1

A solitary figure made his way down the narrow mountain track
and into the clearing above the small village of Aoyama. He was
dressed as a *Yamabushi* priest– a mountain ascetic. Not
uncommon in the area, as there were many secluded temples
high in the mountains. He was wearing the traditional
ceremonial costume including a blue silk overcoat, wide *Hakama*
pants and a *Tengai* woven hat, which covered his head and face.
He was carrying a *Shakujo* staff, with a brass fitting on the top
and six brass rings that rang out as they bounced against each
other when he walked.

As he neared the village he saw a small boy playing in the dirt by
the large *Tori* gate, signifying the entrance to the village. The boy
would have been no more than three years old and was wearing
an oversized jacket to protect himself from the cold morning air.
As the *Yamabushi* approached, the boy looked up and smiled.

"Good morning young man," the *Yamabushi* said to him.

The boy didn't respond, instead he looked him up and down,
seemingly fascinated by the priest's strange attire.

The boy had built what seemed to be a fortress out of sticks and
small stones.

"What are you doing?" the priest asked, hoping this time to get a
response.

"I am playing samrai," he said matter-of-factly, mispronouncing
the name of the notable warriors.

"Really?" the priest responded, showing an interest in his activity.

"Yes", the boy responded, moving a small stick that represented
one of his *Samurai* warriors.

"Do you like the *Samurai?*" the priest asked.

"Well, some are good and some are bad," he responded, surprising the priest with his mature answer.

The priest was just about to ask him another question when a female voice sang out from the village.

"Kansai! Kansai!" she called making her way towards the two of them. Hearing that name shook Yamakiri to the core of his being. Unsure what to expect next, he braced himself. As the young woman came closer, he recognised a familiar face, it was someone he once knew from his past. Her features were fine and delicate, her beauty radiated from her as if she had the sun at her back.

"Kansai is that where you got to, what are you doing?"

Yamakiri was about to respond, when the little boy spoke.

"Playing, Mother and talking to this funny looking man," he responded, smiling and looking up at the *Yamabushi*.

"You need to go inside now and get ready for your lessons," his mother instructed.

"Yes mother," the boy said, standing up and running back to his house inside the village.

She moved her attention to the *Yamabushi*, looking him in the eyes.

"Good morning," she said.

"Good morning," Yamakiri responded, surprised that she hadn't recognised him.

"I am Mariko Yamada, and your name is?" she asked.

The past came flooding back to him; not only was the environment familiar, but the names were as well.

"Yamakiri," the priest responded.

"That is a very interesting name," she said, aware that it was not uncommon for priests to adopt a pseudonym as part of their faith.

"It means 'Mountain Mist' doesn't it?" she asked, looking up the track towards the trees and mountains and the thick covering of low cloud covered the higher peaks.

"Yes, that is right," he responded.

"Would you like some water?" Mariko asked, aware that he would have travelled a long distance.

"Yes, I would be very grateful, thank you," he responded.

"Please come with me?" she asked him, attempting to lead him inside the village.

He turned and as he looked at the village, he froze. It was as if some invisible force was stopping him from entering.

"Ah, I will wait here, if you don't mind," he said, untying his water flask and handing it to her.

"As you wish," she said, taking the flask and walking back to her house.

Yamakiri scanned the area, it was familiar, but in some ways quite foreign to him. As he looked down the road and, he saw a small fenced cemetery next to the village.

In no time Mariko returned and handed him back his now full flask.

"Is there anything else I can get you?" she asked.

"No thank you, but I am very grateful for the water. However, I would like to pay my respects to your ancestors if that is acceptable?" he responded, hesitant to stay any longer than necessary.

"Yes, of course," Mariko replied.

Yamakiri bowed and moved off in the direction of the cemetery. He opened the low gate and began looking among the headstones. It was customary to pay your respects to the dead when passing through an area, especially if accepting any offerings. This was a way of acknowledging that the offerings are only possible because of the sacrifices made by the ancestors.

As he looked along the row of *GoRin-to*-traditional headstones representing the elements, the first one had the name Saito Yamada; immediately he knelt down and bowed his head. Behind him Mariko arrived with some fresh flowers and waited patiently to gain his attention. Turning around she offered him a bunch to place on the graves. Yamakiri took the flowers and placed one on the head stone, bringing his hands together and making a prayer.

"He was my husband's father and a very brave warrior," Mariko said, referring to the man buried there.

Yamakiri smiled, but purposely said nothing; he stood up and moved on to the next headstone. The name on this read, 'Yumi Tokugawa'. He sank to his knees as his legs buckled at the sight of the name. All the time he was trying not to let on that he knew anyone here; he had a good reason for this.

Even with all of his training, he was not able to prepare himself for what he was experiencing; he attempted to prevent the thoughts rushing through his mind, from turning into emotion, but the connection was far too strong. He placed a flower before the headstone and stood up; in a conscious effort to disconnect himself from the tide of emotion welling up inside.

He was just about to leave the cemetery when he saw a smaller headstone in the far corner. Intrigued he walked over to it. The name on it struck him like a thunderbolt, nearly knocking him over, it read Kansai Tokugawa. A rush of emotion swirled through his body like a whirlpool intent on dragging him under. Seeing the unmistakable look of shock on his face, Mariko walked around the low fence, "Are you all right?" she asked, concerned for him.

"Who was this?" Yamakiri asked, steadying himself against the fence.

"He is very famous in the area, my son Kansai is named after him; I am sure you must have heard of him," she said.

Yamakiri paused, trying to regain his composure and thinking of what to say.

"Um no, I cannot say I have," he responded, trying to conceal what he knew.

Mariko found his reaction strange and yet he had said he had no idea who this was. Questions raced through his head, but now was not the time to seek answers. He bowed, took a large mouthful of water and quickly headed for the gate of the cemetery.

"Thank you, I must leave now," he said, hastily closing the gate.

"All right, but my husband will be back soon; are you sure you wouldn't like him to take you to the next town?" she asked.

"No thank you, I prefer to walk," Yamakiri responded, turning and making his way down the steep winding road in the direction of the village of Nabari.

Mariko bowed; but as she looked up, was surprised to see him already a long way down the road.

For Yamakiri, it was hard to conceal how he felt; it was a though he had just seen a ghost and in some ways, this wasn't too far from the truth.

Meanwhile, Watanabe Yamada had been up early and was making his way up the steep road from Nabari to Aoyama village. As he rounded one of the last corners before the village, he saw a solitary figure walking down the road. As he came closer, he could see it was a *Yamabushi*; he hadn't seen any in these parts for quite some time and was intrigued by his presence.

Watanabe kept his gaze on him, trying to attract his attention. He was well aware of their level of awareness and was in no doubt that not only did he know he was there, but may have even sensed him before he even saw him. However the *Yamabushi* didn't look up, instead his eyes remained hidden under his wide *Tengai* hat. Watanabe stopped the wagon just before the *Yamabushi* passed, in an attempt to make contact with him. Being the village representative, he made it his business to speak to anyone who passed by, especially from the mountains. This was very important from a security perspective, as several years prior an entire army had used the pass to surprise and oust the ruling *Daimyo* of Iga.

"Good morning," Watanabe said.

Yamakiri stopped next to the wagon and responded, "Good morning," keeping his face hidden.

"Where are you going?" Watanabe asked.

"I am going to Ueno," he responded, in a tone that indicated he wanted to continue on his journey quickly.

"Ah, I see," Watanabe responded, aware that anything the *Yamabushi* did was not treated lightly and with a three hour walk ahead of him, there must be a good reason.

"Well, I am going there tomorrow if you would like to wait, I can take you," Watanabe said, offering his services.

"No, that will not be necessary, but thank you for the kind offer," Yamakiri responded, turning and continuing on his way down the steep road.

As he walked away, Watanabe had a strange feeling that they had met before, but because he didn't get to see his face he couldn't be sure.

Little did he know, he had just met a ghost from his past also.

Chapter 2

Several years earlier, Yamakiri had retreated to the mountains.
This followed the successful mission to capture Saigo Sakamura,
the brutal *Daimyo* of Iga. However, during the mission,
Sakamura's five year old daughter had been tragically killed;
Yamakiri had blamed himself for this. He had also lost his entire
family during this time, both his mother and father dead; the
futility of war leaving him disillusioned and angry. He had been
told that his father had been heavily involved, but reports of his
death had been sketchy, leaving a lot of questions unanswered.
With the decimation of his village by Sakamura's troops, he had
been left with no place to call home. So he had fled into the
mountains, living off the land as his uncle and others had taught
him. Purposely avoiding any human contact, he chose a life of
solitude in the mountains for over two years, in the hope of
making sense of what had happened and being able to move
forward. Even discarding his given names in favour of the one
his Martial Arts *Sensei* and uncle had given him during their years
of training-Yamakiri.

He made a small cave his home and from here he could observe
the comings and goings of people along the road to Koga to the
north. He watched intently as traders and *Samurai* passed by,
their casual attitude reflective of the relative peace that had
prevailed over the land after the instatement of the new *Daimyo*
under Go-Daigo.

He found solace in the training ritual that his *Sensei* had taught
him and that he had promised to do every morning. This kept
him fit and strong, maintaining a high level of martial arts skill
that would make him the envy of any warrior. However, no
matter how hard he tried, he was unable to rid himself of the
haunting nightmare of that fateful morning.

During his escape from the *Samurai* several years earlier, his uncle had taken him and his cousin to Ōminesanji, a *Yamabushi* temple high in the mountains to the South of their village; there he had been impressed with the monks rituals and training. Furthermore, he suspected they had techniques that would help to control the mind and in his case, free it of the demons that were haunting him. He had learnt some of these, but obviously not to any extent as to help him in his current plight; so he decided to move on and to seek help by finding such a temple.

The *Yamabushi* monks he had met seemed to live in a different reality to others. They were more like observers of the world than participants, and this appealed to Yamakiri. He felt that his problems were the effect of man's greed and ego. Such characteristics were alien to the *Yamabushi* and their beliefs, which were based in Buddhism and Shintoism.

However, he was loathed to return to Ōminesanji. Though it had been several years since he was there, he didn't want to go where he would be known. Until he could truthfully reconcile what had happened, familiar places such as that would surely bring back more memories and cause even more mayhem in his mind. Instead, he decided to move northward in the direction of Mt Hiei. He had heard that there was a *Yamabushi* temple there and a place where he could seek help.

He made his way through the dense Cyprus forest, avoiding established paths wherever possible, but following the sun. Walking for most of the day he arrived at the temple in the late afternoon. The temple was on the top of Mt Hiei, on the border between the towns of Otsu and Kyoto. However, there was something strange about it, considering it was supposed to be a place of peace and learning. The first thing he noticed was the high perimeter walls, constructed in the same fashion as the walls the *Samurai* used to surround their homes and castles. It was obvious these were erected as some form of protection. The name above the fortified front gate read Enryaku-Ji temple.

From the outside it appeared to be a large complex, much bigger than the temple that had harbored him some years ago. As he approached, the gate opened and a monk appeared dressed in the traditional *Yamabushi* attire.

"Greetings," he said bowing.

"Greetings," Yamakiri replied, bowing back.

"My name is Kenjo Sumiyama, and you are?" the monk asked, smiling.

"Yamakiri," he responded, "Please call me Yamakiri"

"Interesting name," the monk said.

"Yes, it was given to me by someone very special," Yamakiri replied, his thoughts turning to his uncle and martial arts *Sensei*.

It was customary for temples to welcome travellers with offerings and hospitality, in recognition of their effort to make it to the temple. In the case of Enryaku-Ji, this was atop the high mountain and was surrounded by steep and narrow paths, making the ascent difficult.

"Please come with me and I will see that you are fed and looked after," Kenjo said, smiling again.

Yamakiri was led through the large temple complex. As they passed by the large courtyard, he saw a large number of monks practicing martial arts This caught his attention. There were at least 100 of them if not more, all moving in perfect unison. Noticing Yamakiri's interest, Kenjo stopped, encouraging him to do the same.

"I see you are interested in this, Yamakiri?" Kenjo asked.

"Yes, sort of," Yamakiri responded.

"These are *Sohei*-warrior monks; they help to protect the temple from danger," Kenjo added.

"Danger, from whom?" Yamakiri asked.

"We have been attacked on many occasions by *Samurai* loyal to Takauji Ashikaga. The abbot here is Prince Morinaga, the son of Go-Daigo, so we are considered loyalists to his cause by them."

Yamakiri found it strange that *Samurai* would choose to attack a religious temple, but he was aware how far the *Samurai* would go to gain power.

He watched intently as the *Sohei* went through a series of *Katas*, blocking, kicking and punching in complete harmony, led by a senior monk at the front. He was intrigued at how a peaceful place such as a temple would need to revert to violence to defend itself.

To his surprise, Yamakiri noticed a familiar face- it was Morehei Tomada, a monk he had met at Ōminesanji temple several years earlier. Yamakiri watched him intently, thinking about their last conversation and how he had advocated for peace over violence. Yamakiri couldn't help but think how times must have changed since he had been in seclusion.

He thought better than try to attract the attention of his old friend and instead moved off with Kenjo through the temple grounds. He couldn't help but be impressed by the size of the central *Pagoda,* its series of tiers towering over everything else, including the mountain and valleys below. Atop the roof was a glistening brass structure he knew as the *Horin,* a series of nine rings and the *Hoju* at the very top; it seemed as if it was reaching for the sky. Not only did the temple reside on the boarder of the two regions, but it appeared to float above them in a fashion, representing a potentially neutral standpoint.

"So what brings you to this temple, Yamakiri?" Kenjo asked.

"I am interested in *Shugendo,*" Yamakiri responded.

"Ah, in what respect would that be?" Kenjo asked, alluding to the arduous discipline.

"I want to become a *Yamabushi,*" Yamakiri responded enthusiastically.

"Hmm. That is a very difficult path, are you sure?" he said, smiling.

"Yes, I believe so," Yamakiri replied.

"We, will see. You must meet with Prince Morinaga first, he is the Abbot here; he insists on seeing everyone who arrives as a matter of security," Kenjo said, leading him in the direction of a small house to the side of the *Pagoda*.

"Please wait here," Kenjo said, as they reached the steps, indicating for Yamakiri to wait at the bottom.

Walking up the steps, he knocked twice and then once more on the wooden door. The heavy door swung open; standing in the doorway was a large figure Yamakiri assumed was the Prince. He couldn't hear what was being said, but twice the Prince looked over at him; he shut the door and Kenjo returned.

"He is busy, but will see you very soon. In the meantime, come with me and I will provide some food and refreshments for you," he said, walking off and motioning for Yamakiri to follow him.

They walked over to the outdoor dining area; there were several rows of tables under a large veranda. "Please wait here, I will organise some food," Kenjo said, pointing to a seat.

He walked over to a large opening in the wall and attracted the attention of the cook, a fat man wearing a badly stained white apron.

After waiting for a short time Kenjo returned with some food; this included a bread roll and a bowl of *Miso* soup.

"Here Yamakiri," Kenjo said, startling him as he had been staring at the ornate buildings around the large courtyard.

"Thank you," he responded, as the tray was placed in front of him.

"Something catch your attention, Yamakiri?" Kenjo asked.

Yamakiri was reluctant to say anything, especially being in an unfamiliar place and company. His *Sensei* had taught him that it was better to just observe in such situations and to disclose as little as possible, until you could be sure that it was safe. Even though this was a temple and from his understanding, a place of peace and serenity, his introduction to the *Sohei* seemed to indicate otherwise.

They sat there, Yamakiri sipping the hot *Miso* while Kenjo watched him, smiling at his appreciation of what he had to offer.

"Have you travelled far?" the monk asked, familiar with greeting people who sought a change in their lives.

"Yes, quite far," Yamakiri responded, his gaze fixed on the floor.

Sensing his guarded response, Kenjo decided not to push him for a more concise answer, though he knew that his master Prince Morinaga would not be satisfied with Yamakiri's vagueness. There had been several raids on the temple recently, which up until now had been successfully defended, but it was only a matter of time before the enemy tried other tactics. The temple was in an attractive location, especially from a tactical standpoint, providing excellent defence opportunities for anyone who occupied it.

The cook interrupted the silence, bringing out a plate with a *Tamagoyaki* omelette cut into several pieces and carefully arranged on the plate to form three perfect hearts. Yamakiri smiled as he looked upon it, in some ways reluctant to disturb the cook's artistic masterpiece.

"Please enjoy," Kenjo said.

"Thank you very much." Yamakiri responded, looking across at the cook and bowing, the cook smiled and bowed in response. Yamakiri was half way through the omelette when something caught his eye from the direction of the Prince's house; standing on the doorstep was another large man-definitely not the Prince.

He had emerged from the house and had bowed to the Prince as if to say goodbye.

Yamakiri stared at the figure, his profile seemed familiar and as he turned and walked down the steps, he immediately recognised him as Masashige Kusunoki. Yamakiri had met him years before and had been part of a group that had helped Kusunoki to secure the region of Iga under his command. Kusunoki looked in the direction of the kitchen and made his way towards them. Yamakiri felt uneasy, unsure if he would be recognised. He was trying to avoid anything to do with the past.

"Do you know Kusunoki?" Kenjo said, noticing Yamakiri's stare.

Yamakiri said nothing and returned to eating his meal, finishing the rest of it hurriedly.

"Ah Sumiyama san, good afternoon," Kusunoki said in a cordial manner as he came towards them.

As Kusunoki stepped onto the wooden deck they both stood up and bowed, he bowed back; Yamakiri was reluctant to lift his head in case he was recognised.

"Sit, sit down please," he said, looking in the direction of the kitchen and waving his finger. The cook, who had seen him coming, had already started to prepare his meal; increasing his tempo to expedite the process.

Kusunoki sat next to Yamakiri; who hadn't washed for several days and was aware he smelled quite bad. He had tried to keep his distance from everyone, but on this occasion, had no choice. He looked across the table at Kenjo and could hear Kusunoki sniffing him.

"Master, this is Yamakiri," Kenjo said, directing his attention towards him.

"Just Yamakiri?" Kusunoki asked, staring at him.

"We are waiting to meet with the Prince," Kenjo interrupted, before Yamakiri had time to speak.

"Ah yes, well we have discussed much this afternoon, including the training of the *Sohei*, Kenjo san. He tells me that they will not be ready for another month. This is disappointing," Kusunoki added.

"Yes I am sorry master, but the last attack saw some of our best warriors killed and it has taken time to train these men up to a proficient level." Kenjo responded.

"Have we met before Yamakiri? You look familiar." Kusunoki said, changing the subject.

Yamakiri had been introduced to Kusunoki at Ōminesanji temple well over two years ago while with his uncle. He wasn't sure what to say, as he wanted to keep his past as secret as possible. However, it would have been considered rude not to acknowledge that you had met someone of Kusunoki's standing, if you had, this would not be something you would easily forget.

"Possibly at another temple," Yamakiri responded, hoping he wouldn't want to go into more detail. Just as Kusunoki was about to ask another question, the cook arrived with his meal; he looked up and acknowledged him, taking the large plate in his hands.

"Excuse me," Kusunoki said, taking no time in starting on his meal.

"Yes of course master, we have to see the Prince anyway," Kenjo responded standing up and offering relief to Yamakiri's apparent discomfort.

"So be it Sumiyama san. Oh, and nice to meet you, Yamakiri. Maybe we will meet again soon," Kusunoki said, bowing as they stood up.

"Come please, Yamakiri," Kenjo said, leading him in the direction of the Prince's house.

As they walked away, Kusunoki sat deep in thought as he devoured his meal, trying to think where he had met Yamakiri before.

Yamakiri and Kenjo stood on the door step of Prince Morinaga's house as Kenjo announced their arrival with two sharp knocks to the solid wooden door. Almost instantly the door swung open, revealing the Prince. He was dressed in ornate clothes, an embroidered cloak with several large ivory buttons securing the front. The Prince was the eldest son of the emperor Go-Daigo and had been appointed the abbot of the monastery several years earlier. Because of this association, the temple had been attacked twice in recent times by troops loyal to the *Bakufu*, the currently ousted Minamoto *Shoguns* from the north led by Takauji Ashikaga. Go-Daigo had tried to keep the country away from a cloistered form of ruler hip, but the begrudged Minamoto were in no hurry to surrender their hard fought positions of power without a fight.

"Come, please," the Prince said ushering them inside.

Yamakiri and Kenjo removed their sandals and donned a pair of indoor slippers and quickly shuffled inside the small but comfortable house.

"Please be seated," the Prince requested.

The two men sat down at the small table in the centre of the room; Yamakiri couldn't help but think, how only minutes before the great warrior Masashige Kusunoki had occupied the same seat.

"Sir, may I introduce Yamakiri," Kenjo said.

"Ah, yes. The warrior from the mist," the Prince responded.

Yamakiri smiled but said nothing; he knew better than to respond until he was addressed personally.

"Yamakiri would like to practice *Shugendo* sir, he tells me that is why he is here," Kenjo said.

The Prince looked directly into Yamakiri's eyes, as if searching for something. His expression changed from inertness, to a probing stare, like that of a knife, the point meeting in the centre of his head behind his eyes. Yamakiri wasn't sure what to do. He had never met someone so intense before, although he had never met a Prince either.

"Hmmm, of course it is your choice to do whatever you choose in life, but the environment dictates what is required of one first, Yamakiri," the Prince said, looking back at Kenjo.

Yamakiri was confused, all he had wanted was the opportunity to become a *Yamabushi*, he felt he didn't need a lecture on anything.

"I am not sure what you mean, Sir," he responded.

Seeing Yamakiri's apparently bewildered expression, the Prince continued.

"Yamakiri, this country is in a time of transition. Although the Minamoto *Shogunate* has been dismembered and forced out of Kyoto, there is still much uncertainty. My father Go-Daigo is trying to establish a fairer system of government in Kyoto, but is coming up against some very tough opposition. We have come under attack several times and at present I am more concerned with bolstering our defences than promoting religious practices," he said, frowning.

Yamakiri thought about what the Prince had just said and was not sure if he should respond. He recalled a conversation he had had with a monk at Ōminesanji temple. The monk was upset by the number of warriors that the temple was housing at that point in time. These were not only Kusunoki's troops, but also a small group of *Ninja* from the villages of the region. The monk could not understand why something that required a political solution needed military intervention first. Yamakiri had tried to explain to the monk that he had been taught that sometimes the will of your opponent needs to be softened to change their resolve; but Yamakiri had also been taught that brute force was usually met with brute force, resulting in far more casualties on both sides. The monk had argued that peace could be attained through dialogue, but Yamakiri had expressed the idea that they must be willing to listen first.

Yamakiri had witnessed first-hand the brutality of conflict and in some ways was a casualty himself. This was the main reason for his escape to the wilderness, he had seen too much and at such a young age, maybe it was too soon for him to fully comprehend.

"So you are saying there is no opportunity for me to become Yamabushi?" Yamakiri asked.

"Unfortunately not at present Yamakiri, the temples defence and the training of *Sohei* must take priority over everything else at present; we cannot sustain security here without them," the Prince replied.

Yamakiri felt he had no choice but to keep searching for a temple that he would be accepted into to learn *Shugendo*.

"I am sorry then Prince Morinaga, I will continue on my way," Yamakiri said reluctantly.

"I am very sorry to hear that Yamakiri, we need all the warriors we can get at this time," Prince Morinaga said, bowing as they both stood up.

"Good luck in your endeavours then.".

"Thank you once again – I sincerely hope you can find a peaceful solution," Yamakiri responded, standing up, bowing and opening the door.

They silently walked outside and down the steps. As he made his way across the courtyard, Yamakiri could see Kusunoki was still eating his meal; as they passed he looked up and smiled at them. They were just about at the main gate when from around the side of a building emerged a familiar face, it was Morehei Tomada, the monk that Yamakiri had met at Ōminesanji temple several years ago. He stopped, surprised to see Yamakiri.

"Ka…," Yamakiri stopped Morehei, "It is Yamakiri," he said, before he had a chance to finish.

He looked surprised for a moment, but respected Yamakiri's obvious wish to be addressed by this name.

"Yes of course, Yamakiri, so good to see you again," Morehei responded, bowing and smiling broadly.

Yamakiri had purposely travelled a long distance from his region to try to start a new life and forget his past, but seeing Kusunoki and then Tomada he now understood why he had always been told that the past is not something you can run away from.

"Well, Yamakiri, it has been a pleasure meeting you. Good luck for the future," Kenjo said, sensing that Yamakiri felt uncomfortable in such company; he bowed and walked away.

"You are not staying?" Morehei looked back puzzled,

"No Tomada san, I must move on," Yamakiri replied.

"But you came here for a reason?" Morehei asked.

"Yes, but it seems that the temple is not training *Shugenja*, this is what Prince Morinaga has just told me," Yamakiri responded, disappointment on his face.

"You want to become *Yamabushi*?" Morehei asked.

Yamakiri nodded and frowned; meanwhile Morehei's face lit up and he started laughing.

"There is some irony in this. Here I am training to become a *Sohei* warrior and you as a warrior, want to become a *Yamabushi*," Tomada said, continuing to laugh to himself.

Yamakiri couldn't see the funny side of it and remained stone faced.

"My apologies Yamakiri. I see this means a lot; I didn't mean to belittle or humiliate you. Please come over here, where we can talk," he said, ushering them over to a large boulder at the entrance.

"The *Yamabushi* here have been convinced to take up the cause and fight for Go-Daigo and Kusunoki. They were reluctant at first, but they wanted to fulfil the emperor's wishes even though they don't like violence. When the prince was installed here as the new abbot by his father, they really had no choice. We are training as *Sohei*, but only in a defensive role, however Kusunoki has insisted that now we focus on developing offensive skills as well." Tomada said.

"Why is that?" Yamakiri asked.

"I believe he wants our assistance to take back Kamakura from Takauji," Tomada continued.

"There is a huge difference between defence and attack; surely Kusunoki of all people should know that!" Yamakiri whispered loudly.

"Of course he does, but at the request of Go-Daigo he has no option but to try to make it work any way he can. Besides, he believes that the *Sohei* will be able to summon divine support to help him in his cause."

"Only if it is just," Yamakiri responded, resolute in his words.

"Ah –so what is just Yamakiri? I sometimes have difficulty understanding this anymore," Morehei said bowing his head.

Yamakiri was surprised by such a statement, considering what he knew of Morehei. When they had first met he was devout in his beliefs and would never have shown any form of doubt or insecurity; he was not sure what could have changed his outlook.

"And here is me wanting to become the opposite of what I have been taught, Morehei," Yamakiri said.

"Times change and people along with them, it is a fact. Many good people died for Go-Daigo's cause, it is a worthy one to stand up for," Morehei said, smiling.

Yamakiri felt his heart sink, as he thought back to that fateful day in Ueno. He had thought that his time in solitude had helped him to get over his grief, but it seemed that the more he saw and heard of his past, the more of a hold it had on him. He wanted so desperately to move on, but as his past kept reminding him, the gods were not going to let things go as easily.

"Tomada san, it is good to meet you again, but unfortunately I am on a quest to find somewhere to practice *Shugendo* and it seems that this is not the place, contrary to what I had been told," Yamakiri said, obvious disappointment in his face.

"Unfortunately this country is in state of transition and there are powerful forces on either side and both are pushing for the change in their favour. The Minamoto shoguns were never going to relinquish their power without a fight and so far many have died on either side seeing to this."

"But fighting is not always the answer Tomada san, you said that yourself at Ominesanji," Yamakiri said.

"Ah, I did say not always, not never, Yamakiri. Different times and situations call for different ways and means to deal with them," Morehei said, holding his finger in the air to emphasise his point.

"But surely fighting should only be a last resort Tomada san," Yamakiri responded.

"Hmm, maybe before you leave, it may be good for us to talk about what is happening in Kyoto with Go-Daigo; please stay for some tea," Tomada requested.

"Very well- I would be interested to hear what is going on, as it seems things have really taken a turn for the worst," Yamakiri responded concerned.

"Excellent, come with me then, it may well be that we could need your help," Morehei said, leading him by the arm back into the temple complex.

Chapter 3

The conversation between Masashige Kusunoki and Prince Morinaga had become quite heated. The Prince had received orders from his father Go-Daigo, ordering him to commit his warrior monks to attack Takauji in Kamakura and remove him from power. Go-Daigo suspected that Takauji's ties to his family and the ousted Minamoto shoguns were stronger than he had initially indicated, his suspicions bolstered by reports that Takauji refused to return to Kyoto. He felt betrayed. He had sent Takauji to Kamakura in good faith, on the premise of setting up a wing of his government in the region, what's more, he had given his word that he would remain faithful.

Kusunoki is a warrior and not a diplomat, Morinaga reminded himself, he has little or no idea of compromise or negotiation. His role is to soften the enemy' resolve to enable a diplomatic solution, something he is very good at.

Kusunoki had pressed Prince Morinaga to use his *Sohei*, despite protests from him that they were not warriors, but more defenders of the temple, but he was not prepared to accept that. Furthermore, he was not impressed with Morinaga's insolence when it came to his father's orders and was insistent on following these at any cost. Little did he know that such resolve would not always serve the purpose for which it was intended.

- * -

Yamakiri sat across the table from his old friend Morehei Tomada as he prepared the tea for them. He watched intently at the care and grace with which his friend carried this out, being respectful not to say anything until after he had finished. In the meantime Yamakiri scanned the small room, until stopping and fixing his gaze on an ornately decorated chest, sitting atop it were two swords, a *Katana* and a *Wakazashi,* the longer and shorter swords traditionally worn only by the *Samurai*. Yamakiri was

37

intrigued as to why his friend had these in his possession, considering when they had first met at Ōminesanji he seemed to despise the *Samurai*.

"Hmm, I see you are interested in my swords Yamakiri?" Tomada asked, handing him the hot cup of green tea.

Yamakiri paused for a moment.

"Well actually I am more intrigued about why you have weapons of the *Samurai* in your possession and proudly displayed, Tomada san," Yamakiri said.

"They were actually a gift from Kusunoki," Morehei responded.

"As I have said, times have changed since we last spoke. In the past this area had only one *Samurai* clan, the Minamoto, however they have been challenged and dislodged from their position of power. The problem we now face is that they are slowly clawing their way back, using Kamakura as their base of control," he continued.

"So it seems the sacrifices and hard work that was done in Ueno was all in vain, Tomada san?" Yamakiri asked, referring to his involvement in the past.

"No no, Yamakiri, that is not the case at all. Iga and Koga are still under the control of Go-Daigo and his *Daimyo*, that has not changed" Morehei said defensively.

"In fact, this area has provided a secure base from which to operate, even though it is some distance from here," he continued.

Yamakiri thought about the situation and how things had changed. Even though he had never been to this region before, he felt isolated and was unsure of where to go next. His wish to become a *Yamabushi* and follow a peaceful path seemed more distant than he had expected.

"Tomada san, do you see *any* chance of me studying *Shugendo* here at Enryaku-Ji?" Yamakiri asked, emphasising the word any.

Morehei thought deeply; he had heard the heroic account of Yamakiri and had been highly impressed. In fact he was surprised that Kusunoki hadn't recognised him when he arrived, since he had been actively involved in securing Ueno a few years earlier under his command.

"Actually, we do need someone with your skills. Our *Sohei* are more adept at defense than the role that Kusunoki wants us to play, that of offence. I will suggest to the abbot that I conduct your *Shugendo* training in return for your *Ninjutsu* training, "Morehei responded.

"Are you suggesting that I train the *Sohei*, Tomada san?" Yamakiri asked, considering his current position.

"Yamakiri, you are very skilled in the *Shinobi* arts, this is what we require at present. Our *Sohei* are expected to fight well trained *Samurai*, you more than anyone would know what tactics and strategy is required to defeat them."

"Yes, of course. But I also know that violence only perpetuates more violence and retaliation. Is there no prospect of a more diplomatic solution?" Yamakiri asked.

"Emperor Go-Daigo has tried this. In fact Takauji was sent to Kamakura for such a mission, but double crossed him. He has the support of many disaffected Minamoto *Samurai* and does not seem open to any sort of compromise," Morehei asserted.

"I will need some time to consider this offer, Tomada san, and of course you will need permission from Prince Morinaga. In the meantime, I will leave and return soon – I have much to think about," Yamakiri responded.

"Of course Yamakiri, I have no doubt that in our present situation the Abbot will have no issue with such an arrangement," Morehei said.

"Good, I hope so," Yamakiri responded, standing up and bowing to Morehei. He followed suit and seeing him to the gate, bid him a safe journey.

Meanwhile, in Kamakura, Tadayoshi Ashikaga sat in silence before his younger brother Takauji as he considered the current situation. The trust that Emperor Go-Daigo had placed in his brother to secure Kamakura had been foolish, considering his past loyalties to the old *Shogunate.*

"So, my brother, what is your plan for Go-Daigo?" Tadayoshi finally asked.

"I believe he is desperate and does not have anywhere near the support he needs to defend Kyoto," Takauji said staring out of the door in the direction of the official capitol.

"Hmm, well yes, I suppose that could be assumed from his misguided trust in you," Tadayoshi responded, aware of the sting in his comment.

"Trust is a two edged sword my brother; never forget how he was behind the trickery of seeing Sakamura removed from power in Iga. He is far from immune when it comes to honesty and we shouldn't forget that," Takauji added, reprimanding his brother.

"Well then, we must not forget that he has Kusunoki on his side and he is prepared to die for Go-Daigo's cause," Tadayoshi replied.

"I am not fearful of Kusunoki; his methods may be considered unconventional, but he is not the only one who can summon such skills," Takauji said.

Their conversation was abruptly interrupted by a knock on the door.

"Come!" Takauji called out.

The large doors swung open to reveal an attractive young woman holding a wooden tray. She made her way over to the two men and placed the tray on the table before them; on it were the implements for making tea and three cups.

The extra cup instantly caught Tadayoshi's attention; he looked up at his brother.

"Are we expecting company?" he said inquisitively.

Takauji smiled and looked at the young woman.

"In these times, I would only consider drinking tea with those who were friendly and sympathetic to our cause," Takauji responded, smiling.

"Of course, so who will be joining us?" Tadayoshi asked, curious.

Takauji was well aware of the impatient nature of his older brother. In fact, he attributed many of his failings to this aspect of his nature, failings he had never been comfortable with. He hesitated, long enough to see that his brother was getting uncomfortable, even looking in the direction of the door for another person.

"You see brother, often we look so hard that we fail to see what is right in front of us, but this is not always a bad thing," he added, looking at the young woman as she prepared the tea.

"Kusunoki may be the biggest threat to our success, but he is by no means infallible," Takauji continued, smiling.

Tadayoshi felt uncomfortable with his brother's disregard for discussing such matters in front of the servant. He was so uncomfortable that he leaned over and took hold of his arm. "What do you think you are doing?" he whispered angrily between his gritted teeth.

"What do you mean?" Takauji asked, well aware of what he was referring to; looking at the girl, he nodded.

The girl reached out and seized Tadayoshi by the shoulder, staring into his eyes, her intention drilled deep into his psyche. She opened her mouth and although there was no discernible sound; instinctively he cupped his ears to protect them, however it was not so much noise as it was more of a vibration that resonated deep inside his head. Tadayoshi felt a strange sensation envelop him, as if caught in the grasp of something stronger than he was able to resist-he was paralysed, unable to move.

"Enough! I think we have made our point," Takauji ordered.

Immediately, she let go of him, he collapsed backwards supporting himself on the floor; he had a strange ringing in his ears and for a moment the entire room seemed to be spinning. Shaking his head he pushed himself up off the floor and stared at the girl, she smiled back. For an instant her face seemed to change, it became pointed and her ears moved to the top of her head, it was as if she had morphed from a human into that of an animal, specifically that of a fox.

The young woman smiled again and returned to preparing the tea for them as though nothing had happened.

"You see brother, I may be younger than you, but by no means underestimate what I am capable of and what lengths I will go to regain control of the *Shogunate*," Takauji said.

Tadayoshi looked dishevelled as he tried to regain his composure, unsure of what had just happened. He had heard stories of *kitsune-mochi*-powerful sorcerers that summoned the cunning of a fox to employ their powers, but had always believed these to be myth. He looked at Seiko again, but she didn't respond, seemingly engrossed in the fine art of the tea ceremony.

- * -

Yamakiri walked down the narrow mountain trail away from Enryaku-Ji temple on mount Hiei. He was deep in thought about what he had just discussed with Tomada san. He had come in search of a peaceful life and had walked into the middle of a military conflict. He thought about his time in isolation and what this had meant to him. Maybe Go-Daigo was naive to think that after his efforts in Ueno some years before, the *Minamoto* shoguns would just stand aside and hand over power to him. He thought back to a lesson his uncle had conducted early in his martial arts training.

He was alone in the *Dojo* warming up and waiting for his *Sensei* when a strange feeling over came him. The small *Dojo* was illuminated by a single candle at one end which left the other in relative darkness, being windowless. The candle was on the *Kamidana-* a shelf that held various items of past generations and the *Kamiza* – a small shrine.

Yamakiri felt a cold breeze on his neck and looked around to see a dark shadow in the corner of the room rising out of what seemed like the floor. He was unable to make out anything distinctive, then realised it was a plume of smoke. Quickly it filled the small room, drifting down from the rafters, enveloping him completely as it swirled around him. It was a foul smell, like that of rotten eggs. To his left, Yamakiri heard a loud click and turned to see what it was, but the smoke was too thick to see anything. Then came another click to his right, with one more behind him. Twisting this way and that, he realised he had become disorientated and had no idea in which direction he was facing.

Suddenly, from out of the smoke, the end of something solid hit him in the ribs. As he turned to protect himself, he was hit in the back by another strike. This continued several times, with the smoke still lingering he was unable to pinpoint the origin of each attack. He thought about another lesson his *Sensei* had taught him about the nature of smoke and fire and suddenly dropped to the floor. To his surprise the smoke had not yet reached the floor and he could see his attacker's feet, just in front of him. Rather than engage him, he rolled to the front of the dojo and made his exit through a trap door under the *Kamiza*, enabling him to exit the *Dojo* outside via a secret tunnel. Coughing, he reached the end and fresh air. Taking several large gasps, he made his way home.

The next afternoon when he arrived for training, his *Sensei* was sitting in the middle of the *Dojo* waiting for him.

"Ah, nice of you to join me," he said, a big smile on his face gesturing for him to sit before him.

"So the training yesterday was very brief, but I am sure the lesson made up for that?" he said, questioning his student.

Yamakiri thought for a moment and recalled how he felt; his teacher was always playing what it seemed were tricks on him, but always highlighted the meaning behind them.

"The smoke confused me, *Sensei*," Yamakiri responded.

"Yes, go on," his teacher urged him.

"I realised how vulnerable I was by being hit, so I escaped," Yamakiri replied, hoping he had the right idea about what his teacher was asking.

"So you didn't have the urge to stay and fight?" his teacher asked.

"No *Sensei*, I felt it was too dangerous to do so."

"Good, this is the purpose and nature of *Metsubushi,* to cloud the mind and confuse your opponent. In this case you escaped and came back when the smoke had cleared; this provided an opportunity for more clarity, this is what is sometimes required in such situations." his teacher concluded.

Yamakiri thought about the confusion he had left behind in Iga by fleeing into the mountains some years earlier. But he was beginning to realise that maybe the confusion was more in his mind and the way in which he had interpreted things. He desperately wanted the smoke to settle in his head and had hoped that he would be able to move on and find peace within himself. However he was now being asked to train others in the arts of war, which was contradictory to his goal. So once again the confusion seemed to be all around, even in what he had expected to be the most peaceful place of all- Enryaku-Ji temple.

There was no stability in the governance of the country, the egos of several powerful men were in a perpetual struggle for power. He had learnt early in his life that power has the potential to corrupt; he somehow felt a sense of responsibility that he had helped to put one of these men into power. Needless to say, he was unsure how or even if he wanted to assist his old friend to train more warriors who, given the power, could also go down this destructive path. He had been taught that the skills passed down to him by his *Sensei* should only be used for good. He felt it was time to seek the guidance of an old friend, but this would mean travelling back to Iga. Reluctant as he was, he knew in his heart it was time to confront his past. He headed back to the small cave where he had concealed his belongings; unaware that his movements were being tracked by several sets of dark eyes hidden in the shadows of the dense forest.

Chapter 4

Night set in over Enryaku-Ji temple, the light of the sun was replaced by the luminous reflection off the full moon. The leader of the small group of *Ninja* had planned this moment carefully to coincide with this lunar event. He was well aware of the spiritual significance that the full moon represented, being the climax of something significant and the potential for a favourable outcome. He was also aware that any adversary would not expect such an action, as a new moon with its natural darkness was usually a better option for attack. This was why all of his men were dressed in a light grey coverall and head cowl, totally opposite to the common practice of hiding in the shadows; they would use the illumination from the moon to conceal themselves. Also in their favour was a wide area around the temple with a broad strip of raw Inada granite rocks. This had been strategically placed to expose anyone trying to make it to the base of the temple walls from the edge of the forest-if they were dressed in dark colours, of course. As the group advanced, one person remained stationary, his job was to scan the walls of the temple for any movement. To guide them, he made a series of clicks, one to move and two to signal to hold position. They were well aware that the guards were monks, not warriors, and although trained to defend the castle, they would never expect such a brazen assault.

As the last of the group made their way to the base of the perimeter wall they regrouped, the motion akin to that of air that expanded as exhaled and compressed when inhaled-they used this feeling as their example. There were few guards around, as their timing was also planned to coincide with meal time, preceded at this stage of the lunar calendar by the ritual chanting of *Buddha's* name; this provided a noisy backdrop to conceal any noise.

The group formed a small three tier pyramid against the wall, which had initially been built to define the perimeter, not as fortification. The fortifying addition has been added only recently and as a hybrid of both, the structure had several built in weaknesses. The last person scaled the human pyramid and disappeared over the wall. Sliding down the inside they made their way to the unattended gate, walking sideways so they could scan for any threats as they went. As he opened the gate, he counted the last one of the seven inside, shutting it silently behind him.

They made off in a line skirting the perimeter wall around the rear of the buildings, their mission to hide and wait in silence until the moment was right. Their target was Prince Morinaga, the Abbott of the temple, and, more importantly, the son of Go-Daigo, the current emperor. They were each promised a large sum of money if they succeeded in bringing him back alive to Kamakura. The value was in his capture, not so much in the bounty, but strategically it removed the safety of the sanctuary for Go-Daigo to use in the event of a threat. Undetected, they positioned themselves in various locations, each ensuring they could see at least two other group members. Like a group of cats observing their prey, wide eyed they watched and waited for the signal from their leader.

Prince Morinaga had finished his dinner, returned to his small hut and was preparing to go to sleep. The discussion that day with Kusunoki had upset him; especially his insistence to provide *Sohei* to help his father to take control of the region. This troubled him deeply, because it would also leave the temple vulnerable to attack. However, he was unable to consider the options as he was tired. He slowly drifted off to sleep.

Observing the extinction of the light in the Prince's hut, the leader of the group began counting. His training had taught him to observe such things as the time between Morinaga's entry into the building and how long it had taken for him to go to bed.

This time was usually proportional to how long it would take for him to reach a deep sleep, essential to the success of their mission. He patiently waited until the time expired.

Satisfied the time was right, he signalled his men to move forward and into position. From the side of the building he squeezed through the gap in the banister and on to the small wooden deck. It was his job to open the door, which he had been informed, would be locked. Out of his jacket pocket, he pulled out a *Kunai*-a small metal spade shaped tool, at the same time two other members flanked the doorway, crouching down. Placing the *Kunai* in the door jam, he prised it open and sliding it up disengaged the locking mechanism. He was very aware of the door's large metal hinges as he opened it, conscious that these could squeak loudly, especially if affected by the damp mountain air. He was also careful not to let any moonlight into the room and quickly filled the open space with the mass of his body, easing the door closed behind him. Crouching down in the corner, he waited; firstly to allow his eyes to adapt to the darkness of the room and secondly to ensure the Prince had not been aroused by his presence.

Observing his body and listening intently, he monitored the unbroken rhythm of Morinaga's deep breaths, indicating he was in a deep sleep state already. He made his move, walking like a crab on all fours to keep his bodyweight centered and low. Crouching over him like an animal observing its prey before seizing it, he reached into another pocket in his jacket and pulled out a small bamboo tube. Removing the cap he poured some of the liquid contents onto a length of cloth he had tied around his hand, until he felt wetness. He waited until his victim breathed out and as he placed the cloth over his mouth and nose, he pressed down on his chest, knowing the sudden compression would cause a reflexive action for his body to suck in more air-in this case filled with the fumes of the powerful sedative. Its composition would have a twofold affect, causing immediate unconsciousness and also rendering his vocal chords useless and inoperable, should he try to sound an alarm. Immediately

Morinaga's eyes opened wide and as the poisoned air filled his lungs, his eyes rolled back in his head. The masked figure placed his two fingers on Morinaga's neck to monitor his heart rate. There was an increase as he opened his eyes, but it was now slowing down as he sank into unconsciousness.

Once satisfied Morinaga was in the appropriate state, he withdrew the cloth from his face and moved over to the door, opening it slightly and signaling to his men. The two figures quickly moved inside as the door closed behind them. Each of them carried pre-cut lengths of bamboo and rope, which they began tying together. Resembling a ladder, they secured four cross members, measuring them as they went to coincide with strategic parts of Morinaga's body and to provide the best position in which to secure him. Once complete, they nodded to each other and then rolled Morinaga onto it, securing his body so it wouldn't move as he was transported.

Once complete, they were now ready to move their prisoner out of the complex as they had rehearsed many times; this they would do by carrying him with one person at each end with another to monitor him and make sure he remained unconscious. But first they needed a distraction; the head of the team eased open the door and looked across to one of his men positioned on the roof of the cookhouse and waved. In response, he dropped a handful of powder down the chimney and onto the burner below. Immediately there was a loud explosion and sparks flew around the kitchen; causing the cook and the diners to jump in shock. Taking advantage of the chaos, the door was quickly swung open just wide enough for the men to carry the makeshift stretcher out and across to the position of the first changeover. Meanwhile, everyone else's attention was directed to the kitchen; some had already run inside and were trying to extinguish the small fires caused by the explosion. Satisfied that they would go unnoticed, the group hurried silently out of the doorway from Morinaga's room and down the small set of steps. They headed quickly towards the back of the buildings, returning the way they had come. The last man closed the door behind him, intentionally leaving it unlocked. The mission had not only coincided with a full moon but also was the *Nichiyobi*– or the day of the Sun, the only day of the week where the Abbot rose late, giving them more time to escape.

They had made it undetected half way around the compound, when one of the escorts halted them and signaled for them to hide. The men carrying the stretcher placed it upright in the shadow of a building, cast by the intense moonlight. Morinaga's body was so well secured that he easily stood nearly vertical against the wall, his rigid form making it not immediately obvious to anyone that it was in any way human. The men carrying Morinaga dropped to the ground, their clothing blending perfectly with the light grey dusty ground by the light of the moon.

One of the monks ran past, nearly standing on one of them. He was in a hurry, probably in search of something to help with the emergency in the kitchen. Fortunately for the *Ninja,* the reflection of the moon off the walls and ground caused a whiteout effect and he was unable to see anything clearly. Once the signal for the all clear was given, the group set off again with their captive, strictly adhering to the well rehearsed routine they had practised relentlessly. Each man's adrenalin surged at the monk's sudden appearance, something they had been trained to use, to make double time to their next way-point by the gate.

As the first man rounded the side of the building he was surprised to see that there was a guard now stationed there. This was not entirely unexpected but would mean a change of plan for their escape. The lead man turned and made a series of hand signals indicating the situation and the need to alter their strategy. After each nodded, they moved into position, four of them providing a human ladder to ascend the wall behind the building, not far from the gate. Once the ready signal was made, one of the men ran up the structure and over the wall, landing silently on the other side. His mission was to get the guard to move away from the gate to allow the group to pass through undetected; however this depended on the guard's gullibility and commitment to his task.

The *Ninja* on the outside hugged the wall and moved around to the gate, ensuring no-one could see him. He knocked once; the guard responded by opening the small shutter to see who was there. As he did this, the *Ninja* hugged the gate to avoid being seen from the inside. Then he counted down and knocked again at the set timing. The guard looked again and still saw nothing, but he was as curious as they had hoped, opening the gate and proceeding to look out through the narrow gap. From out of the darkness, a hand reached around behind his head and smothered his face; in a panic the guard took a deep breath, filling his lungs with the powerful concoction and instantly falling unconscious. He was dragged inside and propped up against the wall, so that as he woke, he would assume he had fallen asleep.

From their position, the rest of the men watched and waited. The signal was given and they made their escape, rushing ahead to the open the gate and provide a seamless exit for the rest. Within seconds, the group, along with the Prince, were outside of the temple.

Hours later as the early morning sun heated the damp roofs of the temple buildings, steam rose into the air. Morehei Tomada heard a knock on the door; this became louder with each moment and more insistent, followed by someone saying, "Tomada San, please open the door."

Eventually he opened the door to see one of his men with a panicked look on his face.

"Tomada san please, the abbot is not in his house," he said, urgency in his voice.

Morehei was already dressed and made his way over to the small group of monks standing outside the Prince's door waiting for his arrival.

"He had not shown up for morning prayers, master," one of them informed him.

"Also, his door was unlocked, so we entered as he did not respond to our knocking," he added.

Looking inside, he saw that there was no sign of Morinaga in the small room, his bed was empty and showed no signs of a body. He slowly surveyed the room, for any clues as to what may have taken place, but nothing seemed out of place, except for the empty bed.

"The explosion in the kitchen-that must have been a diversion. Did anyone see Prince Morinaga leave-who was guarding the gate last night?" he asked angrily.

The monk who had been on the gate stepped forward,

"I was," he said bowing his head. He believed he had fallen asleep and didn't want to be reprimanded.

"Well, did you see anything?" Morehei asked.

The monk said nothing for a moment.

"I am sorry, I cannot remember," he said, bowing his head again.

Morehei brushed the matter aside, it was no use trying to get an answer from him; it was obvious whoever had taken Morinaga had deceived him.

"You must ride to Kyoto and inform Go-Daigo that the Prince is missing! Also ask that Kusunoki send some men to help bolster security and search for him," he said, turning to one of the monks.

"Yes sir," came the reply; the monk ran off towards the stables to ready his horse.

Moments later the messenger on horseback exited the gate to the temple and made his way swiftly down the narrow tree lined track towards Kyoto. As he rounded the first corner, he saw the body of a man lying in the middle of the road. He stopped his horse and leapt off holding its reigns as he cautiously walked over to it. As he knelt down, he felt a shaft of cold steel penetrate his back; this quickly changed and felt intensely hot. As he attempted to cry out, his mouth was quickly covered; the razor sharp knife was twisted inside his body, ensuring his quick death. As one figure dragged him off into the dense forest, the other checked the area and covered up any evidence of what had just happened.

Once his body was concealed, they both mounted his horse and cantered off; content that their mission to stop the message reaching Kyoto had been a success.

- * -

Later that morning at Arashiyama palace in Kyoto, Masashige Kusunoki had met with Go-Daigo regarding Takauji and his apparent betrayal to repatriate Kamakura under the control of Go-Daigo. Instead reports had reached him that he had refused to raise Go-Daigo's flag and that he was rallying some of his former Minamoto co-operatives to rise up against him to take Kyoto.

"Kusunoki san, we need to find a means to overthrow Takauji from Kamakura before he is able to rally support for his cause," Go-Daigo said, with a concerned look on his face.

"I believe that it may well be too late master, according to my sources," Kusunoki responded.

"What have you heard?" Go-Daigo asked.

"My sources tell me that many of the *Daimyo* who initially agreed to support you, have been engaged in secret meetings to undermine your push for a fairer government, Master. I believe this was instigated by Takauji himself," Kusunoki responded.

"So what do you propose I do to fix this?" Go-Daigo asked, looking for some sort of military solution from his commander.

"If you think military intervention is the answer, I am sorry but I beg to differ. Attacking Kamakura will not only lead to more discontent, but in my opinion could well be suicidal," Kusunoki replied, pushing his objection to such a solution.

"I am presently working on a plan to entice Takauji to his own demise master, but this is taking longer than expected to prepare for it," he added.

"This is involving the use of Morinaga's *Sohei*?" Go-Daigo asked with an air of cynicism.

"With all due respect master, you ask such a question as if you are sceptical of me being able to succeed," Kusunoki responded, trying to conceal his frustration.

"So how is the training progressing?" Go-Daigo asked, direct in his question.

Go-Daigo had recently met with the Prince and already knew the answer to his last question, but he wanted to hear it from Kusunoki to enforce his belief that this was not an option this time.

"I believe conventional warfare will not work against the numbers that Takauji is able to rally to his side master," Kusunoki responded, trying to avoid the question.

"Besides, it was very successful against Sakamura and Shinsui at *Iga*," Kusunoki added.

"Yes, I will concede it was, but the way I see it, the circumstances are much different this time. Takauji has already gained momentum and this grows daily with his support. As you say, we don't have the luxury of time in this instance," Go-Daigo responded.

Kusunoki had no answer to this; the *Sohei* training was not progressing quick enough to carry out his plan. But what Go-Daigo was proposing was also not feasible, as it was reported that Takauji already had over 10,000 men under his command, whereas Kusunoki would be lucky to rally any more than half that number. Some of this situation Kusunoki believed was attributable to Go-Daigo taking the soft approach to his initial takeover attempt. He respected his master's wish to use minimal force to overthrow the old *Shogunate*, but Kusunoki knew that it was dangerous to leave some of the armies intact; relying solely on the loyalty of their masters to dictate their allegiance. All it took was for their leaders to change direction and the rest would follow, that was essentially the dilemma he found himself in at present.

"Please master, I need to meet with my commanders and discuss our present options," Kusunoki said excusing himself.

"As you wish, I am sure as always, you will come up with a strategy to see the outcome fall in my favour. My faith in your abilities have never failed me before," Go-Daigo responded, smiling.

"Yes of course, master," Kusunoki replied, bowing as he left the room, feeling the pressure to succeed bearing down on him.

Chapter 5

In Kyoto, Seiko made her way through the narrow congested streets. She moved in harmony with the tempo of the crowd, sometimes walking beside people to give the impression that she was with them, other times turning off in different directions, all the time keeping alert and with the intention of moving unnoticed. Her training had taught her to avoid making an impression on those around her, in this way being invisible and in situations where she was unable to avoid such attention, making use of her environment to blend in. Her mission involved Arashiyama palace, home of the Emperor Go-Daigo. Her first objective was to infiltrate the palace and get as close to Go-Daigo as she could.

She followed the narrow canal that she knew led to the palace gates, as it rounded the corner amidst the line of *Sakura–* cherry blossom trees, she could see its entrance way. She came closer and stopped at what she considered to be a safe distance from the two *Samurai* guarding its large doors. Posing as an artist capturing the scenery on some paper she had brought with her, she sat down and observed their movements.

- * -

Walking briskly down the hill from his old village of Aoyama, Yamakiri thought about the people he had just encountered. Disguised as a *Yamabushi* priest, he hadn't been recognised, even by his cousin Watanabe, though they had grown up together. For now, this was the way he wanted it. He had so many questions that remained unanswered and knew that every step closer to where these events had taken place could prove painful; however, once again he had been spurred on by the plight of Kusunoki and the call to help him. Walking for over an hour, he rounded the corner of the road to see the *Tori* gate, signifying the entrance to the small village of Nabari. He had been here a few times as a boy, but it was nothing like he remembered it. In fact there were only three houses in the entire village from what he could see. This was in stark contrast to the bustling trading village he had seen before as a boy. Everywhere else, there were empty plots of land; tall grass grew up between the remains of old house foundations. As he walked into the village, he caught the attention of a young man, tending his garden at the side of his house.

"Good morning!" the young man called out.

Yamakiri had no option but to respond. "Good morning."

The young man put down his trowel and walked over to Yamakiri.

"Greetings *Yamabushi*," he said, bowing twice.
Yamakiri bowed in response, but waited for his introduction. It was customary in such situations to expect an introduction from what was in this case the host.
"I am Kazuki Satoru," the young man said enthusiastically, bowing once more.

Yamakiri had never seen him before and thought it safe to respond; he needed answers to so many questions and his training had taught him that wherever possible, talk to the locals of the area.
"My name is Yamakiri," he responded.

"Would you like some tea, Yamakiri san?" he asked, pointing towards his small house.

Yamakiri hesitated for a moment, before accepting his invitation.

"Yes, that would be good, thank you," Yamakiri responded.

"Come then, come inside please. I do not get many visitors," Kazuki said, ushering him on to the verandah of his house.

Yamakiri slipped off his sandals, took off his hat and made his way into the small front room of the house. Sitting in the middle of the room was a small table and some cushions, Yamakiri waited for Kazuki to ask him to be seated.

"Please be seated, I will fetch some tea," Kazuki said, walking backwards into the doorway leading to the kitchen.

While he was gone, Yamakiri took the opportunity to look around. The room was small and had very few things in it, other than the furniture and small shrine in the corner of the room. In the opposite corner, he noticed a *Katana* resting up against the wall. It seemed familiar and as he looked at it, he tried to recall where he had seen it before. It had a gold lacquer *Saya*-the outer sheath embellished with an intricate black dragon figurine. He thought hard and then realised he had admired a similar sword worn by a local *Samurai* called Hideo Shimada; he had been the brutal commander of the *Daimyo* – Sakamura before he had been overthrown. In fact, Yamakiri had personally witnessed his death during an ambush on the other side of Ueno.

Kazuki returned to the room carrying a tray with tea making implements and a pot of steaming hot water.

"So you have an interest in *Samurai* weapons I see, Yamakiri san?" Kazuki said, noticing Yamakiri's gaze on the sword.

Yamakiri was aware that the *Samurai* believed their sword was one with their soul and that if the *Samurai* was killed in battle, his sword would carry the curse until its master's death was avenged. "Where did you get that?" Yamakiri asked.

"I was given it by a trader some time ago," Kazuki responded.

"Do you know who it belonged to?" Yamakiri asked.
"Yes, it belonged to the man who killed my parents and destroyed the village" Kazuki responded.

"Can I ask who that was?" Yamakiri asked innocently, seeing how much history Kazuki knew of the incident..

"His name was Hideo Shimada, have you heard of him?" Kazuki asked.

The name echoed loudly through his head, he saw the vivid image of Shimada collapsing, as his throat was ripped open; blood gushing all around him. Yamakiri suddenly stood up, his head spinning as he lost all sense of composure. It was as if the spirit of the sword had reached out and somehow taken control of his being.

"I am sorry Satoru san, I must leave," Yamakiri said, bowing, urgency in his voice.

With that Yamakiri rushed out the door, quickly putting on his hat and sandals, he walked briskly back onto the road, in the direction of Ueno. Once again, he found himself trying to run from his past, but it seemed around every corner, even more presented itself, seemingly challenging him. He was well aware that going back to Ueno was going to be his biggest challenge yet, he knew that he had to find someone who would be able to explain the past and hopefully help free him from his inner demons.

- * -

Meanwhile in Kamakura, Takauji Ashikaga was anxiously anticipating the arrival of his special guest, Prince Morinaga. Although he had no proof that Morinaga was involved in any plot to overthrow his father, this was his justification for having him seized from *Enryaku-Ji* temple. Takauji knew that removing him would weaken the *Sohei's* ability to provide protection for the emperor as they had in the past. Takauji was bitter for what he believed to be a plot to oust him of the power he felt he deserved. In response to this, he saw no option but to drive Go-Daigo out of *Kyoto* and take it for himself. To further justify his actions, he had the backing of many powerful *Samurai* angered by

Go-Daigo's arrogance in believing he could take over the *Shogunate*.

However, the real thorn in Takauji's side was Nitta Yoshisada. Yoshisada had been instrumental in taking Kamakura from *Hojo* Tokiyuki the year before, but was incensed that Takauji had betrayed his and Go-Daigo's trust, by claiming it for himself. Takauji's plan was simple, but extremely brazen. He would use the same strategy that Go-Daigo used several years earlier to weaken the *Shogunate*. That was to dismember, limb from limb, the body of power that stood between him and the control of the country. This included the plan to break down the cohesion between Go-Daigo, Morinaga and Kusunoki, a task he knew would not be easy.

The knock on the door he had been waiting for broke the silence.

"Come!" called Takauji.

The doors opened to reveal two of his men holding a third man with a hood over his head. His body looked weak as they supported him under each arm.

"Bring him forward," Takauji ordered, waving his hand.

The men dragged him in front of Takauji and sat him down, removing the hood. This exposed a disheveled Morinaga, his long black hair matted in front of his face and his eyes bloodshot. After being snatched from his home at Mt Hiei, he had not had been allowed to sleep since he had regained consciousness.

"Ah Morinaga, so nice to have you to come and see me," Takauji said in a welcoming tone.

"As if I had a choice," Morinaga responded in a disgruntled tone, looking through the mess of his hair.

"Choice-we all make choices, some not always popular with those closest to us, Morinaga," Takauji responded.

"Like your choice to come here in an attempt to betray your father," Takauji continued.

"What! Do you think my father will believe such nonsense, Takauji? It is obvious you had me kidnapped," Morinaga responded angrily.

"Hmm, obvious? The fact that you deserted your position to come over to my side, Morinaga, is obvious," Takauji insisted.

"That is preposterous, no one will believe that!" Morinaga responded, his rage building.

"Do you really think so? That would depend on the circumstances surrounding your sudden disappearance from *Enryaku-Ji*, especially when he hears of your proposal to me," Takauji responded.

"What proposal?" Morinaga enquired, becoming even more frustrated at his captor's insinuations.

"Never mind, but I warn you that once Go-Daigo hears of your intentions, he will beg me to take your head," Takauji responded, smiling

Morinaga felt he was in no position to argue, even though what Takauji was saying was a complete lie. As far as he was concerned, there was no reason for his father to believe any of this.

"Take him away," Takauji ordered, smiling as Morinaga was lifted and dragged from the room.

Chapter 6

Yamakiri made his way north along the road to Ueno. Each time he heard someone coming he concealed himself along the side of the road, avoiding the prospect of unnecessary contact with anyone. It was not that he didn't want to talk to people. It was more that after so much time in isolation, he had realised it was often better to remain in the background than it was to expose oneself. However, he knew this would be difficult in a large town such as Ueno, where everyone wanted to know everyone else's business. This was a legacy of the old *Daimyo's* rule and stemmed from the need to understand where one was safe, or more importantly, in danger.

Knowing the old regime had been ousted some years earlier did give him some comfort, but he still felt the need to be careful. A *Yamabushi* may attract unwanted attention and questions, so he decided to change his attire. Just before the town entrance he slipped into the trees on the side of the road. He had intended to stop here, to pay his respects to someone he had known. Making his way through the trees, he proceeded to one particular tree; seeing it, he crouched down. Memories came flooding back and he saw the image of his uncle lying there, dying.

"*Sensei*, I am sorry I let you down, please forgive me," he whispered, as tears started to roll down his face.

"I realise that I must make sure that your sacrifice is not in vain and will honor your wishes," he continued.

"I ask that you please help me and guide me in my travels," Yamakiri asked, placing his hands together.

He said a prayer and was just about to stand up, when a small bird swooped down and perched itself on a branch just in front of him. For a moment it was silent and sat there just staring at him; Yamakiri stared back. Then it launched into song, its high shrill song breaking the relative silence of the forest. It was as if it was trying to speak to him and was somehow connected to his dead uncle.

Yamakiri thought back to his time at Ōminesanji temple and when he first met Morehei Tomada. He was standing on the steps, when he began to be overwhelmed by all sorts of animals from the nearby forest. What was even more impressive was that he seemed to be able to communicate with them. This experience had intrigued Yamakiri so much that it inspired him to seek the ways of the *Yamabushi;* their connection to nature and peaceful outlook on life appealed greatly.

Breaking his daydream, a voice said, 'What you have been taught is not about fighting, Yamakiri. Please remember this.' Yamakiri was sure someone else had said this, but apart from the bird, there was no one else around. He stared at it, its eyes became very intense, then suddenly it flew off into the trees. Yamakiri sat there for a moment, thinking about the voice and how it was exactly what his uncle had taught him. Maybe it was the bird that had spoken to him and maybe somehow it was the *Kami* – the spirit of his uncle.

Yamakiri stood up and removed the *Yamabushi* clothing and hat, replacing it with the clothes of a commoner. He knew this would help to blend in better and not attract attention to himself. Hiding his things under a fallen tree, he made off for town, in search of an old friend and some help.

- * -

In Kyoto, Seiko had been observing the guards at the palace gates for some time while she pretended to draw. She knew at noon the guards would change over and be replaced with new ones, so she quickly moved away to acquire the items she thought would assist in her entry. When Seiko returned just before noon she saw, as she had expected, the thick wooden doors open and two guards emerged to relieve the outgoing two of their post. Seiko waited, and just before they had settled in, approached them.

"I am back now," she said, holding out a small box in front of the bigger guard, who obviously enjoyed his food.

"Back? I have never seen you before," he said.

"Oh, of course not. You are not the same guards that I spoke to earlier on today. I am very sorry; I promised I would bring something for them, if they would let me see the emperor's head cook. But since you are not the same guards, I suppose this will not still be the case," She said, knowing all too well she had already captured their interest in the box.

"Wait, maybe I can help," the larger guard said, not wanting to miss out on the obvious bribe Seiko had in the box.

"Umm, are you sure?" Seiko said innocently.

"Yes, well, actually my sister is a cook in the kitchen," he said. Seiko pretended to look surprised at such a coincidence.

"But first you have to show us what you have for us in the box," the guard continued.

"It is a sample of my work," she said prying open the box. Inside were several colourful rows of *Wagashi* – sweets, made from *Azuki* beans, finely crafted to reflect the various seasons. The guard looked inside and his eyes lit up.

"Did you make these?" he asked, as he surveyed the colorful contents of the box.

"Yes, of course; would you like to try some?" Seiko asked, knowing all too well that these would be irresistible to them. The guard reached in and took one of the cakes; after sniffing it, he took a large bite. Seiko passed the box in front of the other guard, who seeing his partner devouring one and rolling his eyes, could not resist missing out on the same pleasure.

"These are very good. Much better than anything made here," the guard said, after swallowing the last of it.

The other guard was chewing on his; nodding his head and snorting in agreement as he devoured the tasty treat.

"Wait here; I will get someone to fetch my sister. As long as you can guarantee a steady supply of these for us, I will make sure she hires you," the guard said smiling.

"That would be much appreciated," Seiko said, smiling back.

Meanwhile in Kamakura, Takauji sat discussing the details of the raid on Enryaku-Ji temple with Ryushin Yakushimaru.

"So Ryushin, your mission went without any complications?" Takauji asked, smiling.

"Yes master and I am certain my men have left no trace of our presence there," Ryushin said confidently.

"Good, that will help in my plan to convince Go-Daigo that his son is involved in a plot to overthrow him," Takauji said, tapping his fan on his leg.

"So what is our next move master?" Ryushin asked.

"Now we wait. Time has a way of distorting reality in the minds of men. I am sure Kusunoki will be despatched to find Morinaga soon enough. If he is alerted to his whereabouts in Kamakura and with the hatred he has for me, he will show little hesitation in sending a force to attack," Takauji said, a confident smile on his face.

"But I believe Kusunoki has only a small garrison of *Samurai*. I would be certain that he would never launch such an attack with so little resources, Master," Ryushin said, with a concerned look on his face.

"That may well be the case, but Kusunoki's loyalty to his master may see him act otherwise-especially if he is ordered to do so," Takauji added.

"I don't understand," Ryushin said.

"Hmm, you are still young, Ryushin. There are ways men act that other men cannot understand," Takauji said, emphasising the term men, referring to the 17 year olds immaturity.

Ryushin was not going to show he had been offended by such a statement. He had spent many years studying martial arts and strategy from his grandfather and also Shugendo from his father. He felt he was well travelled and highly skilled at what he did.

"It is men as you say that cause and fight wars Master, not young people," Ryushin retorted, making his point around why Takauji had Morinaga kidnapped.

"Strangely enough, it is men who are sometimes easy to influence and sway, especially with the correct motivation Yakushimaru san," Takauji said, referring to Go-Daigo and smiling to himself as he looked towards the west.

Chapter 7

Yamakiri made his way through the bustling town of Ueno. He had chosen this time, to make it easier to blend in with the busy townsfolk. The mood of the town was calm; people were happy and courteous to each other as they went about their business. Yamakiri's destination was the castle on the western side of the town. This had been built by the last *Daimyo,* Saigo Sakamura not only for his protection, but seemingly also as a statement of power and control. Its huge walls towered over the town. Yamakiri had been inside only once, and that was several years ago. As much as the castle stood for Sakamura and his oppressive ways, it also had many weaknesses and was by no means as impenetrable as Sakamura believed. Yamakiri had been taught that things such as this were a reflection of their creator and that in this way it was easy to determine their *Tsuki* – weakness. In Sakamura's case, his demise had come from not securing the foundations and therefore failing to see how anyone could attack from below. Along with his blatant arrogance, he had underestimated the power of the people.

Yamakiri approached the solitary guard at the gate.

"Greetings," the guard said.

"Greetings," Yamakiri responded, bowing.

"I wish to speak with Harada san, if I may," Yamakiri continued.

"Hmm, that name is not familiar to me. Please wait here and I will get someone to see if they can find him," the guard responded.

"And your name is?" the guard asked.

"Ah, Yamakiri Tokugawa," Yamakiri responded, reluctantly; hoping that adding that last name may help to jog Harada San's memory should he be announced.

The guard knocked on the gate and as it opened, he leaned in and spoke quietly with someone on the inside. Poking his head out of the gate, another guard looked Yamakiri up and down and then continued talking. The first guard nodded several times, before closing the gate and returning.

"I am sorry, but Harada San is not here anymore," the guard said apologetically.

Yamakiri felt the disappointment surge through his body. He had come a long way, only to find that Harada was not there.

"Did he say where I could find him?" Yamakiri asked.

"I was told that he left here several years ago, but no one knows where he has gone. I am very sorry," the guard added.

"Ok, well, thank you for your time," Yamakiri said, bowing and walking away.

Yamakiri was not sure where to go next. He desperately needed to find his old friend Kito Harada. Despondent, he walked back into the town, finding it hard to conceal his disappointment. He was deep in thought when he bumped into an old man, who was crossing the street in front of him, nearly knocking him over.

"Watch where you are going, will you!" the old man said angrily.

"I am very sorry, sir," Yamakiri responded, bowing several times. As he looked up into the eyes of the old man, he saw him staring back at him as if studying a fine piece of art.

"You look very familiar, boy," the old man said, looking Yamakiri up and down.

Yamakiri was confused; he had only been to Ueno a couple of times, the last over three years ago.

"I am sorry, I don't know you, I am not from around here," Yamakiri responded.

"Hmm, you look like someone I once knew, well you have the same features as him anyway. His name was Yoshiakai Tokugawa, do you know him?" the old man asked.

Yamakiri's heart raced, Yoshiakai was his father and the village trader; so he would have come into contact with many people in Ueno. But Yamakiri did not want to tell this stranger that. He had been taught to keep such things close to you, until you could establish who you were talking to.

"So you say you are not from around here?" the old man asked.

"Yes, that is right," Yamakiri responded guardedly.

"I am looking for someone, but it appears he is not here any more," Yamakiri continued.

"And who might that be?" the old man asked.

"His name is Kito Harada, sir," Yamakiri responded, hoping the old man might recognise the name.

"Ah yes, Harada San. He was a commander here after the demise of the tyrant Sakamura," the old man said.

"Was?" Yamakiri asked.

"Yes, he left shortly after. As far as I know, he has never been back" the old man said.

"Do you know where he went?" Yamakiri asked.

"Yes actually, he went North," he said, pointing in the direction of the northern gate.

"Are you sure?" Yamakiri asked.

"Certain. Apparently he went in search of Hideo Shimada's daughter. She had left town after her father was killed. Nasty man he was."

"And her name was?" Yamakiri asked.

"Umm, Akiko, yes that's right. Akiko," he said, his smile revealing his missing front teeth.

"Thank you for that, sir," Yamakiri said bowing. "And sorry about bumping into you."

Turning, he headed off towards the North happy that the gods had sent this man to help him find his old friend. At least he had established that he wasn't in Ueno, but he would still need some luck to find him. However, this was surely a good omen, Yamakiri thought to himself.

_ * _

Meanwhile, at Enryaku-Ji temple, Morehei Tomada was becoming more concerned for the safety of his master the abbot, Prince Morinaga. Without any clear indication of what had happened, he had no idea where to start searching for him. All that he could hope was that Go-Daigo had received his message and was responding with a search party. However, it was mid-afternoon and still he hadn't heard or seen anyone.

He was about to despatch another messenger to Kyoto, when the guard on the gate called out, "Kusunoki is approaching!"

Morehei thought to himself maybe Kusunoki had taken all this time to rally his troops, hence the delay. But as the guard opened the gates to let him in, only Kusunoki rode through. Morehei met him as he approached.

"Greetings Kusunoki San," Morehei said bowing.

Kusunoki dismounted and bowed.

"Greetings Tomada san," he said smiling.

"I have come to see Prince Morinaga."

"Oh, Kusunoki san, I am very sorry, didn't Go-Daigo receive my message?" Morehei asked.

"Message? I was not told anything, has something happened?" Kusunoki asked, now very concerned.

"Yes, he has gone missing and seemingly without a trace," Morehei continued.

"Missing, how?" Kusunoki asked.

"He disappeared from his house last night some time," Morehei responded anxiously.

He led Kusunoki over to Morinaga's hut and told him what they had found; he looked around the room, hoping to find some clues to Morinaga's sudden disappearance.

"Was the door locked this morning?" Kusunoki asked, aware of how the abbot always locked himself in.

"No, Master," Morehei responded.

"And did anyone hear or see anything out of the ordinary last night?" Kusunoki asked.

"No, Master and no-one saw him leave, if that is what you mean," Morehei added.

It was then that one of the men made his way to where Kusunoki was; his head down.

"I am sorry master, it is my fault," he said respectfully.

They both looked at him confused.

"What is your fault?" Kusunoki asked.

"Well, I was on guard duty last night and fell asleep for a short time, anything could have happened," he added.

Kusunoki was not so sure Morinaga had left of his own accord. It was too much of a coincidence that the guard had fallen asleep, the messenger had not made it to Kyoto, and now he was missing.

"I must inform Go-Daigo of this matter immediately," he said, mounting his horse and turning around.

"In the mean time, bolster your security Tomada san," he added, ushering his horse off in the direction of the main gate.

- * -

Earlier that morning, Watanabe Yamada had returned to Aoyama from his overnight visit to the north. When he arrived, he was met at the gate by his wife, Mariko, and their son, Kansai.

Kansai ran up to him and jumped on the wagon.

"Daddy," he called out as he clambered atop the high seat.

Watanabe gave him a big hug and several kisses. Kansai sat down and took the reins, pretending to drive the wagon like his father. Watanabe stepped off the wagon, leaving Kansai to play..

"Greetings," he said, as he kissed his wife.

"Hello my dear, you must be tired," she said.

"Well, more hungry than tired," he said, as she led him off towards the house.

Mariko turned to make sure Kansai was okay.

"Mummy, tell Daddy about the funny man that talked to me," Kansai said.

"Who, the *Yamabushi* that I passed on the road this morning?" Watanabe asked.

"Yes, I gave him some water. He had come down the mountain track, obviously from one of the temples," she said.

It was not unusual to see *Yamabushi* in the area. They had become less aloof after the removal of the old *Daimyo* from power. He despised them, probably because of his deep seated

73

superstitions towards them. But since they had been instrumental in helping to remove him from power, the new *Daimyo* imposed no such restrictions and they were free to come and go as they pleased.

"He also paid his respects to our ancestors," Mariko added.

"Of course," Watanabe responded, inferring this was customary to do so.

"He said his name was Yamakiri," Mariko said.

The mention of that name echoed through Watanabe's head. Could it be just a coincidence that he had used a name that was given to his cousin by his late father? He thought back to his brief meeting with him on the road and how he felt as if he had met him before. How could this be possible, after all his cousin was buried in the cemetery after his body was found in the hills, mauled by a wild animal.

"Are you all right Watanabe?" Mariko asked, referring to his change in demeanour.

Watanabe said nothing, he was focussed on the past and the thoughts flooding his mind; had this ghost from the past come back to haunt him?

Chapter 8

Yamakiri had been walking for over an hour along the dusty road
when he was approached by a *Samurai* on horseback, coming
from the opposite direction.

"Greetings," he said, as he rode up to Yamakiri.

"Greetings," Yamakiri responded, bowing.

"You seemed to be ill-equipped to be travelling so far out of
town," the *Samurai* said.

"Actually, I am looking for someone," Yamakiri responded.

"His name is Kito Harada sir, have you heard of him?" he
continued.

"Ah, Harada san, yes, of course. He is a bit of a recluse though,
you will be lucky if he lets you on his land," the *Samurai*
responded.

"Can you tell me where he lives then?" Yamakiri asked hopefully.

"Yes. If you continue along this road for about another one *Ri*,
you will come to a sharp bend to the right, there you will see a
track on the left heading up into the hills. Follow this to the end
and it will lead you to Harada san; but I will warn you, he is not
very receptive," the *Samurai* said.

"I will try my luck. Thank you for that," Yamakiri responded
bowing several more times.

Yamakiri followed the *Samurai's* instructions and made his way
up the narrow track, unsure of what to expect. He had not seen
Kito for over three years and wasn't sure he would want to see
him. As he rounded a corner he saw a makeshift hut made out
of roughly cut timber and trees. It was surrounded by a low
fence and had a small fire smoldering to one side, the smoke
indicating that someone was there, or had been very recently. He
cautiously made his way through an opening towards the
entrance. This had a thick piece of canvas draped over the small
entranceway, he suspected to act as a door. He looked around,
but couldn't see any signs of life. He knocked on the hut's wall

several times and waited, but no-one answered. Suddenly he felt a strange feeling on the back of his neck, as if someone was watching him, but turning around, couldn't see anyone.

"Kito, are you there?" Yamakiri called out and waited for a response, but nothing, so he called again. He hadn't come this far not to see him, especially as he had so many questions that needed answering.

He sat down on the cold stone steps and waited, searching the surrounding trees for any sign of life.

Finally a male voice called out,

"Who are you and what do you want?"

Yamakiri felt uncomfortable. He knew he had been watched since his arrival and was unsure why Kito hadn't shown himself.

"I am looking for Kito Harada; I need to speak with him," Yamakiri responded cautiously.

"Why?" the person replied.

"We were friends once and I need to talk to him," Yamakiri said anxiously.

There was another long silence, then from behind a large tree a man appeared. He was bearded and covered in dirt; he was dressed like a hermit and his eyes were bloodshot.

"Who are you?" he asked, keeping his distance, like a cautious wild animal.

"It is me, Kansai Tokugawa," Yamakiri responded, using a name he may have been more familiar with, unsure if this was the man he had come to see.

"Impossible; he is dead!" the man responded.

Yamakiri was shocked and unsure why he would say such a thing. However he had been away for a long time and in his absence, the space could have been filled by all sorts of stories and rumors.

"Are you Kito Harada?" Yamakiri asked.

For some time the man peered back, as if trying to distinguish the true identity of Yamakiri.

"Kito, what has happened to you?" Yamakiri continued.

Kito slowly moved out and stood upright.

76

"It is you, Kansai," he said, finally recognising the young man in front of him.

"Well, yes; but I prefer the name Yamakiri," he responded.

Kito sank to his knees and began to weep, the tears flooding out of his bloodshot eyes as he looked up at Yamakiri. It was as if Yamakiri's appearance had released some deep seated emotion that Kito had been holding back. Yamakiri walked over to him and crouched down beside him.

"Kito, what has happened? I can't believe it is you," Yamakiri said quietly.

Kito looked into Yamakiri's eyes as if searching for something.

"I am haunted by demons from the past, Yamakiri," Kito finally responded.

"No matter how hard I try, I am unable to free myself from their grasp. This must be my *karma* for doing so many bad things," Kito continued.

Yamakiri thought for a moment about the man before him and how he had lost his vibrancy. The Kito he once knew seemed to be lost inside this sorry figure. He had no problem recalling the last time he saw Kito. It was in Sakamura's castle in Ueno; together they had taken Sakamura hostage and had forced him to open the gates so that Kusunoki and his troops could enter the castle. However in the chaos, a stray arrow had accidentally struck Sakamura's five year old daughter, killing her instantly. Although it was an accident, the image of the innocent little girl with an arrow embedded in her tiny body had haunted Yamakiri in the form of nightmares ever since. The fact that he was holding her at the time only added to his pain.

"Kito please, we cannot go back in time and do things differently and I know that you didn't do anything bad," Yamakiri said, trying to reassure his old friend.

He approached Kito slowly and held out his hand.

"Kito, good and bad people are hurt or killed in wars, that is just the way it is. There is no point being bitter or having regrets," Yamakiri said, touching him on the shoulder.

Yamakiri listened to himself as he spoke. It was as if he was

giving guidance as much for Kito as for himself. He recalled
something his *Sensei* had once told him, 'What we teach is what
we need to learn the most for ourselves'. At the time Yamakiri
was young and didn't understand what he meant, but as he
matured this started to make sense.

"Look at you, you lost your entire family, Yamakiri. Did it have
to be this way?" Kito asked.

The bitterness was obvious about what he had been asked to do
in the past. As Yamakiri listened he found it hard to believe that
this was the same person who he had known several years ago.
He was not sure what had happened after he had left Ueno that
day, but if he wanted Kito to help him, he would need to help
him out of his bad state first.

"Come Kito, we need to talk. I really need your help and you are
the only one I can trust," Yamakiri said, lifting him to his feet.

- * -

Kusunoki returned to Arashiyama Palace in Kyoto where Go-
Daigo had been awaiting his return. He had sent him to discuss
the idea of re-locating to the temple for his security as he felt
vulnerable in the city. However, as he entered the courtyard, the
look on his commander's face was far from what he had
expected.

"Kusunoki san, your return from Mt Hiei is quicker than I
anticipated," Go-Daigo said nervously.

"Master, there has been some trouble there. Morinaga has gone
missing, I suspect it is the work of Takauji."

"Missing, how?" Go-Daigo asked, shocked at the news.

"I am not sure Master, but it looks like work of *Ninja*. It was not
discovered he was missing until sometime this morning,"
Kusunoki said as he dismounted from his horse.

"So what do you suggest we do?" the Emperor asked.

"I believe we need to bolster security around the palace first, to
keep you safe. Moving you to Mt Hiei is out of the question at

present. The *Sohei* are no match for the cunning of the *Ninja* and I cannot guarantee your safety there," Kusunoki added.

"So what about Morinaga, do you think he is still alive?" Go-Daigo asked.

"Yes. If someone wanted him dead, they could have easily killed him as he slept. I believe we will hear soon enough, Master," Kusunoki said.

As Kusunoki followed the Emperor inside, they passed two young servant girls going in the opposite direction down the long corridor. They both bowed as they approached and as they passed one of them looked up, following their movement as they made their way towards the security of the inner palace. Little did Kusunoki know, the Emperor was far from safe even within the security of his fortified home.

- * -

Meanwhile in Kamakura, Takauji had had Morinaga dragged from his cell and brought before him. His underclothes were stained and tattered, a testament of the treatment he had been subjected to after being kidnapped. As he was seated, he looked up at his captor with bloodshot eyes and felt rage growing inside him.

"What do you hope to achieve by this, Takauji?" the Prince asked.

For a moment Takauji refrained from answering, instead he stared deep into Morinaga's eyes, as if savouring the moment of his vulnerability.

"What do I hope to achieve?" Takauji responded sarcastically.

"The fact that you have approached me with a plan to overthrow your father clearly shows no intent on my behalf of any sort of a plan," Takauji added.

"Do you really believe that my father will fall for this story? He is not a fool Takauji," Morinaga responded angrily.

"Of course not, in fact I respect his ability to see through such things. He did not get to where he is today by being a fool. But like you and me, he is only human and as such, is not without *Tsuki* – weakness," Takauji responded, smiling.

"And what is that supposed to mean?" Morinaga asked.

"You see, Morinaga, you are a man of religion, rituals and dogma, so I can understand how it would be difficult for you to appreciate his perspective on things; especially matters of conflict and war. Your father believes that he is destined to rule this country as the next *Shogun,* but what he fails to see is the tide of discontent growing. He has made many promises that he has failed to keep and now many have become tired of waiting," Takauji said contemptuously.

"It is hard to keep promises when those he trusts betray him so quickly," Morinaga angrily responded, referring to his present company.

"I too was made many promises, Morinaga, and I am still waiting. But instead he sends Yoshisada to oust me. There is no show of trust in this," Takauji replied, trying to conceal the fact that he betrayed Go-Daigo.

"You have made many choices that you cannot blame anyone else for Takauji, not even my father," Morinaga said angrily.

"Choices? I had no choice-I was forced to take the actions I have," Takauji responded.

Morinaga decided not to engage in any more discussion and to remain silent. He could see that nothing he could say would dissuade Takauji from his plan to take over the *Shogunate,* all he could do was to wait for his rescue.

Chapter 9

Outside of Ueno, Yamakiri looked across at the sorry figure of his old friend Kito Harada. He found it hard to believe that the dishevelled person before him was the same proud warrior he had once known. He had made them both some tea and as they sat there, he considered whether Kito would be the right person to help him. After drinking in silence for some time, Yamakiri spoke.

"What happened to you after I left Ueno that day, Kito?" Yamakiri asked bravely.

There was silence for some time as Kito gazed into his cup and then across at his friend several times. It was as if each sip of the tea gave him strength and the courage to talk.

"I am sorry that you have found me in such a state. Maybe this is why I was always taught not to fight," Kito responded.

"Was there more fighting after I left?" Yamakiri asked.

"Physical fighting – no; but battle has raged in my head ever since that day," he said as sadness swept across his rough features.

"We were supposed to help to make this a more peaceful world, but in doing so, we seemed to have just moved the battle into the heads of those like us who tried to make a difference," Kito continued.

Yamakiri thought about what Kito was saying-it made a lot of sense, especially with him having to deal with his own inner demons. Yamakiri paused before responding.

"I understand what you are saying Kito, I too suffer from such an affliction," Yamakiri responded sympathetically.

Kito looked deep into Yamakiri's eyes, as if searching his soul for answers, then he bowed his head.

"I killed the *Daimyos's* daughter that day Yamakiri, it was my fault that such an innocent life was taken. In ordering you to seize her, I feel it took a part of your innocence as she died in your arms," Kito said his head still bowed.

Yamakiri reached across the table and placed his hand on Kito's shoulder.

"Choices, Kito. We all make choices and then have to live with the consequences," Yamakiri said, his words echoing in his head.

"The choices I have made haunt me all the time. The look on your face as you carried that innocent girl back to her father was too much to bear. She didn't deserve to die that day," Kito said, as tears started rolling down his cheeks.

Yamakiri didn't know what to say. He had also been haunted by the events of that day in ongoing nightmares. He had hoped that Kito would be able to help him to free him from his inner demons, but looking at the sorry sight before him, now he was not so sure.

- * -

In Kyoto, Seiko believed she had successfully infiltrated the castle just in time. She watched on from the window as Kusunoki ordered extra guards to the gate and perimeter of the palace.

"What is going on?" she asked, as one of the servants also paused to watch.

"I am unsure. I saw Kusunoki return and meet with the Emperor, something bad must have happened for them to increase security," she said.

Seiko thought back to her past. Her father had been the *Daimyo's Samurai* commander in Iga several years earlier. As a young girl, she had witnessed him drag people into the town square, torture and in some cases, decapitate them, in front of the crowds that gathered. She despised his brutality and found it hard to understand how someone could be so cold hearted. So much so, that when she had been approached by someone to help overthrow the *Daimyo,* there was no hesitation in offering her assistance.

However, he had gone missing after an ambush and although she had been promised his life would be spared, she never saw him again. It was after that she was told that he had been killed by the very person who promised to keep him safe- Kito Harada. What was more, she and Kito had been lovers at the time, and this left her confused about the true basis of their relationship. This, to her, was an act of betrayal that motivated her to seek revenge on those who had orchestrated it. So fleeing her home, she sought the help of someone with skills in the dark arts, with the sole intention of destroying those who had deceived her. Her prime target was the man she was now looking at below in the courtyard – Go-Daigo. As she saw it, if he hadn't tried to take over the *Shogunate* from the Minamoto clan, her father would still be alive. Now she found herself in a perfect position to not only carry out her goal, but with the assistance of others, to see the demise of his entire organisation.

- * -

Back in Kamakura, Ryushin Yakushimaru was getting restless. He and his men had successfully kidnapped Prince Morinaga from his temple at Mt Hiei, but in the light of this, he needed something to keep feeding the fire of control he felt with such actions. However, he had been told by Takauji that it was important to wait now and to see what manifested out of his successful action. However, Ryushin was not a person who had much patience.

At 18 he was reasonably young, but having been taught the martial arts by his grandfather from early on, was considered highly skilled and his talents much sought after.

As he sat staring out the door, his thoughts turned to the 17 year old girl who had come to his family several years earlier. His mother had found her wandering in the forest near their home, distraught and confused, so she had taken her in and looked after her. She had said her name was Seiko and that she had fled

Shiga, after all of her family had been killed in the skirmish between Sakamura and Kusunoki's troops. However she was reluctant to disclose much else. His mother had insisted on making her comfortable and seeing that she was well taken care of. Ryushin was her only child and she had always wanted a daughter, and Seiko seemed to fill that void for her.

However, Ryushin had seen another side of Seiko, in contrast to the innocent person she portrayed. One day while walking in the forest, he saw someone in the distance through the trees. As he moved closer he saw it was Seiko. He observed her from behind a large rock and was disturbed by what he saw. It appeared she had trapped a small animal and had killed it, its entrails strewn on the ground before her. She seemed to be immersed in some sort of trance and was naked from the waist up. She was smothering the dead animal's blood all over herself, at the same time; her head rolling around in circles as she revelled in the macabre ritual. Then in a final act, she raised the animal's heart in both hands high above her head and stared at it for a moment, before bringing it to her mouth and tearing it apart in a mad frenzy like a hungry wild animal unsure of its next meal. As she bit into it, blood squirted out across her face and ran down her chin onto her heaving chest and small breasts. She devoured the heart without stopping and once finished, rubbed the blood over her face, laughing out loud as it filled the joins between her teeth. Then suddenly her eyes rolled back into her head and she collapsed onto the forest floor.

Ryushin was unsure what had just taken place and decided not to announce his presence. Leaving her there he made his way back to his village. It was over an hour before Seiko returned; but when she did, she acted as though nothing had happened. She had cleaned herself up, leaving no sign at all of what had just taken place. When Ryushin's mother asked where she had been, she told her she had been walking in the forest and after sitting down under a tree, fallen asleep. This explanation seemed to satisfy Ryushin's mother, but obviously left him with more questions about her than he had answers.

He was aware that she had been despatched by Takauji to infiltrate Go-Daigo's palace and to carry out his orders, but Ryushin was concerned that she might have her own agenda.

- * -

Kusunoki was talking to his head guard in the courtyard of the palace. Being a residence with little means of fortification, it would prove difficult to secure it from any sort of invasion or attack. The outer walls were wooden; also, there were no ramparts on which to stage guards to repeal an attack. This was not good, Kusunoki thought to himself.

"We can place men here and here," he said, pointing to an area within the gates.

"Also, we will place two men at each of the corner points of the outside moat and two between them," he continued. However, he was far from comfortable with what he had to work with, especially as he was in charge of Go-Daigo's safety.

He shook his head as he tried to make some sense of how to protect his master, but it seemed fruitless. He knew that if he could move him to another location in secret and offer the illusion that he was still there, then at least he would have better control of security. It was no secret that Go-Daigo was in Kyoto and from a political perspective, that was the way he wanted it. It was crucial that he was seen to be in residence in Kyoto, given that it was the capitol, it sent a message to his enemies about who was in control. At least, that was what he wanted them to think.

"Set about staging your men as discussed," Kusunoki said to his commander.

He thought about where he could move Go-Daigo to ensure his safety. Enryaku-Ji temple was his first option and even though Morinaga had disappeared from there, it still afforded the best place to ensure the Emperor's safety. However, he would need to bolster security there first, and judging by recent events, would need warriors more skilled than the *Sohei* to protect it.

His thoughts turned to the events surrounding the capture of Iga several years earlier and the highly skilled warriors who made that possible. He would need to find Kito Harada, this was a man he had respected most highly for his loyalty and skill. Kito had impressed him and Kusunoki knew that if anyone could help, it would be him.

Chapter 10

Yamakiri also needed the help of Kito, but in his current state, he appeared to require more assistance than he could offer.

However, Yamakiri had many unanswered questions. These left a large void in his life, which stopped him from moving on.

With all of his family dead, he hoped the man before him may have the answers he so desperately sought, but it was obvious that getting such information was not going to be easy. Yamakiri poured his old friend another cup of tea and handed it to him, an offering that he hoped would help to relax him.

"Kito, I need to ask you some questions about what happened to my father," Yamakiri said settling back down on the large log beside the small fire.

Kito looked up, his bloodshot eyes reflecting the lack of sleep he continually suffered. In response he appeared to recede back into himself, as if regressing into the past.

"Yamakiri, your father was a very skilled and honourable man; he didn't deserve to die the way he did that night," Kito said as a tear ran down his cheek.

Yamakiri braced himself. He had never been told how his father had met his fate or any of the circumstances around his death, but at last he was about to discover the truth.

"Kito, I am sorry if this causes you pain, but I must understand how and where my father died," he responded, urging his old friend on.

Kito sat motionless for some time before continuing. It was as if the truth needed time to make its way to the surface.

"Your father was the best *Genin* I had ever known," Kito finally said.

This was a surprise to Yamakiri. He knew the term *Genin* referred to the foot soldiers of a *Ninja* clan, these were the warriors that were called upon to carry out the missions. As far as Yamakiri had known, his father was just a trader for their village.

"He was *Genin*?" Yamakiri responded, his head flooded with images of his father.

"Yes, he was a very brave and careful man who loved his family dearly, Yamakiri," Kito added.

Yamakiri didn't miss the emphasis on Kito's reference to his father being careful.

"You said he was careful, Kito. Yet he was killed and never came back. Did he make a mistake?" Yamakiri asked, pressing for an answer.

Kito broke down as the reality of the situation hit him hard.

"I am sorry, my friend," Kito said, finding it hard to express the words through his sadness.

"Sorry for what?" Yamakiri asked, pressing him for more answers. Now it was obvious that Kito knew more than he was saying.

"What, Kito, why are you sorry?" Yamakiri asked again, his anguish beginning to take over.

"Please Yamakiri, please forgive me," Kito pleaded, bowing his head to hide his face.

Yamakiri waited. There was no point in pressing him, it was obvious that whatever he knew was considerably painful to talk about. He waited patiently.

"Your father was sent out on a mission that was not meant to succeed," Kito finally said, as tears streamed down his face.

Yamakiri struggled to make sense of what he was saying. He knew nothing, except that he hadn't returned home that night.

"What mission? Please Kito, I need to know." Yamakiri said pleadingly.

"I didn't know it would end that way," Kito responded.

"I didn't know he would be sacrificed."

"Sacrificed for what?" Yamakiri asked, as his anguish turned to anger. "You are not making sense Kito."

Suddenly Kito stood up.

"Please wait here," he said, as he walked inside his shelter.

After a few moments, he returned and handed a crumpled up

piece of rice paper to Yamakiri. He sat back down and watched as he straightened it out to read it.
The writing was faint, he could just make out the message:

Servant's quarters, east wing, before dusk-ensure window is unlocked.
Immediately after dusk, ensure door is secured and locked.

"What is this?" Yamakiri asked.
There was a long pause as Kito thought hard about what to say next. He took the piece of paper from Yamakiri, his hand shaking, and stared down at it.
"This is why your father died and why he never returned," Kito said, his tears dripping on to the note.
"I don't understand Kito, what does this mean?" Yamakiri protested.
"Your father was betrayed, Yamakiri. By the very people he trusted.
Yamakiri's heart sank. He had been searching for answers to what had happened to his father. But he now realised, maybe he wasn't ready to hear the truth.

- * -

Kusunoki and a handful of his men prepared to set off from Arashiyama Palace. Disappointed by the *Sohei's* inability to keep Prince Morinaga safe at Enryaku-Ji temple, he needed to find some expert help.
"Master, I am going to Ueno to seek out someone who will be able to train the *Sohei* better and quicker than they have been so far," he said as he mounted his horse.
"And who would that be?" the Emperor asked.
"I have spoken of him before, Master. In fact it was his efforts

that saved me from having to take my men into battle to secure the castle from Sakamura, His name is Harada san," Kusunoki responded.

"The *Ninja*?" Go-Daigo replied sceptically.

He was uneasy with the way the *Ninja* operated. He believed that their methods caused too much uncertainty and room for the enemy to regroup. In fact, he felt that in some ways, the uprising that was now in progress arose from the lack of certainty that a full scale attack and subsequent massacre of any opposition would have afforded him years earlier.

"Excuse my directness, Master, but I sense that you are unhappy to engage the services of these men again?" Kusunoki asked.

Go-Daigo paused for a moment before responding.

"Kusunoki san, such men are neither soldiers nor nobility and therefore have little understanding of the ways of war," Go-Daigo said, rubbing his hands together.

Kusunoki was taken aback by his master's statement and was not sure how to respond. He didn't share Go-Daigo's view on the *Ninja* and was perturbed by his sheer arrogance. However, he consoled himself in the fact that conventional war never had any true victors and that diplomacy was a far more effective weapon than one made of steel.

"I beg to differ with you, Master, the *Sohei* are sadly lacking in the skills required to keep the temple safe," Kusunoki said, bowing his head in respect.

"Kusunoki, I have always trusted you and your judgement and if you believe this is what is required, then so you must go. But be warned, Takauji is not one for diplomacy. He is a cunning and ruthless adversary, who will stop at nothing to get his way," Go-Daigo responded.

"Yes of course, Master," Kusunoki said, bowing once more and directing his horse towards the large gates of the palace. But he felt uncomfortable with the current situation, especially his master's lack of recognition in what the *Ninja* had done to see Iga fall to him. In some ways, the true battle was not between his

master and Takauji, but between his master and his own
ignorance.

- * -

In Kamakura, Takauji Ashikaga sat with his brother, plotting
their next move in their plan to take over Kyoto and to oust Go-
Daigo. Part of this plan had been to kidnap his son Prince
Morinaga from Enryaku-Ji temple on Mt Hiei. Without him
there to provide a safe haven if Go-Daigo had to flee Kyoto, it
would leave the Emperor exposed and vulnerable.
"What is your next move?" Tadayoshi asked his older brother.
Takauji looked into his brother's eyes. He was well aware of
what he wanted, especially if he was to seize power from Go-
Daigo. Tadayoshi craved power, but Takauji believed that this
obsession somewhat clouded his true judgement on things and
made him vulnerable to losing himself in his own self
importance. Takauji had to temper his brother's ego, but he was
also aware that he needed his help. Unlike Takauji, Tadayoshi
was a brave warrior, but he lacked the sound judgement required
of Takauji's other commanders.
"We wait to see Go-Daigo's reaction to Morinaga's move to
betray him. Our spies will let us know if this ploy has been
successful or not," Takauji said.
"Why don't we just kill Go-Daigo and get him out of the way?"
Tadayoshi asked naively.
Takauji tried not to show his frustration at his brother's lack of
understanding.
"Because Go-Daigo still has many followers and the loyalty of
the people. There is still a place for an Emperor in this country,
but certainly not one who also holds the position of _Shogun_.
Furthermore, the vacuum created by his death would send this
country into complete turmoil," Takauji responded, referring to
people like his brother, especially with his thirst for power.
"No, Go-Daigo needs to be put in his place. If I can do this,

then the people will follow and settle down. This requires a diplomatic solution. We must let them see that he has no skill in running the country and that having him in power is detrimental to its future," Takauji added.

"How do you propose to do this then, brother?" Tadayoshi asked.

"You will see soon enough. Ryushin is making his way to Kyoto as we speak," Takauji responded smiling.

Chapter 11

Yamakiri sat staring at the hills across the valley. His old friend Kito's revelation that his father had been betrayed, causing his death, was hard to believe and even harder to accept. But he had known Kito for some time and had trusted him with his life on several occasions.

"I am sorry my friend, I didn't believe it until I saw the note for myself," Kito responded in a quiet and compassionate voice.

"Where did this come from Kito?" Yamakiri asked, examining the note for any clues.

Kito paused for a moment and then responded.

"It was given back to me by our spy in Ueno, after the incident there," Kito responded.

"Given back, you are saying that you originally gave this to them then, Kito?" Yamakiri asked anxiously.

"Yes, I am sorry, Yamakiri. I had no idea at the time of the orders, or their implications for your father. I was just ordered to pass it on, that was all," Kito responded.

"By who?" Yamakiri asked, his brow creased as he tried to comprehend the impact of the situation.

Kito paused again. He realised the implications of what he was about to tell his friend and was unsure how to proceed.

"Before I tell you this, Yamakiri, you must remember that this was in very dangerous times and required the utmost secrecy. As you were well aware, we were never told why we had to do things or who was involved in it-this is the way of *Ninjutsu,*" Kito said, trying to set the scene.

"What are you trying to say, Kito?" Yamakiri asked, anxious for an answer.

"Just that you may never find the truth," Kito responded.

Yamakiri stared intently at his friend, as if trying to delve into his mind and comprehend what he was trying to say.

"Please, go on," Yamakiri urged.

"This was given to me to pass on by the *Chunin,*" Kito said reluctantly.

Yamakiri understood this to be his superior, someone higher up the ranks than him. He had expected this to be the case and also understood that it was common not to know the identity of such a person, especially in times of conflict. This ensured the safety of everyone else and the bigger plan.

"I suppose you do not know who that was, Kito?" Yamakiri responded, ready to accept that he may be at a dead end.
Kito's faced changed, his cheeks dropped as he felt the sadness come over him.

"What is it, Kito?" Yamakiri added.

"Yamakiri, it was given to me by your uncle – Saito Yamada," Kito said, unsure of what Yamakiri's reaction would be.

"I don't understand; my uncle ordered my father's death-he was the *Chunin?*" Yamakiri said.

Yamakiri's mind raced, he stood up, but staggered sideways, ending up propping himself against a nearby tree. The impact of what Kito had told him was too hard to comprehend standing up, his body slid slowly down the trunk until he came to rest on the ground at its base. He sat there motionless, dazed and staring at the ground.

_ * _

Watanabe Yamada walked out through the gate to the village in Aoyama and over to the edge of the road. From here he could see right down the Kaochidani valley and the road leading towards the large town of Ueno. He stared out as if searching for something in the distance. As he stood there, he heard the voice of his father calling him from the village. Turning around, he thought he saw him standing on the porch of what was their house some years earlier. All around him the scenery blurred, he was being drawn down a long tunnel, as if looking back in time. To the right of the house was the house of his uncle, Yoshiakai Tokugawa, his wife and his cousin Kansai. He thought back to a martial arts lesson that his father had given him and his cousin in his dojo one particular day.

Watanabe was facing Kansai with a bamboo *Shinai* raised high in the air in a *Dai-Jodan* posture. His father had told him to strike at Kansai at any time and try to hit him. Watanabe looked intently into his cousin's eyes, looking for an opportune moment to attack. What he was unaware of, was that his father had given Kansai a leather *Shuriken;* Kansai had this concealed in his right hand by his side, so it was impossible to see. He was also told to show *Tsuki* – weakness, and to draw Watanabe in to attack. Because Watanabe and Kansai had grown up together, Watanabe felt that not only did he know his cousin well enough to know his weaknesses, but also that he could force him into a position where he opened an opportunity for attack. Staring intently, he flinched, projecting his body forward, as if in a motion to attack. However Kansai also knew his cousin well enough to know that he never did things in half measures and that if he was intent on moving, it would be hard for him to hide his intention. Watanabe was just about to reset from his feint, when something hit him in the face, causing him to recoil in surprise. Before he had time to recover fully, he felt the soft end of a *Shinai* press against his throat. Watanabe stepped back in an attempt to parry it away, but suddenly realised that he no longer had his weapon. Not only had his cousin taken his balance, but in the confusion, also stolen his weapon without him realising it.

"Very good!" Saito called to Kansai, moving in and patting him on the back.

"Of course, there were many factors that have made this possible, the most important is that you know your opponent."

Both boys looked at him and nodded. For Watanabe, who had always believed he was better than his younger cousin, it was somewhat embarrassing to be defeated in such a manner. "The lesson here is to know your enemy; their strengths and their weaknesses," Mr Yamada said, smiling.

Watanabe snapped out of his day dream, and looking around, was drawn to the small cemetery to the side of the village. He walked over and opened the gate. Directly in front of him, was his father's headstone. He knelt down before it and bowed his head, bringing his hands together prayerfully as he did so. He felt a surge of energy rush through his body, as if someone or something had passed through him.

"Thank you for everything, Father," he said, looking up at the headstone.

As he sat there, his attention was drawn to the small headstone in the corner of the cemetery. The headstone read 'Kansai Tokugawa'. His cousin's remains had been found in the forest and brought to the village by someone he had known some time ago. Half-eaten by what he had been told was a bear, he had been away at the time and didn't get to see the remains or the burial. But hearing about the accident in Ueno and Kansai's subsequent disappearance, it made sense that he had committed *Seppuku*-suicide.

However, with the appearance of the *Yamabushi* that morning, he was now confused. His father had given Kansai the warrior name of Yamakiri at the beginning of his training, and it seemed too coincidental that now someone had mysteriously appeared with the same name. Many unusual things had happened around the time his cousin had gone missing and Watanabe had never heard exactly what had happened to Kansai or his father. However, he had been told that Kansai had killed Mariko's father while trying to save his uncle's life. Mariko had never been told this.

Suddenly, he felt a hand on his shoulder. He turned to see Mariko standing behind him. Her face was veiled in shadow as the sun beamed out from behind her.

"Your father was a good man, Watanabe," Mariko said reassuringly.

Watanabe said nothing; he was still immersed in the past and the events prior to the raid on Ueno. He had known Mariko before this, but after rescuing her she had no recollection of him or the training they had undertaken together. This disturbed Watanabe He could not help but wonder what she had hidden in her mind; locked behind an invisible barrier that his father had placed there to prevent her from remembering. This was an aspect of his father that he had never understood, and he knew it was only a matter of time before the truth would have to come out; this would surely shatter the peaceful existence he had tried so hard to build for himself and his family.

- * -

In Kyoto, Seiko was helping out in the kitchen of Go-Daigo's Arashiyama palace. She had been accepted into the establishment just before Kusunoki had increased the security around the Emperor. Her mission was to fit in, and therefore become invisible, until she was given orders to move; a *Chitsumushi* - a bug concealed in the grass. This required time and patience on her behalf, but she knew all too well that the more time spent on preparation the more favourable the outcome and effective the end result.

She thought back to how she had ended up in this situation. How she had been betrayed by the very person she loved and trusted. How his deception had lured her into setting up a situation that saw her father killed, despite a promise that his life would be spared. What was even worse was he was the one who had killed her father in cold blood. He had told her how he had died and claimed it was an accident, but she didn't believe him, her trust was eroded as he pleaded for his innocence. She had grown up surrounded by *Samurai,* but never really understood their ways or means. The sheer brutality of their methods made no sense and she found it hard to see how such violence could ever lead to a peaceful life. She had observed how war perpetuated revenge, which in turn brought more violence and hatred. It was a vicious circle. That was why she had decided to help the *Ninja* when approached several years earlier, to help with a peaceful resolution, or so she had been told.

However, now she found herself working for the Ashikaga *Samurai,* the supposed enemy. She tried not to dwell on it too much, the confusion of who seemed to be right wasn't blurred. But she had another agenda; ironically, for her it was about revenge. But in her case, it was far more simple, to see justice done on those who had betrayed her father and had caused his death through deceptive means. Although they were carried out by the very person she had fallen in love with, she knew the orders had come from a man in the very place she had infiltrated. Her intention was to work her way down through the hierarchy and to punish those people systematically with her own methods, using the mind. The last, her father's murderer, him she would savoir as she made him suffer. She knew where to find him, but time was on her side. For now her father's killer – Kito Harada- would have to wait.

Chapter 12

Yamakiri had struggled to regain control his thoughts after Kito had told him that the death of his father had been intentional.

"You do not seem concerned by what you have told me, Kito san," Yamakiri finally asked.

Kito did not respond, it was as if he was giving Yamakiri time to digest what he had just told him.

"And what of innocent people like Mariko Yokoku? She has no recollection of what she has been through, or of me; her memories erased, for the sake of what?" Yamakiri added.

Mariko had been used to aid the *Ninja* in carrying out their plan; she had been hypnotised into believing she was another *Daimyo's* daughter. However, her father, who believed she had been killed, had sought revenge on Yamakiri's uncle for orchestrating such a plot: killing him and in turn being killed by Yamakiri.

"Well, that is exactly the point, she remains unaware and innocent of what took place," Kito responded.

"And everyone else?" Yamakiri asked, referring to the state he had found Kito in, staring him in the eyes.

Kito recoiled, as if something had clicked in his mind.

"We are warriors, Yamakiri; this is our path. To move forward, *Sutemi* - sacrifices must be made sometimes," stressing the word *Sutemi*.

Yamakiri felt uncomfortable with the reference to being a warrior. He had spent several years in the mountains trying to free himself of the nightmares and memories of the past. But with constant reminders, he felt trapped and even worse, vulnerable.

However, he had surfaced to witness a change in the state of the country, back to one of conflict and seeming chaos. But now it seemed even worse, conflict had affected the very path that he had wished to follow, to free himself of the past. It seemed his desire to follow the peaceful path of the *Yamabushi* was becoming nothing more than a distant dream.

- * -

In Kamakura Takauji Ashikaga sat with his brother Tadayoshi, he had entered the room just as Ryushin Yakushimaru was leaving. As they had passed, Ryushin looked at him and a big smile lit up his face. This had made Tadayoshi feel uncomfortable; he didn't completely trust his brother and his methods, especially some of the people he had employed to bring his plans to fruition.

"You seemed disturbed by the presence of Ryushin," Takauji said.

"Hmm, well, I am not sure his methods are the most appropriate to remove Go-Daigo from power," Tadayoshi responded, his concern obvious.

"You quickly forget how he destabilised Iga and Koga, by using unconventional methods himself Tadayoshi. This is war, we are fighting for what was taken from us, our birthright," Takauji quickly responded.

"That is exactly my point though, Takauji. I don't consider the *Ninja* noble or worthy of the description of warriors, they do not fight fair on an open battle field, but instead choose the hide in the shadows and stab people in the back," Tadayoshi responded.

Takauji thought for a moment before responding.

"Maybe you are just old fashioned, brother, we must move with the times. The lines of battle are no longer defined and explicit as they were in the past and our enemies no longer wear the same uniform and regalia to be easily identified. Go-Daigo has successfully managed to weaken those lines and lure some of the *Daimyo* by the promise of power. So we must play to this weakness to be successful," Takauji said, looking out the window.

"And how do you propose to do that?" Tadayoshi asked.

"We must meet him on his own terms and fight the way he wants to fight," Takauji said, returning his attention to his brother.
"I have sent Ryushin to Kyoto to lure Nitta Yoshisada away from his master. Without his loyal service and with Kusunoki otherwise occupied, it will weaken Go-Daigo's ability to rule, especially if he is unable to focus on retaining the interests of his followers," Takauji continued.

"And how do you intend to do this? Yoshisada is no fool," Tadayoshi responded.

"Ryushin may be young, but he is cunning and clever. I have every faith that he will be able to achieve what I have asked of him," Takauji said, smiling.

Tadayoshi said nothing, but stirred as an uncomfortable feeling enveloped him; once before he had come face to face with Nitta Yoshisada and knew better than to underestimate his abilities, or any opponent for that matter.

- * -

Masashige Kusunoki and six of his men rode into the large town of Ueno. It was noon, and people going about their business stopped and dropped to their knees as the seven passed. But times were different; when they were under the control of Sakamura, such a gesture was made to ensure their lives were spared, but this time it was out of gratitude and respect. Kusunoki smiled as he enjoyed the adoration, but in the back of his mind he knew that his mission would not have been possible without the assistance of a group of *Ninja*. After all, this was their land and they had the biggest incentive to oust Sakamura. Once again, he was here to seek their help, but this time it was to find Prince Morinaga and return him to Mt Hiei.

Stopping at the feet of an old man with his head bowed, he dismounted his horse.

"Excuse me, I am looking for a person named Kito Harada. I believe he lives near here? Kusunoki said, urging the man to stand up.

"I am sorry, I am not familiar...." he was stopped by a younger man behind him.

"I know where to find Harada san," he interjected, bowing several times, in respect of the impressive figure before him.

"Please, can you show us the way then?" Kusunoki responded, urging him to mount his horse beside him.

The man mounted his horse and looked back at Kusunoki.

"This way," he said, tapping his reigns on the side of his horse's neck.

He led Kusunoki and his men out of the town through the large northern gate.

After riding for a while, the young man stopped them at a sharp bend.

"Up there, Master," he said, pointing up a narrow track that disappeared into thick brush.

"Thank you, we will be fine from here," Kusunoki said acknowledging his help with a bow.

Kusunoki looked up the hill and could make out a wisp of smoke rising from the trees; he knew this would be where he would find Kito.

"Wait here, and water the horses over there" he said to his men, pointing to the river.

He made his way through the brush up the slippery track, purposely making as much noise as possible to announce his arrival and to not get caught up in any misunderstanding.

Eventually he reached the makeshift hut. At first it appeared as if no-one was there, but upon seeing who it was, both Kito and Yamakiri appeared from behind the small building at the same time, surprised to see the large solitary figure standing before them.

Kusunoki instantly recognised Yamakiri from his encounter several days earlier at Enryaku-Ji temple. However, the unkempt man to his left, bearded and unwashed, didn't resemble the Kito Harada he had known and was looking for.

"Greetings, Master," Kito said, bowing his head.

Kusunoki bowed in return and then looked up.

"It has been a long time, Harada san," he said, referring to his present state.

"But not so long for you," he continued, looking across at Yamakiri.

Yamakiri said nothing, but bowed in response.

"I come here seeking your help, Harada san. We need someone of your skills to find Prince Morinaga, he has disappeared and I suspect has been kidnapped," he said.

Kito looked back at Yamakiri. He was intrigued as Yamakiri had asked something different of him and this made Kito suspicious. "Did he send you here?" Kito asked, referring to Yamakiri.

"No, no, of course not, Kito," Yamakiri responded, trying to reassure his friend.

"No, he didn't. I have come because I need your help," Kusunoki said, staring at Kito.

Yamakiri was taken aback. Only the day before, he had met with Kusunoki at the temple and at that stage had seen that its defences were well covered.

"Missing? But I just saw him there only yesterday," Yamakiri said, surprised. .

"Yes, well, he vanished without a trace during the night," Kusunoki continued.

"Why do you think I will be able to find him, Kusunoki san?" Kito asked.

Kusunoki paused for a moment before responding, he knew that if he wanted to get any assistance he would need to choose his words carefully.

"I suspect it was the work of *Ninja,* as he vanished without a trace," Kusunoki responded.

Kito looked at the imposing figure before him. Kusunoki was legendary throughout the country for his heroism and skill as a warrior, but the look on his face was one of anguish and helplessness. Years earlier, Yamakiri and a group of *Ninja* had assisted Kusunoki to overthrow the *Daimyo* in Ueno, but he suspected that their part in that had remained relatively unmentioned; not out of disrespect, but more so to keep their identity safe. After all, most of the people involved in that were locals and had to consider their security going forward.

Kusunoki looked back at Yamakiri.

"Ah, now I remember you, seeing both of you together just reminded me of where I have seen you before," Kusunoki said, staring intently at Yamakiri.

"You were at Sakamura's castle the day we rode in and took over, were you not?" Kusunoki continued.

Yamakiri looked away and then bowed his head. That was a day he had tried to forget for so long. A tide of emotion swept over him like an uncontrollable surge of water, this quickly turned to anger.

"With respect Kusunoki san, what did we actually achieve that day?" Yamakiri asked, a cynical tone in his voice.

Kusunoki looked at the saddened figure before him and considered his response carefully. He had never been confronted like this before, especially from someone so much his junior. He also felt the anger brewing inside him, but unlike Yamakiri, he had trained for many years on how to keep his composure. This was the greatest skill a warrior could possess and was what had made him famous throughout Japan.

"Peace," Kusunoki responded. He was well aware that in times such as these, the idea of any sort of peace was short lived.

Kusunoki had made the connection with Yamakiri and now recalled his past. How he had been brave enough to breach Sakamura's fortified castle and in doing so, prevent an all out confrontation; thereby preventing a massacre.

He needed these men and their skills more than ever, but it was obvious that coercing them was not going to be as straight forward as he had anticipated.

Chapter 13

Ryushin Yakushimaru had made his way to Kyoto; his mission was to lure Go-Daigo's loyal follower and protector Nitta Yoshisada away from him. He knew as soon as it was discovered that Prince Morinaga was missing, Kusunoki would be occupied on finding out his whereabouts-now he needed to deal with Yoshisada.

He tied his horse to the banister of an old inn on the city's outskirts. As he made his way through the narrow streets, Ryushin kept his eyes to the ground. His many years of training had taught him that by not engaging with people, he could remain relatively invisible and unseen. He knew Go-Daigo would have spies everywhere, but Ryushin was able to spot them long before they noticed him and take the appropriate measures.

After an hour of walking, he came to a large house in the eastern part of Kyoto; this he knew to be Yoshisada's residence. He casually surveyed the building; it was fronted by a large solid wooden gate. He could tell it was heavily fortified by the large number of metal studs peppering its exterior. However, Ryushin was well aware that where there was fortification, there was also *Tsuki* – weakness. This he had learnt not from his years of martial arts training, but from the study of *Shugendo* – the disciplines of becoming a *Yamabushi*. Ryushin had difficulty understanding how these so-called warriors didn't know such things, but on the other hand he was grateful that it enabled people like him to successfully ply their trade.

He made his way down the narrow lane. Beside it a high stone wall provided security, capped by an overhanging wooden walkway designed to be difficult to assail. Ryushin smiled to himself as he walked its length; maybe this would deter a *Samurai*, but it certainly wasn't much of a challenge to him.

As he approached the corner, a guard rounded it; he was dressed in armour and was carrying a *Yari* – spear. Ryushin had nowhere to go but straight ahead; he knew any sudden change in his demeanour would surely raise the alarm. However, his lack of surprise gave the guard immediate cause for suspicion.

"Stop there!" the guard said, dropping his *Yari* in Ryushin's path.

Ryushin knew this weapon well, he also knew that *Samurai* never carried a weapon unless they were also very adept at its use. But his mind was put at ease by the way the guard had halted him, without preparedness for any sort of confrontation.

"Do you have permission to walk down this lane?" the guard asked.

It was obvious the guard was bored and was trying to goad Ryushin into a response. Having to walk guard duty around the house would have been some sort of punishment for an indiscretion and he would be keen to elevate his status in any way possible. What was more, Ryushin knew this was a public lane.

"I am sorry sir. I had no idea I could not go this way," Ryushin said apologetically bowing several times.

He was well aware that each time he bowed, he showed his inferiority and weakness to the guard. In fact, he could feel the guard's sense of power growing. Ryushin had been taught this technique as a young boy by his grandfather, who had explained it best with the example of a cat and a small bird that had been trapped. The more the bird acted submissive and defeated, the less interest the cat had in it. However, Ryushin sensed the opportunity to take control of the situation and help him towards his goal.

Ryushin looked up and stared intently into the guard's eyes, locking his psyche and drawing him in. The guard had no choice but to surrender to his influence.

"Remove the *Yari*," Ryushin ordered him.

Without hesitation, the guard lifted the *Yari* from in front of Ryushin and stood at attention, his eyes looking ahead in a daze.

"At noon tomorrow, you will attempt to kill Yoshisada, but will not be successful. Do you understand?" Ryushin commanded.

The guard nodded, confirming his orders.

"I am going to leave now. You will count to ten and then keep patrolling. You will not remember me being here or anything I have said. Do you understand?"

"Yes, I understand," the guard responded.

"Alright, begin counting now," Ryushin commanded and walked down the lane past him.

As he reached the corner, he turned to see the guard break his posture and continue on his way; oblivious to what had just happened.

Ryushin smiled to himself as he made his way through the narrow lanes, satisfied that he would be able to make the next part of his plan work.

- * -

Seiko had quickly settled into her job in Arashiyama palace. However, she was well aware that it took more than high walls and guards to keep someone safe. In her training as a *Kunoichi*-a female *Ninja,* the principles of her art looked not just at the physical methods of protection and their inherent vulnerabilities, but more so, at the mind and its weaknesses. She thought how easy it would have been to simply kill him, having seen several opportunities to do that already, but this was not why she was here. She had been constantly reminded by her teacher about *Nagare* – the flow of things and how to appreciate this. Like water, if you try to cut off its path, it will eventually find another way and in most cases, with more violent urgency. No, her masters didn't want that; if they could change Go-Daigo's way of thinking then it would alter his direction and intention; an intention that presently saw him trying to take control of the *Shogunate*.

Her mission was to get close enough to ply her trade. She understood how to access and traverse the labyrinth of the mind; to navigate into parts of the sub-conscious that had developed long before man had evolved into the so-called civilised creature he now was. A lot of this had come naturally to her. Tormented as a child by the death of her mother at such an early age, she had found solace in exploring such regions that others would have avoided.

Seiko's mission at this stage was to observe and to find patterns of behaviour in her target. She found this was far from difficult, especially where so much of Go-Daigo's actions were dictated by form and the expectations thrust upon him by his followers.

She followed the procession of servants down the long corridor towards Go-Daigo's dining room. Although she had been in the palace only a few days, she had been called in to substitute one of the servants who had suddenly fallen ill; an opportunity easily created and subsequently taken by Seiko. Unlike the other servants, Seiko noted as much as possible on her way to Go-Daigo's location; the width of the corridors; height of the ceilings and the coverings on the floor all committed to memory along the way. She had selected her victim well, knowing that in the hierarchy, she would be afforded the most freedom, placed at the back as the order of her importance dictated. Ironic, she had thought to herself, about how such a tradition had presented a weakness that was easily exploited by those who needed to do so.

Finally the head of the procession reached the large wooden doors to Go-Daigo's room; it was flanked by two large guards. The more senior guard looked intently at the group of the five servants, scanning for anything out of the ordinary. His glance turned to Seiko and for a moment remained fixed, as if to force some sort of reaction that could allude to anything untoward.

However, Seiko was well aware of this and stared at the back of the servant directly in front of her, this satisfied the guard that she had been well trained and was trustworthy. The guard moved his attention back to the head servant and nodded.

"Alright-go," he said bowing and turning back to the other guard for him to open the doors. The last thing he wanted was to be responsible for his master's dinner getting cold.

Seiko shuffled into the room behind the rest of the group. It was large, with a high ceiling. The walls were embellished with many large paintings (some depicting battle scenes), calligraphy and wall-hangings. At the front of the room was a solitary figure, sitting behind a long table. Although there were five servants carrying an array of dishes, it was usual to provide far more than Go-Daigo could eat. The rationale was that it was better to have too much, than to provide not enough and upset him.

She waited her turn, taking the opportunity to survey the room. To her left was a large window, its wooden shutters closed to keep out the cold and further along, a small door. She assumed this was an escape exit to be used in times of danger. This was a common feature in rooms such as this and only a select few knew where it would lead to.

"Come, come," Go-Daigo called her forward as the servant in front of her moved to the side.

As Seiko came forward, Go-Daigo looked her up and down. Never having seen her before, he was curious to find her in his presence without the formal screening process he usually carried out to ensure his security.

Seiko placed her tray of *Wagashi* down on the table; all the time under close scrutiny. As she stood up, she smiled and bowed, exuding the confidence of someone who was meant to be there. Go-Daigo was caught off guard by her brashness. As she took up her position at the end of the line, he ushered the first servant forward.

"What is this?" he whispered to the head servant beside him, looking back at Seiko.

He had hoped that Seiko's presence would have gone unnoticed, but this was obviously not the case.

"I am so sorry master, one of the servants had suddenly fallen ill and I needed a substitute he said, shaking as the gravity of the situation set in.

"I have never seen her before," Go-Daigo said, tempering his anger. He referred to the fact that he insisted on personally meeting anyone who would serve him food.

"She has just started in the kitchen," the servant said, trying to shift responsibility to the head chef.

Go-Daigo moved her to one side with a flick of his hand and shifted his attention to Seiko.

"You-come forward," he said, nodding to her.

Seiko quickly shuffled forward and dropped to her knees, bowing, conscious of the need to place herself lower than Go-Daigo.

"What is your name?" Go-Daigo asked.

"Seiko, Seiko...Harada," she responded nervously.

Go-Daigo looked into her eyes and was immediately swept up in her apparent innocence. Her intention to present the persona of a shy young girl was working. She thought back to her childhood and the times where she had managed to coerce her father into submission with the same manipulative technique, but she was well aware the importance of this moment and the reason she was here. She was aware of the imminent danger she was in and suppressed any thought of this. It was easier than having to hide it once it became an emotion.

"Hmm," Go-Daigo responded, looking back to the head servant.

She had a nervous look on her face. She had breached protocol and prepared herself for the consequences.

Go-Daigo looked back at Seiko.

"You work in the kitchen, I am told?" he asked.

"Yes, Master," Seiko responded meekly.

"What do you cook?" he asked, not expecting any sort of definitive response.

Seiko looked down at the table between them.

"Well, I am told I make good *Wagashi* cakes," she replied.

"You made these?" he asked, pointing to the plate of sweets.

Seiko nodded.

Go-Daigo picked up one of the colourful cakes and taking a big bite, chewed on it thoughtfully. Time seemed to stand still as he looked at Seiko and the other servants while finishing the cake.

After swallowing the last mouthful, he looked back at Seiko and smiled.

"That is the best *Wagashi* I have ever tasted," he said, some of the pink remnants of the cake still between his teeth.

"Well, you better get back to the kitchen, Seiko and make some more," he said, sealing her acceptance.

Then he looked back at the head servant. She knew she had made a big mistake, but also from his smile, sensed she had somehow been redeemed.

"Yes, Master," Seiko responded, standing up and joining the rest of the group.

As they marched out of the room, Seiko smiled. *Tsuki,* she thought to herself; to have infiltrated Go-Daigo's so-called impenetrable fortress and what's more, his inner-sanctum, with little effort, made her appreciate her years of training and unique skills. She was in control and exactly where she was supposed to be at this point in time. Now the real work could start.

- * -

Outside Ueno, Kusunoki had resigned himself to the idea that Kito Harada was not going to assist him to find Prince Morinaga.

"So be it then, Harada san," Kusunoki said, bowing and walking off down the narrow track in the direction of the main road. He was a man of few words and had to keep going; the longer Morinaga was missing, the less chance he had of finding him alive.

Kito looked at Yamakiri; the look of guilt at the prospect of letting Kusunoki down obvious. After all, Kusunoki had sought him out, amongst all of the other warriors in the region and he was someone who would remember such things for a long time.

"Wait, please, Kusunoki san," Kito shouted, breaking the unbearable silence.

Kusunoki immediately stopped and turned around, looking over his shoulder.

"I will help you to find Prince Morinaga," Kito said confidently.

"But under one condition," he continued.

Yamakiri was taken aback. Here was his old friend trying to do a deal with one of the most powerful and respected *Samurai* in Japan. What was he doing?

"Go on," Kusunoki said, surprising both of the young men at his readiness to negotiate.

"That Yamakiri is granted his wish to train in *Shugendo* and become a *Yamabushi*," Kito responded, unsure of how Kusunoki would respond.

114

Kusunoki paused for a moment, as if thinking how he could make this happen. However, his influence was huge and he was sure he could achieve it.

Yamakiri felt a nervous rush of energy sweep through his body, he was taken by surprise at Kito's request.

"You don't have to do this," Yamakiri whispered back to Kito.

"I know I don't, but this is what you want, isn't it?" Kito responded smiling through his unkempt beard.

"*Henka* my friend," he added.

"Yes but…" Yamakiri was about to respond, when Kusunoki interrupted.

"Very well-I will make my way back to my men at the bottom of the track and await your arrival."

Yamakiri said nothing as he waited for Kito to gather his things; his mind immersed in the prospect of what was before him. On his visit to Hieizan temple Prince Morinaga had said he was able to practice *Shugendo* only if he was able to train the *Sohei* in *Ninjutsu*. However, with the sudden disappearance of the Prince, everything had changed. He thought back to a lesson his *Sensei* had conducted early in his training on the idea of what Kito had just said-*Henka*.

Yamakiri was practicing a technique with his cousin when he was stopped abruptly.

"Ok –very good," his uncle said, looking at both of them.

"But now I want to see as many *Henka* as you can do from this one technique."

Yamakiri was confused. He had never heard this expression in training before, but knew this word meant change. However, in the context of his training, he suspected it held a much deeper significance.

Seeing the look on Yamakiri's face, his uncle did what he always did and confronted him.

"Ok, *Tsuki* now," he commanded, asking that Yamakiri attack.

Yamakiri knew better than to hesitate, as on a similar occasion he had waited too long and instead of attacking, had been attacked first.

Yamakiri punched with intent, in response his uncle moved to the side, striking him in the arm and then throwing him across the small *Dojo*. Yamakiri performed a forward roll and came up on his feet, facing back towards him.

"Once more!" he ordered.

Yamakiri moved back in and attacked. Again and again he was thrown and each time he got up and returned to perform another attack. After about five throws he stopped Yamakiri.

"So, what did you notice about those techniques?" his *Sensei* asked.

Yamakiri thought for a moment and then responded.

"They were all different?" he responded, not completely sure if this was the answer he was looking for.

"That is correct," he said, smiling back at his student.

"And how do you think this relates to the idea of change?" he added.

"Um, that you changed the technique each time I attacked you," Yamakiri responded again.

"Yes very good –*Henka* in *Budo* means 10,000 changes. In this example, from one technique, comes 10,000 changes; and more importantly, as you have just experienced many different responses to those changes."

"Did you notice that each *Ukemi* you did was different-unique, to my technique?" he continued.

Yamakiri hadn't really noticed, but upon reflection realised that he had in fact performed many different rolls from his teacher's throws.

"Yes *Sensei,*" Yamakiri responded.

"Training in this way will prepare you for anything and make you more accepting of change-this is the nature of *Henka.* Do you understand now?" his teacher asked.

"Yes, I do," the words echoed in his head as he withdrew from his daydream.

Yamakiri knew better than to argue the point with Kito. He had spent some time with him in the past and had the highest respect for him. Also the fact that a person such as Masashige Kusunoki had sought him out for help said so much about the confidence he had in his abilities; in fact it was these that had brought Yamakiri here as well.

The young men made their way down the narrow track and out onto the road where Kusunoki and his men were waiting. He had sent one of them off into Ueno as soon as he had returned and he had returned with horses for each of them. They said nothing as they rode off in the direction of the town, following behind the group. Yamakiri looked at his friend; the wind blew his long scraggly hair back behind him, waving like flames from a fiery torch blowing in the wind. However, Yamakiri couldn't help but think back to the last time he had encountered Kusunoki; he hoped this time it would be a better outcome.

Chapter 14

In Kamakura, Prince Morinaga had once again been brought before Takauji in what seemed like a campaign to humiliate and embarrass him; however, he was still unsure of the motives of his captor.

"What do you hope to achieve by all of this, Takauji?" the Prince asked, the frustration obvious in his voice.

"Hope? I hope to achieve nothing. More importantly I will be successful in getting back what is rightfully mine, Morinaga," he responded angrily.

"Do you really think my father would bend to your threats just because you are holding me hostage?"

Takauji was silent for a moment as he considered what his captive was saying, seemingly giving importance to what the Prince had to say. However, he was much too arrogant for that and Morinaga knew that once he had set his mind on something, he would stop at nothing to see it through to fruition.

"Go-Daigo is no fool Morinaga San, I am well aware of this and in a strange way respect him for what he tried to do. But I am also aware of how he betrayed me and others in his bid to oust the Minamoto clan from the *Shogunate*. To try that without earning the respect of the people was not only foolish, but also fraught with danger," he said, shaking his head.

"So you believe that kidnapping me and holding me ransom is an honourable way to regain the peoples respect for you, Takauji?"

"There is no ransom, Morinaga. You have come here of your own free will, seeking my support to betray your father," Takauji replied angrily.

Morinaga's eyes bulged wide as the rage swelled inside him. He knew that Takauji was pushing him to react, but decided not to respond; he also knew deep down that this would be pointless. Nothing he could say would make a difference to Takauji's plans. If there was one aspect of him that Morinaga had to respect, it was his resolve. However, one thing in Morinaga's favour was his father's loyal commander Kusunoki and his unequalled skill as *Samurai*. He knew that Kusunoki would not easily fall for any ruse that Takauji and his followers could try to present. However, what Morinaga didn't know was how he had been kidnapped and the people that Takauji had employed to carry out his plan. Skilled in the arts of *Ninjutsu*, both Ryushin Yakushimaru and the Kunoichi, Seiko was not only highly trained, but had scores to settle against both Go-Daigo and Kusunoki for their past actions. This made for a deadly combination that would surely end in bloodshed.

- * -

Kusunoki, Kito, Yamakiri and the rest of the group rode north towards Kyoto. It had been several years since Kito had passed this way, the last time just prior to his seclusion to his hilltop retreat. He had made his way to the province of Shiga in search of his lover Akiko Shimada, the daughter of the last *Daimyo's Samurai* commander in Ueno. However, there was no welcome for him upon meeting her; she had discovered that her father had been killed by Kito in an ambush and sought revenge for his death. She had attempted to attack him with a knife, but Kito had moved quickly enough to avoid any serious injury, receiving only a minor cut to his forearm before she fled. Kito rubbed the scar on his arm as he thought about how someone he had loved could do such a thing.

"Does this place remind you of something, Kito?" Yamakiri asked, noticing Kito lost thought.

"Unfortunately war has its unexpected casualties, Yamakiri san," Kito responded.

- * -

It was nearing noon and as Ryushin Yakushimaru had anticipated, Go-Daigo's commander Nitta Yoshisada was about to make his way from one side of his houses courtyard to the other to where he dined. Ryushin had concealed himself under a buttress on the inside of the wall before daylight had set in. He performed numerous exercises to keep his blood flowing as he hung upside down, ensuring he would be able to move quickly when the time was right.

The guard he had confronted the day before was nowhere to be seen, but Ryushin had every faith in his abilities and knew he would be there as instructed. Scanning the compound, his senses were heightened by the effects of the dried *mushrooms he* had consumed. He had been careful to measure the amount, otherwise the hallucinogenic effects could easily take over, distorting his perception. His timing needed to be perfect, too soon and he would be discovered, too late and Yoshisada could be killed.

While Ryushin was intently watching the doorway of Yoshisada's house for any sign of movement, his agent suddenly appeared. He moved into position and was waiting around the corner to ambush his target, his hand at the ready on his *Katana*. Ryushin calculated the distance from his position to where Yoshisada would pass. He waited, hoping his agent would use his training in the manner he expected and as trained by his masters. This would be in typical *Samurai* fashion of confronting his opponent face on and presenting a formal challenge before attacking.

There was a stirring in the doorway as Yoshisada appeared, moving onto the step and pausing before making his way across the courtyard. As his assailant caught sight of him he made his move, shuffling forward to cut off his advance. Ryushin knew there would be little dialogue before the ensuing attack, so had to time his movement perfectly. He scanned the area, checking to see that he wouldn't be noticed. Satisfied, he dropped silently to the ground like a cat stalking its prey, hiding behind a large urn.

The guard pushed Yoshisada backwards, in an obvious move to gain distance. Unarmed, Yoshisada looked confused and obviously found it hard to understand why one of his men would be doing this. As the guard drew his weapon, Ryushin swung into action-leaping out from his hiding position and dive rolling towards Yoshisada. Rising from the ground, he leapt up, and kicking with both feet, hit the guard in the chest, sending him flying backwards into a group of tables and chairs. Yoshisada leapt back into the safety of the doorway as the guard regained his balance and lunged at Ryushin. He responded, twisting his body sideways and securing the handle of the sword, taking hold of the blade from the top. He kicked the guard in the stomach, causing him to lose his grip, then followed up by twisting his body and swiping the blade across the neck of the guard. The sound of tearing flesh filled the air as the cut severed his throat. The guard fell to the ground, holding his neck as the blood spurted out between his fingers. He attempted to get up, but Ryushin stood on his jacket, pinning him to the ground. He convulsed several more times, but as his blood spurted out onto the ground, so did his life and as he gasped his last breath, he died, his mouth and eyes wide open.

Ryushin looked up at Yoshisada, he appeared to be in a state of shock at what had just taken place. He had no idea what had motivated his own guard to attack him or where this stranger had appeared from just in time. They both looked down at the dead guard and then Yoshisada looked up at Ryushin.

"Thank you, you saved my life," Yoshisada said bowing, slightly embarrassed that he had been caught so off guard in a supposedly safe place.

Ryushin bowed in return.

"I am thankful that I was able to be of service, Master," he responded, his serious look reflecting the gravity of what had just happened.

"And you are?" Yoshisada asked.

"Ryushin Yakushimaru, Master. I came here to seek a position as a guard," he said, smiling.

He knew that in the wake of what had just happened and the fact that he had somehow been in the right place to save Yoshisada's life, he would not be subject to the same scrutiny as normal.

"Hmmm, I am curious how you managed to get past my security without my knowledge, Ryushin," he responded in a cautious manner.

"Well in fact, it was this man who let me in. He had told me to wait nearby, then I saw him try to kill you," Ryushin said tentatively, staring down at the dead man.

Yoshisada paused, he was no fool and Ryushin had been taught never to underestimate anyone.

"Thanks to you and your skill he didn't succeed and for that I am very grateful," Yoshisada said, bowing.

"I am only thankful I was in the right place at the right time, Master." Ryushin returned the bow. He was content that his plan to gain the confidence of one of Go-Daigo's top commanders and quickly earn his trust had been a success.

Chapter 15

In Kyoto, Kusunoki and his party rode through the gates of Arashiyama palace. The emperor had been alerted to their arrival and made his way down into the courtyard to greet them. Upon seeing him, they leapt off their horses and knelt on the cobblestones, bowing their heads in respect.

"Up, up," Go-Daigo commanded, gesturing with his *Tesson*, expediting the protocols to hurry things along.

Go-Daigo looked at Kito, his unkempt appearance causing him to frown. Go-Daigo was accustomed to seeing his *Samurai* immaculately dressed, so to see this somewhat smelly bearded man wearing dirty and torn clothing did not amuse the emperor. He glanced over at Kusunoki, as if seeking re-assurance that this was actually the man he had sought to help him in his endeavours. Kusunoki bowed in response and accepted that his master judged people on their appearance above anything else. "Master, this is Harada san, the gentleman I have spoken of," Kusunoki said, feeling the necessity to fill the space.

"Hmmm," Go-Daigo uttered to himself, as if displaying his disapproval of Kito.
"And who is the *Yamabushi*?" he said, looking at Yamakiri.

Yamakiri knew better than to speak until he was spoken to and waited for Kusunoki to introduce him.

"This is Yamakiri, Master," Kusunoki responded, realising that he had no idea of his last name and the importance of this, in regards to establishing his status with his master.
"At your service Master." Yamakiri bowed once more.

Go-Daigo grunted, as if frustrated with his commander.

"We need to talk," he said, ushering him away from Kito and the rest of the group.

Kusunoki followed his lead, turning his back on the two men.

"You bring me these two...men, to help us-a hermit and a *Yamabushi*?" Go-Daigo whispered cynically.

"Yes, Master, but with respect, appearances can be deceiving," Kusunoki responded, trying not to be condescending. "Appearances are a reflection of what is inside. Looking at these two, am I supposed to trust a hermit- obviously ill-disciplined-and divine guidance from the other. This is hardly what I need to ensure my control of the *Shogunate*," Go-Daigo said, his anger obvious by his tone.

"Please Master, please trust my judgement. I will not let you down," Kusunoki pleaded.

Go-Daigo looked back at the two and shook his head.

While Go-Daigo and Kusunoki were engaged in conversation, Kito happened to look up at a window on the first floor of the palace just in time to see a female figure looking down at them. As soon as she saw him, she quickly ducked back behind the shutter. Even though he only had a fleeting glimpse, Kito was sure he recognised her,. His attention was interrupted by the return of Kusunoki, and at the same time Go-Daigo turned and walked back inside.

"The Emperor does not look happy," Yamakiri said.

Kusunoki paused before responding. He was well aware that the two young men before him would not take Go-Daigo's assessment of them lightly.
"Well, I am afraid we have some work to do to gain the Emperor's confidence and trust," Kusunoki said cautiously, not wanting to upset the men.

"Trust? What was the point in bringing us here, if he doesn't trust us?" Kito asked, disappointed at his comment.

"Don't worry, I will sort this out. In the meantime let's get you some food and refreshments. And maybe a bath, Harada san," Kusunoki said with a grin.

- * -

On the other side of Kyoto, Ryushin Yakushimaru had been invited inside Nitta Yoshisada's house and was seated in a small tea room beside the *Samurai*. As the servant conducted the tea ceremony, Yoshisada was curious to observe how Ryushin would behave; this was a quick way to assess his status and upbringing.

"That was a very interesting technique you performed on my attacker," Yoshisada said, referring to Ryushin's speed and the way in which he had despatched the assailant.
Ryushin nodded his head to acknowledge the compliment, but purposely said nothing.

"Obviously this was from no formal *Bujutsu* training, can you tell me where you learnt it?" Yoshisada asked inquisitively.
"From my grandfather, he was a master of *Hakuun Ryu Ninjutsu*," Ryushin responded cautiously.

Yoshisada was from very traditional *Samurai* lineage and had difficulty understanding some of the martial arts practiced outside of mainstream *Bujutsu,* if he was honest, because he felt threatened by what he didn't know. But after having Ryushin save his life, he had to concede that such systems not only had their place, but also merit. Little did he know, it was the same system that had enabled Ryushin to infiltrate his security and earn his confidence in a very short space of time.
"Hmm, maybe you could prove useful, have you heard of Takauji Ashikaga?" Yoshisada asked.
Again Ryushin paused, acutely aware of how important his timing was, especially in conversation.

"I have only heard the name in passing, Master," he responded, concealing the truth by his confident expression.

"Well, I may have something I need you to do for me. That is if you are interested, Ryushin."

"I came here to be of service, so yes, of course."

"Good, first I will see that your needs are taken care of, then we can discuss the details."

"Thank you, Master," he said bowing, concealing his satisfaction at successfully completing another stage in his mission.

- * -

Meanwhile, after Yamakiri and Kito had cleaned themselves up, they were taken by Kusunoki to the emperor's *Ohiroma* – audience room. As they entered, Yamakiri was immediately overwhelmed by the display of wealth around the room. There were large paintings of scenery and golden statues, but one thing Yamakiri noticed very quickly was there was nothing to do with the *Samurai* or war in general. This was obviously a man who dealt in politics and never got blood on his hands, he had others to do that for him. This made sense, because it was the commander Kusunoki who had led the uprising in the province of Iga and had employed the skills of the *Ninja*, including Yamakiri's father and uncle-both of whom had been killed during the takeover. Consequently, Yamakiri had a lot of reservations about providing support to Go-Daigo's cause. For him, war seemed not only to be a futile exercise, but one that propagated more wars, ultimately causing pain and unrest to the people who fought at the front; including himself and his current predicament.

"Come, come," Go-Daigo said, ushering them before him.

He had purposely excluded Kusunoki from this meeting so that he could assess these men for himself.

"Firstly, I would like to personally thank you for your help in Iga. I realise that both of you made great personal sacrifices for me to see that Sakamura could no longer continue his reign of

128

oppression," he said, smiling as he looked backwards and forwards between them.

Yamakiri thought that this was a strange introduction, considering that was over three years ago. He wondered why Go-Daigo would refer to something so long ago and more importantly, what the significance was to what he was about to say next.

"Thank you, Master and…" Kito started to respond, but was interrupted.

"You see, war has never been a good solution for me in resolving political matters. It is far too messy and leaves more problems than it solves in its wake," Go-Daigo added, totally ignoring Kito. He had obviously rehearsed his speech and wasn't going to be interrupted by anyone.

"That is why my Kusunoki recommended you two to find my son Prince Morinaga. He holds you in high esteem and believes you will be able to find him and bring him back safely to me. I believe he is a prisoner of Takauji and is in Kamakura. I am still unsure of Takauji's motives for kidnapping him, as I have had no request for a ransom," he added.
"With respect Master, are you sure he is a prisoner under Takauji?" Kito asked.

"Prisoner-no. Let's just say that my son's loyalty to me has not always been as obvious as it could be. So I need to make sure that he is a prisoner, before I make any damning accusations. Do you understand?" Go-Daigo asked.

"Yes, Master," Kito said bowing. Seeing Yamakiri wasn't following suit, he elbowed him. Yamakiri jumped and realising Kito's acceptance, he had no other option but to go along with it.

In the meantime, Seiko had seen the arrival of Yamakiri and Kito from the window of the palace. She had found it hard to suppress the anger welling up inside her. Not only did it rekindle memories of how Kito had betrayed her, leading to her father's death, but it also presented an opportunity to get the revenge that she had longed for-even though such a move could jeopardise Takauji's plans.

As she waited in the kitchen for her tray to be filled, she thought how easy it would be to poison any of its recipients, now that she had the trust of Go-Daigo and access to his inner sanctum. This would be too easy, however, and was not the way she had been taught by her master.

His words echoed in her mind - 'Attack when it is least expected, in this way you will not only have the element of surprise, but it will be far more difficult to identify the attacker and give you more time to vanish.'

As she waited she prepared herself mentally; breathing out the emotions and thoughts and filling the void with calm. She knew she needed to trick others into believing she was someone else-especially Kito Harada.

She focussed her mind as the cook filled her tray and drew in the confidence from past successes. Using this technique would be the ultimate test of her skill, to fool someone who had not only been close to her, but someone who she had shared intimacy and love with.

As the procession of servants marched down the hallway towards Go-Daigo and his guests, Seiko focussed on the present. As much as she had despised Kito for what he had done, she had a mission to complete and could not let her emotions jeopardise it. She had been told that if successful, Takauji would provide her with anything she wanted. Her mission was to trick Go-Daigo into thinking he was being betrayed by his son, this could not be rushed and require the right timing.

As the line of servants entered the room, she completely ignored Go-Daigo's company. However, what her training hadn't taught her was that the chances of success rested on one's ability to take advantage of the form that bound such people as the *Samurai* and upper ruling class. By following their strict protocols, she understood where to conceal herself and carry out her work. What she had failed to appreciate was that the two young men with Go-Daigo had not been trained as *Samurai* and were not bound by such rules.

Seiko waited patiently as the servants in front of her took turns at placing their trays on the table before the three men. As she moved forward and knelt down, she avoided eye contact with anyone. Once she had placed her tray on the table, she stepped back into line and prepared to leave the room. Although she was content that she had managed to keep her identity secret, she suddenly felt a surge of energy envelop her.
Unaware of what was happening, Go-Daigo smiled "Here-please enjoy."

Kito looked up at the line of servants on their way to the door and shouted "Stop there!", much to the surprise of Go-Daigo and Yamakiri.

"What are you doing?" Yamakiri whispered loudly, grabbing Kito's arm and trying to restrain him as he leapt up.

Go-Daigo was about to reprimand his guest when Kito turned back to him.

"Master, this woman is an imposter," he said pointing to Seiko and moving towards her.

Seiko turned around and delivered a powerful front kick to Kito's groin. Unable to avoid it, his knees gave way and he collapsed to the ground in agony. She was about to deliver another kick to Kito's head when she was struck in the side of the face by a plate, thrown by Yamakiri. The blow sent her reeling backwards as it cut into her cheek. She looked up to see Yamakiri leap over the table and dive roll towards her. Looking to escape, she turned towards the door, only to find it blocked by the head server. She stepped to the side and kicked the woman in the head, sending her flying across the room and into the wall. Quickly opening the door, she exited, slamming it behind her. Yamakiri rose to his feet and leapt over Kito, pulling the door open and expecting to see the woman on the other side. However, as he looked down the long corridor it was empty, to his surprise. It was as if she had vanished into thin air.

Coming back into the room, he helped Kito get up off the floor. Go-Daigo made his way towards them.

"What was that all about?" he demanded, glaring at the two men.

"I am sorry, Master. But I believe you had an assassin here," Kito said regretfully.

"Assassin-that's impossible!" Go-Daigo responded angrily.

"No, Master, I know that woman and what she is capable of," Kito responded, correcting Go-Daigo.

"How do you know such things?" Go-Daigo demanded

"Because I trained her, Master," Kito said, bowing his head.

Go-Daigo looked back at Yamakiri and then at Kito, his eyes wide in disbelief.

"I am sorry, she got away. Shall I go after her?" Yamakiri asked.

"No point, Yamakiri, she would be well gone by now," Kito said.

"Although I am not sure she would have carried out an assassination, as she has had the chance before. I do wonder what her intentions were. I suppose I need to thank you for saving my life, Harada san," he said.

"You are welcome, Master, but I think from now on we need to be extra vigilant. If there is one, then there are likely to be more," Kito replied, frowning.

_ * _

Nitta Yoshisada had no idea what his master Go-Daigo's plans were for Takauji, and had his own agenda to fulfil. He had heard that Takauji was giving away his family land in return for loyalty and that had to be halted. However, the demise of Takauji needed to appear as if it had come from within his own family and as he knew only too well, his brother wanted his position, so it would need to point back to him. He was planning an assassination, which would frame his brother. Once successful, Yoshisada would seize the opportunity to revenge Takauji's death by executing his brother and then taking over power. This he felt would be possible, especially with the help of the highly skilled young Ryushin seated before him.

"Yakushimaru san- you said you had come here seeking to work from me, and after witnessing your skills first hand, I would like you to carry out a very important task for me. Furthermore, it be must carried out with absolute secrecy," Yoshisada said, unaware of the connection Ryushin had to Takauji.
"Yes, Master, I am more than happy to serve you. You can depend on me," Ryushin responded.

"I need you to stage an assassination on Takauji Ashikaga and make it look as if his brother was responsible," Yoshisada said, resolute in his request.
Ryushin intentionally paused for some time, as if to give the impression he had been taken aback by such a request.
However, he had been told by Takauji that Yoshisada was planning something like this. Yoshisada believed that Kamakura was rightfully his and was determined to see it back in his hands at any cost. Ryushin thought to himself how foolish and desperate Yoshisada must be, so deep down he was not surprised to hear of such a plan.
"This could be difficult, Master," Ryushin responded, giving the impression that he knew little of Takauji.
"I am sure you are more than capable, Yakushimaru san," Yoshisada concluded, affirming this more as an order than a request.

"I will do my best," he responded, happy that Yoshisada had so openly exposed his plans.

"Good, I will see that you are supplied with everything that you need to complete your mission."

"Yes, of course," Ryushin responded, smiling.

Chapter 16

After a meal and some preparation, Yamakiri and Kito set off for Kamakura. They trotted off down the well worn road from Kyoto. Kito had noticed that Yamakiri had been very quiet and had hardly said a word.

"You seemed reluctant to go on this mission, Yamakiri?" Kito asked.

Yamakiri said nothing for some time, purposely avoiding eye contact with his friend; instead looking into the trees on the side of the road.

"Who was that woman?" he finally asked.

Kito chose to remain silent. He didn't want to discuss the subject, especially as she had been partly responsible for the death of Yamakiri's father some time ago.

"Well?" Yamakiri demanded, stopping his horse. He suspected that the reason Kito had been reluctant to talk about the incident in Go Daigo's palace was because he was trying to conceal something and he wanted to know what it was. However Kito kept on riding, as if such a gesture would prove enough to avoid talking about it, but Yamakiri had been searching for answers and was not going to let it go.

"Right, I am not going to help you unless you tell me what is going on," he insisted.

Kito finally stopped his horse and turned around, however instead of answering, he looked beyond Yamakiri as if something in the distance had caught his eye. Yamakiri looked at him puzzled and then turned around to see a lone person on horseback approaching them. As he came closer they could see it was a young man, probably in his late teens.

"Greetings," he said in a friendly voice bowing.

As he caught up, Yamakiri followed him with his stare. "Greetings," Yamakiri said, bowing and returning his gesture.

The young man looked at the pair and from their body language knew that they were having some sort of disagreement.

"I am sorry, am I interrupting something?" he asked cautiously.

Kito looked at Yamakiri and then back at the young man.

"Um, well nothing that cannot wait for another time," he said, straining to smile.

"I am Kenji Shimada from Kamakura," he said, introducing himself and bowing once more.

"Kito Harada, from Ueno," Kito responded.

He looked across at Yamakiri as if to prompt him to introduce himself. Yamakiri thought for a moment then responded.

"Yamakiri," he said, obviously reserved in giving any more information than he had to.

"Okay," Kenji said smiling.

"I take it you are off to Kamakura?" Kenji added.

"Maybe," Yamakiri responded.

"Well, I am at your service, if you need any directions. I grew up around here and can guide you safely," Kenji said.

There was an obvious tension in the air between Yamakiri and this stranger. Sensing this, Kito rode back.

"Yes, that would be much appreciated. I hear there can be bandits on these roads," he said, staring back at Yamakiri as if to break his bad attitude.

"Very well then, shall we continue?" Kenji asked, turning his horse in the direction of Kamakura.

"Fine," Yamakiri uttered, not completely happy with this arrangement. There was something about this person that he didn't like, but he was unsure what it was.

136

As they rode off, the young man made sure his riding style was not reflective of his true expertise with horses, or any other skills for that matter; the last thing he wanted was to disclose his true identity to anyone unnecessarily.

- * -

Seiko had made her way to the outskirts of Kyoto. She was angry with herself, being unable to conceal her true identity from Kito Harada. What was more, she had compromised her mission and would have some explaining to do to her masters.
 She had underestimated his skills, as she had the day she had tried to kill him. Now it was unsafe for her to be seen in Kyoto, but her duty was to return to Takauji and inform him of her failure, this would then call for a new plan. She was also disappointed that she had not had time to discover why Kito was there and knew that his presence could only be to conduct some sort of mission-why else would he be in the company of Kusunoki? Her mission had been to manipulate Go Daigo into sending Kusunoki to Kamakura and ultimately into a trap.

From the cover of some trees, she surveyed the road towards Kamakura and seeing several people pass by in a short space of time, decided to lay low and rest until night fall. She made her way to the top of a small hill, from there she had a good view of the road in both directions, not that she would expect anyone to come looking for her, but more out of habit. Lying down under a large shrub and out of sight, she closed her eyes and attempted to get some sleep.

- * -

In Kamakura Takauji Ashikaga was sitting with his younger brother in a large room, its large doorway leading to a balcony that overlooked the sea in the distance. He seemed transfixed and in deep thought as he stared at the river mouth where the Namerigawa River spilled out into the ocean.

"Is something troubling you?" Tadayoshi asked his older brother.

Takauji heard the question, but ignored him, as if to give more importance to himself and consequently less to his inferior sibling.

"Hmm," Takauji finally uttered to himself, turning to face Tadayoshi.

"These are interesting times and what happens next is pivotal to returning Japan to its rightful ruler," he continued arrogantly.

"Yes, I am well aware of the situation. Even though you have excluded me from most of the details," Tadayoshi responded, as if disappointed.

"Well, there is a good reason for that, there are many other things that are happening as well," Takauji said, forcefully slapping his fan in the palm of his hand.

"I am like that river there; my flow is like this –indomitable. The governance of Japan can only be by *Samurai* to be proper and effective. Go-Daigo believes it is time for diplomacy and political control; however he fails to recognise the foundations of this country are forged in blood and not on paper," Takauji said loudly, banging the end of his fan on the table, causing a deep impression.

The loud crack echoed through the room, filling the silence. Takauji stared at the dent in the ornate table, as if admiring his work. Then without warning he swept aside the small pile of paper that his brother had placed there some minutes before, some of the pages were swept upwards and then floated down like blossoms on a spring day.

"Here is proof-see for yourself brother. Where is the impression made by your paper-? It does not exist. Not like the *Tesson,* its impression is permanent," he said, smirking.

Tadayoshi knew better than to respond to his brother's taunt and knew this was his way of asserting his power. However he had to concede that the past few years had seen nothing but violence in the country, as each faction vied for control. Furthermore, he could only hope that by agreeing with his brother he would be awarded some degree of control and ultimately be left to his own devices-as dangerous as that could potentially be.

Chapter 17

During the long ride to Kamakura, Kito attempted to make conversation with their self invited guest. Although initially he had been openly willing to share the journey and provide guidance, he had gone quiet, as if trying to avoid conversation. All along Yamakiri had ridden behind the two men and as he had been taught, observed the newcomer for anything that may prove different to what he had said about himself. One thing Yamakiri had noted was the manner in which he appeared to be riding. It was as if he kept changing his style and rhythm every so often. Yamakiri had been taught to look for the subtle things that alluded more to changes in thinking, more so than in habit. Finally, he turned and stopped, waiting for Yamakiri to catch up. "Is there something about me that makes you uncomfortable, Yamakiri San?" Kenji asked.

Kito also stopped and waited a few feet ahead of the two.

"I am not sure, should there be something to be weary of?" Yamakiri responded.

This comment surprised Kito, who unlike his partner, had no reason to be suspicious. Kenji intentionally paused before committing to an answer.

"There is a crossroad up ahead, make sure you take the right road, it will be much safer. Maybe we will meet again, *Sionara*," Kenji responded bowing to both of them. Then before anyone could respond, he turned and cantered off down the dusty road; the cloud of thick dust kicked up by his horse covered his sudden departure.

Kito turned back and looked at Yamakiri.

"What was all that about?" he asked, obviously confused at Yamakiri's strange comment and behaviour.

"Maybe we should take the left road then Kito," Yamakiri said, looking past Kito and into the settling cloud of dust.

"What! Why would you propose such a thing?" Kito responded angrily.

"Okay, we will take his advice then," Yamakiri conceded, in an obvious effort to keep the peace.

However, his instinct told him otherwise and he had learnt to trust this over the years of solitude in the mountains. He had to also respect Kito's judgement and needed him to unravel the circumstances of his father's death, but as they rode on, he prepared himself by reciting a *Mantra* over and over, its purpose, to provide protection should they encounter any danger. He also decided not to tell Kito of the several attempts he had sensed from this man to penetrate his psyche, knowing that Kito would be unaware of anything of this nature.

Eventually Yamakiri and Kito came to the crossroads that Kenji had warned them about earlier. There was an obvious tension in the air as Kito considered the right road to take. He stopped and looked back at Yamakiri, well aware that any decision he would make could have repercussions in the future. Once again, Yamakiri was not going to argue.

"Go, go," he said, ushering his horse past Kito and onto the right fork in the road, against his better judgment.

"Stop!" Kito shouted, causing Yamakiri to pull up his horse.

"We will go the other way then," he added, pointing towards the left fork.

Kito still had no idea why Yamakiri didn't want to trust Kenji's directions, but at the same time, he needed to make the point that they were equal and that it was crucial to show that. However, what neither he nor Yamakiri had realised was the true ability of this man to penetrate Yamakiri's mind, in such a way that Yamakiri truly believed he had made this decision himself. This was a higher level of *Ninjutsu* called *Ninpo;* neither of them had seen it, but Kenji was a master.

- * -

In Kyoto, Kusunoki was engaged in discussion with Go-Daigo. He had been asked about the plans Kusunoki had made to deal with Takauji and the two young men's roles in this. It was evident from Go-Daigo's temperament that he was not too pleased with the lack of progress being made, and Kusunoki's choice of people to carry out his plan.

"Master, I would recommend that we move you to Enryaku-Ji come nightfall," Kusunoki said as tactfully as possible.

This comment was out of context to what they were discussing and had taken Go-Daigo by surprise; consequently he paused before answering.

"What are you trying to say, that you cannot ensure my safety?" Go-Daigo responded, seemingly annoyed by his suggestion. Go-Daigo was well aware that he needed to remain in Kyoto to ensure its control under him. Furthermore, any sign of *Tsuki,* would send a signal to Takauji that he could be easily unseated from the power he had fought so hard to acquire.

"As I suggested-under the cover of darkness and without anyone knowing," Kusunoki responded.

Go-Daigo was not used to concealing his movements for security, after all, he believed he had moved on from this and had the people on his side.

"And what of my affairs here in Kyoto Kusunoki san-who will see to these?" Go-Daigo asked.

"I will see that anything of urgency is forwarded to you, Master. As far as anyone will know, you are ill and require complete rest, this way you have an excuse for not being disturbed. I have also organised a stand in for you, Master," Kusunoki responded.

Go-Daigo's anger was obvious in his face. Kusunoki had already pre-empted his plan and had things in place to carry it out, without any consultation from his master. However, Go-Daigo had previously given Kusunoki authority to ensure his well-being and to take any steps necessary to make this happen.

"Very well, but I must still be seen to still be in control," Go-Daigo sighed-expelling the feeling of helplessness.

- * -

It was early afternoon by the time Ryushin Yakushimaru arrived at Takauji's castle in Kamakura. He had galloped away from Yamakiri and Kito and made good time. He wasn't that concerned about getting there before the other men, as he had misdirected them, sending them down the opposite road he had suggested. This required a river crossing that would slow them down considerably. He smiled to himself as he rode through the fortified gates of the large castle, content in the belief that he could control any person and subsequently, any situation. However, due to his youth, he was yet to fully appreciate the responsibility that came with such power.

Chapter 18

It was late afternoon; the sun was licking the top of a large ridge, preceding its inevitable handover to the night. Seiko stirred as she took some much needed sleep. It was unusual to allow herself the luxury of drifting this far down into her psyche, especially with the prospect of confronting some of the disturbing images and feelings of her unsettled past. She had made a grave mistake, by failing to consider the full impact that seeing Kito could have on her and the memories associated with that.

As she dreamed, she found herself walking out of a darkened cave and into the main street of Ueno, but unlike the usual bustling hub that the town usually was, the streets and lanes were empty and devoid of life. As she passed a street leading to the town square, she could see a crowd of people in the distance. She turned and walked towards them; coming closer she was able to see the focus of their attention. On a raised platform stood a tall man-a *Samurai*, he was waving his unsheathed *katana* high above his head and was shouting something at the crowd. As she came even closer, Seiko recognised him. It was her father. His gaze turned to her solitary figure in the street and he stopped talking, as if he was transfixed and time had suddenly stood still. A feeling of vulnerability swept through her as the crowd turned around and also stared at her, their attention seemingly directed by an invisible force. She turned her attention back to her father. In response he leapt from the platform and made his way towards her, parting the crowd as he swept his sword from side to side, hitting people with the back of it and narrowly missing an elderly man who ducked just in time to avoid its finely crafted blade.

Seiko wasn't sure what to do. It was obvious her father had become angry at the sight of her; she was about to try to talk to him when out of the corner of her eye she noticed a figure step out from the shadows from under the shade of a building. By this stage, her father was about 50 feet away, striding towards her and still waving his *Katana* in the air. Her eyes flickered between the two as each approached, both seemingly intent on reaching her first. She looked around to her left and now could make out the face of the man-it was Kito Harada, but her attention was quickly redirected to her father, who was now running. Her instinct told her to move to a safe position, but as she attempted to move, she couldn't —as if frozen, her muscles were deaf to any command she tried to give them.

Suddenly Kito changed direction, this time moving to occupy the space between her and her fast-approaching father. Appearing to be unarmed, he would be no contest to her highly skilled father, who had now raised his sword in preparation to strike him down. Kito looked back and shouted to her "Go, run!"

His intention was obvious, to provide a buffer between herself and her father to enable her to escape. As he turned back, the blade was already slicing through the air towards his head.

She tried to warn him by screaming, but it was too late. Her body shuddered violently as she woke. Her immediate reaction was to instinctively draw up her legs and try to rock away the intense influence of what she had just experienced.

- * -

Yamakiri and Kito had finally reached the outskirts of Kamakura. It was a large town and provided many an opportunity for distant traders to do their business with those from the northern regions. Throughout their journey the young men had been careful not to arouse suspicion or bring undue attention to themselves; choosing to ride some distance apart and appear as if there was no connection between them. This was necessary in such a region where commoners were deemed suspicious if seen together, even if there were only two of them. As agreed, he

146

waited out of sight, concealing himself in a small patch of trees on the side of the road.

As he saw Kito approaching, Yamakiri placed a leaf to his mouth and sent out the signal his partner was expecting. Kito looked around, and once satisfied no-one would see him, leapt off his horse and quickly pulled it into the dense foliage.

Kito could make out a pair of eyes peering out through the leaves of a small shrub, and ducking down, smiled to confirm their connection.

"I thought you may have gotten lost," Yamakiri whispered to his friend, indicating the length of time it had taken him to catch up.

"You can never be too cautious, Yamakiri," Kito responded-as if echoing something he had taught him a few years ago.

Those words resonated with Yamakiri and provided a quick reminder of why they were there and their mission for Kusunoki. They were to locate Prince Morinaga and report back to Kusunoki. A task that that would require them to utilise skills they had mastered during their time in the mountains of Iga, in preparation for their last mission.

They had at least an hour before the sun would disappear and quickly set about preparing. This involved reviewing the plan of the town given to them by Kusunoki and ensuring that they could communicate silently as they moved through the streets in search of their target. Also, it was important to allow their eyes to adjust to the fading light as darkness set in, each of them going through a series of exercises designed to enhance their night vision. This was why Kusunoki had sought them out, because of such unique skills-their arts of *Ninjutsu*-enabled them not only to conceal themselves in the darkness, but to disappear and become night itself.

- * -

Ryushin presented himself before his master, Takauji, bowing as was custom before seating himself directly in front of him. To Takauji's left sat his brother, positioned to acknowledge respect for his older brother, but more so the power he had over him and the provinces.

"Well, Ryushin, what have you to report from your mission to Kyoto?" Takauji asked, attempting to smile and disguise his mistrust of the person before him.

Ryushin had thought carefully about this meeting on his way back from Kyoto. His purposeful deliberation about it had been further influenced by his chance meeting with Kito and Yamakiri, along with the request from Yoshisada to kill Takauji and to frame his brother for it. He didn't believe in chance or coincidence and knew only too well that there was a very good reason for all of this.

"I believe Go-Daigo is planning an attack, Master," Ryushin responded.

Takauji's eyes immediately lit up and the smile was replaced by an overwhelming expression of satisfaction.

"Attack, are you sure about this?" Takauji asked, hopeful of more details.

"Yes Master, he was assembling his troops as I departed, and in fact I encountered some of his spies along the road, heading in this direction."

"Spies? What are these spies?" Tadayoshi spoke out, looking across at his brother for some form of acknowledgement.

"I suspect they are *Ninja*, Master," Ryushin added, purposely leaving out any more information than need be.

Ryushin was in the perfect position to play one master off against the other. With each sentence he cleverly gauged his audience's reaction and was able to steer their emotions, like the captain steering his ship in rough seas. He needed something of substance to ensure that when this was over and his services were no longer needed, his reward would not just be what Takauji would give him.

Takauji stared out through the large windows towards the west and the mountain range separating them from Kyoto.

Finally he focussed his attention back to Ryushin.

"You have done well so far, Ryushin, I am sure your skills will be no match for these *Ninja* and I will not have to concern myself with such pathetic attempts to disrupt my cause. In fact, I want you to capture these agents and bring them to me," Takauji said, removing his *Tesson* from his belt and pointing its blunt tip at Ryushin's face.

"Yes, Master," Ryushin responded, concealing any concerns he had about Takauji's request.

Ryushin may have been young, but he had been taught from the very start of his training never to under-estimate any opponent. He was not completely sure what Yamakiri and Kito's plan was, but he had sensed that Takauji was the target. And with that knowledge, he also knew that to catch them, he would need to remain close.

He bowed, shuffled back and quietly exited the room.

Tadayoshi looked back at his older brother, as if posing a silent question about his plans now that they had heard the news from Ryushin.

In response, Takauji returned a stare that intimated his authority over his brother.

"You are not concerned that your life may be at risk, brother?" Tadayoshi finally asked.

"Do not forget –I am first and foremost *Samurai*, why would I fear death? Besides, I have every faith that Ryushin will do what I ask of him," Takauji responded.

Tadayoshi however, was not completely convinced of the young man's loyalty to his brother. In these times, loyalty had its price and therefore anyone with the right amount of money could buy it. But he chose not to express his concerns, this was not the time or the place. All he could do was to stand back and observe how history would unfold.

- * -

Chapter 19

Seiko had semi-recovered from the bad dream about her father and Kito, and was quietly making her way through the long grass towards the roadside when she heard the distant sound of horses approaching from the direction of Kyoto. She had chosen this time to move, as being dusk, most people would have settled in for the evening and would be occupied with eating dinner.
She crouched beside a large tree and listened intently, ensuring it would provide good cover from someone approaching from the west. Almost immediately she was able to make out more than one horse as their trotting hooves clipped in and out of time with each other. This also told her that these horses were probably not from the same stable; this had been an aspect of her training that had fascinated her from the very outset and she had spent endless hours familiarising herself with such nuances of nature. As the horses passed she noted the riders, one was obviously *Samurai* and even in the dim light, it took less than a second to conclude that this was Masashige Kusunoki. She had spent every opportunity studying as much as she could about him and his habits. The second person, also male, was dressed in a large old hooded jacket that concealed his face. His style of riding, posture and even position in relation to his riding partner, indicated that this person was higher in authority than Kusunoki; this could only be one person-Emperor Go-Daigo.
Immediately she decided that rather than continue her intended journey back to Kamakura, Seiko now had another mission; to follow Kusunoki and Go-Daigo. She waited until they were further on down the road and then set off. Although on foot, she was more than fit enough to keep up running for some time. After following discretely behind them for some time, she stopped at the start of a long stretch of road. Her training in *Chimon* – Geography had provided an insight into the lay of the land and the fact that half way along this stretch was the intersection

to the road to Mt Hiei and at the end of this, Enryaku-Ji Temple. Her feeling that they were going to turn up this road was confirmed as the pair steered their horses to the left. This made complete sense now, Kusunoki was moving Go-Daigo to a safe location-especially after her mission had been compromised by Kito back in Kyoto. She vaulted over a nearby fence and moved quietly between a group of horses, until she found one that didn't seem as shy as the rest. Leading it to a weak area in the fence, she held it by the holster as she kicked down the flimsy railing. Then jumping on its back she proceeded quietly to round up the remaining horses and herded them out through the gap. This way, the farmer would not suspect that one had been taken and that instead, it had just gone missing.

Seiko made her way through the chaos of the escaping horses and cantered off in the direction of Enryaku-Ji temple.

- * -

Kito and Yamakiri were in the final stages of preparing their mission to find the whereabouts of Prince Morinaga in Kamakura. Kusunoki suspected that he had been kidnapped and was being held captive somewhere; but due to the absence of any demands, he didn't believe this was for any form of a ransom. As the light dimmed and gave way to the darkness, Kito looked across at Yamakiri, who looked worried.

"If you are uncomfortable with doing this, I will go alone Yamakiri," Kito said, looking intently into his friend's eyes.

Yamakiri knew Kito was not just being polite and was concerned with the potential for their mission to go wrong, especially if he was not completely focussed on the task at hand.

"I have to be honest, this was not what I wanted, Kito," Yamakiri responded.

"As you had already made it clear my friend. But sometimes the pathway to peace is not as easy as we would like. Besides, our mission is just to find Morinaga and report back. That is all," Kito said, trying to settle Yamakiri.

Yamakiri said nothing.

"That is also why I will have you keeping watch for me, I will do the risky part," Kito added reassuringly.

Yamakiri knew that things did not always go to plan and that a situation could change within seconds, but he had to learn to trust people again and in Kito's case, even more so.

He had spent a lot of the last three years thinking about what had happened in Ueno and how the Daimyo's daughter had been killed in the chaos.

'Fate', he thought to himself.

"Alright, it is time to go," Kito said, looking up through the trees into the darkening sky.

The two young men made their way to the edge of the trees by the road; each looking left and right for any sign of life, at the same time listening intently- the only discernible noise, was that of thousands of cicadas, providing a wall of noise, something to assist in their concealment. Kito nodded and tapped Yamakiri on the shoulder twice, one by one they disappeared into the shadows, becoming invisible and blending into the night.

- * -

Inside Takauji's stronghold, Takauji was seated with Prince Morinaga, having had him retrieved from his cell in the lower part of the fortress. An elaborate feast had been prepared and laid before them on the large table, something that Morinaga would have been well accustomed to. Takauji's plan was simple, to secure the support of his captive and use this as leverage to sway Go-Daigo to relinquish his drive to secure the northern regions of the country. However, achieving this would require an entirely new tactic, something that had the potential to backfire and cause even more mistrust between himself and

Morinaga.

What Morinaga couldn't see was the darkened figure waiting in the wings behind one of the elaborate thick curtains. The figure listened intently as Takauji attempted to engage his guest in conversation.

"Please, eat Morinaga, you must be hungry," Takauji said, well aware that Morinaga had been intentionally deprived of food in his cell.

Morinaga said nothing, instead he stared at the floor as if in a show of disinterest in the food and Takauji's futile attempt to control him.

"Please," Takauji said once more, trying to sway his resistance. However, Morinaga didn't move or change his posture, obviously intent on ignoring Takauji's offer.

Takauji restrained himself from becoming frustrated; he was no fool and had been prepared for Morinaga's refusal to co-operate. He raised his two fingers to his temple, rubbing them against his smooth skin as he drew them down his cheek. Almost immediately there was a shallow pop from behind the curtain, then a light thud as the sharp point of the dart pierced the tight skin of Morinaga's neck; its poisoned tip allowing the flow of blood to deliver the powerful neurotoxin to its victim's brain. The effect on Morinaga was instant. He looked up at Takauji and opened his mouth to speak, but it had already taken over, causing him to fall backwards onto the floor.

The figure emerged from his hiding place and shuffled over to the lifeless body of Morinaga.

"You haven't killed him, have you?" Takauji asked nervously. Ryushin ignored his master's question and his obvious distrust of his skills. Instead focussing his attention on his victim and what he had been asked to do.

He leaned over the body and removed the dart from Morinaga's neck, replacing it with two fingers; firstly to stem the trickle of blood oozing from the small puncture wound and secondly, to feel his pulse. Ryushin looked up at his master and nodded to confirm he was in control of the situation.

Reaching into his jacket pocket he removed a bamboo tube and pulled out a cloth saturated in a pungent liquid, its smell quickly filling the air. He looked across to Takauji and urged him to make some space by waving his hand. Takauji responded by shuffling back, narrowly avoiding the effects of the powerful concoction. However, Ryushin was not affected; he had prepared himself by blocking his nostrils with small wads of cloth and holding his breath.

He passed the cloth across Morinaga's nostrils and looked for a response; they flared out as his body tried to make sense of the situation. The concoction would enable Ryushin to control the level of consciousness of his victim, to a point where he was totally susceptible to suggestion via the sub-conscious.

As Ryushin worked on Morinaga something caught his eye from the open window, but he kept going as it was essential to complete what he had started. He positioned himself in such a way as to keep an eye on the window and Morinaga at the same time, without making it too obvious. Once he was satisfied Morinaga was in the ideal receptive state, he leaned over and whispered in his ear. Morinaga nodded in response. Takauji sat back and watched intently as Ryushin worked his magic.

Suddenly Ryushin dive rolled towards the window, and in one fluid motion reached out and pulled in the darkly clad figure who had been perched on a ledge to one side. Caught by surprise, the *Ninja* had not had time to prepare for Ryushin's rapid advance; as he was pulled through the opening he crashed onto his side, sending both of them rolling towards Takauji.

Surprised, Takauji had stood up and tried to move away, but had been caught up in the melee. His legs were swept from under him, causing him to crash to the ground. By that stage both of them had risen to their feet and in the chaos, Ryushin had managed to pull off the head cowl of his opponent. As they both stood up, he was able to identify him as one of the men he had met on the road. It was Kito Harada.

Ryushin was about to speak when Kito lashed out with a stomping kick, he needed to create some distance from his opponent. Ryushin twisted his body and punched the kick away; a technique he had practiced numerous times, his strategy to expose his opponents flank and minimise his potential to counter attack. However, Kito continued the motion, and taking advantage of its momentum, executed a sideways roll, coming up off his shoulder and executing a side kick to Ryushin's face from the ground. This hit him with such force that he reeled backwards and tripped over the still motionless body of Morinaga, falling to the floor. He lay there as Kito leapt over Morinaga to deliver a stomping kick to his head. However, he responded by raising his leg up and embedded it deep into Kito's midriff; rolling backwards to throw him over his body. In response Kito altered his balance and flew into a handspring, bouncing off the floor and back onto his feet.

In the meantime, Takauji had made his way to the door and was about to open it to alert the guards. Kito had to stop him, so as he came back to his feet, he delivered a punch to the back of Takauji's head, instantly knocking him unconscious. He fell to the floor in a crumpled heap.

By this stage, Ryushin had recovered and as he rolled over Morinaga's body, he seized the cloth on Morinaga's chest as he advanced towards Kito. As Kito turned, Ryushin flicked the end of the cloth, its whipping motion catching Kito in the eye, its impact and the effect of the solution it was soaked in momentarily blinding him.

Kito lashed out with a punch, but with no depth, he was unable to judge the distance accurately and he missed Ryushin all together. In response Ryushin hinged in and struck Kito in the throat with a *Shuto*-knife hand strike, crushing his larynx. Kito stumbled backwards until he hit the wall behind him. Seizing the opportunity, Ryushin leapt in and driving his thumb into Kito's solar plexus forced the air out of his lungs. Gagging for air and winded, Kito had no option but to try to gain his breath; now the fight was no longer just against his opponent, but also his body, for life itself. Knowing this, Ryushin smothered his face with the cloth and as Kito breathed in; he was quickly enveloped by the intoxicating effects of the neurotoxin and collapsed.

Chapter 20

Kusunoki and Go-Daigo arrived at Enryaku-Ji Temple under a veil of darkness and secrecy, the absence of a moon assisting with this. Approaching the large gate, they were well aware that the now vigilant eyes of the *Sohei* were upon them. Kusunoki's expectations of the monks to provide better security than had been afforded to Go-Daigo's son Morinaga had been well spelt out and even though it was obvious who he was, he still expected to be challenged.

He dismounted and leading his horse to the gate knocked three times loudly, then stepped back and waited. He counted to 20 and then stepped in and knocked again four times. Almost instantly and without a fuss the doors swung open, the two of them entered the welcoming opening. As Go-Daigo's horse passed through the gate, it abruptly stirred and in the process nearly knocked the guard off his feet. However he quickly recovered, and in the same motion, swung the gate shut behind the horses. What he had failed to see was the shadowy figure roll off to the right and keeping below eye level, moved into the shadow of the high stone wall.

Go-Daigo flicked his hood off as they made their way to the centre of the complex. It was late and most of its occupants were either asleep or standing guard; however Tomada, the head monk in charge in the Abbot's absence, was waiting to greet them. As the men approached he dropped to his knee and bowed, and although he had never met Go-Daigo personally, it was obvious to him who he was.

"Please," Go-Daigo said, urging him to stand.

" Yes, Your Highness. I am very sorry, Master, we were unaware that the Emperor was coming," Morehei responded, looking across at Kusunoki and taking hold of Go-Daigo's horse's bridal to keep it steady.

"That is good, his presence here has to be kept secret for his safety," Kusunoki responded.

"Yes of course, Master," Tomada bowed, acknowledging him. What any of them had failed to see was the dark, still figure less than a few feet from their position. Like a wild animal stalking its prey, it listened and watched intently, then subsided into its hiding place to wait for an opportune time to make its move.

- * -

In Kamakura, Yamakiri waited patiently in a large tree for Kito's return. From this position he had seen Kito scale the high wall of the palace like a lizard and at the top slide effortlessly over, ensuring his low profile did not give away his human form. From there he had momentarily disappeared and then came into view again as he scaled the sheer face of the high building behind it.

Now Yamakiri focussed on the point where Kito would again become visible, signalling the success of the mission. At the same time he monitored the surrounding area for any sign of life. He had kept still and waited patiently, as he had been taught, unsure of how long he would have to hold his position. To his surprise, the figure of a man broke the form of the wall for a moment as it passed along the narrow ledge leading to the row of windows. Strange, Yamakiri thought to himself, Kito hadn't taken anywhere as long as he had expected. This was a good thing, however, as the quicker they could move, the less chance of being compromised. Seeing this, he slithered down the smooth tree trunk to the ground in preparation for Kito's return. Once Kito was opposite to him across the road, they both moved off, keeping pace with each other; eventually they reached their starting point and regrouped.

"Come, I must report to Kusunoki," Kito urged, tapping Yamakiri on the arm.

Before Yamakiri could ask what he had seen, Kito quickly led Yamakiri back to where their horses had been waiting and mounting them, cantered off in the direction of Kyoto. Things were moving so fast that Yamakiri barely had time to think, let alone notice the change in Kito's demeanour.

- * -

Seiko lay in darkness under the large wooden structure. Her situation had changed dramatically from one of failure to having the potential to once again succeed. She looked up to the stars, as if to thank the gods for this second chance. She watched intently as Go-Daigo closed the door to what was usually Prince Morinaga's residence, leaving Kusunoki standing on the wooden porch. Her initial mission had been to infiltrate Go-Daigo's castle and alter his perception in such a way as to persuade him to change his plan to take over the *Shogunate*. However, after being compromised by Kito she needed another plan to satisfy Takauji and his expectation of softening Go-Daigo's resolve, making him more open to negotiation.

However, in the back of her mind she had the memory of her dead father and Go-Daigo's part in all of that. Like her, he had also been betrayed and revenge was something that had to be carefully considered and never taken lightly. The consequences of such action were as complex as the deed itself, as her *Sensei* had emphasised many times in her training. He had quickly sensed that she had sought him out to learn the skills necessary to enact her revenge, and had been quick to make it clear this was forbidden. He had even gone to the extra lengths of openly blocking her with a curse that would see any such action punished and her abilities severely weakened. Seiko had seen these powers first hand and had used them herself, and so was under no illusion as to their effectiveness.

She intently traced the movements of Kusunoki as he walked down the small set of steps and moved across the open compound. He too had had a part to play in the events some three years ago in Iga. In her eyes he was partly responsible for the death of her father, although somewhat more indirectly.

161

He made his way to the canteen area, where he caught up with the monk who had opened the gate. From her position, Seiko was unable to hear anything, so she had to move closer. Retreating, she curled up and turned, making her way under the building towards its rear. Once there she checked the open area and surveyed the shadowy areas for a good hiding position and a path that would provide the maximum level of concealment.

She crept up under the large wooden deck where Kusunoki and the monk were seated and from the ongoing pauses in conversation it was obvious they were eating.

"I have asked Go-Daigo to remain hidden here and not to reveal himself to anyone, so I need you to see he is kept comfortable," Go-Daigo said between swallowing his next mouthful of food.

"Yes, Master. But with all due respect, how does the Emperor feel about this?" the monk asked.

"The Emperor has entrusted his security to me and as much as it may not be to his satisfaction, this is not just about his safety, but the continuation of an emperor for this country," Kusunoki responded.

"Further to this, I am worried that an assassination attempt may be made on his life. He needs to remain here until it is safe and the threat is eliminated," Kusunoki added.

There was silence after this statement; Seiko contemplated the weight of what Kusunoki had just said and although there could have been several contenders for the *Shogunate,* she knew that Kusunoki was talking about Takauji. Once again this changed the present scenario and provided Seiko with even more information to provide to her master. She had to make her way back to Kamakura to inform Takauji immediately. With that, she withdrew from her position and made her way to the back of the compound. Silently, she made her way up the steps to the rampart on the high perimeter wall and checking she would not be seen, lowered herself down on the outside and disappeared into the night.

Chapter 21

Yamakiri and Kito had been travelling all night and most of the following day without stopping, except to water the horses when the opportunity arose. Every time Yamakiri had attempted to engage Kito in conversation, he had ignored him. This was beginning to unnerve Yamakiri.

Then without warning, Kito came to a halt in the middle of the road, dismounted and pulled his horse off to the side of the road into a thicket of trees. Yamakiri seized the opportunity to speak to him.

"Look Kito, I am not sure what you saw back there, but unless you tell me I cannot see any point in me being here."

Kito started back at him; his usually bright eyes seemed to recede into his face like bottomless pits. Yamakiri had been taught to read a person by looking into their eyes, but the absence of anything revealing in Kito's was something he had never seen before.

"What do you want to know?" Kito responded, surprising Yamakiri.

"Well, what I just asked you?"

Kito stared back at Yamakiri, as if looking straight through him.

"I saw Prince Morinaga in the company of Takauji," Kito said assertively.

"And he is being held captive, as Kusunoki suspects?" Yamakiri enquired, happy to now have some form of response from Kito.

"No, that is not the case at all. In fact he has joined sides with Takauji and I heard him, was plotting against his father and to bring him down."

Yamakiri paused for a moment, as he considered the situation and how strange it seemed. He had only met Morinaga once, but even so, could not see how the Prince could betray his own father.

"That does not make any sense, why would he want to do that?" Yamakiri asked looking puzzled.

"Look. We were asked to find out where Prince Morinaga is-that was all. It is not for me or you to try to make sense of the reasons behind this. Now, I suggest we get some rest, we still have nearly a day of riding to get back to Kyoto," Kito responded resolutely, as if to deter any more conversation.

"Of course," Yamakiri responded, not wanting to push his friend or their friendship any more than necessary.

- * -

A thick mist hovered above the Kamo River as the morning sun heated the air surrounding it. Masashige Kusunoki looked out through the window across the city of Kyoto and contemplated his next move. After delivering Go-Daigo to Enryaku-Ji, he had returned to Arashiyama Palace, making sure no-one except his most trusted of men had noticed his movements. He faced a dilemma; if he placed extra protection around the emperor at Enryaku-Ji, it would be obvious there was someone important there. Further to this, he would need to send a reasonably large contingent of men, arousing more suspicion. Convinced that Morinaga had been kidnapped, he wasn't confident that the *Sohei* would be able to provide the level of protection that Go-Daigo needed to be safe. On the other hand, if he could create the impression that Go-Daigo was still in the palace, it could be used as a trap for any would be attacker. What he did not know was that his plan had been disclosed and the emperor's security was already at risk.

- * -

Chapter 22

Ryushin Yakushimaru perched himself high on a rock overlooking the large town of Kamakura like an eagle looking for its next prey. He was deep in thought as he considered his current situation, at the same time breathing deeply as if to bring the isolation of the external world within. He had completed Takauji's request to kidnap Morinaga from Enryaku-Ji and bring him to Kamakura. But now he considered Nitta Yoshisada's orders to kill Takauji and frame his brother. This mission would not be that difficult for a man of his skills. However, unlike some, his desires were not purely based on the want for power and domination with no consideration for the long term future. Although this was not his domain, he had been well tutored in the past on what the ramifications of his actions could be and the inherent responsibility he carried with his skills.

There were plenty of *Ronin*– independent and master-less *Samurai* willing to side with the highest bidder as mercenaries, but this was Ryushin's point of difference. He was far more skilled than any *Samurai* and his skills were not just limited to the fighting arts. His teacher had taught him to refine and use the greatest tool that he believed man had: reason. More incisive than even the finest crafted *Katana,* reason provided so many more options than merely cuts delivered from a skilled swordsman and from where he sat at present he literally had the world at his feet.

He thought about the events of last night and how he had managed to convince Takauji that the *Ninja* outside his window had been sent there to kill him, by none other than his arch enemy, Nitta Yoshisada. How naïve Takauji had been to also believe that he had killed the would-be assassin and disposed of his body, before Takauji had had time to regain consciousness.

"Trust", he uttered to himself and smiled. How such an essential aspect of human nature could be used as such an effective weapon against the very people who were foolish enough to subscribe to it. For him, as a *Ninja*, it provided a means of entry and ultimately avoided any need for direct confrontation. Time would tell, as the results of his efforts, would undoubtedly come to fruition.

As for himself, what was he hoping to achieve out of all of this?

'Peace', his inner self responded.

'Peace from what?' he asked.

At this point in time, it was an answer that seemed too far in the distance to be clear. Especially as he not only seemed to be caught up in turmoil and chaos, but in a more than bizarre twist of fate, he was somewhat at the centre of it all.

'Patience', he reminded himself as he stood up and made his way back to Takauji's palace. But as he walked, he tried to make sense of a nagging feeling in the back of his mind. Had he made a mistake and taken advantage of his own ability to control things?

- * -

Meanwhile, Yamakiri and Kito had made their way through the streets of Kyoto and the extra heavy security of the guards around the perimeter of Go-Daigo's palace. The two men had been directed to the kitchen where Kusunoki was having breakfast.

"Morning," Kusunoki said, slightly bowing his head to acknowledge their return.

"Good morning, Master," Kito responded, adding the extra formality out of respect.

"We need to talk Master, I have some disturbing news," Kito said quietly.

Kusunoki looked across at Yamakiri.

"In private," Kito continued, catching Kusunoki's attention and looking back at Yamakiri.

"Very well, follow me," he said, urging Kito in the direction of the main part of the palace.

"Please arrange breakfast for these men," he shouted to the cook as he left the kitchen.

Kito ignored Yamakiri as he followed Kusunoki out of the room, it was as if he wasn't there.

This made Yamakiri feel uneasy, but he took the hint and caught the attention of the cook, nodding to confirm he wanted something to eat and then he glanced back in the direction of the two men as they disappeared around the corner of the narrow corridor.

Kusunoki opened the door to his quarters and gestured for Kito to enter the small modest room.

"Please, be seated," he said, pointing to a small table on the far side of the room.

Kito seated himself as Kusunoki closed the door and made his way to the table. Arranging his elaborate *Hakama* trousers so he could be seated, he sank down like a bird gracefully landing back on its nest. Placing both hands on his knees, he leaned towards Kito.

"What did you find, Harada san?" he whispered to purposely set the tone of the conversation.

Kito stared back intently.

"Morinaga has sided with Takauji and is plotting to betray his father."

Kusunoki lurched forward in response to what Kito had said. "Are you sure?" he asked, his eyes flickering from side to side as he tried to make sense of the situation.

"Yes Master, I saw him in the company of Takauji and heard him making such plans."

Kusunoki sat back and dropped his shoulders, as if a huge load had just been placed on them. His thoughts raced as he tried to make sense of the situation. He had secretly taken Go-Daigo to

Enryaku-Ji for safety, but if what Kito was saying was true and Morinaga had turned against his father, then Go-Daigo was now in grave danger. Kusunoki searched his memory for anything Morinaga may have said that could have alluded to his intention to shift loyalties-but as he reviewed each event, it made less and less sense.

"Please, leave me, I need time to consider my next move, Harada san," Kusunoki said, his face had completely changed from when Kito first saw him, now it was gaunt and his cheeks seemed to be sagging in despair.

"Yes, Master," Kito responded, rising and making his way from the room, leaving a solemn figure staring into the abyss behind him.

- * -

Chapter 23

Ryushin smiled to himself as he made his way down the narrow path from the high rock ledge he had been meditating on earlier. He thought how foolish Takauji had been to allow himself to be manipulated and deceived. He knew this was the intoxicating effect that power had on people, numbing their senses and distorting their sense of reality. As he walked, Ryushin recalled a lesson his grandfather had given early in his martial arts training.

It was a clear sunny morning. Ryushin sat by the side of a large pond, watching with interest as thousands of insects danced across the water in front of him, so still that its surface reflected everything in perfect symmetry.

Ryushin waited patiently for his grandfather to arrive, keeping to his word to be on time to start his training. Although he believed he was well aware of his environment, the arrival of his grandfather startled him; announced by the touch of his firm hand on his grandson's shoulder. Turning his head, Ryushin saw his grandfather's smiling face.

Although just 10 years old, Ryushin was well advanced for his years. He had a natural aptitude for the martial arts and was able to do things effortlessly, whereas others would have taken years to master them. He also had a strong connection to and understanding of nature, inherited possibly from his father, who was a high ranking *Yamabushi*.

His mother had considered Ryushin a gift from the gods. After trying unsuccessfully for so long to conceive she had made a pilgrimage to Enryaku-Ji Temple, where she had prayed to the Yakushi Buddha to become pregnant. Being successful, she had subsequently named her son after the deity.

His grandfather, Dōjitsu, sat down beside him and followed Ryushin's gaze, still focussed on the pond. After some time he spoke.

"What do you notice about the pond, Ryushin?" he asked quietly, breaking the silence.

Ryushin stared even more intently, but was unsure what he was supposed to be looking at. He found these moments quite awkward, as if there was pressure to find the correct answer, so paused before attempting to respond.

However, this time Dōjitsu didn't wait for Ryushin.

"Do you notice how still the water is, Ryushin?"

Ryushin smiled to himself. He had been focusing on this and was prepared for the answer.

"The reflection is very good," Ryushin responded without hesitation, like an archer despatching his target as soon as it had presented itself.

"Yes, yes-good boy," his grandfather said, clapping as if to seal his delight. As he smiled, Ryushin felt warmth come over him and he smiled back.

"So let us think of the water as something other than just water-like say.....your emotions, calm and still. But what is more important is the clarity of the reflection," Dōjitsu said, looking at Ryushin for signs of him understanding the point he was trying to make.

"Good, now looking at the water, keep an eye on the reflection in the water," Dōjitsu said, pointing to the middle of the pond.

It was not hard to discern what his grandfather was referring to. A small black pine tree, about five foot tall was the only thing in view.

As Yamakiri stared, he began to feel warmth emanating from his grandfather. Out of the corner of his eye, he could see that he had clasped his fingers in front of him and was pointing at the pond.

"Watch, watch the reflection of the tree carefully," Dōjitsu said, as if sensing his grandson was not completely focused.

As Ryushin stared, he noticed that what had once been the distinct reflection of the tree was becoming distorted and transforming into something else. He blinked as if to reset his mind, but nothing changed. The water was still calm, but the image was now starting to resemble something of a more familiar form.

Ryushin shook his head again, the tree had disappeared and had been replaced by the image of a young woman, dressed in a very ornate *Kimono*. He looked up, but the real tree had not changed-how could this be?' he thought to himself.

"We see through our emotions, Ryushin, like you see in the reflection of the pond. By changing the nature of the water, we can change the perception of the seer," Dōjitsu said smiling.

Ryushin tried hard to grasp what his grandfather was saying-but confusion was all over his face.

"Do not try to understand Ryushin, one day I will teach you more and with practice, you will master these things," Dōjitsu said as the waters once again became still.

This lesson had set Ryushin on his path to learn more and to master the arts of *Kuji-in* – mind control.

As Ryushin made his way through the Palace gates, he recalled the warning Dōjitsu had given him later on as he taught him these particular skills.

"Never forget that everything you choose to do carries great responsibility and eventually you will be held accountable for your actions".

His grandfather's words echoed loudly in his head as he made his way up the stairs towards Takauji's chambers.

- * -

As Yamakiri slept, he was immersed in a dream that saw him standing high on a mountain, looking over what he recognised as Kyoto. In the distance he could see large plumes of smoke rising high into the air, the intensity of the fires beneath evident by the speed of the rising plumes. It wasn't hard to discern that this was the product of unrest. As he stared he felt his chest tighten and the constricted feeling quickly spread across his body, causing an uneasy tension. Looking across a small rift he could see the rooftops of the temple complex of Enryaku-Ji. As if in contrast to the turmoil below, he could sense the calm of the mountain retreat and as if to support the fact, a faint hue seemed to provide a protective shell over it and its occupants. He projected himself forward and as he passed through this protective shell his demeanour changed instantly to one of utmost calm. Immersed in this feeling he drifted into another realm, to a place he yearned for in his sub-conscious and in his life; for peace and serenity.

Suddenly his sleep was interrupted by a deep thud-instinctively he sat up and looked around the room. Being early afternoon, the artificial darkness created by the heavy wooden shutters was pierced by a thin shaft of light, its iridescent ray illuminated the wall opposite the shielded window. Part of the beam rested on the area where Kito had been sleeping, but his *futon* was empty.

A rush of adrenaline swept through Yamakiri's body, he stood up just as there was a loud scream from outside. Its resonance cut through Yamakiri like a *Katana* through the air. He raced to the window and flung open the shutters; a swathe of bright sunlight temporarily blinded him, but led by the direction of the scream he looked down into the small courtyard to see a group of people gathering around something on the ground.

As they jostled around, he recognised the shape of a body and to his shock, he could see the clothing was the same as that worn by Kito during their journey to Kamakura. As he stared, one of the people on the ground looked upwards, making direct eye contact with him, then the rest followed; completely ignoring the body lying motionless on the ground. Yamakiri knew this meant only one thing. Kito was dead.

Chapter 24

Ryushin sat before Takauji, the seriousness on his face made him look much older than a young man in his teens. But somehow he had been chosen for this life, his youth denied for a greater cause than he was aware of.

"I have presented you with an enviable opportunity Master," Ryushin said, smiling and breaking the silence.

"Yes of course you have," Takauji said referring to his work on capturing Morinaga.

"With respect, this is not something you would know about, but I am sure you will be pleased."

Takauji was taken aback by the forthright attitude of the young man. He was not comfortable in letting others make decisions or acting without his approval, but he also knew he had to be tactful with someone like Ryushin. With his youth and obvious skills, Ryushin was not someone you would want to upset. In fact he felt the best approach was to treat him in the same manner as a *Shinken* –a live sword.

"I hope so," Takauji responded, reservation in his voice.

"Nitta Yoshisada is on his way to take over your position here for Go-Daigo," Ryushin said.

"Yoshisada-how do you know such things?" Takauji responded in surprise.

It was Yoshisada and Takauji who had worked together to retake Kamakura from Hojo Takatoki. Yoshisada wanted control of the area for himself, but upon returning to Kyoto with the news of their conquest, both he and Go-Daigo soon found out that Takauji had decided to go against Go-Daigo's wish to have Kamakura under his control and take it for himself.

"So you have orchestrated this?" Takauji asked.

"Yes Master, but there is more. Yoshisada has been led to believe you are dead and therefore Kamakura is his for the taking."

Takauji stared deep into the eyes of the young man before him, as if trying to gauge his resolve and conviction.

"You say this with much surety Ryushin, how can you be certain that is his intention?" Takauji asked.

"Because he sent me to kill you." Ryushin responded with a degree of arrogance in his response.

Takauji leaned back and sat upright, looking around the room as if to search for a way out. What Ryushin had said made him very uncomfortable, but he tried hard not to show it.

- * -

Earlier that day, as he observed Yamakiri sleeping, Kito listened intently to the rhythm of his friend's breathing. From the length of each breath and his training he knew that he was in a deep sleep. Kito moved silently to the door and harmonising with Yamakiri's breathing, opened it silently, easing his body into the corridor. He moved undetected through the palace and making it outside without being seen, made his way to the other side of Kyoto.

Kito arrived at the home of Nitta Yoshisada and approached the guards on the gate.

"Yes?" one of the guards said, positioning his arm across his body and placing it on the handle of his sword in preparation to draw it.

"There will be no need for that," Kito responded, looking down at his hand.

"I would like to speak with your master," Kito asked the guard.

"And you are?" The guard asked tentatively.

"Just tell him that I have a message from Ryushin Yakushimaru," Kito responded.

The guard whispered into the other guard's ear and then knocked on the gate twice, immediately it opened and the guard disappeared through the narrow gap.

Within a few moments, the gate opened again and the guard re-appeared.

"Come, Yoshisada will see you," he said, inviting Kito inside.

Only a few minutes passed before Kito exited the gate. He made no attempt to engage the guards, instead making his way briskly down the busy street and back in the direction of Go-Daigo's palace.

- * -

Sometime after this, Yamakiri had hurriedly made his way down to the courtyard, pushing through the small crowd, stood over his friend's lifeless body. A small trail of blood weaved its way through the grooves in the cobblestones, flowing slowly from the back of Kito's skull. Looking up, Yamakiri traced the path of his fall, past the open window of the room where they had been sleeping and to the roof. He must have fallen from there, Yamakiri thought to himself, but why was he on the roof?

It was then that the broad figure of Kusunoki appeared on the other side of Kito from Yamakiri.

"What has happened here?" he asked looking directly at Yamakiri.

Yamakiri's sullen face said more than any words could convey and for once he kept silent, as if disrespecting the position and respect someone in Kusunoki position demanded. Lying before him was not only a friend and someone who in the past had saved his life, but also someone he had hoped would help to unlock the mystery behind the death of his parents. Without Kito, his hopes of slaying his inner demons became less of a possibility and the prospect of being trapped forever by the unknown more of a reality.

Yamakiri crouched down next to the body of his friend. "What happened, Kito?" He asked under his breath as he touched the exposed flesh of his chest. His lifeless body was still warm and his open eyes looked up in the direction of the rooftops. Yamakiri shook as a cold wave of air swept through him, as if his touch had somehow provided a channel for Kito's spirit to leave his body.

As he followed the path of sensation he looked upwards again to the rooftop. Seemingly out of nowhere a white dove had come to rest on the spot where Kito had fallen. It looked down at Yamakiri, and as if satisfied it had his attention, took flight. There was a whistling sound as it flew upwards and Yamakiri was sure he had heard the word 'home' in its departure. Transfixed, he followed its flight. Yamakiri knew this was a sign and sure enough it was clear it was heading south, in the direction of Iga and Yamakiri's home, Aoyama village.

"Please excuse me, Kusunoki san, I must take him home," he said bowing.

"Yes of course, I will arrange horses and provisions for your journey, that is the least I can do," Kusunoki responded, placing his hand on Yamakiri's shoulder. With that he turned and began issuing orders to his men, each dispatch saw them run off in different directions. As Yamakiri stood up, a solitary tear ran down his cheek. Looking into the sky to the white speck of the departing dove, he uttered to himself-'I'm coming home'.

Chapter 25

Yamakiri woke in a cold sweat. He quickly sat up and looked across the room, to where Kito had gone to sleep some hours before. To his surprise, he saw the shape of a person under the blankets. What was more, as he watched for signs of life, he could see it rising up and down.

Yamakiri quickly realised he had only dreamt about Kito's death. He sighed as the reality hit home, but he also knew that there was a very distinct message in the vivid and disturbing images.

He sat there for a moment and contemplated what the dream had meant in regards to Kito; was he in danger?

Yamakiri somehow felt responsible for him. After all, he did come back into Kito's life with the intention of finding his own truth-maybe unfairly, Yamakiri thought. Like him, Kito was obviously trying to escape his past and maybe this was why they were once again together, through their similar circumstances.

The image of the white dove represented peace to him, something he needed to find to become complete again. After all, it was a black dove that had signalled the start to this journey, a journey that had culminated in the loss of his family and him being thrust into the dark side of humanity, with its lust for power through the brutal aspects of war.

Yamakiri crawled across the room and knelt above his friend. Just as he was about to put his hand on his shoulder, Kito's eyes opened wide.

"What are you doing, Kansai?" he asked without thinking-his consciousness between the sleep and awake realms.

Yamakiri shifted backwards, pulling his hand back and placing it under his armpit, as if attempting to ease some sort of pain.

Kito looked back at his friend, his face had somehow morphed into the young man that he had met and helped train several years earlier. Along with this, was the distinct change from a person who had seemed to be in control of himself to one far more meek and vulnerable. As Yamakiri sat there staring at the floor in front of him, Kito knew what his friend had to do.

"You need to return to Aoyama, to put Kansai to rest-providing that is what you want," Kito said in a quiet voice.

At that moment Yamakiri realised the extent of the denial he had immersed himself in and how much he had been running away from reality. The longer and further he ran, the greater the pull to return to the source. The nightmares and the inference from Kito was far too obvious to ignore. He knew he could run no longer.

Although Yamakiri felt nothing more needed to be said, Kito placed his hand on his shoulder.

"Look my friend, I knew if you returned from the mountains someday, this moment would come. In fact I am not alone in that. Your uncle and I made a pact and prepared the way for your return. Our fate is not always ours alone, we have to trust in the spirits of our ancestors to guide us and to honour their traditions. Of course you will not find Kansai Tokugawa buried at Aoyama, but more so, your legacy. If you choose to venture that way then you owe it to your parents and your uncle to look further," Kito said, smiling.

Yamakiri paused before responding.

"And what about you, Kito?" he asked.

"My past lies here with Kusunoki and Go-Daigo. This is something you need to do alone, but I will be with you in spirit and will be here if you choose to return. Now go, Yamakiri," Kito said, removing his hand.

Yamakiri began packing up his things in preparation for his departure as Kito lay back down and appeared to go back to sleep. However, there was something else that had wanted Yamakiri out of the way and had found opportunity in this moment-something far beyond Kito's level of understanding.

Chapter 26

In the trees outside Enryaku-Ji, Seiko stirred as dusk set in. She had consciously switched her body's internal clock into nocturnal mode, triggered by the sudden change in temperature from the sinking of the sun. Before going to sleep, she had affirmed to prepare herself for the mission ahead and although oblivious to any visual recollection, felt different. More energised and alert than usual, her training had once again served her well.

She re-tied her clothing to streamline her movement and crawled the short distance to the edge of the trees. Her vantage point had been chosen carefully, to give her a clear view of the front gate and down the length of the perimeter wall. As the light of day was slowly replaced by the darkness, she was careful to minimise the amount of light entering her pupils, thereby retaining maximum visibility as the night set in.

Another reason for choosing this point was her knowledge of the wind and as she raised her head, her nostrils flared, like a wild animal scanning the area for any sign of prey. Prior to this, she had enhanced her sense of smell by rolling some fresh camphor leaves between her hands and inhaling the rich fumes, a technique taught to her by her master to not only clear her nostrils, but also her mind.

As expected, she was able to discern the various cooking smells wafting from the canteen inside. Her knowledge and experience told her that people were more relaxed and less alert after the evening meal – this was *Tsuki*, a weakness that was not only understood, but the one of the most reliable tools in a *Ninja's* arsenal.

Seiko waited for the right time to move, as if monitoring the breath of an opponent during combat. In fact, her master had used this as a metaphor when explaining how to make the most of this moment. The inhale was the eating, providing essential nutrients to the body. However, there was the digestion, which was the consolidation period-like an exhale, this was when a person was at their weakest. However, the *Sohei* –were not to be underestimated, their ability to provide a solid defense from intruders had been proven on many occasions. Seiko watched and waited for the appropriate moment before making her move.

- * -

Yamakiri had made his way along the road from Kyoto to Iga province. He had intentionally avoided the small settlements and towns along the way, including the larger town of Ueno, instead, taking a lesser known route that bypassed it altogether.

As he approached the last corner before the small village of Nabari, he stepped off the road and made his way up a small embankment where he stopped. Lying down, he peered through a tuft of thick grass.

He was looking for any signs of life, but as the sun went down the only activity was the rising of thick smoke from the half a dozen or so houses in the village. He focussed on one house in particular-that of Kazuki Satoru, the young man he had met several weeks earlier. The chimney of his house, unlike all the others, was devoid of any smoke. This unnerved Yamakiri; it would have been far more desirable to see smoke from this home as well, indicating Kazuki was at home. Nevertheless, he needed to move on. As he crawled back down to the cover of the bank, something caught his attention, and looking to his right, he saw the figure of a man.

"Er, hello," the man said.

Yamakiri turned to see the very person he had been trying to avoid-it was Kazuki Satoru. He had a somewhat puzzled look on his face.

"Oh it is you-Yamakiri?" he said, forcing a smile.

"Yes, that's right, Yamakiri responded, turning and sitting on the embankment.

Yamakiri tried to act innocent as he sat there.

"I was seeing."

"No need to explain yourself to me, Yamakiri. I am just heading back home from Ueno, you are welcome to come for dinner-presuming you are hungry?" Kazuki interjected, seeing his discomfort.

"Well," Yamakiri said pausing.

The memory of their last meeting stirred in his mind, specifically the feeling he received from Shimada's sword, immediately returned as if in a defiant challenge. Although this was in his past, it was still affecting the present and until put to rest, would control his future.

He recalled something during a lesson his uncle had said, 'there will be many times where you need to summon the courage to enter danger.'

He had then proceeded to show Yamakiri how to do this.

He had Watanabe his cousin attack with a knife to the abdomen. Initially Yamakiri moved to the side to evade the thrust, with this his uncle pointing out that the space created opened him up for an easy counter attack.

"No no, you must move into the attack-watch," he said, having Watanabe thrust at him and successfully defend his advance.

"Look," he said, referring to the cross posture he had made with arms, "you can move in, but always make sure you are protected, both physically and spiritually," and he turned to show Yamakiri the cross he had made.

"This is your spiritual protection-trust in this and no harm shall come."

Yamakiri knew he had to confront the fear he was experiencing, and with his uncle's lesson he had no excuse. One other thing his uncle had taught him was that you are never given a test without having the ability to solve it.

"Yes-thank you for your offer," Yamakiri finally responded as he slid down the embankment.

"Very well," Kazuki said, smiling and leading off around the corner of the road.

Catching up, Yamakiri visualized himself in the cross combat posture his uncle had displayed.

Immediately a rush of energy overcame his body, not only filling his being, but also providing an invisible outer shell of protection. 'I am ready' he said to himself.

- * -

Back in Kyoto, Kusunoki had summonsed both young men to his quarters and was surprised when the door opened to only see Kito enter the room.

"Where is Yamakiri?" Kusunoki asked.

"He had to leave, Master, and return to Iga," Kito said bowing.

Kusunoki was not happy and it showed on his face. He had wanted to send both of them to Enryaku-Ji to provide protection for Go-Daigo.

Kusunoki paused, as if rearranging his plans.

"Alright, well I need you to do something for me, Harada San," he said after closing the door.

"I want you to go to Enryaku-Ji Temple, to provide security for Go-Daigo. I have taken him there in secret for his protection. Do you understand?" Kusunoki asked in a soft voice.

"Yes of course, Master," Kito responded.

Kusunoki's words echoed in his head. It was as if his will had been redirected and tightened like a bow, ready to be released. Kito struggled to contain his composure, but something deep down had control and wasn't letting go.

"Best you leave immediately," Kusunoki said, moving towards the door.

Kito stood up and bowed, "Yes Master," he said, quickly exiting the room.

He was on a mission and although Kusunoki had sent him, there was some other force driving him. An invisible force, beyond his conscious will, with its own agenda and with a totally different objective, the outcome having the potential to throw the country into total disarray. With Yamakiri out of the way, this mission had no reason to fail.

Chapter 27

It hadn't taken Kito long to reach Enryaku-Ji; cantering most of the way. His intention was to reach it before nightfall-however, dusk had already begun to set in. Only slowing once, he reached the large wooden gate to the complex, dismounting before his horse had come to a complete stop. Moving forward, he knocked twice on the gate, paused, and then knocked three more times. This was the code Kusunoki had given him, based on the month and day, it was simple except to the uninformed and provided a means of identifying who could be trusted. The guard stationed behind immediately swung the gate open and bowed, without even looking to see who it was. As soon as Kito and his horse were inside, it was pushed shut and secured with a large pole.

Kito had only walked a few paces when he was approached by one of the monks. As he drew closer, Kito recognised the familiar face.

"Greetings, I am Tomada Ryuku" he said, bowing.

"Yes, I know," Kito responded, returning the bow.

For a moment Tomada looked confused and as he stared at Kito, he reeled back in surprise.

"Is that you Harada san?" Tomada continued in surprise.

They had met several years earlier at another temple and Kito had helped to train a group of them in self defence techniques to help defend the temple.

"Kusunoki has sent me," Kito responded, avoiding any conversation of the past.

"He couldn't have chosen a better man." Tomada responded, smiling and acknowledging Kito's legendary skills.

"Come, come, I will see you have some food and a place to sleep," Tomada added, taking the reins of Kito's horse.

"I will have something to eat, but I am not intending on getting sleep tonight," Kito said, walking towards the open kitchen with Tomada.

"Very well-he is in the Abbot's hut," Tomada said nodding in the direction of the small building to their left.

Kito looked around, making the most of the remaining light, surveying the building for any weakness or entry point. Looking up to the roof, he gazed along the tiled ridge for anything unusual, but all was as expected, or so he thought. However, a dark set of eyes peered back, through what from a distance looked like one of the ridge tiles. Cleverly concealed, Seiko had already breached security and was in place for her next move.

- * -

In the village of Nabari, Kazuki and Yamakiri had made their way to Kazuki's small house. Donning a pair of house slippers, Yamakiri followed him inside, conscious of what stood in the corner of his main room.

"Please, make yourself at home, Yamakiri," Kazuki said, gesturing him to be seated at a small table in the kitchen.

As Yamakiri moved closer to the doorway into the living room, he felt a presence, as if someone was in there waiting for him. This made him very uncomfortable, however, he knew he had to stay this time and confront it.

Kazuki stoked the embers of the small fire in his stove, feeding it small pieces of dried bark with the intention of graduating to small then larger pieces of firewood.

"So Yamakiri, we didn't have much of a chance to talk last time. I don't get many visitors and would welcome some conversation," he said, smiling as he filled a large kettle with water.

"Yes, well," Yamakiri said as he moved his attention from the doorway

"Have you been here long?"

"Well, for the last three years I have lived here permanently. I rebuilt this, my parents' house, after it was burned down by Sakamura's men. I believe it was in revenge for an attack on his castle in Ueno by *Ninja*," Kazuki said, bowing his head.

Yamakiri could see and feel he had recalled something painful and knew that it must be substantial to affect him still, even after some time had passed.

"There is more, isn't there?" Yamakiri asked.

Kazuki put down the kettle he had just picked up, as if to compose himself.

"Yes, Yamakiri, there is. You see they also killed my parents that day and all of the other villagers, in cold blood," Kazuki looked across at Yamakiri, as tears filled his eyes.

"All of them?" Yamakiri asked.

"Well, nearly, with the exception of one couple that had managed to hide away and then escape into the hills," he added.

Seeing how distraught this had made Kazuki, Yamakiri was not sure he should ask any more about what had happened, but he also knew that the events of that day had connected many people throughout the province and that his village had suffered the same fate. It was very personal for him, as in the same series of raids he had lost his mother and had been forced to escape to the mountains with his uncle and cousin.

"I suppose, this is our karma, coming from our reluctance to stand up to the oppressive *Shogun* and his *Daimyo*," Kazuki sighed.

Something urged Yamakiri on, he had come this far and needed to find the truth. Seeing Kazuki in this state, he knew as much as it caused him pain, he needed to talk about it as well.

"How about you Yamakiri, what brings you back this way?" Kazuki asked, trying to change the subject. Yamakiri had to respond, as hard as this was proving to be.

"I suppose I am searching, Kazuki," Yamakiri responded honestly.

"Searching for what, may I ask?"

Yamakiri knew that the raid on Kazuki's village was directly connected to his past and could help to fill many of the gaps and questions that needed answering. However, he was unsure how much of his past he could expose, something he had kept so well concealed over the years.

"You said one family escaped?" Yamakiri asked as Kazuki knelt down to pour the boiled water into a tea pot.

"Yes, Sendo Yokoku and his family," Kazuki responded.

Yamakiri froze as a cold shudder went down his spine.

"They also had a daughter-Mariko. I knew her and her parents well. She is now at Aoyama village and is married to Watanabe Yamada, the village trader there. Strangely enough, I have seen Mariko on several occasions, but she doesn't recognise me, even though we grew up together," Kazuki continued.

Yamakiri's heart raced as he recalled his last brief meeting with Mariko and how strange it was that she had never recognised him either, especially as they had once been very close.

"Her father was also the trader here; a very quiet man who kept mostly to himself. However, shortly after the raid, I was asked by someone to help find him. Seems he had been so angered by what had happened that he had gone crazy.

He used to keep birds-doves actually, and would let several out each morning, to fly off in different directions, but I never saw any of them come back. He even had a very rare, black one," Kazuki recalled.

"A black dove?" Yamakiri asked.

"Yes, that's right," Kazuki responded.

Yamakiri was stunned. It was a black dove that had appeared at his village before the raid by Sakamura's men. It could only have come from Nabari and this man Sendo Yokoku, but why?

The image of Sendo flashed before his eyes; more specifically the scene just as he had killed Yamakiri's uncle and he had, in turn, been killed by Yamakiri.

Yamakiri was finding it difficult to maintain his composure, but he had come this far, he needed to keep going. *Gambatte,* he said over and over, as if to strengthen his resolve.

Chapter 28

On the rooftop of Go-Daigo's hut, Seiko pulled the metal *Kunai* from her belt and began to systematically pry off the tiles by working down from the top. Every once in a while she would stop to peer over at the young man eating outside the kitchen.

Once she had removed just enough tiles for her to fit through, she pulled back the rest of the structure, carefully prying up several batons before tackling the final layer into the ceiling space. Checking once more on the position of Kito and pausing to listen for any activity inside, she slithered down through the hole and into the ceiling, feeling her way and recounting the strong points of the inner structure which would support her weight. Once inside, she supported herself across the bearers, careful not to make contact with the paper thin ceiling material or make any noise. Any miscalculation now could compromise her mission. Most crucial to this was to remain invisible and on her exit not to leave any clues to her being there. She lay there completely still, as she calculated her next move.

- * -

Oblivious to Seiko's presence, Kito had finally finished his meal. During this, Tomada had watched in silence and surprise as Kito satisfied what seemed to be a relentless appetite. Swallowing the last mouthful of rice, he burped and wiped his mouth with his sleeve, smiling as if to show his contentment.

Out of courtesy, Tomada waited before saying anything.

"How many people know of Go-Daigo's presence here?" Kito asked, looking across at the building housing him.

"Only me," Tomada whispered.

"What if he needs to eat or go to the toilet?"

"I have all of that sorted. All the cook knows is that there is someone in the house, but has no idea who it is," Tomada said, smiling.

"So I am best to keep very discreet about my purpose here," Kito asked.

"Yes, of course. I will tell the others that you are here to train our *Sohei* in Martial arts," Tomada responded.

"That sounds good, however, I will need to have somewhere to sleep where I can keep an eye on the building," Kito said, briefly looking in the direction of the house.

"Although, I do not plan to sleep at night and will keep watch," he added.

"You can stay in the guard's hut over there if that suits. With the wide doorway, you get a clear view of the Abbot's house."

"Please excuse me. Go-Daigo's dinner is ready and I must deliver it to him," Tomada whispered, standing and bowing.

Kito also stood up and bowed. As Tomada moved off to collect the tray of food from the serving area, Kito made his way to the guard's hut.

Seeing it was empty, he rolled out the mattress in the corner and prepared his sleeping area as if he was going to sleep-however; this was the last thing on his mind.

- * -

Back in Nabari, Yamakiri sat watching Kazuki pour the tea. He thought back to his home and how dramatically things had changed after the appearance of the black dove that day, especially the look of terror on his mother's face as she saw the bird.

"Did you ever recall meeting the trader from Aoyama village, Kazuki?" Yamakiri asked in a casual tone.

198

"Hmm, well not actually meeting him as such, but I did see him on several occasions. In fact he passed through the day before the village was ransacked and my parents were killed," Kazuki responded.

Yamakiri tried hard to keep his composure. The revelation that Kazuki may have been one of the last people to see his father alive shook him to the core. As he got closer to Aoyama village, the truth of what had happened to him was becoming clearer, the pieces of the puzzle starting to come together.

"Being such a small village, you must have known him well, Yamakiri?" Kazuki asked, seeing his reaction.

Yamakiri paused, thinking about what to tell Kazuki. However, he needed to know the truth. Something deep inside told him it was time to drop his guard, as this was the only way he would find it.

"His name was Yoshiakai Tokugawa. He was my father," Yamakiri said slowly as if to solidify the reality of that fateful period in his life.

"Was?" Kazuki asked, referring to the past tense of his response.

Yamakiri stared up at a scroll hanging on the wall, as if searching for something. It was a piece of calligraphy and contained the characters *KoKu*-which he understood to mean 'Big Space'. As he scanned the lines of the painting he stopped on a small speck of ink under the bottom character. It seem to draw him in and as he concentrated more and more on the dot, it morphed into a face and as he looked harder, he realized it was the face of his late father. Surprised, he jolted his head back, bringing it back into perspective with the character *Ku*. It was as if someone was trying to tell him something. Searching for some meaning, he considered how insignificant the small image of his father's face was to the bigger picture, yet here were two people whose lives had been completely altered by the actions of one person. A wave of guilt swept over him. Sensing this, Kazuki sat back and looked down as if to give Yamakiri space.

"Sometimes space is what we need, Yamakiri," Kazuki said, referring to his interest in and reaction to the wall hanging.

Yamakiri recalled a lesson his uncle had once given him and his cousin in the *Dojo* during one of their training sessions.

He was talking about how important the space between you and your opponent was and how this changed during a combat situation.

'It is like breathing' he said, emphasizing this by expanding his arms in and out with his breath.

"Sometimes we need to be big and sometimes we need to be small,' he continued.

Seeing confusion on his young students' faces, he knew a practical demonstration would help to emphasize this.

He stood front on to Yamakiri and raised his hands to form a circle in with his head in the middle. Yamakiri knew this as *Hoko no Kamae* – bear posture.

'Attack,' he said to Yamakiri, urging him in with his fingers.

Yamakiri knew better than to disobey his teacher's request and moved in to punch. He was confident he would hit his uncle as he appeared to be such a large target. But as he got to the point where he was sure he would make contact, his uncle seemed to vanish before his eyes. He hadn't seen him drop to the floor or curl up into a small ball and roll off to his blind side.

So he was surprised when he heard a voice from the far corner of the room, ask him to turn around.

"You see-what you may perceive as being very large, may not always be so. It is only your perception that governs this," he said concluding the lesson.

200

Yamakiri realised that his uncle's lesson that day had come back when most needed. Not to haunt, but to help. Silently he thanked him.

Chapter 29

As the nearby cicadas sang loudly, Seiko lay in wait inside the ceiling. She had made a small hole in the thin material and was able to see Go-Daigo sitting at a small table below writing some notes. He had finished the dinner brought by one of the monks several hours before and appeared to be getting sleepy. 'Patience,' she told herself-as she waited until he was asleep to do what she needed to do.

As she watched, Go-Daigo rolled up his papers, and tucking them to one side, blew the large candle out.

For the next phase Seiko's timing needed to be perfect, she needed to capture his mind at the precise moment of his sleep state-she listened intently to the rhythm of his breathing to indicate this.

Someone else had also been monitoring the situation and had noted the thin sliver of light disappear from under the door of the hut. Kito knew that this was also a signal for him to carry out his move. He pulled on his heavy jacket, then stood up and moved to the kitchen area, which at this time of night was deserted. As he passed one of the small buildings to his right, he heard the faint sound of someone moving inside. Instinctively, he dive rolled towards the corner of the building and spun around on the ground, extending his body and rolling under the structure just as the door slid open.

From below, he could see up through the floorboards of the deck and make out the silhouette of a man. He watched as the man walked to the edge of the deck above him and as he grunted, a thick stream of urine hit the ground. At first it made a patting sound, but this quickly changed into a splash as a pool formed. The warm liquid splashed up, hitting Kito in the face.

In response he slowly turned his head, but not before receiving several more splashes to his face.

The man let out another grunt and then returned to the warmth of his bed. Kito waited until all was quiet inside, before making his next move. He scanned the area for any other signs of life- but his surroundings were still and noiseless. 'Time to move', he said to himself as he rolled out from under the hut, avoiding the small pool of steaming urine and rising to his feet.

He hugged the wall and took advantage of the shadows. Although it was only a few feet from where he was to the Go-Daigo's hut, he knew better than to run across open ground and instead slid his way along the wall to the rear of the building. From there he dropped down and kept low, crawling across the divide. His mission was uncertain at this point, as Kito was not in control. Instead something more powerful was driving him; a supernatural force beyond his comprehension-he was merely the vehicle of its manifestation.

Meanwhile, Seiko had been observing the rhythm of Go-Daigo's breathing as it slipped into a sleep pattern. Drawing his mind into hers, she assessed his state of consciousness. As his mind flickered between various thoughts like a pendulum slowing down and coming to equilibrium, she prepared herself to move.

Slowly she crawled along the rafters, only the balls of her feet and palms making contact with the roof structure. In the available light, she had familiarised herself with the layout of the building and Go-Daigo's location below, so now in complete darkness, she was able to navigate successfully. Reaching the access panel at the end of the ceiling void, she carefully pried it open and lifting it, placed it to one side. After each movement, she paused to take stock and listen for a moment, before continuing.

Putting all of her body weight forward, she drew her feet up and skilfully placed them on the same rafter as her hands. She then stood up and leaned over the access way, testing the strength of the rafter she was about to place all her weight on. Satisfied it was strong enough, she took her entire weight with her arms and carefully lowered herself into the room, like a spider descending down its silver thread. Dangling in the air, she dropped onto the floor, cushioning the impact by absorbing the shock with her knees and sinking into the shape of a small ball in the corner of the room. There she waited, her piercing eyes drawing in every possible bit of light and enabling her to make out the form of her intended target. Her heart raced as she realised the importance of her mission. Before her lay one of the most powerful men in Japan. Not only was his destiny in her hands, but what she did next could change the course of history. Little did she know, she was not the only one with this power in the vicinity; furthermore, their intentions were much different.

- * -

In Nabari, Yamakiri was finding his time with Kazuki trying at best. He had already resigned himself to the idea that he would need to confront things from the past to enable him to let go and move forward. His escape to the mountains had been just that;, stemming from a deep desire to evade it and alleviate the pain that went with it. Now his resolve was being tested as he made his journey not just back to where he grew up, but more importantly for him, back into his past. He knew his greatest tool was courage and as he sipped his tea, he was well aware that something was pushing him towards an aspect of his past that had to be dealt with before moving on.

"Kazuki, there is something I would like to see," Yamakiri said, carefully placing his cup down on the small table.

Kazuki looked back at him curiously.

"Yes, Yamakiri?" he asked.

Yamakiri looked into the next room through the open door way. From his position, he was unable to see the sword that he had seen last time he had been there, but once he focused on it, it seemed to be calling.

"You showed me the sword of Shimada, last time I was here-do you still have it?" Yamakiri asked cautiously.

"Yes, of course, Yamakiri," Kazuki responded with a smile.

"Would you like to see it?"

Yamakiri took a deep breath to center himself. Shimada had been the commander of the brutal *Daimyo* Sakamura. What was more, Yamakiri had been there when he had been killed and was instrumental in this. However, there was something else that Yamakiri had been seeking. His uncle had assumed the identity of Shimada after he had been killed and also taken this sword. What Yamakiri seemed to have experienced last time he was in its presence, was not only the spirit of Shimada, but also the spirit of his uncle and more importantly the conflict between the two. Now it made sense. His uncle had died while wearing this and Yamakiri believed he had been cursed by Shimada, causing his subsequent death.

"Please." Yamakiri responded.

Kazuki stood up and exited the room, returning almost instantly with the sword. Sunlight from the window reflected off the shiny lacquered *Saya* as Kazuki passed it to Yamakiri. Not being able to feel the energy of the sword, Kazuki was oblivious to its influence, affording him some level of protection. However, the same could not be said for Yamakiri. As he took hold, a rush of energy surged through his arms and into his torso, but it did not stop with his physical being; it seemed intent on driving to his very core. The sensation was similar to something Yamakiri had experienced as a young boy.

He had been riding his horse in the hills above his village, when it had been spooked by a large snake coiled up in the grass. This had caused the horse to bolt, tearing down the narrow track towards the village with Yamakiri just managing to hold on, but at the same time feeling completely out of control.

Yamakiri closed his eyes and was instantly overwhelmed with rolling images of his past, some that he did not have time to make sense of. There were *Samurai* engaged in battle, people with limbs cut off and dead on a battlefield. At the same time, screams and voices echoed in his head like a deluge of rain in a monsoon shower.

Out of the chaos, Yamakiri could make out something familiar; it was someone calling the name *Fudo Myoo* – the immovable god. Yamakiri on many occasions had used his essence to center himself and to regain control. He knew what he needed to do; he began to breathe deeply.

Cutting through the images he created a sliver of pure white light, like a razor sharp *Katana*, from the top of his head and through the center of his body. At the same time he chanted a mantra, charging the light and giving it ethereal substance. Each chant saw the light widen and solidify, and his body began to take on a resonance that pulsed with the rhythm of his mantra. A feeling of confidence and composure filled his being; each breath enveloped him within an invisible shell of pure white light.

Yamakiri opened his eyes and looked down at the weapon that had caused so much chaos and misery. Kazuki looked on, although unable to understand what Yamakiri was doing, he knew enough to remain silent out of respect. Without hesitation he drew the weapon, the sound of the blade disengaging from its *Saya* was hardly discernible, hinting at the craftsmanship that had gone into its making. Kazuki was taken aback by Yamakiri's promptness at exposing the blade. This was usually never done without permission from the owner, by tradition, had to be followed by the drawing of blood. Kazuki knew this and so had never dared to remove it from its sheath.

Yamakiri discarded the *Saya* and held the sword vertically in front of him, its razor sharp tip directed at the ceiling as its side bounced the last remnants of light off the setting sun around the room. There was no true owner now. At least, not in this physical realm, but he had felt a presence draw near as he exposed the blade, as if to challenge him.

Yamakiri held fast, his strength drawn from his belief in the power of his god. Once again he closed his eyes and projected the pure light into the weapon, the shining metal replaced by a glowing incandescence lighting up the darkness.

In his mind's eye he saw a dark figure approaching from his left. He remained steady, resolute, as the figure of a *Samurai* drew closer and through its *Menpou*-the menacing face mask he saw a set of red glowing eyes. He had already recognized the warrior from the distance-it was obvious it was Shimada, the owner of the sword and he was coming to claim its spirit.

Yamakiri removed his right hand from the hilt and with two fingers drew a grid of nine overlapping lines, with each stroke he uttered a single syllable word, empowering his creation. Next he traced the *Kanji* characters *Ka* and *Go,* onto the grid to provide divine protection, finally sealing it with a shake of his hand in the direction of the grid.

The spirit of Shimada stopped suddenly, his path blocked by the grid. His evil essence was unable to pass through the wall of divine protection. He stared at Yamakiri through the ethereal wall of light, his eye burning with rage at the sight of what was, he believed, rightfully his. Yamakiri seized the opportunity at his pause and leaped to his feet, clutching the glowing *katana* and passing through the grid. Instinctively he made cut after cut through Shimada's spirit, the path of the blade leaving behind the characters for killing evil. As soon as Yamakiri had completed the last cut, Shimada's spirit was drawn backwards at high speed, pulled swiftly by an invisible force that left his arms and legs flailing uncontrollably like flags in a strong wind, finally disappearing into a small point of light.

Yamakiri shuddered as his eyes opened wide. Exhausted, he collapsed, falling sideways on the floor. Kazuki looked on, as Yamakiri fell at his feet. Unsure what to do, he leaned over the still body and felt his neck for a pulse. As hard as he searched he was unable to find one.

- * -

Chapter 30

Seiko observed Go-Daigo sleeping from the dark corner of the room. She knew her timing had to be impeccable if she was to capture his sub-conscious and embed the seed in his mind. However, as she waited, her attention was drawn to a presence on the other side of the door, given away by a creak of a loose floorboard.

The door latch flicked up; she had already responded by drawing in her entire essence to a single point, rendering her body a lifeless and inanimate object and undetectable to even the most gifted psychic.

The door eased open, the usual creak of the metal hinge rubbing together was stifled as it was lifted to reduce the friction. There was a pause as a dark figure peered around the room, sniffing the air like a wild animal seeking the scent traces of its prey. Satisfied that the only discernible presence was the sleeping emperor, the figure in the form of a small man entered the room, closing the door carefully behind him.

Seiko remained completely motionless as she observed him move silently across the floor towards Go-Daigo, still unaware of her presence. He stopped beside the sleeping emperor. Seiko could just make out him reaching into the darkness of his jacket, followed by the unmistakable sound of a knife being drawn from its scabbard. The presence of the weapon was confirmed as it reflected the sliver of moonlight coming through a small crack in the shutters.

Seiko's heart began to race as she realised what was about to happen: this was an assassin and their target was obvious. Nothing stood between them and the death of the emperor, except her. This was not what her masters wanted or needed. Although Go-Daigo was a threat to their goal of taking back control of the country, he needed to be kept alive. If not, his death would cause a vacuum and with all the other factions vying for power, an all out civil war.

As the figure bent over Go-Daigo, Seiko swung into action; it was as if the building itself had come alive. She reached out and secured the arm holding the knife, driving her thumb deep into the pressure points, one between the bicep and tricep and the other sliding down to the wrist until finding the base of the thumb. As she applied pressure, she felt the arm give way, the nerves over-riding the signal from the brain to the muscles in the arm and hand-sending the fingers flaying outwards and causing the knife to fall to the ground. The assassin instantly responded, manoeuvring his free arm under his body and securing the knife in the other hand just as it hit the floor. Seiko released the arm and leapt back, just in time to avoid the upward thrust of the knife and the attack that would have surely pierced her lower abdomen.

As she braced herself against the wall, she peered at the shadow before her, trying to catch his identity. Then her eyes flicked across to the now stirring Go-Daigo, the last thing she wanted was for him to wake up and sound the alarm. Even more pressing, however, was the assassin and his potential to throw the entire nation into chaos. Apart from the rise and fall of his body with each deep breath, the assassin stood still and listened, seemingly waiting for the next move. Seiko stared back, as if to engage in a form of psychic combat. Her intention was however not as simple as that, she needed to get to Go-Daigo before the assassin did.

Seiko had already concluded that her opponent was highly trained in the arts of *Ninjutsu*, by the way they had entered the room and countered what for her would have been a solid technique left no doubt in her mind. She weighed up her options. Meanwhile, Go-Daigo was still stirring. This was the last thing Seiko needed-the odds were against her and she had to escape now.

She rolled to her right to draw the assassin in, but he didn't move. She hadn't really expected him to follow, at best she hoped to draw his attention. She ended up in a kneeling position and struck Go-Daigo on the inside of his exposed shin. The strike caused him to react just as she had planned-he kicked out in response, at the same time yelling out in pain. This distracted the assassin for just enough time for her to move in, grab his wrist and execute a *Shuto* strike to the side of his neck. As he flinched she wrenched the knife from his grip and slashed it across his neck. The sound of tearing flesh followed by the hissing of his blood spurting from the severed artery filled the room. He fell backwards, onto the Emperor, reeling as the blood drained quickly from his body. Seiko executed a backwards roll and coming to her feet, ran up the wall, projecting herself through the open manhole and pulling it closed behind her.

Within a matter of seconds, guards were already entering the room, alerted by the shout of Go-Daigo. Seeing the emperor struggling to free himself and stand up, one of the guards assisted him. Meanwhile, the assassin jerked uncontrollably on the floor, like a fish out of water. As the room was illuminated, it became apparent that there had been some sort of struggle-streaks of blood coated the walls, leading to a large pool which had formed around the dying man in the middle of the floor. With all of the attention focussed inside the small hut, no-one saw Seiko make her escape over the wall.

Turning his attention to the black masked figure, Go-Daigo leaned over and pulled the blood soaked material from the now still body on the floor. He took hold of a lantern from one of the monks and leaned back in surprise. He recognised him instantly, but struggled to comprehend what the man was doing inside his hut and how he had met his fate.

- * -

Yamakiri slowly opened his eyes to see a man standing over him and shaking his shoulder. He quickly looked around the dim room, as if searching for someone or something. His eyes fell back on Kazuki's anxious face..

"Yamakiri, I thought you were dead," Kazuki said, resting back on his knees.

Yamakiri took a moment to gather his thoughts and to recollect what had happened. Then he looked down and at his side and saw Shimada's unsheathed *Katana*.

"You nearly killed me with that," Kazuki said, smiling nervously.

"Ah, I am very sorry," Yamakiri said bowing his head.

"I better put this away," he added, picking it up and sliding it back into its *Saya*.

He handed it back to Kazuki, but Kazuki kept his hands down in his lap.

"No. Yamakiri, I think you should take it. I never felt comfortable having it here anyway," he said.

Yamakiri placed it on his knees and looked down as if to admire its craftsmanship; its brown lacquered *Saya* glistened in the light. 'How could such a thing of beauty bring so much sorrow to so many?' he thought to himself.

However, this was not the first time that he had seen this sword, just never this close before. Shimada would pay regular monthly visits to his village to collect taxes from the people. Most times Yamakiri would hide himself from the *Samurai* and watch, but there was something that always drew his attention to the sword in his hands.

Yamakiri closed his eyes to get a better sense of its energy. Now the feeling was entirely different. The turmoil had gone, as if he had exorcised the demons residing in the blade.

214

He recalled the discussion he had had with a *Yamabushi* monk, years earlier. He had been taken to see a special ceremony called *Katana Watari*–a ladder of swords.

A group of monks lined up to ascend the ladder, comprised of thirteen live blades, each razor sharp. Even though they had bare feet, not one of them suffered any injury. He was told it was the combination of faith and the purity of the swords.

However, on an earlier occasion, several monks had suffered deep cuts to their feet; it was later discovered that the offending blade had been used to kill a dog and had not been purified.

Yamakiri also recalled that his uncle had been wearing this very sword when he had been killed. It seemed as if it had cursed him-or at least Shimada had and caused his tragic death.

"Please take it," Kazuki pleaded.

Yamakiri knew he had no choice in the matter, it was his destiny. He placed it down by his side and smiled back at his host.

- * -

Earlier in the night, in the total darkness of a cave Ryushin Yakushimaru prepared himself. Breathing deep and rhythmically he flooded his body with oxygen, with each breath he became more and more light-headed. He was well aware that this practice had been passed down from teacher to student for centuries, its origins buried in the mists of time. He had been taught by his grandfather when he was just entering adolescence, traditionally, he was told, the best time to master it.

The pitch black environment of the cave, devoid of any light, provided the best conditions for what he was about to do. Here, the distinction between the outer shell of the physical body could easily be disregarded, therefore providing a oneness with the inner and outer worlds.

He suddenly ceased the deep breathing and replaced the breath with the rocking of his body. Like a butterfly shedding its chrysalis, he moved back and forth. Each time his astral body moved further from the outer bounds of his physical body, until he felt the distinct feeling of disconnection- he was now free to go wherever his thoughts dictated.

In an instant he was outside the cave entrance, its dark depths framed by the rock face. Spiralling back into the darkness was a silver cord, connected at his end to his solar plexus; this was what his grandfather had told him was his lifeline. He had also warned him that this technique had many dangers, especially for the remaining physical shell. As he had been taught, Ryushin had placed a shell of protection around himself before leaving his body.

In an instant he was in the compound of Enryaku-Ji –completely invisible. He scanned the area, looking for signs of life, but more specifically, one person in particular. His senses told him that Kito Harada was there somewhere. Ryushin's intention was for Kito to find Go-Daigo, now he was there to ensure his plan came to fruition.

Looking towards the guard house, he saw Kito lying down, but wide awake. Instantly he was above him; Kito was totally unaware of Ryushin's presence. Despite his training, he was not at a level to sense such things.

Ryushin repeated an incantation in his mind and projected this to Kito. Almost immediately, Kito swung into action, making his way towards the building housing Go-Daigo. Ryushin's mission was for Kito to kidnap Go-Daigo and from what he knew of his skill, had no doubt he would be able to deliver him to Takauji. However, Ryushin was unaware that Seiko was also there to carry out her orders from Takauji. Confident his plan would work and that Kito was off to complete his mission, he returned to his body in the cave. He began to go through the process of waking up, at this stage unaware of what had actually transpired at

216

Enryaku-Ji. He was also unaware of the karma between Kito Harada and Seiko-something remiss in his plans. It was Kito who had killed her father, Hideo Shimada, there was a debt to be paid. As skilled and influential as Ryushin was, he was no match for the gods and their powers.

Chapter 31

The following morning, Yamakiri woke from what was a rare undisturbed sleep. He had accepted Kazuki's offer to spend the night in Nabari before going on to Aoyama village, another three hours' walk away at the top of the valley.

Kazuki was already up and cooking breakfast-a mix of *Tamagotchi* omelet and *Tempura*. Sensing Yamakiri's awakening, he looked around and through the small doorway.

"Good morning, Yamakiri," he said smiling and wiping his hands on his oil stained apron.

Yamakiri rubbed his eyes and stretched out his arms, like a cat waking from its sleep.

"You slept well, my friend," Kazuki continued.

Yamakiri looked out through the open kitchen window to see the sun above the mountains; it must have been at least mid-morning. He tried to recall any dreams he may have had, but his mind was blank. It was unusual to have no recollection, let alone having one of the re-occurring nightmares that had haunted him for some time.

Yamakiri sat up and put on his jacket, tying it firmly across his body. He walked into the kitchen and following the smoke from Kazuki's cooking, stared out the open window. The south facing view framed the mountains and something close to his heart-the village of Aoyama. Although he had passed through several weeks earlier, he felt completely detached at that time, alienated by the events of the past. But now the feeling was different, there was a distinct compulsion to go home.

The tops of the high mountains were shrouded in cloud, as if concealing another world only available for those who dared to venture there. His father had told him that no real *Samurai* would, their mix of superstition and the lack of the opportunity for safety in numbers precluded their ascent. Yamakiri thought about his own journey into the mountains and how his uncle had given him his new name, now in hindsight he could see how it may have been more prophetic than just coincidence. That fateful day Yamakiri was forced to leave Aoyama and head into the safety of mountains with his uncle, he had ascended into the mist. Perhaps symbolic of the journey was the fact that it had left him with more questions than answers. But now it was time to find the truth, something that had so far taken much courage to do. The pull became stronger with each revelation, as if some invisible force was calling him home.

- * -

Seiko had been heading north since her hurried escape from Enryaku-Ji, only stopping to water her horse at the opportunity of a stream or river. Rounding a bend, she could see smoke rising from the side of the road. She knew this road well, especially where there were villages and houses- more for the sake of avoiding them-but here there were no houses, so it must be someone camping. Rather than trying to avoid them, she carried on making her way along the road. As she came closer, she caught a glimpse of a horse tied to a tree, then another, which was being fed by a large *Samurai.*

As she came parallel with the camp, she saw that there was a small group of around 15 *Samurai,* busy going about their morning and preparing to break camp. Noticing her presence, one of the *Samurai* called out to another and from behind a horse another man appeared. He had a small well manicured moustache and wore a pointed hat, signifying his position as a high ranking *Samurai.*

Seeing Seiko, he walked towards her. She had stopped by this stage and dismounted, continuing her downward motion and dropping to her knee out of respect.

She watched the ground in front of her as the *Samurai* approached, until he stopped directly in front of her.

"Hmm, who do we have here?" the *Samurai* asked in a deep and authoritative voice.

Seiko looked up and then quickly bowed her head again.

"Seiko Harada, Master," she responded nervously.

"Do you know who I am?" he asked.

Seiko had seen this man once before, at Go-Daigo's palace in Kyoto. From the manner in which they had been talking, it was obvious he was someone who was well respected.

"No, sir- I apologise, I do not," Seiko responded, aware that it was disrespectful not to know people in high positions.

"Well, since you are young, I will be lenient on you this time. But I want you to remember me, as in future you will come to know me as *Shogun* – Go-Yoshisada," he said assertively.

Seiko was intrigued by his frankness and confidence, especially how he believed he would be the next *Shogun*. This didn't make sense to her.

"Yes, Master Yoshisada," she responded, looking up, then bowing her head again.

"So where are you going?"

"Kamakura, Master," she responded.

"Can you cook?"

"Yes sir."

"Good, then you can travel with me and be my cook until we reach Kamakura," he said with no consideration for any other plans she may have had.

Seiko looked up again, squinting as Yoshisada moved his head, allowing the morning sun to bathe her face in intense light.

"It would be my honor, Master," she said, smiling.

She was well aware of the on-going struggle for power within the regions and recognized the opportunity to get close to one of Go-Daigo's loyal followers. She was intrigued to see that this man had no military backing to take on Takauji, obviously he believed that he could walk into Kamakura unchallenged. Although Seiko would have liked to make a speedy return to Takauji to report Go-Daigo's whereabouts and more importantly, his current vulnerability, she knew that things would need time to settle after the incident at Enryaku-Ji. Also she was well aware that it was fate that brought about this encounter-*Nagare* –flow, she reminded herself. Move along the path of least resistance-a concept that had been taught to her from a young age.

- * -

In Kamakura, Ryushin had been summoned to Takauji's palace. As he entered the large room he saw Takauji and his brother seated at the far end. He slid the door shut behind him and dropped to his knees, ensuring he followed the strict protocol of being lower than his hosts. It was unusual for Takauji to have his brother present at such meetings, as he was more of an administrator. It was obvious that Takauji didn't want him to know everything, after all, knowledge was power.

"Come come, Yakushimaru san," Takauji said, urging him forward.

Ryushin shuffled up to an area in front of the two men and dropped to his knees once again.

"My spies tell me that Yoshisada is heading this way. Is this correct?" Takauji asked confidently.

Although Ryushin had not been made aware of this by any of his sources, he trusted Takauji's information.

"That would be correct, Master," he responded.

"He is travelling very lightly as well," Takauji continued.

Ryushin avoided smiling, even though deep inside he was happy that not only had his plan worked, but also that his credibility had been bolstered by the news.

"As you requested, Master," Ryushin responded bowing.

"What's more, Go-Daigo will follow shortly after," he added.

Tadayoshi quickly turned and peered back at his brother.

"Go-Daigo, here-how so?" he asked, looking surprised.

Takauji smiled back, pausing briefly as if to saviour the moment.

"It is not what you may think. I want to him to negotiate a truce with me and when he sees how his son Prince Morinaga has been plotting to betray him, he will have little option but to side with me," Takauji said, his smile even wider.

Tadayoshi looked at him and then across at Ryushin. Thick lines formed on his brow as he tried to comprehend the sheer brashness of his brother's plan.

"And what about Yoshisada?" Tadayoshi asked.

"I will arrange a welcoming party for him. Seems he may want to negotiate a truce as well, but in his case, I will be in no mood to talk. I have a score to settle with him." Takauji said, slapping his closed metal fan on his palm.

Tadayoshi knew better than to question his brother's plans, to do so would be nothing short of treason. However, he did have concerns around his brother's choice of agent for all of this and turned his thoughts to Ryushin. He was uneasy that the future of this country was being twisted and turned by the actions of a young man.

Ryushin felt a surge of energy from Tadayoshi and turned to look at him.

"You seem to have doubts in my ability, Ashikaga san?" Ryushin asked.

Surprised, Takauji stirred.

"Just remember who you are working for Yakushimaru and show some respect to my family," Takauji said, his smile changing to an angry stare.

Ryushin bowed his head.

"I am sorry, Master," he said apologetically.

Although he was confident that Kito Harada would bring Go-Daigo to them, still there was a niggling doubt in the back of his mind. What even Ryushin failed to acknowledge was that his power was being limited by forces far more powerful than any mortal being.

Chapter 32

Yamakiri made his way up the hill towards what had been his home some three years earlier. Looking down he saw the well established grass on the tracks of the narrow road, testament to limited use it had. Rounding a sharp bend, he caught his first glimpse of the *Tori* gate, marking the front entrance to the village. For a moment he stopped, as if to take stock, while at the same time searching for any sign of life. He looked up into a large cedar tree, where many a time he had climbed as a boy and then to the meadow beyond the village where his father had played with him and taught him to ride horses. A warm feeling flooded his being as he recalled some of the happier days of his childhood, growing up in such an idyllic place.

By this stage it was late morning and with the sun shining he could make out wafts of steam rising from the long grass on the side of the road. In that moment he became acutely aware of the subtle forces at play, in and around him. They came from behind him, as if he was being pushed along by the ghosts of his past and also from in front, a strange feeling: anticipation mixed with fear. Trapped in some sort of psychic stalemate, he took a deep breath and charged his will. He knew it was too late to turn back now and that the force in front of him was created of his own mind-it would take the same to overcome it.

He pushed on; with each step he felt his resolve grow. The road was fairly steep, but he knew this as he had often come down it as a small boy, running up the high bank to stop his hurried descent. Looking to his left, he could see small footprints in the soft earth, not his after all this time, but from some other young boy who had found pleasure in the same idea.

As he drew closer his heart raced. At the top of the hill, to his left, was the cemetery he had visited some months earlier and next to that the high fence, broken by the large opening of the gateway. He was now in a position to look into the compound, searching with each step for anything familiar to him. Through the opening he could see the large Cryptomeria tree he used to climb as a boy and below it a large wooden water barrel. Sitting beside it was a young boy, oblivious to his presence. He appeared to be playing in the dirt around the barrel, using a large stick to gouge out the earth. Suddenly he looked up and stared straight at him, his face devoid of any expression. As Yamakiri's stare intensified he was able to make out the boy's face – to his surprise it was as if he was looking back into the past, at himself. As Yamakiri became transfixed on the boy, their surroundings blurred, as if a tunnel had appeared between them. Suddenly a voice came out of nowhere, breaking his trance.

"Excuse me," a deep male voice said to his left.

Yamakiri turned and looked in the direction of the voice. The person coming towards him stopped as he caught sight of the young man. Yamakiri immediately recognised him, it was his cousin, Watanabe Yamada. Watanabe's jaw dropped. He had believed that not only had Yamakiri been killed some time ago, but he had often sat in front of his grave and tried to talk to him.

"Kansai-is that you?" he asked, his voice rattling with surprise.

For a moment Yamakiri didn't know what to say, but somehow the silence between them was appropriate, as if rekindling a connection that had been forged through growing up together.

A tear rolled down Yamakiri's face, followed by a second, then more, suppressed by years of denial and guilt.

Watanabe ran towards him and embraced his younger cousin, tearing at his back as if to reassure himself that the person before him was in fact there.

"We thought you were dead." Watanabe said as tears formed in his eyes.

Yamakiri became limp, as if surrendering to the moment, his eyes rolled backwards and he collapsed, his body completely supported by Watanabe. He was finally home.

- * -

Kusunoki had just arrived at Enryaku-Ji. Something had told him he needed to check on Go-Daigo, so he had made the early morning ride up the steep mountain track to the fortified gates.

Before he had time to dismount they swung open widely. Hurriedly urged inside by one of the young monks Kusunoki bowed his head as he passed through the wooden opening. Kusunoki made his way directly to the hut where Go-Daigo had been secretly hidden. To his surprise the door was wide open, the Emperor was standing on the front porch.

Upon seeing him, Kusunoki dismounted; surprised by Go-Daigo's willingness to expose his presence.

"Master, I have…." Kusunoki was about to air his disappointment, when he was interrupted.

"Stop!" Go-Daigo said angrily, waving his *Tesson* while marching towards him.

Kusunoki looked up as his master stood over him.

"Come, we urgently need to discuss what we do next," Go-Daigo continued.

"What is this-what happened?" he asked, back at the open door of the house.

"That I cannot tell you, Kusunoki san, but one thing is certain: your plan to keep me safe here was not a good one," he said, his face changing to an expression of disappointment.

"I am sorry, Master," Kusunoki said apologetically, bowing his head, but still unsure what had transpired.

He turned and walked up the steps and through the door, looking around the room as he entered.

The first thing that struck him was the amount of blood splattered on the walls; he followed the small droplets as they changed into larger splashes, then into a stream of a thick congealed mass. All of this was predominately around the bed Go-Daigo had been sleeping in. Across the bottom of the bed lay a large mass, covered by a bloody sheet.

Kusunoki stepped forward and pulled back the stained cover; instantly he recognised the face. A set of wide and lifeless eyes stared back at him, but of more prominence was the large gash in his throat and the trail of blood that had obviously squirted from it.

"Hmmm," Kusunoki said to himself as he looked up and around the room, trying to make sense of the scene.

"Why would he try to kill me?" Go-Daigo asked from behind him.

Go-Daigo walked in and stood next to him.

"Did you kill him, Master?" Kusunoki asked cautiously.

Go-Daigo shook his head, "Definitely not, what is more the door was locked from the inside."

His head started to spin as he tried to comprehend the situation; the more he learnt, the less sense it made. Scanning the room, Kusunoki looked up, his attention drawn to the manhole in the ceiling. He moved forward, and studying it closely, he could make out two imprints in its soft surface. Looking at the wall underneath it, he saw another imprint like that of a foot, then another. Stepping back he drew his *Katana;* and thrusting it upwards, pushed open the hatch cover. Instead of the darkness one would expect from within the enclosed ceiling space, there was a stream of light that bounced off the wall above them.

"This is how the assassin managed to enter the room undetected," Kusunoki said, turning to Go-Daigo.

"Assassin?" Go-Daigo said, surprised.

"Then why is this man dead?"

They both looked down at the body. Kusunoki knew his master was demanding answers, but he was unsure what to say next. The only explanation he could offer, considering the amount of confusion around this, would not be helpful in guaranteeing the protection of the Emperor, but he was sure Go-Daigo had already come to the same conclusion.

"This could only be the work of a highly skilled *Ninja*, but I am confused why this man is dead in your house." They looked down at the body, his wide open eyes providing little clue to his fate. Both of them recognised to dead man before them.

"As far as I was aware, Tomada was one of your most loyal followers and had taken a vow to protect you. Him lying here before us makes no sense at all," Kusunoki said, studying the face of the dead man as if hoping he could tell them something.

"Well, if this is the best protection you can offer, I would be better to have stayed in Kyoto," Go-Daigo said angrily, then he stormed out the door.

Kusunoki didn't dare respond. He had seen even some of Go-Daigo's loyalist followers put to death for less insolence; however, the death of the *Sohei* monk Tomada and the absence of the man he had sent to watch over Go-Daigo did concern him deeply.

Kito Harada was nowhere to be seen and entering the room in such a fashion was definitely the work of a *Ninja*, it didn't look good. However, why was Tomada dead and not the Emperor? If Kito had aimed to kill him he would surely have succeeded, he tried to assure himself. He had to find Kito Harada, but for now he needed to remain close to his master to protect him.

To the north, Seiko had attached herself to Nitta Yoshisada's small band of men. She rode at the back of the contingent and watched carefully as the horses' tails swished from side to side in rhythmic unison.

One of the benefits of being a woman was that she was expected to follow behind and be at their beck and call. This worked well in her favour, providing the perfect excuse to remain out of sight and more importantly, out of mind. Little did her host know that with each mile they travelled, she gained much more information about him. To Seiko this was a tool that with the right timing she could use to her advantage, or even better, as currency for payment for something else.

However, she also endeavoured to keep within earshot of Yoshisada, well aware that anything he said would be important to not only the recipient, but also to others. Yoshisada was a man of little words, favouring action instead.

One thing she had noted early on was the absence of any signs of readiness, in the case of trouble. She knew the area well and saw no reason for complacency; bandits were known to frequent the roads and sought any opportunity to ply their extortionate ways. Yoshisada and his men either seemed oblivious to this, however, or considered their presence enough of a deterrent to any would-be attacker. Seiko thought how ironic it was that she alone could have taken out this man before he took a second breath, but that was not her mission.

As they drew parallel to a small stream beside the road Yoshisada raised his hand to signal to the others to stop. He dismounted and led his large horse down to the water's edge; instinctively it bowed its head and began to drink. All of the men followed suit, as did Seiko, however as she dismounted she froze, as if in response to an invisible air of uncertainty.

As one of the men led his horse towards the water, a loud swish followed by a crack broke the peaceful song of the stream. The man moaned and his knees buckled as he fell to the ground, the well targeted arrow stood upright in his back, like a flag marking its territory. Yoshisada spun around to see his man drop to the ground, at the same time placing his hand on his *Katana* in readiness for an attack. His eyes darted from side to side as he tried to discern the origin of the attacker's position, but there was nothing, just silence.

By this stage all of his men had transformed into a heightened state of readiness, each clutching their swords; some already had them drawn. Seiko had crouched down behind her horse, making herself a smaller target. She also scanned the surrounding trees for any sign of life. Looking back at the man on the ground, she immediately understood. This was a strategic attack, the accuracy of the arrow could have easily been directed at Yoshisada, but this was obviously not the intention. By this stage Yoshisada had drawn the same conclusion, if this was supposed to unnerve him, he wasn't about to show it. In a show of defiance, he turned back to the stream and admired the form of his drinking horse.

Seiko looked across at his men; each seemed to be in a state of catalepsy, frozen and unable to move and unsure what to do next. Then as one of them finally moved towards the dead man, Yoshisada called out "Leave him!"

Suddenly a second arrow whistled through the air, striking another man in the chest and piecing his heart. He fell to the ground, clutching the arrow and writhing in pain as a dark stain rapidly spread across his chest. Defiantly, Yoshisada kept staring at the flowing water. The other men could not hide their shock at the attack, knowing that at any moment their life too could easily be snuffed out. This time Seiko had traced the trajectory of the arrow back to what she believed was its point of origin: a large tree on the other side of the stream. The other men were still frantically searching. Seiko glanced back at Yoshisada, it was clear that he had drawn even more confidence from the second attack and the obvious fact that he had not been targeted.

She was about to move forward when she heard the whistle from an arrow, then a thud just below her foot. Looking down she saw an arrow firmly embedded under her foot in the soft soil. However, this had not come from where she had thought the other attacks came from. Tracing its path back into the trees, Seiko saw that this arrow had come from the same side of the stream as they were on. Yoshisada, alerted by the sound, stared across at her. Meanwhile, the other men had moved into position around their master, their hands on their *Katanas* while they intently scanned the area.

Then a small figure holding a bow casually walked out of the trees and into the middle of the road. At first he was hard to see, his speckled green and brown clothing blending perfectly with the trees behind him. His face was also disguised in the same way, making it impossible to distinguish his identity.

In response, Yoshisada's men repositioned themselves in front of their master to form a line of protection.

Yoshisada's men began to advance in order to provide a buffer, but Yoshisada called out "Wait!" and halted their advance.

Moving forward he pushed apart his men and stood out in front.

"What do you want?" Yoshisada shouted.

While this was happening, Seiko had pulled out the arrow under her foot and examined its craftsmanship. Unlike most arrows, this had five sets of quills arranged perfectly around the shaft. These were no ordinary weapon and, as she had been taught, such an array would have ensured the pinpoint accuracy she had just witnessed.

"You are to come with me, Yoshisada san," the man shouted back.

Immediately Seiko's suspicions were confirmed-it could only be Ryushin Yakushimaru, someone she had come to know years earlier.

Suddenly one of Yoshisada's men shuffled forward. In response Ryushin pulled an arrow from over his shoulder, loaded and fired it. It whistled past Yoshisada and embedded itself in the *Samurai's* right hand, splitting the handle of his sword in the process and embedding the tip in his hip. The *Samurai* reeled and spiraled to the ground while trying to dislodge the arrow from his body.

"I don't want any more trouble. Yoshisada is leaving with me," Ryushin shouted, moving towards the group.

"Kill him!" Yoshisada shouted, receding back and pointing at the advancing figure walking towards him.

As his men moved into position, Yoshisada mounted his horse, turned around and started riding in the opposite direction back towards Kyoto.

Ryushin had already hit three of Yoshisada's advancing men as they ran towards him. Dropping his bow, he reached into his shirt and pulled out a small stack of *Shuriken*, throwing each in swift succession into the faces of his attackers. Some dropped to the ground as others stumbled forward. With less than 20 feet between them, there was a large crack in the air followed by a thick cloud of smoke; totally immersing what was left of the advancing men and their target. One person delivered a cut where Ryushin had been standing moments before. Several others ran through the thick cloud, turning and positioning themselves on the other side. Breathing heavily with their swords drawn, they waited for the smoke to clear.

As the smoke finally dispersed, it revealed two of the men on the ground, one dead and the other writhing while holding his neck and trying to stem the flow of blood. What was very apparent was that Ryushin had vanished, leaving the remainder of

Yoshisada's men standing around and looking for any sign of his escape.

In response to Yoshisada's escape, Seiko mounted a horse and set out after him. Galloping at full speed the horse snorted heavily with each stride. In the distance Seiko could see Yoshisada stirring up a tail of dust in his wake as he disappeared around a sharp bend in the road.

As Seiko turned the corner, she could see a long straight, but the dust cloud that should have followed the escaping Yoshisada had stopped abruptly. Pulling up her horse, she looked around at the thick trees on either side of the narrow road. Suddenly she was beset by someone from behind her; they jumped onto the hindquarters of her horse and pulled her to the ground. The two of them landed with a thud, Seiko was rolled onto her back and found herself underneath someone who was sitting astride her and pinning her arms. Looking up, the first thing she saw was a set of dark brown eyes, and looking at his face, she instantly recognised the man above her. It was Kito Harada. She attempted to struggle, but Kito was far too strong for her to break free.

For a moment there was complete silence as the two stared at each other, frozen in time as if their past connection had reconsolidated their beings together.

"Watch out!" came a call from the side of the road; it was Yoshisada. Kito looked up to see Ryushin stop his horse and leap off.

Yoshisada was confused; he had been pulled aside by Kito Harada, who had been following Seiko from Enryaku-Ji overnight.

Kito quickly stood up, giving Seiko the opportunity to roll away and get to her feet as well.

"Ryushin- It has been some time," Seiko called out across the distance, weary of his intentions.

"You-Ryushin Yakushimaru?" Yoshisada said, somewhat confused.

"Why did you kill my men? I thought we had an understanding?"

Yoshisada was referring to the contract he had made with Ryushin to stage the murder of Takauji in Kamakura and frame his brother for it.

"And you, I thought you were working for this man as well," he said, looking back at Kito.

Kito also looked confused.

"I have no idea what you are talking about, I have never met this man before in my life," Kito responded.

Suddenly a roar of horses' hooves grew louder-it was the remainder of Yoshisada's men. Ryushin turned and as if by some invisible force the horses stopped suddenly.

Meanwhile, Kito peered back at Seiko, the look on his face one of searching. She glared coldly back, the scars of her father's betrayal as fresh in her mind as the day Kito had told her he had been responsible for his death.

"Kill him!" Yoshisada shouted to his men, pointing at Ryushin.

Yoshisada turned around just as Seiko drew a *Tanto* from inside her clothing. Pushing it to his throat she moved in and wheeled around behind him, placing it against the tight skin of his neck.

"Do not move another foot or I will kill him!" she shouted through gritted teeth, her eyes bulging like a demon.

Kito moved forward.

Seiko turned to look him in the eye. "That goes for you as well Harada, stay where you are!"

Ryushin casually moved towards Seiko and Yoshisada, leaving his men frozen and helpless behind him.

Seiko said nothing as Ryushin came closer, testament to whose side she was on. He looked beyond her and stared intently at Kito behind her. Kito swayed as if being pushed by an invisible force. Then Ryushin stopped, and waving two fingers in front of Kito, he uttered an incantation. Kito suddenly stood bolt upright.

"Kill his men," Ryushin whispered to him.

With that Kito rushed past Yoshisada at the same time drawing his *Katana*.

"Tie him up, Seiko," Ryushin added, turning and throwing a rope to her.

Yoshisada tried to struggle, but Seiko pushed the knife against his throat harder.

"I wouldn't, if you want to live," she said.

Meanwhile Kito ran like a madman at full speed towards Yoshisada's remaining men, his *Katana* raised above his head. Two of them had already dismounted, but before they had time to draw their swords, they were cut down. Kito was unstoppable, his skill matched with his lack of fear was no contest for the rest of them. Within a minute, he had successfully despatched all nine of Yoshisada's men and was standing amongst a scene of carnage; blood and body parts littered the road.

He looked back at Seiko, who had just finished tying up Yoshisada.

"You deliver Yoshisada to Takauji since you seem to be able to control him. Do you know if Go-Daigo is still at Enryaku-Ji?" Ryushin asked.

"Yes, I believe so," Seiko responded.

"Good. Tell Takauji I will have a greater prize for him soon," Ryushin said, smiling and turning his attention to the bound Yoshisada.

"You will not be able to capture him as easy as you may think," Yoshisada said angrily.

"With traitors like you by his side, how hard could it be?" Ryushin responded arrogantly, pressing the point that it was Yoshisada who had employed his services to go behind Go-Daigo's back and kill Takauji.

Yoshisada sneered and spat on the ground in front of him.

Seiko pushed him towards his horse and helped him get into the saddle. Yoshisada knew better than to resist, at least he was still alive and able to negotiate in this state.

"You!" he called out to Kito, "Come with me."

Kito responded instantly, running towards Ryushin.

"This time we will make sure your mission is a success," he said as Kito mounted the nearest horse.

As he caught up with Ryushin, they both rode off in the direction of Enryaku-Ji.

Chapter 33

Yamakiri opened his eyes to see a small pair staring straight back at him, their innocence capturing his attention for a moment.

"Kansai, please," a soft voice called out; as the small boy stepped back he revealed the face of a beautiful woman. Many times in his dreams he had seen this face before him. Her innocence was something Yamakiri had desperately sought, but he knew deep down that once it was lost, it could never be restored.

"Mariko?" Yamakiri asked as he sat up.

"Yes, you remember my name?" she asked surprised.

Yamakiri was about to respond when someone else entered the room carrying an armload of firewood, it was his cousin Watanabe.

"Ah, I see you have woken up. Please Mariko, I need to speak with him," Watanabe said, urging her to leave the room.

Mariko bowed her head, "Come Kansai, help me to prepare dinner," she said, taking the little boy's hand and leading him out of the room.

Watanabe stood and watched, then once they had left, moved over to Yamakiri and knelt down beside him.

"What happened to you, Kansai?" he whispered.

Yamakiri stared back at his cousin for a moment, the name he had been known as before echoed in his mind.

The last time he had seen Watanabe was over three years ago. He had obviously aged, but looked a lot older than the 21 year old that he was.

Yamakiri thought back to that fateful day and all of the carnage he had seen.

He had witnessed Kito kill Shimada, Sakamura's *Samurai* commander, and Seiko's father. They were followed later that day by the death of Watanabe's father, Saito Yamada, and while trying to save him he had killed Mariko's father. In that one day, he had seen more death than a young man should ever have to, and still to this day it hadn't made sense to him.

"What happened to everyone the day of the ambush, Watanabe?" Yamakiri asked, shaking his head and staring blankly at the floor in front of him.

"Kito told me you were dead. He actually even brought your body back and we buried you alongside your parents," Watanabe responded.

Yamakiri thought back to his parents, there were so many unanswered and puzzling questions about that time.

"My father always said if you are going to die, die fighting for something you believe in, but I don't understand why so many had to die that day, Watanabe," Yamakiri said shaking his head.

Suddenly Kansai, Watanabe's son came running back into the room, followed quickly by his mother. "Stop Kansai!" she called, catching up and securing him around the waist.

"I thought," Watanabe said, about to reprimand Mariko for interrupting them.

"No please, it is okay-come, come Kansai," Yamakiri said, urging the young boy forward.

For a moment Kansai didn't move, even though his mother had let him go.

"Come Kansai, I won't bite," Yamakiri said smiling.

Kansai looked to his father for approval.

"It is okay Kansai, this is your uncle," Watanabe said taking his hand and directing him towards Yamakiri.

As Kansai slowly moved towards him, Yamakiri felt a warmth sweep over him. It was in this very village some time ago that he had lost contact with his parents and would never see them again. Something else that disappeared that day-his sense of family. Looking at Kansai reminded him so much of himself when he was young, ironically they shared the same name.

Yamakiri reached out his hand and in response, Kansai placed his much smaller hand in his uncle's. The contact with someone so young and innocent was invigorating and was something Yamakiri had been yearning for all these years.

"I wonder if it really matters what happened in the past Watanabe, after all, it cannot be undone." Yamakiri said as Kansai came closer, finally raising the courage to climb onto his uncle's knee.

"I see you still carry a lot of the past with you," Watanabe said, looking over at Shimada's *Katana* resting against the wall.

Yamakiri turned around, and realising what Watanabe was referring to, looked back.

"That has taken many lives and brought countless misery to many people, yet you choose to carry it?" Watanabe continued.

Seeing his father's reference to the sword, Kansai stood up and wandered over to it; however, he knew better than to touch it without permission.

Kansai stood there admiring it from a safe distance. It was taller than he was and its highly lacquered surface reflected the light from the window and the setting sun.

Yamakiri thought back to the days when he too had been fascinated by this weapon.

"That may be the case, but it was not only the weapon that is responsible. Your father once taught us that the sword represents truth; however, it is the beholder who chooses how it is used, not the sword. Maybe it has come into my possession to serve a greater purpose than killing and causing misery," Yamakiri said, looking at Kansai.

"All war causes misery and distrust, to one side or the other. The only thing we can hope for is peace," Watanabe responded.

"And what of you, have you found peace, Watanabe?" Yamakiri asked.

Watanabe looked towards the doorway of the kitchen, where Mariko was preparing the evening meal.

"I am not sure any more," Watanabe said, looking back at his cousin.

"What do you mean?" Yamakiri asked.

"Your arrival here is no chance happening. In fact Kito Harada alluded to this when he brought your body back to be buried. He refused to show me what he said were your remains and made sure who or whatever he buried was done so quickly," Watanabe responded.

"I don't understand," said Yamakiri.

Watanabe stood up and walked across the room to the far corner. He pushed a narrow wooden panel in the wall causing the top of it to open up and expose a small shelf. He pulled out a rolled up piece of paper tied with a silk ribbon and handed it to Yamakiri.

"Kito had said to me that if Kansai was to be reborn I was to give this to him. I now realise that he was talking about your return and did not mean anything to do with my son Kansai," he said taking a step back and placing his hand on his son's head.

"What is it?" Yamakiri asked.

"I have no idea, but it was obviously meant for your return."

Yamakiri looked down at the scroll. Written on the outside in fine calligraphy were the characters for *Yamakiri*.
Seeing the characters, Watanabe looked surprised.

"Strange, I am sure that was not there when Harada san gave it to me," Watanabe said, looking confused.

Yamakiri slid the ribbon off the end of the scroll and uncoiled it, stretching it out in front of him-he read it out.

Yamakiri, if you are reading this, then you could only have survived the test of time. Your future awaits you, if you choose to go down this path. Kansai Tokugawa is dead and buried, but never forgotten. It is dangerous to dig up the past, but in this case you would be digging up the future. The choice is yours.'

It was signed Saito Yamada-Watanabe's father.

Yamakiri looked up at Watanabe. "Do you know what this means?"

"Well, it is obvious that you are not buried in the grave we were told you were," Watanabe responded.

Yamakiri looked back surprised. He knew what the note meant and what his dead uncle had asked him to do.

"We all have choices, cousin. You do not have to accept this," Watanabe said reassuringly.

"Do you really think so?" Yamakiri asked.

Watanabe didn't answer, he already knew what it was. The discussion was interrupted by Mariko.

"Excuse me, I have some dinner for you," she said innocently.

Yamakiri looked up at Mariko; -her beauty radiated from her as she smiled.

"This is not just about me; our pasts are all intertwined together, as are our futures," he said looking across at the young Kansai, standing next to his father.

"Thank you Mariko, I look forward to it," Yamakiri said smiling back.

As Mariko responded and turned around to bring in the dinner; Watanabe looked back at his cousin, unable to hide his concern for what was to come next.

During the meal no one said a word; although there was the odd grunt and burp as each man showed his appreciation. Yamakiri looked across the table at Mariko and in response she smiled back. Looking into her eyes, he saw her sense of detachment from him, in distinct contrast from the last time he saw her. After training together in his uncle's *Dojo* she had confessed that she had fallen in love with him, then her eyes had sparkled like jewels as they gazed into his. But now there was no such sparkle, as if any memory of that period of her life had been erased. If this was the case, Yamakiri thought, by who?

Yamakiri turned his attention to young Kansai, sitting at the opposite end of the table. He was completely engrossed in trying to control a big piece of *Tempura* with his chopsticks. Suddenly there was a loud clunk as it dropped on his plate. For a moment he froze and stared downwards, as if waiting for someone to say something. Slowly he looked up and peered at Yamakiri as a big smile grew across his face, then he began giggling. At first Watanabe looked back at him and looking to his right saw that Yamakiri was also smiling. Seeing this as acceptable, he looked back at his son and smiled as well.

Kansai's giggling echoed in Yamakiri's head and suddenly connected with the nightmares he had been having since secluding himself in the mountains. A shudder ran down his spine as the realisation hit; although the dream had been about Sakamura's daughter being accidentally killed, he now realised it was far more symbolic-it was the death of his innocence.

- * -

Having sent Seiko to Kamakura with Yoshisada as her prisoner, Ryushin and Kito had made good time in the opposite direction along the road back to Enryaku-Ji. During the ride, there had been no talk between the two and from Ryushin's perspective that was as he wanted it. He had Kito under his control and was well aware of his skills. To him, he was much more effective than any well-honed weapon.

At the intersection of the track that led to the top of Mt Hiei, Ryushin stopped and as Kito halted his horse, he issued him with a series of orders. As each instruction was given, Kito nodded. Receiving the final one, he pulled the reigns around and rode off up the track at speed in the direction of the temple. Ryushin waited for a moment before following.

After an hour's ride Kito approached the gate, conscious of how he would be received. The two *Sohei* brandishing *Yari* stood at the ready, pushing the tips of their weapons out in front as soon as they heard the sound of his approaching horse.

Kito stopped and jumped off.

"I must see Kusunoki now," he said, urgency in his voice.

The two men looked at each other; they had never seen Kito before and were apprehensive, what was more, they had been issued with orders not to let anyone in.

"And you are?" one of them asked.

"Kito Harada," he responded.

"Wait here please!" he said, knocking on the gate three times with the tip of his spear.

The sound of the large wooden bolt being drawn across the backside of the door was followed by a creak as it was pulled slightly open.

The guard leaned in and said something to someone on the other side. Then the door slammed shut and the guard turned back to Kito.

"Please wait, Kusunoki will be here shortly," he said, re-assuming his position.

Kito waited patiently, it wasn't long before the sound of the door latch sliding across and the large figure of Kusunoki appeared from behind the opening. The look on his face reflected his disappointment.

"Why were you not here guarding Go-Daigo as I had

instructed?" Kusunoki asked angrily.

"Master, I was, but after the attempt on his life I made sure he was safe and followed the assassin to try to catch her," Kito responded bowing his head.

"Her?"

"Yes Master-the same woman that had infiltrated Go-Daigo's palace a few weeks ago."

"And did you manage to catch her?" Kusunoki asked.

"Yes Master-I killed her after a brief struggle."

Kusunoki looked down at Kito's clothing, noting the dried blood all over it.

"Do you know who sent her?" Kusunoki asked.

"Yes, Master-she confessed under torture that she was working for Takauji Ashikaga and err.." Kito responded.

"What?" Kusunoki demanded.

"Prince Morinaga," Kito said, hesitantly.

"What?"

"Yes. It seems that the information I provided can be substantiated. He has in fact defected and is plotting to kill his father and take over his position as *Shogun*."

Kusunoki seemed astounded, in total contrast to his usual calm demeanour.

"We must not let Go-Daigo know of such a plot until we are absolutely sure this is the case," Kusunoki responded.

"Well, he is safe here, Master," Kito said.

"It seems he is not safe anywhere, Harada san."

"At least there are better fortifications here than there are in Kyoto," Kito said, glancing across at the guard to his left. The guard re-adjusted himself in response.

"Alright, although I am unsure what it will take to convince Go-Daigo that he needs to stay here for now," Kusunoki said, prompting the guard to open the door.

As Kusunoki walked back through the open gate, Kito adjusted his saddle, to signal success. Across the road in the trees, Ryushin Yakushimaru receded -he needed to prepare for the next phase of his mission.

Chapter 34

"Now that you have returned, there is something that we need to do, Yamakiri," Watanabe said, distracting his cousin from his dinner.

"How did you know that would be the case, Watanabe? I could have chosen to never return," Yamakiri responded.

Watanabe looked across at his son Kansai, engrossed in trying to stab another piece of *Tempura* with his chopstick.

"Sometimes the choices we make are not our own, Yamakiri," Watanabe said turning back and looking him in the eyes.

Yamakiri was confused by this statement and wasn't sure what to say next.

"As much as we may think we are free to do whatever we want, there are things that our ancestors have done that we must address," Watanabe responded, turning his attention to Mariko. Unaware of what he was referring to, she smiled back.

"Come, we have something we need to do," Watanabe said standing up.

Yamakiri looked up, uncertain of what was expected of him. "Come, come," Watanabe urged.

As he led Yamakiri out of the back door and down the steps, he pointed over to a large shovel leaning against the low garden fence.

"You will need that."

Yamakiri picked up the shovel, then swinging it over his shoulder, followed Watanabe out of the gate in the direction of the graveyard.

Watanabe stopped under the village gate.

"I suppose we do have choices in life. You could choose not to dig up what is there and turn your back on what it may be that is buried there," Watanabe added.

"And if I do?" Yamakiri asked.

"That is not for me to say, or to know for that matter. I was just instructed to show you," Watanabe responded.

Yamakiri felt a cold breeze rush past him, even though the nearby trees were still. He thought about the events that had culminated in him coming back to Aoyama. He knew at each stage he could turn around and walk away, however, he also knew that without confronting his past, he could never be truly free.

"I will leave you to do this alone," Watanabe said, turning and making his way back to the house.

Yamakiri watched him disappear inside, then he turned his attention to the grave; Watanabe's words echoed in his head. In reality he knew he had no choice, to turn his back would be a dishonour to his family and to his teacher.

He pushed open the gate and entered the small enclosure. Walking past the grave of his uncle he stopped and bowed, then without hesitation, began removing the dirt from what was marked as his grave.

He had only dug down about a foot when his shovel struck something solid; a deep thunk indicated that it was made of wood. Dropping to his knees he pushed away the dirt from the top and traced the extent of its sides. It was around two feet long by about one foot wide.

He looked back towards the village as if looking for approval, however no-one was there, he was all alone.

Reaching down, he pried the box from the grasp of the soil and slid it alongside him on the edge of the hole.

Brushing the top clean, he could see something carved into its lid. It read 'Yamakiri'.

He shuddered as a surge of energy rushed up his spine; he slowly prised opened the lid. Looking inside, he saw various items, including scrolls wrapped with ribbons and weapons- a *Tanto* and several *Shuriken*. One of scrolls stood out: it was much lighter in colour than the rest, as if it was more recent than the others. As he turned it over, he saw that it too had his name on it.

He quickly removed the ribbon and unravelled the paper. It was a letter signed by his uncle.

Yamakiri
It is good that you have returned to claim what was destined to become yours.
Our family has a deep tradition of honour and service to this country and
with what I am passing on to you, I know that you recognise this too.
I was well aware that you have been searching for answers on the fate of your
father. He too believed in service to his country and to justice and gave his
life for this. He was a Ninja of the highest skills and used these to keep
others safe from oppression.
Unfortunately our master required that he be sacrificed for the greater
purpose, and he was captured and put to death by Sakamura. This was
necessary to lay the ground work for the series of events that you were also
part of.
Success is not always measured in ways that we can understand or that are
obvious to others, but I have taught you to look beyond that and to
appreciate that we serve a divine purpose known only to god.
So I pass on the lineage and mechanism of such service to you, so that others
may benefit. The Densho contained in this box are yours to understand,
revise and pass on to the next generation. Please treasure and protect them
until then.

Signed - Saito Yamada - Spring 1333

Yamakiri looked at the other items within the box. Most prominent and consuming much of the space was a set of scrolls: three in number, all tied together. He recalled his uncle referring to something similar during his years of training with him. He would place them to the side of the *Dojo,* demonstrate a specific technique and then refer back to them-nodding or shaking his head if he was happy or unsure.

Yamakiri unraveled the binding releasing them and selecting one, opening it in front of him. It was quite heavy and the paper wrapped around a thick wooden dowel.

As he looked at the first section of the scroll he read the title *'Hakuun Ryu Ninjutsu-Densho'.*

This was something he didn't understand as his uncle had never mentioned anything about it that he could recall. Looking further along the scroll he could see that it did have details of all of the techniques that he had been taught. He rolled it back up, and looking at another, saw it had the same title. Instead of techniques, he saw it had written *'Menkyo Kaiden'* followed by his name, Yamakiri, given to him by his uncle.

Yamakiri sat back in shock, realising that what he had before him was in fact a license awarding him *'Soke'* of the school; making him in effect the next grandmaster. However, he knew he had a choice: ultimately the balance of this didn't rest solely with him and he knew it. He had been taught how important tradition was within his family and the need to carry it on; he also knew that denying his responsibility to his uncle would not come lightly.

As he looked through the box he found several more documents, one was distinct with a gold ribbon and a note wrapped around the outside. Examining it more closely, he saw it also had his name on it. Pulling it from the ribbon, he unfurled it and spread it out before him.

Yamakiri-these documents are of the greatest significance to our country and need to be kept safe. Furthermore, they belong to the Emperor Go-Daigo and should be returned to him when his safety can be assured. This was my promise to him and for you to follow through with this mission.

Yamakiri looked up at the sky, the setting sun illuminated the clouds, painting them in iridescent swathes of reds, yellows and oranges. Then he turned his attention to the north and the direction of Kyoto-he knew what he had to do, but also knew that he couldn't do it alone. Putting the scrolls back into the box, he stood up and made his way back into the village.

- * -

Atop Mt Hiei night started to close in, the sounds of the song birds gave way to the sounds of the night. Ryushin knew it would be easier to take Go-Daigo in the night, especially under the protection of Kusunoki. He was after all Samurai and their ways meant he wasn't adept at operating at night. However, Ryushin knew better than to use this as an excuse to drop his guard, after all he was noted to be one of the best swordsmen in Japan.

The *Sohei* on the other hand could prove more difficult. They were well trained in defense and knew how to read nature and what it could tell them. Fortunately their understanding of such things came from the same source as Ryushin's, *Shugendo* – the roots of the *Yamabushi*. However Ryushin also had the fortune of being trained by his grandfather – a master of *Ninjutsu*. His men would arrive soon; he had already taken Morinaga from the temple, but knew his next target would not be as easy. However, he had inside help that no-one suspected.

Inside the temple grounds Kito had followed Kusunoki's instructions to remain vigilant. Go-Daigo had been convinced to stay at the temple by Kusunoki with the assurance from Kito that it was far safer than his residence in Kyoto. Besides, any attempt to relocate at this point in time would be extremely dangerous-or so Kito had convinced Kusunoki.

Chapter 35

"We must leave now, Watanabe," Yamakiri said with urgency as he entered the small house of his cousin.

"What?" Watanabe asked, surprised. Mariko turned around also surprised by the request and looked at Yamakiri.

"We must leave for Kyoto, Watanabe. I will need your help," he said.

Mariko made her way into the room with Kansai following close behind. She stopped and picked him up.

"Your father has asked me to return some very important documents to the Emperor," he said, holding the small box in front of him. Watanabe looked back at his family, as if to ask for permission. Deep down he knew that his father's involvement in Go-Daigo's last attempt to secure the Shogunate was by no means the final Chapter in the story. After hearing of his trouble with Takauji, he had been waiting with some trepidation for someone or something to pull him back into the recent power struggle. The arrival of Yamakiri had alerted him to that and had shattered the shell of denial that he had shrouded himself in.

"I am sorry, my love. I must honour my father's wishes and help Yamakiri," he said regretfully.

A solitary tear ran down Mariko's cheek, leaving a shiny ribbon in its wake on her delicate skin. Kansai looked up and seeing the tear his smile changed.

"What's wrong, Mommy?" he asked.

She looked at Yamakiri, then back at her husband.

"Come with me, she said, taking hold of his tiny hand and leading him away into the kitchen.

"I am sorry Watanabe, I had no idea this was going to turn out this way," Yamakiri said regretfully.

"Maybe things would have been different if Sakamura's daughter had not been killed that day," referring to the tragedy in Ueno years earlier.

Watanabe paused before answering.

"Maybe many things would be much different," he said looking at Mariko, who was leaning on the windowsill and staring outside with her chin propped up on one hand, her distress reflected obviously in her blank gaze.

Yamakiri knew what he was implying. Years earlier, when Mariko had spent time training in his uncle's dojo, she had confessed that she had fallen for him. But through a series of events, her training and any past memories had been somehow erased from her mind. Along with this had been the memories of the circumstances surrounding how Yamakiri's father had lost his life. After the death of his uncle, she was the only one who could tell him what had happened.

"It is not time to dwell on the past now. We must make our way to Kyoto immediately," Yamakiri said, urging his cousin on.

"Yes, we must. Let me say goodbye to my family first," Watanabe said.
Yamakiri couldn't help but think back to that fateful day when his uncle took him away from the very same place they were in now. Had he known he would never see his parents again, he may have decided against it…Never have regrets, he told himself, echoing the words of his mother.

- * -

At Enryaku-Ji, Kito settled down for the night outside the small hut where the Emperor was preparing to go to sleep.

He was instructed to remain vigilant at all times and be on his guard. Across the courtyard from him were several men, each tasked with keeping their eyes on a particular section of the complex. At the sign of any movement, they were to signal Kito.

Kusunoki had despatched a messenger to Kyoto to request a troop of his finest *Samurai* to help escort Go-Daigo safely back to his palace. Go-Daigo had taken heed of Kito's warning not to ride the steep mountain trail without protection at night, but as if exercising his power, he had insisted on returning to his palace in the morning.

From the trees Ryushin had watched the messenger pass, but had chosen not to thwart his mission. He suspected he was heading for Kyoto, though he wanted it to appear as if their route back to Kyoto would be unimpeded and so watched him disappear down the narrow trail. He would wait until daybreak and the arrival of his men before making his move; this way he would be better placed to play out his strategy.

- * -

At the same time that the sun was going down over the mountains in Iga, Yamakiri and Watanabe set off for Kyoto. For a moment Yamakiri had experienced a strange feeling that he had been here before, as if history was somehow repeating itself. Glancing back over his shoulder he saw the two of them standing there like statues frozen by the reality and weight of the situation. He couldn't help but think back to that day when he had been in the same position as a young boy watching his father steer his cart full of goods to be traded out of the gate and down the steep road towards the north. One of his regrets was that he never had the opportunity to say goodbye to his father as he embarked on the mission that would seal his fate and one that he would never return from.

What was more, later he had learned that these trading missions were not as they seemed or were portrayed. His father had been a *Genin*-a foot soldier and active *Ninja,* carrying out his orders from above. This had also troubled him; he knew that it was his uncle who had given the order for that fateful mission and he had since learnt that his father's life had been sacrificed for the greater cause.

As they made their way down the road, he couldn't help but see Mariko's face in his mind's eye; it was one of pure innocence and unknowing, even though she had been there the night his father had been killed. Somehow she had survived. It was also obvious that the memory of what had happened had been hidden from her to protect her, but from Yamakiri's perspective, it had also removed any possibility of him ascertaining the truth.

"You are very quiet, Yamakiri," Watanabe said, breaking the silence.

Yamakiri said nothing at first.

"Silence is sometimes the best way of protecting the truth, Watanabe," Yamakiri finally responded, seemingly restrained in his tone of voice.

"Hmm, sometimes the truth can be a double-edged sword," Watanabe responded.

Watanabe's words echoed in his head, as if recalling something significant his uncle had taught him and had referred to many times during his training. To demonstrate this he had brought out a *Tsurugi*-the doubled edged sword always seen in the hands of the god Fudo Myoo. He had taught them how this was a weapon only for highly spiritual martial artists. His emphasis was on the exposed edge while cutting and how it could also cut the user.

Yamakiri found himself intrigued by that comment. He had been searching for the truth and had first hand experienced the pain of the so-called back edge of the blade and so instantly recognised this analogy.

"So why do you think the truth is hidden from so many?" Yamakiri asked, stirring in his saddle.

Watanabe knew what he was driving at and had no patience for playing with words.
"Look Yamakiri, we were all part of something bigger in that time and we each played our part, why cannot you accept this?" Watanabe scoffed.

"And you-you have just accepted this?" Yamakiri responded angrily.
"I look at Mariko and see the innocence in her eyes, as if nothing happened. Do you think she has been given the opportunity to truly accept all that has happened?"

"She remembers nothing at all."

"Including the fact that it was her father who killed yours?"

"In her eyes, he died a hero," Watanabe retaliated.

Yamakiri could feel his emotions swirling as he thought about what Watanabe had just said. He knew differently about the situation surrounding Mariko's father's death. Yamakiri was about to respond when a dark shadow flew in front of his face. He hadn't heard anything, but his experience told him that it was an owl, setting out on its nocturnal life. He took this as a sign, a sign to change his mind and to not pursue his line of questioning.

"Come, we must make better time," Yamakiri said, flicking his horse's reigns and tapping its body with his heels. As it broke into a trot, Watanabe encouraged his horse to follow suit. The noise of the clattering hooves denied any opportunity for further discussion, for the time being anyway.

- * -

Meanwhile, Seiko and her prisoner Yoshisada had made good time and were already half way to Kamakura. Although he had not attempted to talk up until now, they stopped for the night and as she helped him dismount, he took his chance.

"Can I at least piss in the proper manner?" he asked, alluding to the fact that he had been ignored on the last two instances and ended up soiling himself to relieve the pressure.

"I am happy for you to assist me?" he added, smiling, his inference meant to demean her standing with him.

Seiko scoffed to herself. How pathetic he looked, this great *Samurai* warrior, held captive by a young woman. What was more, he had fallen for the illusion that Ryushin created, believing he could be successful in his plan to take over as *Shogun* by having Takauji killed and framing his brother. With this in mind, she decided to untie him and let him have his wish.

"Ah, so you trust me now," he said sarcastically.

"No more than you master does," Seiko responded.

"Go!" she added, as she finished untying his hands and ensuring her last word ceased any hope of conversation. He was not free however, his arms were still bound tightly around his chest, severely limiting his ability to do anything such as escape. Yoshisada lifted up his jacket and pulled out his penis where he stood. Immediately a strong stream of urine patted on the ground directly in front of him and at Seiko's feet as if in some desperate act of defiance.

Unaffected by his action, Seiko turned away and began searching for firewood.

"We will camp here for the night," she said as she walked away.

Yoshisada was surprised that his captor had turned her back on him and leaving his hands untied he could well escape. He looked around at the terrain, steep hills rose on each side of the narrow road, carved out over the centuries by the bustling river beside it.

"Do not even think about it, Yoshisada. I am well aware of you *Samurai* and your fears," she said, referring to the *Tengu* that were said to reside in the hills and forests of the region.

Yoshisada grunted out loud in response as he finished his

258

business and adjusted his clothing.

However, what Seiko had not known was that Yoshisada and his men were the advance party for a large contingent of around another 5,000 more, heading along the same road behind them. What was more, their forward scouts had seen her and their master in the distance and reported back to their commander.

As she turned around with the load of firewood in her hands, she was surprised to see not only Yoshisada standing there, but another dozen or so men flanking him.

Three of them were archers and drew their bows as she turned, moving forward and around her to ensure that if she moved, she would certainly have been hit.

"You do not think that I would be stupid enough to overthrow Takauji with only a handful of men, do you?" he said, referring to the highly skilled men around her and the hordes of men that followed them along the road.

Seiko carefully scanned the area; she had chosen this place to stop because it afforded little means of escape but now she had been caught in her own strategy.

"Throw down any weapons you have on you," Yoshisada shouted, as one of his men untied him.

Seiko followed his orders and dropped the pile of small branches, then she reached into her jacket and removed the *Tanto* and threw it in front of her.

Yoshisada moved towards her, but his advance was suddenly halted by a high pitched screech of something above his head-jerking back he looked up, searching in the air for its origin. Seiko, taking advantage of the distraction, leapt backwards, hand springing away in the direction of the trees by the river.

What she had failed to see was the water rise behind her and the figure of a dark creature emerge from its depths. The water ran off its hairy matted head as it rose above the surface. There were many stories of *Kappas*-mythical creatures that lived in the lakes and rivers-which had been known to drag unsuspecting humans into the depths. She was overwhelmed by the creature and unable to get her footing as it dragged her backwards into the river, shoulders first. Witnessing this, Yoshisada and his men stood there in shock, unable to fathom what they were seeing.

Seiko gasped for air as the creature dragged her deeper and deeper under the water, but it was too strong to resist and the enveloping water changed to darkness, and then an eerie silence filled the air.

Chapter 36

The sun had completely gone as Yamakiri and Watanabe entered the small village of Nabari. To the left was the house of Kazuki Satoru; the figure of the small man could be seen beside the large pile of firewood by the rear entrance. He looked up and smiled as the two men saw him and deviated from their course.

"Greetings," Kazuki said bowing.

"And so to you," Yamakiri responded and both of them bowed back.

"Ah Yamada San, it is good to see you in the company of your cousin Yamakiri," Kazuki said, looking across at Watanabe.

"Hmm, well more so by volition than by choice," Watanabe responded semi-despondently.

"Would you care to stop for some tea?" Kazuki asked.

"No, I am sorry my friend, we cannot this time. We need to make haste to Kyoto," Yamakiri responded.

"Kyoto-tonight?" Kazuki asked, surprised.

"Well, Mt Hiei, actually," Yamakiri responded.

Kazuki's demeanor changed instantly.
"Do you need some help, Yamakiri?" Kazuki asked keenly.

Yamakiri looked back at his cousin for a response. Since they had only spoken once since leaving Aoyama, Yamakiri quickly considered the prospect of Kazuki as a distraction to the tension between the two men.

"Very well, but you will need to move quickly. We have no time to spare. I can brief you on what we need to do along the way," Yamakiri responded.

"Alright, I will be very quick, I promise," he said excitedly, throwing the small load of firewood he had gathered to one side and rushing around to the back of his house.

Watanabe stared back at Yamakiri as if to question why he had invited Kazuki along.
Yamakiri shrugged his shoulders and pushed out his bottom lip. He believed in fate and for whatever reason, Kazuki had been there at the precise moment when they were passing. This seemed to indicate he was meant to come along; only time would tell why, Yamakiri thought to himself.

- * -

At Enryaku-Ji, Kito had been vigilant on guard all night outside Go-Daigo's temporary accommodation. He had watched the stars as they slowly traversed across the clear night sky and using a reference point was able to count the number of hours until dawn. As each hour passed he would rise from his position and stretch his muscles; this would serve two purposes: firstly, to supplement the internal tension and relaxation exercises he would do to keep the blood flow going, and secondly; to change his vantage point to another location. The last shift put him on the roof of the gate house at the entrance to the complex. From here he had not only a clear view of Go-Daigo's location, but also a view down the track leading down the mountain to Kyoto and beyond. As he lay on the cool tiles, he scanned the surrounding trees for any movement or signs of life. It wasn't long before something caught his eye. Looking for the distortion of the background, he was able to make out a large boar rustling around at the ground below a large tree, its search for worms incessant as it slowly moved forward, burying its snout and large tusks deep into the soft soil. Suddenly it stopped and looked up, raising its sensitive nose to the slight wind blowing across the mountain from the west. It could obviously smell something alien to the environment and perceived it as either a threat or a possible food source. Following the direction of its stare, Kito

262

could see the outline of several figures on horseback come out of the dark background and into a spot of moonlight just before the clearing in front of the temple. Now he was able to make out three men and as he focused intently, the familiar *Tengai* hat worn by the *Yamabushi*. Seeing the prey was bigger than it could handle the boar turned and trotted off into the forest, grunting as if in disappointment.

Kito stood up on the roof to alert them of his presence.

"Yamakiri, is that you?" Kito asked.

"Yes, my friend-and with some help," Yamakiri responded.

"One moment," Kito said, turning and jumping off the roof into the compound.

As the party moved forward towards the gate, they could hear Kito in discussion with someone behind it and then the sound of the large draw bar being slid across, confirming their acceptance.

The large door swung open, revealing Kito standing on the other side.

Kito walked out to meet them, making a beeline for Yamakiri, who had already dismounted.

"Greetings Yamakiri, I was wondering if you were coming back to help me," Kito said, smiling and slapping his friend's shoulder.

"Well, I had some pressing matters to take care of first," he responded.

Looking across at the other men, Kito thought he recognised one of them as someone he had known in the past.

"Yamada san-is that you?" he asked.

"Watanabe to you," he responded, grinning.

Kito bowed as Watanabe approached him. He had spent a lot of time with Watanabe's father and had held him in the highest esteem; this he cordially extended to his family, as was the custom.

"Come, come. Are you hungry? I will wake the chef and get him to make you something," Kito said, ushering them inside and past the guards on the gate, who were busy scanning the trees as they quickly pushed the doors shut and bolted them.

As vigilant as they were, there was no way that they would have seen the large number of eyes peering back through the trees and undergrowth. Like a pack of wild animals awaiting a moment when their prey would be unsuspecting, the group of *Ninja* waited patiently for the order. Each knew that the stakes were much higher than last time and as always, there was no room for error. It also helped that they would not be working alone and would have help from an unsuspecting ally.

Inside the temple, Kito led the weary group over to the canteen area and had them wait while he roused the chef from inside his hut, at the same time he issued orders for the guards to take up various positions around Go-Daigo's hut.

Moments later the overweight chef appeared in the back of the kitchen, his protest obvious by the grunting and flailing arms interspersed with his half asleep attempts to don his stained and dirty apron.

"Right-that is sorted," Kito said smiling as he made his way to the table where they were seated.

"I knew you would be back," Kito said smiling across the table at Yamakiri.

"You mean once I discovered what was buried in the grave with my name on it?" Yamakiri asked.

"Hmmm well, you did have some choices around that."

"Some would say otherwise-as if it was my destiny," Yamakiri responded in a serious tone.

A crash of plates from the kitchen, followed by a series of curses sliced through the serious and intense conversation.

"Good to see you again, Watanabe. It has been a long time my friend," Kito's tone changed as he turned and spoke to him.

"Yes it has. Oh, and this is Kazuki Satoru," he replied, leaning back to expose Kazuki.

"Ah yes-from Nabari, are you not?" Kito asked.

"That is right, how did you know that?" Kazuki asked.

"I heard mention of you, and in fact you helped me some time ago to capture someone in Shiga province," Kito responded.

"I did?" he asked.

"Yes, a man named Sendo Yokoku, from your village. Unfortunately he escaped not long after."

Suddenly Kito realised what he had just said.

"Oh, I am very, very sorry," he said bowing several times to Watanabe.

Sendo Yokoku had been a *Genin* under Watanabe's father during the last uprising. Believing his daughter Mariko had been killed in a failed mission with Yamakiri's father, he had sought revenge on the person who had ordered it. After escaping from Kito he had seized the moment and attempted to kill Watanabe's father. In an attempt to thwart the lethal attack, Yamakiri had in turn killed him.

For some time there was silence, as each person considered the past and their connection to each other. As if on cue, the chef arrived with a tray and several steaming plates that he distributed amongst them. They sat there, seemingly engrossed in the meal, but with each person acutely aware of the connection to each other and the past; something that had once again proved impossible to avoid.

Chapter 37

The 5,000 strong force of Nitta Yoshisada's military had pushed on towards the north during the night. When they were still over a day's ride away from Kamakura, Yoshisada pulled them up near the small town of Mikawa.

Believing that he had the element of surprise, he knew it was important to gather as much momentum as possible once the advance had been set in motion. However he also knew that this needed to be tempered with rest so that upon reaching Kamakura, he still had an army that was fighting fit.

"We will rest here and continue our advance at noon," he told his top commander, looking at the weary troops.

His plan was simple, but differed from the initial strategy of marching into Kamakura and taking over. Now he would need to take Takauji's men by storm and surprise.

From his departure, he had been led to believe that Takauji's brother had killed him and seized power. But with the ambush and attempt to capture him, he suspected that Takauji would be preparing to receive him, but not in any sort of military operation. However, more importantly, he didn't want to lose face by retreating and as far as he was concerned the events of the past day were not enough to deter him from his goal. What he didn't know was that Takauji had already been alerted to his advance and was preparing to meet him not far from his present location.

_ * _

The sound of a million cicadas filled the air as Ryushin and his men settled down to see out the rest of the night. Scattered amongst the undergrowth, each was acutely aware of their role in what was to come next and the importance of its success. That was, all but one.

Seiko was still wet from being dragged into the river by the so-called *Kappa*(which was in fact one of Ryushin's men) and had made her way to his side.

"You set me up," she whispered angrily.

"You of all people should know that things are never as they seem, Seiko," Ryushin replied.

"Besides, no harm came of it now did it?"

Seiko knew better than to argue. Ryushin had his mission and anyone that got in his way would be quickly removed from his path.

"What do you want me to do?" Seiko asked, submitting to his authority.

Ryushin thought for a moment; he hadn't factored Seiko into his plans and didn't want her to get in his way. Although he was well aware of her skills, he knew that as a *Kunoichi* she operated very differently to the way he had been trained. In fact, he had some issues with female *Ninja* from an early age. His grandfather had openly told him the meaning of the term *Kunoichi* – meaning 'nine holes', in reference to the vagina and the complications that came with it-as he had explained, 'maintaining such a mechanism for childbirth.'

"Kito Harada; I believe there is a past connection to this man with you?" Ryushin whispered.

"Yes. He betrayed me and killed my father." Her eyes widened as a surge of rage engulfed her.

"Hmm, so it is revenge you seek? Dangerous, such actions," he said shaking his head.

"Well, shortly he will be surplus to my needs and I have no issue with his disposal. As far as anything else, I prefer to have my men do what needs to be done,"

Seiko understood and confirmed it by shaking her head; nothing more needed to be said and she retreated back into position to wait for her moment.

Inside the walls of the temple Kito and the three travellers finished their early breakfast under torchlight; each pushing their plates to the centre of the table, as if signalling it was time to talk.

"We will be taking Go-Daigo back to Kyoto this morning, just as soon as his escort arrives," Kito said breaking the silence.

"Do you think that is wise, considering his vulnerability when he is in transit?" Yamakiri asked.

"Those are his wishes and we must respect them," Kito responded.

"Hmmm," Watanabe muttered under his breath.

Suddenly there was loud shouting from the far corner of the complex, someone was calling out "Attack! We are being attacked!" It was one of the *Sohei;* as the men stood up in response, they saw his dark figure reel and fall off the wall, where moments before he had been standing watch.

"Quick, over there!" Kito shouted, pointing to the location of the commotion.

Without hesitation, Yamakiri picked up his staff and vaulting the low banister, ran in towards the far corner. He was quickly followed by Kazuki and Watanabe.

"I will ensure the Emperor is safe," Kito shouted.

However, he didn't run in the direction of Go-Daigo's hut, instead he ran in the opposite direction towards the house where Kusunoki was sleeping.

Just as he ran up the steps the door slid open, filling it was the large figure of Kusunoki busy tying his shirt. Kito launched himself, performing a double flying kick to his chest, sending him stumbling backwards onto the floor. Falling backwards, he did a reverse roll onto his feet and ran towards the reeling figure on the floor. As he reached him he kicked him in the solar plexus, kicking the wind out of him. As he raised his head, Kito kicked him in the jaw, as his head flicked back and impacted with the floor, he was knocked unconscious. Drawing his *Tanto* he turned and knelt down to cut his throat.

"Leave him, he won't be bothering us for now!" a voice shouted from the doorway.

Kito looked up to see the camouflaged face of Ryushin.

"Tie his hands, I don't want him killed," he added.

Kito sliced through Kusunoki's belt and after rolling him over, hastily tied his hands behind his back.

Finishing quickly, Kito stood up and rushed out the doorway. An arm reached out, stopping him.

"Now secure the Emperor and make sure nobody gets to him," Ryushin commanded from the shadows.

Meanwhile, Yamakiri and the others made their way to the far side of the compound and were now standing over the body of the dead guard, whose lifeless eyes seemed to trace the arrow embedded between them. By this stage there were well over 50 *Sohei* amassing around the immediate area of the supposed attack. Some crouched on the wall and peered over, as if searching the relative darkness for any sign of a threat.

"Look!" Kazuki shouted as the shadows around the buildings seemed to come alive, the distortion of the distinct lines morphing into the shape of a large number of human figures. They panned out, surrounding the group of men to restrict their escape.

In an attempt to break free, one of the monks stood up and was about to leap off the wall when the sound of a deep thud filled the air. He careered backwards onto the ground and a loud gurgling sound was heard as his severed carotid artery filled his throat and lungs with blood.

In desperation the overweight chef who had seen the *Ninja* expose themselves charged at one of them, his cleaver held high in the air. Effortlessly, his intended target turned,, drawing his sword. He cut the chef across his abdomen, folding him in half as the cut nearly sliced him in two.

"Enough!" Came a shout from behind the darkly clad men.

The solid line of men moved aside to reveal Ryushin.

"There is no need for anyone else to die here!" he shouted.

"We have what we came for," he said, turning and pointing at two men standing in front of the house where Go-Daigo had been sleeping only moments before. The large man was obviously Go-Daigo, his hands bound behind his back. As Yamakiri strained to see through the dim light, he suddenly realised who the person standing behind the Emperor was. It was Kito.

"Is that who I think it is?" Watanabe whispered to Yamakiri.

Yamakiri nodded his head in acknowledgement.

"You appear surprised that your friend is working for me?" Ryushin asked, smiling.

"Everyone has their price."

Yamakiri knew he could not let Ryushin take the Emperor and had to stop him at whatever cost, but it was obvious they were outnumbered. Not only that, Ryushin's men had infiltrated the temple and no-one had known, this would have taken a high degree of skill and he had no doubt this would also be the same for their combat abilities.

Suddenly out of the group of *Sohei* someone called out, "This is not going to happen!"

But before Yamakiri could stop him, he ran at the line of men followed by the rest of the *Sohei,* raising their various weapons in attacking postures.

"No!" Yamakiri yelled, but it was too late and several of them were already engaged in intense combat.

Yamakiri knew it was futile to stop them. Seeing a gap, he ran towards Kito and the Emperor. However he had only gone a few steps when out of the chaos stepped Ryushin. Yamakiri stopped dead in his tracks, behind him Watanabe and Kazuki faced outwards to defend his back.

"I said no-one needs to die, but that seems not to be the case. Do you want to join the dead today?" he asked, smiling.

"Who are you?" Yamakiri asked angrily, pointing the tip of his *Shakujo* at his face.

"That doesn't matter. What is important is that I am here to take Go-Daigo and no-one is going to stop me," he said, drawing his sword and holding it to the side of his body.

Behind them the fight raged on; the clanging of sword upon sword, interspersed with shouts and moans as more *Sohei* succumbed to the superior skills of Ryushin's men.

By this stage, several of Ryushin's men had surrounded the small group and pushed out a space, completely encircling them.

"Well, *Yamabushi,* are you going to try to stop me with your magic?" Ryushin said, slapping his sword against the tip of Yamakiri's staff, causing the rings to rattle loudly.

"Rest assured, my masters do not want to see the emperor harmed, he is far too precious for that. But if you insist on engaging me and my men, then anything could happen. Besides, I am sure you can trust your friend to protect him," he said, smiling and looking back at Kito.

"Get him mounted up!" Ryushin ordered his men and Kito.

"As for you, *Yamabushi*, I suggest you order what is left of your men to stop attacking before there is no one left."

Yamakiri looked around at the carnage. It seemed that out of the 50 *Sohei* that were at the temple, very few were left standing. It was obvious that they had been out-skilled by Yakushimaru's *Ninja*.

"*Yamate! Yamate!*" Ryushin shouted to his men.

Immediately they stopped fighting, although some continued to parry away the odd thrust and punch from the *Sohei*.

Seeing one of the senior *Sohei* close by Yamakiri shouted "Stop your men-it is fruitless!"

He shouted out several times to his men to stop, as most were exhausted or injured, they ceased fighting, some dropping to the ground, others just dropped their weapons. Those who were able ran to the men who were injured.

"This didn't need to happen," Ryushin said shaking his head as he scanned the carnage.

"We will meet again soon," Yamakiri said as Ryushin walked towards Go-Daigo, who was now atop a horse.

"I am sure we will," Ryushin said, waving his sword in the air to call back his men.

Yamakiri looked across at Kito.

Kito stared back, his expressionless face framing his cold black eyes.

"How could he do this?" Watanabe asked, his anger obvious.

"I don't think he had any choice," Yamakiri responded.

"What do you mean?" Kazuki asked.

Yamakiri didn't respond and seemed to be fixated on the group of *Ninja* and Go-Daigo, led by Ryushin, as they rode out of the gates.

His thoughts turned to his arrival in Aoyama that day and how Mariko had greeted him as a total stranger; it was as if they had never met before. Yamakiri suspected she had succumbed to *Saminjutsu* – a form of mind control.

Yamakiri stirred, he was in uncharted territory and needed to understand more to make any sort of informed decision.

"Shouldn't we try to follow them?" Kazuki asked.

Yamakiri shook his head. He knew Ryushin would have his route well covered.

"Anyone who walks out that gate would be dead before their next step. Attend to the injured," he said, making his way to Kusunoki's hut and fearing the worst.

Chapter 38

Nitta Yoshisada and his army had just made their way into Mikawa when a cry rang out from a side road, ordering a charge. Looking to his left, Yoshisada saw Tadayoshi Ashikaga barrelling down the wide road flanked by his men. His standard raised high in the air along with hundreds of drawn Katana reflecting the morning sun-it was obvious he was in no mood to negotiate.

Yoshisada turned to his men and shouted "Prepare for attack!"

Although they were tired, they were well drilled enough in combat to organise their ranks according to the circumstances. However, they were without the advantage of an open battlefield to organise their sections accordingly and the element of surprise on Tadayoshi's side was already paying off.

To combat the horse charge, Yoshisada's *Naginata* and *Yari* soldiers pushed their way to the front to meet the advancing men. However, Tadayoshi had also had time to position his archers up on the embankments opposite and as they came into range, the archers let fly with a hail of deadly arrows.

Instinctively, Yoshisada's commander took charge of his horse, pulling him back into the group and knocking down several of his own men in a bid to escape. He knew that in such a situation, he would need direction from his master and for that he needed him alive.

Meanwhile at the front the two forces clashed heavily, the sound of metal upon metal overshadowed by the screams of *Kiai* from each side in a contest to scare their adversary. As Yoshisada retreated back into the narrow pass, a bodyguard of men closed ranks in front of him as others rushed past to engage in combat. It didn't take long before a pile of bloodied dead and injured *Samurai* littered the road, forming a barrier that Tadayoshi's horsemen found hard to cross. This required the swordsmen on foot to take over, but also by this stage, Yoshisada's men had managed to organise themselves into their respective sections. With the archers now in position, they had begun to drive the close range soldiers backwards.

Yoshisada had no option but to call a retreat so he could regroup his forces. The pass would serve as a natural barrier in defence, but as it was any attempt to advance forward would not only be futile but also suicidal. However, he was intent on making it to Kamakura, driven on by the news that Takauji had been issuing his traditional family land in Kozuke to his own loyal supporters. The news of this enraged Yoshisada so much that he never considered that it was a trap to lure him into battle.

- * -

In Enryaku-Ji, Yamakiri slid open the door of Kusunoki's hut expecting to see the *Samurai* dead inside. However, this was far from the case; he was writhing around on the floor trying to free himself. For a moment Yamakiri paused, considering that it had been Kito who had done this to him. He was not looking forward to explaining his actions and in fact was struggling himself to understand what was going on, but from the lack of connection between them as he last saw him he was fairly convinced that Kito was under some sort of mind control.

Kusunoki's eyes burned with rage; Yamakiri prepared himself as he removed the gag.

"It was Harada who did this to me!" Kusunoki said angrily, enforcing the connection between Kito and Yamakiri.

"Is the Emperor safe?" he asked, as he jerked his hands free from the bindings.

"The Emperor has been taken," Yamakiri responded quietly.

Kusunoki leapt to his feet, pushing Yamakiri aside as he collected his swords from the corner of the room and tucked them in his belt.

"No wonder he had advised me to stay here until the morning-it was all part of his plan!" Kusunoki said, storming through the doorway.

"How do I know you are not part of this as well?" he said harshly, turning back towards him and staring into Yamakiri's eyes as if searching for the truth.

Yamakiri said nothing. He knew better than to attempt to explain such a complicated situation to someone who was so enraged.

A rumble from the direction of the gate caught his attention and he turned to see a large contingent of his men make their way inside the complex; it was the escort he had ordered to take Go-Daigo back to Kyoto. Seeing the carnage and then Kusunoki on the veranda, the commander hastily made his way over.

"Sir, what has happened?" he asked.

"You are too late, the Emperor has been taken!" Kusunoki responded angrily.

"You must have seen them on the road. They have only just left," Yamakiri interjected.

"We saw no-one. However, we took the track directly from Kyoto to save time," the commander responded.

"That explains it then. They will be taking him to Kamakura. Get my horse," he ordered, striding down the steps.

"I will come with you," Yamakiri said.

"No, you stay here and sort out this mess your so-called friend has caused," Kusunoki said emphatically.

Yamakiri surveyed the area. A feeling of sadness and anger filled his heart. It was Kito who had caused all of this. He tried to search his mind to when he had changed or could have been influenced. Then it struck him, it was after their mission in Kamakura; Kito had returned from Takauji's castle and had not been himself since then. Yamakiri suspected something must have happened to him, and a feeling of disappointment in himself took over. He should have seen this coming and stopped it, but what he had to remind himself was that there would always be things out there that were beyond his control. The best he could do now would be to make amends by following Kusunoki's orders.

- * -

Meanwhile, Ryushin and his men had concealed themselves and the Emperor as they watched Kusunoki's men ride past on their way up the mountain. They were not going in the direction of Kamakura as Kusunoki had expected, but instead were heading back towards Kyoto.

As they rode down the narrow track Ryushin looked over his shoulder to see Seiko at the back of the pack, he nodded to her and then looked at Kito.

"Stop there," he said.

Instantly Kito pulled up his horse and let the procession of men past.

As Seiko drew alongside she kicked Kito, sending him flying off his horse and tumbling down through the trees. She leapt off her horse and skipped through the undergrowth to catch him. By the time she reached him, he was standing and trying to make sense of what had happened. Seiko kicked out, but Kito twisted to the side to avoid the attack and as she passed he struck her in the neck with a thumb strike, sending her backwards. He leapt forward and placed his foot on her heaving chest.

"Stop this! Why are you attacking me?" Kito asked, restraining her with his foot.

As she looked into his eyes she couldn't see the man she had once loved, in fact there was no sign of the Kito she had known at all. It was as if he was a totally different person, and in some way he was.

She could easily have continued to fight to avenge the death of her father, but in this state of mind, revenge didn't seem right to her.

She centred herself and stared deeper into his eyes. She was surprised by the ease at which she had made the connection; he had obviously been taken over by Ryushin and his powerful influence.

She struggled with him mentally to find an in-road into his psyche and unlock Ryushin's control. It was only fair that if she was going to kill him he knew the reason for his death.

All she needed was to re-establish the link between them from the past when they were in love. Time seemed to stand still as she reached deeper into his past, watching the subtle changes in his eyes like flicking through the pages of a book. Then suddenly, her cue-"Kito!" she shouted, rupturing the shell holding his mind and pulling his memories back into his consciousness.

Kito shook his head and stared intensely at her. She had only been told of this technique and never had the opportunity to apply it, so she found herself in uncharted territory and unable to prepare herself for what would come next.

"Akiko?" Kito responded, referring to a name he had known her as from the past.

The look of confusion on his face said it all, her technique had been successful, however, there was something else. She managed to regress his mind and now his eyes sparkled, as lovers do when staring into each others.

He quickly removed his foot and crouched down beside her, rubbing her shoulders.

"Are you alright?" he asked, looking over her body.

Seiko had been warned about the dangers of performing this sort of so-called magic and now looking at Kito and his behaviour, she understood why. She had regressed him back to the time when they were lovers, obviously before she had tried to kill him for killing her father.-This now presented her with a dilemma, who actually was he?

Suddenly there was a loud thud as Kito was violently launched away from her, landing on his side. Seiko looked up to see Yamakiri standing above her, his sword drawn with its tip pointing at Kito, who was slowly recovering from the kick to the side of his head. He stepped back so that he could cover both of them in his field of vision.

"Kansai-what are you doing?" Kito asked innocently as he stood up and brushed off the loose dirt.

Yamakiri was confused, he had gone against Kusunoki's orders and taken it upon himself to find Kito. He needed to understand what had happened so he could try to rescue Go-Daigo. But coming across Kito and the woman he had fought in Kyoto now embracing, told a completely different story to what he had been led to believe. Kito had never referred to him as Kansai and he knew this was a name and life he had chosen to leave behind.

Seiko tried to sit up, but Yamakiri moved in, redirecting his sword at her.

"Stay where you are," he said.

"Wait Kansai, Akiko has been helping us, she is on our side," Kito pleaded.

Seiko looked up and noticed Yamakiri was holding something very familiar. It was her father's *Katana,* the skill in its craftsmanship and design on the *Tsuba* unmistakable.

"Where did you get my father's sword?" she asked angrily.

Yamakiri's mind began to swirl as Seiko delivered her well timed assault on it. Her strategy was to use the past not only to confuse Yamakiri, but also to capture him.

"Did you take it from his dead body after Kito killed him?" she asked, looking back at Kito.

Yamakiri flicked his head, as if discarding the invisible demon that Seiko was trying to unleash on him.

"Kito had not intended to kill your father, it was an accident. He was never meant to die, in fact our orders were to take him prisoner," Yamakiri responded defensively.

She looked back at Kito, searching for his response to what Yamakiri had just said. Kito bowed his head, as if to confirm what he had tried to tell her all those years ago.

"You can confirm what happened, Kansai?" she asked Yamakiri.

"I was also there, with Kito. Shimada resisted, as if not under the influence of the narcotic like everyone else," Yamakiri said defensively.

Seiko thought back to that day and the circumstances surrounding it. The night before she had been handed a powerful drug to lace the *Miso* at breakfast. This caused everyone who consumed it to succumb to its effects. However, her father had never had any as he had an allergy to the fish that was included in it.

"Your father was one of the few who still had the fight in them," Yamakiri added.

"So it was true, what you told me, Kito?" She asked, her shoulders sinking as she felt the weight of that moment on her. What was more, she was the one tasked with deploying the drug and was told it needed to be given to everyone. The realisation now struck her-she had in fact caused her father's death by not carrying out the orders.

Tears ran down her face as she wept uncontrollably. All these years she had fooled herself into believing that her father had been killed intentionally, when this was never the plan. What was more, she had not believed Kito and had unjustifiably sought revenge for his death.

Yamakiri re-sheathed his sword as Kito moved in to console her. The events of that day had not only taken a father from the woman before him, but also Yamakiri's innocence. Seeing a man cut down before him had had a much deeper effect than he could have known; Seiko was not the only one who had lost something back then.

Kito had told him about his father's mission to Ueno and Sakamura's castle. How he had never returned that morning and how the arrival of the black dove had signalled his failure. He also needed to know the truth about what had happened that night, though this was not why he had come searching for Kito.

"Where is Go-Daigo being taken?" Yamakiri asked.

Kito stared back at him, his lack of understanding obvious.

"Well Seiko, or whatever your name is, we need to know," he insisted

Seiko looked up at him, tears streamed down her face.

"I do not know, but I suspect to Takauji- I overheard Ryushin telling one of his men," she replied.

There was an anxious pause as Yamakiri evaluated this information. It didn't make sense, this was not how Ryushin, being *Ninja,* would operate; it was far too obvious and predictable.

"Come on, we need to get back to Enryaku-Ji.

Are you okay?" Yamakiri asked Kito.

"I'm not sure," he replied, the confusion obvious on his face.

Yamakiri looked at Seiko, he needed Kito, and more importantly, his mind, back.

"Don't worry, I will take care of it," Seiko said, nodding in response.

"Come, time is not something we have a lot of at the moment," Yamakiri urged, moving in the direction of the track leading back to the fortress.

As they approached the fortress gates, they were stopped by a guard.

"Why isn't that prisoner bound?" he asked nervously, referring to Kito.

"He is no prisoner, that is why. Now open the gates," Yamakiri said forcefully.

The guard was understandably defensive, not long before that he had seen Kito involved in the capture of Go-Daigo and the slaughter of several of his fellow monks.

"Look, I have no time to explain, but we need your help," Yamakiri pleaded.

"I will vouch for him, now let us in, we have no time to waste."

There was a pause and some discussion from behind the gate, then the sound of the draw-bar sliding across. As soon as it opened, Yamakiri and his companions rushed inside.

"Please, gather all of the capable *Sohei,* I need to talk with them," Yamakiri said.

From the far corner of the complex Watanabe and Kazuki appeared and when they saw Yamakiri and Kito they ran towards them.

"What is going on? What is he doing here?" Watanabe asked, referring to Kito.

Kito looked back at his old friend.

"He has no memory of what has happened, Watanabe. It was not of his doing," Yamakiri defended him.

Kito was about to say something when Seiko stepped in.

"Look, all of you need to realise that Ryushin has some very strong techniques for influencing and controlling people. Any of us could fall under his control with such techniques, so we have to be very careful. I can help to combat this," she said, looking back at Kito.

"Alright, we need to ready ourselves to free Go-Daigo. That includes you two," he said, referring to Kito and Watanabe.

They shook their heads in agreement; maybe it was just as well Kito had regressed to his old self. Yamakiri knew he would be far more effective in this state.

Chapter 39

Masashige Kusunoki and his men arrived at the crossroads at the base of Mt Hiei. To the left was the road to Kamakura and to the right, the road back to Kyoto. His feelings were still very mixed. Of course, he was angry that his master Go-Daigo had been taken prisoner and had been betrayed by someone he thought he could trust. And furthermore he had been taken by someone that Kusunoki had never heard of, and right from under his nose. He had employed the *Ninja* before to help destabilise Iga and its surrounding regions, but now the same skills had worked against him. What was even more significant, however, was that Kito Harada had been one of them. Uncertainty and change was something he didn't deal well with. Loyalty to his master was of the utmost importance, as this followed form and was something he had been taught from an early age.

He had been surprised that they had not seen any sign of the kidnappers as they rode down the narrow path; this incensed him as well, the fact that these men didn't have the courage to fight face to face. However he had failed to see the irony in his own tactics, using *Ninjas* and their ability to employ guerrilla tactics and monopolising on the vulnerabilities of their opponents.

He shook his head, as if to cast off the incessant torture of his predicament, resisting the subtle urge to go right, in the direction of Kyoto. He tugged hard on his horse's reins, steering it in the opposite direction and cantered off, followed by his large contingent of men.

- * -

Ryushin was making his way down the mountain in the opposite direction towards Kyoto. To most this would have seemed the most unfavorable option, especially as Go-Daigo had many of his loyal followers there. However Ryushin knew the area well and had spent many a day surveying the terrain-this was *Chi-mon*, to understand the lay of the land, a skill he had been taught and was well versed in. Besides, their route would take them around the town's limits and through the myriad of tracks that skirted the populated areas. His destination was the residence of one of the past emperor, Kanzan, on the western outskirts of the city. He had secured this earlier by ensuring the caretaker was moved on and one of his men put in his place. He was also well aware that Takauji's ultimate plan was to take over Kyoto and therefore to be seen to hold power over the country.

Several times during the journey Ryushin stopped, and like a wild animal raised his head in the air, closing his eyes and sniffing several times. In some cases this would be followed by him drawing symbols in the air, at the same time uttering an incantation. He finalised it by tensing his entire body as he pointed his clasped hands ahead of him.

At one point he looked across at his gagged captive, who was shaking his head as if he wanted to say something. Obliging, Ryushin leaned across and pulled down his gag to allow him to speak.

"So you believe the gods will help you in your attempt to kidnap me?" Go-Daigo said angrily, referring to his *Kuji* hand spells and incantations.

Ryushin paused for a moment before answering.

"The gods, as you call them, are impartial and will assist anyone, Go-Daigo," he responded.

Go-Daigo sneered back. The arrogance of Ryushin's tone for someone so young was something Go-Daigo had seen far too often.

"That may well be the case, but you will still have to face judgement for this," he said thoughtfully.

"I, like you, will be judged not by my actions, but by the outcomes of my actions," Ryushin answered confidently.

"So you believe that what you are doing is with the best interests of this country and therefore you will not be punished?" Go-Daigo asked.

"I make my own choices, Go-Daigo, and I accept responsibility for their outcomes."

"So you believe Takauji's move to take over the country is the right one?"

Ryushin had no inclination to justify his actions, even if it was to the current emperor of Japan. His motives behind helping Takauji were complex and being part of the Minamoto clan, motivated by obligation more than choice.

He reached over, pulled the gag back up over Go-Daigo's mouth and kicked his horse to continue the journey down the narrow track, pulling the bound emperor behind him.

- * -

At Enryaku-Ji Yamakiri had gathered all of the *Sohei* together in a group to address them. Sitting beside him were also Kito, Watanabe, Seiko and Kazuki.

"Firstly I am very sorry for the loss of your fellow *Sohei* during the attack. This highlights just how skilful Yakushimaru and his *ninja* are and furthermore how careful we need to be in our approach to him. Like us, he does not think or act conventionally and therefore has this advantage over conventional forces. We need to be mindful of this and prepare as best we can."

Yamakiri noticed one of the monks staring at Kito, who was standing next to him still confused about how he had arrived there.

"Look, see how he can control and influence even the best warrior," he said pointing at Kito.

"I will go to Yokawa temple to the east and ask the *Sohei* there to help us," one the monks called out.

"Good, I will go with you. The rest of you prepare for training. Master Harada and these men will begin your training in the arts of *Ninjutsu,*" he said looking back at Kito and the others.

"Is that all right with you, Kito?" Yamakiri asked quietly.

"Uh-yes, of course," Kito responded.

"Good, thank you," Yamakiri said, smiling.

"As for you Seiko, are you with us?" Yamakiri asked, turning to her.

Seiko thought for a moment and then responded.

"Yes, but I would like to go with you to Yokawa. I need to talk to you in private," she said looking across at Watanabe.

"As you wish," Yamakiri said, following the monk in the direction of the main gate.

Yokawa was a temple complex a short distance through the forest to the North West. Yamakiri and Seiko followed behind the monk as he led the way.

"When Kito said your real name, I suddenly realised who you were," she said quietly.

Yamakiri looked back at her.

"What do you mean?" he asked.

"Kansai Tokugawa?" she asked.

"Yes. Well, I once was," Yamakiri responded.

"Seems I was not the only one who lost a father in all of this," she said apologetically.

288

It didn't take Yamakiri long to realise what she was talking about.

"What do you know about my father?" Yamakiri asked.

Seiko was silent as she considered the best way to tell Yamakiri what she needed to.

"So you were the one at Kawai, the agent we passed the drugs to?" Yamakiri asked.

"Yes, that was me," she affirmed.

"From Ueno?" he continued, stopping her.

The monk at the front stopped and looked back at them.

"Please, we will catch up," Yamakiri said to him, urging him on.

Seiko knew where this conversation was heading and decided not to prolong it.

"I was there the night your father died, in Sakamura's castle," she said, looking down.

"It was you that stopped his escape by locking the door, wasn't it?" he said holding her by the shoulders and shaking her.

Her body went limp as he shook her for a response.

"Why?" he said angrily.

"I am so sorry. I didn't know that was going to happen." she said in a quiet voice.

"Look at me!" Yamakiri said getting angry.

She looked up, tears streaming down her face.

"It was all a set-up to trap Mariko. Your father was used as a diversion," she said, her voice quivering.

Thoughts raced through Yamakiri's head so fast he had little time to catch them. He let Seiko go and stepped back, leaning on a fallen tree.

The impact on Yamakiri was more intense than she could have known.

"Your father was a very brave man, Yamakiri," she said, trying to soften the blow.

"You say that, yet you killed him!" Yamakiri shouted.

"No, no, I didn't; he killed himself," she said without thinking.

"*Sepukku?* You want me to believe he committed suicide?" he asked defensively.

"He did Yamakiri, I was there when he did it. I saw the whole thing."

Yamakiri placed his head in his hands and closed his eyes. Images of his father killing himself flashed before him. Up until now, he had believed his father had been killed by someone in combat, but suicide?

"What did you see?" Yamakiri asked, as painful as it was.

Seiko tried to settle herself as she knelt down beside him.

"He and Mariko had been sent to kidnap the *Daimyo's* daughter, or at least that is what they had thought they were there to do. However, Mariko had been made to believe she was another Daimyo's daughter once she had been captured," Seiko said, trying to control her tears.

"How?" Yamakiri asked.

"*Saminjutsu* – hypnosis," she responded.

It suddenly occurred to Yamakiri why Mariko hadn't remembered him when he had returned to Aoyama that day-her mind had been altered to make her forget her past. This also explained the recent incident with Kito, and was an area he knew little about.

"He fought hard to escape but when he came across the locked door he was surrounded with no way out," she said, holding back more tears.

"He cut his own throat with a *Yari* and fell on another."

For the first time, Yamakiri had a clear vision of what happened to his father that night. His feelings were twofold; on one hand he felt a strange release that he finally could let go of the inaccurate images conjured up by not knowing, but on the other hand there was anger at who ordered the doomed mission.

"So Mariko knows nothing of what went on?" Yamakiri asked.

"Well, as of now she doesn't, but I suppose the truth is trapped in her psyche," she responded.

Yamakiri's attention now turned to the last time he had met Mariko at Aoyama and how she had not known who he was; despite having professed her love for him years earlier. Now this all seemed lost in the chaos.

"What is more, it is just as well; she was with child at the time of the mission," she added.

Yamakiri stirred, the last time they had met was only a few months before the mission. During that encounter, they had made love. If what Seiko was saying was correct, then it was more than likely this had resulted in her being pregnant.

"But I am unsure if she had the child as I never saw her after the ambush at Kawai."

If she was correct, then the child he had met at Aoyama was in fact his and not Watanabe's as he had assumed.

"Come on, we need to get to Yokawa," Yamakiri urged, standing up and in his way dealing with the truth.

Chapter 40

By the time Ryushin's group and his captive had made it to
Kazanin palace several hours had passed. Somewhat run down,
the old palace had been set up to provide a secure place to hold
Go-Daigo. Ryushin believed that it would not be long before the
city was under the control of Takauji and this was the best place
to keep the Emperor until the arrival of Takauji.

His men pulled the Emperor down off his horse and led him off
through a doorway to the side of the small courtyard. Ryushin
followed them in through the dark corridor and into a small
windowless store room, now a makeshift cell.

"Leave me with him," he ordered, ushering his men out of the
room and making sure the door was shut behind them.

He walked across to where Go-Daigo had been sat down and
removed his gag, untying it and his hands, then he stood back as
if to admire his prisoner.

Go-Daigo rubbed his wrists as he stared back at Ryushin, his
contempt for his captor obvious in his expression. He was
unaccustomed to being alone with strangers, always having
security close by when in such company. He stared at the young
man whose looks betrayed his teenage years.

In response Ryushin dropped to his knee, adopting the custom
of keeping your head lower than the person before you as a sign
of respect.

Go-Daigo sniggered to himself at his situation; here was
someone who had control of him, yet by his actions,
acknowledged the control of his status as royalty.

"It is a little late for respect isn't it?" Go-Daigo asked
sarcastically.

Ryushin looked up, but remained kneeling.

"When Kusunoki finds me, he will have you killed," Go-Daigo continued.

"We all must die sometime, so I am not afraid of this," Ryushin responded frankly.

"However, I don't think Kusunoki will find you any time soon. His skills are those of a conventional *Samurai* and it is difficult for him to think any other way. However, as a warrior I still respect him as a skilled adversary," he added.

"Something you could do well to learn from," Go-Daigo responded.

"Who are you anyway?" Go-Daigo continued.

"I am Ryushin Yakushimaru," Ryushin said proudly.

"Hmm," Go-Daigo said, as if searching for a connection to someone or something.

"However, I do not believe that is of any importance right now. I will see that you are well looked after-we can't have our Emperor being mistreated. I am sure you and Takauji will have much to discuss when he arrives," Ryushin said, standing up and exiting the room.

Go-Daigo watched him leave and listened intently as the door was bolted shut.

- * -

At Enryaku-Ji, Kito and Watanabe had wasted no time in assembling the uninjured *Sohei* for training. They had them in lines, marching backwards and forwards performing a myriad of blocks, kicks and strikes. Although their form looked impressive it seemed to be lacking something, but Kito was unsure what. He had never trained such a large number before and was unsure how this was actually done.

The drills continued for several hours, at a frantic and incessant pace. In fact, they were having their first break when Yamakiri returned from Yokawa with Seiko and at least another 100 monks.

"Good to see you already have them training, Kito san," Yamakiri said smiling and surveying the sweating group of young men.

"Yes, well, there is no time to waste," Kito responded.

"What is your plan for preparing them?" Yamakiri asked.

Kito thought for a moment before responding.

"I will be honest with you, I am a little perplexed as to how we confront Yakushimaru and his men," he finally answered.

Yamakiri looked back at the men he had led from Yokawa and then across at the remaining group.

"We don't," Yamakiri responded bluntly.

"You of all people should know that we cannot employ traditional forms of combat against someone as skilled as he is, it would be suicide."

He had hoped that Kito would have been able to train these men in unconventional warfare but it seemed that his regression had also stripped him of his capacity to see what was required. Yamakiri looked back at Seiko

"We need Kito the *Ninja* back so he can train these men," he said.

Seiko looked across at him and then the men and shook her head.

"I am sorry, I cannot guarantee I can get the results you are looking for," she said despondently.

Yamakiri was well aware that their training would need to be much different to the defensive techniques they had been drilled in to defend the temple. He had watched them as they had been easily overpowered and out manoeuvred by Ryushin's men. One of the things that his teacher had continually emphasised throughout his training was that a technique against one was no different to a technique against 1,000. It occurred to him that this was how Ryushin was easily able to defeat these otherwise excellent warriors.

"You two, please show a technique," he asked, urging two of the monks to his left to come forward.

"You attack," he said to one of them.

Without hesitation, the monk lunged forward at his opponent. Without thinking his *Uke* moved backwards in a straight line, at the same time blocking the punch.

"Continue attacking!" he shouted.

In response the monk lunged again and again, each time he was met with a block but missing was any sort of a counter attack.

He called another pair out and asked the same, again they responded by moving backwards in the same manner with no counter.

"What do you notice about their movements, Kazuki san?" he asked.

Kazuki was taken aback, he had never been trained in the martial arts and knew Kito would have been better equipped to answer such a question.

He thought for a moment and then looked across at Kito.

"No, you answer," Yamakiri urged.

"Umm, all of them moved the same?" he answered, looking back at Kito again.

Yamakiri nodded. "Exactly, they all move the same way. This is how Yakushimaru was able to defeat them so easily."

The *Sohei* had been trained to defend their temples and because of their religious beliefs did not believe in retaliation, which in this case was any form of counter attack.

"Yakushimaru attacked them at their weak points, as any good warrior would. That is how he defeated them so easily, so we must respond differently and be less predictable," he continued.

"How do you propose to change that?" Kazuki asked.

"I am not too sure, but that is enough training for now until I think of a better way," he said despondently.

- * -

Several hours passed as Kusunoki and his men made their way along the road to Kamakura. Every so often they would stop to check for any sign of Go-Daigo or his kidnappers. As they rounded a sharp bend, they narrowly avoided colliding with the fast moving *Samurai* coming in the opposite direction.

He pulled up, coming to a halt just in front of Kusunoki.

"What is this? Kusunoki asked.

"Master-I have been sent to call for reinforcements for Yoshisada," he said, urgency in his voice.

Kusunoki was surprised at his request. As far as he knew Yoshisada was still in Kyoto, why would he be asking for reinforcements?

"We have encountered heavy resistance from Takauji's army near Mikawa," he said, nearly out of breath.

"Where is Yoshisada now?" Kusunoki asked.

"Our forces are about three hours ride from here, Master."

"Alright, we will help him," Kusunoki said, turning to his commander.

The *Samurai* bowed and turning around headed back towards Kamakura. Kusunoki ordered his men to follow as he rode off down the road.

Chapter 41

At Enryaku-Ji things had moved so fast for Yamakiri that he needed time to consider where fate had led him. He sat on a rock next to the canteen, drinking water. Watanabe came and sat beside him on the wooden step.

"We have had little time to talk," Watanabe said, opening the conversation.

"About what?" Yamakiri responded.

"There are things I sense you would like to know about what happened in the past and why things are the way they are now," Watanabe said.

"With you?" Yamakiri asked cautiously.

"Me and Mariko?" Watanabe responded candidly.

Yamakiri stared at the ground. This had been a search for the truth and as he had been warned, it would not be easy. Seeing Mariko after all those years was a shock, but what had shocked him even more was the way in which she had been shielded from the past by others. Now Yamakiri had learnt that the son raised by his cousin Watanabe was more than likely his. It was the fact that someone could live such a lie that was unfair, especially as Yamakiri had chosen the path of truth. However, he also realised that this was not always obvious to the person in the midst of it.

Yamakiri had sensed tension from the moment they met and knew this had to be resolved, especially as they needed to be on the same page moving forward. However, the news of Kansai being his son was something Yamakiri would not disclose. Was he being selfish to want Mariko to recognise their past and the connection they once had? He needed time to think about that.

"Do not think that Mariko has come out of what happened unscathed," Watanabe started the conversation awkwardly.

Yamakiri found this comment strange and obviously a lead into something he wasn't sure he wanted to pursue.

"I didn't. What is your point Watanabe?" he asked.

Watanabe paused for a moment.

"She has nightmares nearly every night about what happened to her, but has no other recollection. It constantly reminds me of how fragile she is," he responded.

"Someone had to be there for her, to reassure her."

"You mean to shield her from the truth?" Yamakiri asked.

"Yes, I suppose so," Watanabe replied thoughtfully.

"Meanwhile she lives her present life as a lie."

This comment incensed Watanabe, although he knew it was the truth. However, for him, this was more about duty than the truth. It was his father that had enlisted Mariko in the mission and to that extent he felt obligated to see that the mess that was left behind was dealt with correctly. That was also why he had not hesitated when Yamakiri had asked him to come.

"Look at yourself Yamakiri, even you live some of that lie. Just by the mere fact that you no longer carry your given name; is not that a lie also?"

Yamakiri was about to answer when Watanabe tapped his arm.

"And look around you," he said, referring to Kito Harada sitting across the courtyard from him.

"This is what happens when people manipulate the truth. Is it right? Look at the outcome Yamakiri, and tell me if it is right?"

Then he stood up and walked across to Kito, leaving Yamakiri to think about what he had just said.

He knew he was right on so many levels. What had transpired was nothing short of a mess, and for the sake of what, he asked himself.

Furthermore he found himself doing the last thing he had wanted, to teach people how to fight.

'What you do not want is sometimes what you need the most', his grandfather's words echoed in his head. These wise words had often stopped him from descending into a state of self-blame. He stood up and threw his cup off to the side, in a symbolic gesture as if to cast his negative thoughts off as well.

- * -

Nitta Yoshisada had regrouped his men west of Mikawa. The ambush of Tadayoshi had taken many casualties, but he was not about to lessen his chances of taking back what was rightfully his. He looked to the east, staring up at the ominous Mt Fuji; its snow covered peak dominating the landscape. This was a prominent feature of the landscape that he had been very familiar with, it was like a guardian and had seen him grow and provide protection to his family. But now things had changed, it seemed like he was being punished for something and denied his birthright. As he stared, he could hear a distant rumble to his rear which slowly increased, becoming louder and louder.

Turning, he searched the road. Suddenly it filled with hundreds of *Samurai,* led by the unmistakable figure of Masashige Kusunoki. Yoshisada was confused, this was not what he had ordered his messenger to do; to draw Kusunoki into this battle. In fact he had tried to keep him out of this campaign. As he saw it this was his battle, to regain what had been taken away from him and to take control back from Takauji.

Kusunoki rode directly towards him, stopping just feet away and bowing as his horse came to a halt. Kusunoki scanned

Yoshisada's men, then focussed his attention back on their leader.

"Thank you for coming so quickly," Yoshisada said, bowing once more.

"I was not responding to any request from you, Yoshisada. I have greater issues than supporting any military campaign that you choose to carry out in secret," Kusunoki responded, pressing the point.

Yoshisada was taken aback by this comment, although deep down he knew it was the truth. He had intentionally avoided telling anyone of this, hoping to overthrow Takauji and then announce his return to power in Kamakura under the Go-Daigo *Shogunate.*

"There was nothing secret about this Kusunoki, I have a right to take back what has been taken from me and my family," he responded.

"And you have the approval of the Emperor to do this?" Kusunoki asked, knowing in fact he didn't, but wanting to see his reaction.

"I am sure the Emperor would approve," he replied.

From this comment, Kusunoki knew Yoshisada had no idea of the plight of the Emperor and obviously hadn't seen him or any of his captors pass by. This was not that surprising, given the skill of Yakushimaru and his *Ninja* though. Kusunoki decided to keep Go-Daigo's abduction to himself for now.

"So what brings you here then Kusunoki, if not to assist me?" Yoshisada asked cautiously.

Kusunoki thought for a moment before responding.

"I have a mandate from Go-Daigo to retake Kamakura in his name."

After hearing about Yoshisada ahead, his new plan was to combine both forces and use these to push forward into Kamakura. However, he had to be careful that Go-Daigo wasn't used as a pawn in any negotiations, or worse, sacrificed to disrupt any potential return to power.

"In the name of Go-Daigo I suggest we combine forces and drive forward to Kamakura. There is more of a chance of success with the larger force we have now assembled. Do you agree?" he said, in not so much of a question as a declaration.

"Of course," Yoshisada said, bowing. He was well aware that Go-Daigo had more confidence in Kusunoki than himself. After all, it was the failing of Yoshisada to secure Kamakura that saw Takauji succeed in his plan to regain control.

"We have already encountered resistance at Mikawa, but together we should be able to push through."

"Yes, I am sure," Kusunoki responded.

Yoshisada was not happy that he could be denied control of Kamakura, instead potentially having to go through the correct protocols to be awarded control from the Emperor. However, he had no choice but to work with Kusunoki. Little did he know that the rescue of Go-Daigo was at the forefront of Kusunoki's plan, not Kamakura.

The combined forces of the two groups were met with little resistance at Mikawa; just a few hundred of Tadayoshi's men engaged them, each side suffering only minor casualties. Such was their success that Kusunoki decided to push forward to the next potential choke point of Ashigara pass in the Hakone Mountains. There Kusunoki expected a lot more resistance, but was confident with the combined force of the two armies he would over-power them. He was conscious that the more time taken to reach Kamakura the more danger his master would be in. Little did he know that Ryushin Yakushimaru had studied much of his history and knew not only how he thought, but to some extent, his next move. As such, he had given advice to Takauji on what to expect and how to prepare, information Takauji knew better than to ignore.

Chapter 42

At Enryaku-Ji, Kazuki had followed Yamakiri to the far side of the large courtyard to where he was sitting with his back to a large boulder. He sat down in front of him.

"You seem to be disturbed by the conversation you had with Watanabe. It is probably none of my business, but it is also not what I came along to see," he said.

Yamakiri stared back at him, surprised that he had ignored his obvious desire to be alone.

"So what are you here for, really?" Yamakiri asked.

Kazuki paused before answering.

"I suspect for the same reason we were drawn together, Yamakiri. After Shimada ransacked my village and killed my parents I was left with nothing, just an emptiness and bitterness. To this day, I still do not understand why it happened. So like you I am searching as well, I suppose," Kazuki said despondently.

Yamakiri thought back to the morning the black dove had arrived in Aoyama and the significance of its presence. Used as a natural means of communicating the failure of his father's mission, he was unaware at the time how it would also signify an abrupt turning point in his life. The surprised look on his uncle's face as he looked up, and the look of absolute shock on his mother's, was something he would never forget. He had seen the smoke rising from Nabari prior to their hasty departure into the mountains with Watanabe and his uncle.

Up until now, he had failed to make the connection. The smoke was Kazuki's home being devastated by Shimada and his men and people were also being killed, including Kazuki's parents. But the hardest fact to face was the news that this had all been triggered by the failure of his father's mission in Ueno, or so it was purported. A sense of sorrow and guilt swept over him. Although he knew his father was not responsible for his own demise that night, he did feel some burden on him to put things right. Looking up and across the ground at Watanabe, Seiko and Kito, he saw more victims, all drawn together by this single event.

He had seen Watanabe's father die before him and he had killed Mariko's father in the same moment. He had also seen Kito kill Seiko's father, but the worst image of all returned to him nearly every night in his dreams: the sight of Sakamura's five year old daughter, lifeless, killed by a stray arrow. He shuddered and shook his head as if to shake off the images of death, but it wasn't working. He collapsed onto his side and struck the ground repeatedly with his fist, harder and harder, at the same time cursing under his breath until he collapsed face first into the dirt.

Kazuki instinctively placed his hand on his shoulder to console him.

"Yamakiri," he said softly, but he failed to respond.

"Please, Yamakiri," he said insistently.

Yamakiri stirred and slowly pushed himself up off the ground and looked up at Kazuki, his face half covered in dust as it stuck to his tears. He looked into Kazuki's eyes, but instead of the confident man Kazuki had come to know, he saw the eyes of a young boy forcing his way through from the depths of his psyche. Although Kazuki didn't know it, what he was staring back at was something that Yamakiri had had stolen from him that fateful morning in Aoyama-his innocence. What was more, it had been tarnished by all of the loss and carnage he had been exposed to in such a short space of time.

Kazuki leant forward and embraced him tightly, as if sub-consciously emulating the embrace of his long lost family.

306

"It is okay, my friend. We will get through this together, I promise," Kazuki said, reassuring him.

Kito had started to stand up at the sight of Yamakiri breaking down, but had been pulled back down by Seiko.

"No-please Kito, leave him," she said, understanding the situation was far more complex than Kito could understand in his current state of mind.

Just as Kito sat back down two monks walked over to them.

"Excuse me please, can we have a talk?" he asked.

"Yes of course, please sit down," Seiko said.

They sat down in front of them, smiling.

"I am Kasagi and this is Dharma Rinpoche," he said, introducing the other monk to his left.

"Rinpoche?" Kito asked, enquiring about his non-Japanese title.

"Ah yes, he is not Japanese, he is Tibetan," he responded.

Kito had met many Buddhist monks over the years, only once had he met someone with the title of 'Rinpoche' but he knew that this title meant 'precious one' and was only given to someone of high standing in Tibetan Buddhism.

Dharma seemed a lot older than any of the other monks, but it would have been impossible to guess his age.

"Pleased to meet you," Kito said, bowing deeply.

"I am sorry, he does not speak any Japanese, but I can translate," Kasagi responded.

Kasagi turned to him and uttered several words in Tibetan, to which the lama turned and smiled through his stained yellow teeth, nodding at the same time.

"He has been observing your training and believes he may have a way of defeating Yakushimaru," Kasagi said casually.

Kito looked him up and down; he was very thin and certainly didn't look anything like a warrior should.

Dharma shook his head convincingly and stood up, urging Kito to do the same.

Kito looked back at Kasagi, who also nodded.

"Please, he wants you to try and attack him so he can show you."

Kito stood up and looked back at Watanabe, somewhat confused, then turned his attention towards the frail looking lama standing there with a big smile on his face. Reluctantly and with some reservation, Kito punched at the man's body. Before he could make contact, his attack came to an abrupt halt, his punch hitting what appeared to be thin air about 6 inches away from the lama's body.

The lama roared with laughter as Kito stood there confused.

"You could at least try to hit him Kito," Watanabe said from where he was sitting.

"I did," he responded.

"Please, he wants you to try again," Kasagi requested.

This time Kito decided to try and hit him with much more force. He lunged forward at speed but instead of stopping, he was thrown backwards, ending up on his backside. Dharma let out another loud cry of laughter as he looked down at Kito on the ground. Kito looked flustered as he stood up and brushed the dust off his behind. He was very skilled in the martial arts, but had never encountered something as strange as this before.

"Please, you try," he said, pointing to Watanabe.

Watanabe wasn't sure he wanted to, but his curiosity had the better of him. He quickly stood up and faced the lama. Without warning, he lunged at him in the same manner that Kito had just done. However, this time the lama moved to the side and with a quick flip of his fingers, sent Watanabe tumbling across the ground. A plume of dust rose into the air as he came to a halt.

Seiko had watched in silence as this was going on.

"What is this martial art called?" she asked, breaking her silence.

Kasagi conferred with the lama before answering and then responded.

"Dharma has told me he knows nothing of the martial arts at all. This is what is known as *Mikkyo*, it involves the use of the gods to assist in an outcome."

"But is this something we can learn and teach to the *Sohei*?" Watanabe asked.

There was small conference between the two men in Tibetan and various shaking and nodding of the head from Dharma, then Kasagi turned back to him.

"He says it is something that can be taught, but not something that can be learned easily, if that makes sense. There is great responsibility in using this and it is not for everyone," he said.

Yamakiri and Kazuki had seen what was going on and, intrigued, had made their way across the courtyard. Yamakiri looked at Watanabe, who was still brushing off the last of the dust from being thrown around.

As they arrived, Dharma stared intently at Yamakiri as if studying him and then traced the outline of his body with his finger. A big smile lit up on his face, then he turned to Kasagi and whispered in his ear.

"Dharma says you have some interesting skills," Kasagi said bowing to Yamakiri.

Yamakiri was surprised by this comment, and at the same time was unnerved as the monk kept on staring at something around Yamakiri's body.

"What is he doing?" Yamakiri asked finally.

"He seems to be fascinated by your aura," Kasagi responded.

Then Dharma turned again and made some comment to Kasagi, prompting him to ask Yamakiri a question.

"He wants to know if you are aware of the elements – *chi, sui, ka, fu & ku?*"

Yamakiri thought for a moment, then nodded.

"Yes, my uncle had mentioned these and shown some examples once."

Without warning, Dharma positioned himself behind Yamakiri and placed his hands on his shoulders. Then he whispered in Yamakiri's ear the word *'Chi',* meaning earth. Yamakiri looked back at Kasagi.

"He wants you to concentrate on this, as if you were a big rock," Kasagi responded.

No sooner had Yamakiri imagined himself as this, than he felt a surge of energy rush through his body and down through his feet-with this he felt incredibly solid and heavy.

Dharma looked over at Watanabe and nodded, motioning for him to attack Yamakiri.

Taking his cue, Watanabe stepped forward and prepared to attack. Yamakiri shuffled his feet, as if to prepare, but was immediately restrained by Dharma, who said something to Kasagi.

"He's saying 'Don't move'," Kasagi said and then nodded for Watanabe to continue.

Watanabe rushed in, punching at Yamakiri's face. Preparing to be hit for the sake of the exercise, Yamakiri closed his eyes and anticipated the strike, but there was nothing. As he opened his eyes, he saw Watanabe sitting on the ground in front of him.

Dharma took his hands off Yamakiri and walked back some way from him across the courtyard. Stopping, he called out the word '*Ka*', meaning fire.

Once again, Yamakiri closed his eyes and visualised being immersed in fire and again felt a surge of energy from the direction of Dharma.

Watanabe looked up at Kito, as if to signal him to attack instead and stood up to make a space in front of Yamakiri. "Me?" Kito asked nervously.

"Yes, you try," Watanabe responded.

Without any hesitation, Kito moved forward and prepared to attack. As he began to move, Yamakiri felt a rush of energy flood his body and keeping his eyes open this time, witnessed Kito being violently thrown backwards. His feet left the ground, giving him just enough time to roll out of the throw.

Dharma walked back to the group smiling at everyone, as if nothing had happened.

Once more he turned to Kasagi and spoke.

Kasagi turned to the group. "Dharma says that with the gods on your side, so will success be."

With that he knelt down and drew a character on the ground representing '*Shin*' heart.

Then he looked up and asked "Okay?"

Everyone nodded, confirming they understood.

The he drew directly above this the word '*ha*' – blade, and looked up.

Yamakiri recognised this as the kanji for *Nin* – the blade over a heart-and was part of the *Kanji* for *Ninja*.

Dharma pointed to each component and then circled it with his finger, at the same time explaining something to Kasagi.

"He has explained that this has a twofold meaning; one is how the blade cuts through evil wielded by a pure heart and the opposite meaning of how a bad heart will be cut by the blade if misused. This is his warning to you in choosing to use this power. Do you understand?" Kasagi translated.

Seiko stepped forward. She had been quietly observing the demonstration, but said nothing until now.

"I know Ryushin and what he is capable of, how can you be sure that this will work against him?" she asked.

Kasagi looked at Dharma and asked the question. The smile on his face instantly disappeared and replaced with one of complete seriousness.

"How does he suggest we train to acquire such skills in a short space of time? That sort of skill can take decades of training," she said.

"He has offered to help prepare the *Sohei* in their training, it will not take long," Kasagi replied.

"I do not understand," Kito interjected.

He said something to Kasagi, who nodded in response.

"The *Sohei* are all well versed in the ways of the *Yamabushi* and understand the laws of nature, this is the next stage of their development and it is timely that Dharma has just arrived," Kasagi said confidently.

Yamakiri was impressed with what he had seen and had always believed that there was a higher purpose to his training. His uncle had alluded to this when he was younger and had often said that the goal of their training was not to fight. Now he believed he understood what he had meant.

"*Ninpo*," Yamakiri uttered under his breath.

"What was that?" Kito asked.

"Beyond technique," Yamakiri responded.

"Yes, that is correct. What he has just demonstrated is *'Mu'*," Kasagi said as Dharma nodded, recognising this word.

"Does *Mu* mean not 'emptiness'?" Kazuki asked.

"On one side it does, but on the other it means strength. So it actually refers to strength from nothingness."

"Dharma Rinpoche would like to rest now, please. He would like to commence training at first light," Kasagi said, smiling; Dharma's face lit up also.

They all bowed as Kasagi and Dharma walked away.

Yamakiri thought about what he had just witnessed and realised that his wish to become a peaceful warrior was now possible; it was as if Dharma had manifested from another realm in response to his prayers.

Just as he was about to walk away, a cold breeze swept past him. This was unusual as the high walls of the fortress protected those inside from such things. But as soon as he registered it, it was gone again.

Suddenly Dharma stopped walking, clasped his hands at his front and said something, then drew something in the air and cast it away, like a fisherman casting his rod.

Then looking back at Yamakiri he smiled, bowed, and then continued on.

- * -

Meanwhile Ryushin Yakushimaru had left Kazanin palace and walked into the lower reaches of the nearby mountains, following a crystal clear stream until he reached a high waterfall with a large boulder at its base. Removing all of his clothes he waded into the deep pool surrounding the waterfall and climbed onto the boulder, positioning himself directly under the falls. Although the water was freezing cold, he had done this so many times that he had mastered the technique to nullify its effect.

The water cascaded off his head as he prepared himself for the *Yamabushi* ritual of *Misogi*-water purification, taught to him as a young boy by his grandfather. Feeling the icy cold water beating on his head, Ryushin visualised all unwanted energy being washed away and flowing back to the sea. He engrossed himself in the feeling of complete freedom, with no ties to anything except what he had raised in due obligation to his masters. As the water spiralled down his body like a serpent coiling down a tree, the liberation also freed his spirit from its bodily encasement.

Now he could choose his destination by the mere projection of his will, confident that the water would not only anchor his physical being to the place but also afford protection for its shell.

Instantly he was present at Enryaku-Ji, or at least his astral body was; weaving through the ethereal fabric of the people there-unseen, or so he thought. However, there was a brilliant glow of light from across the courtyard and as he passed by one person, he could see it emanated from someone he had not seen there before; a highly spiritual being. What was more, he tracked Ryushin's spirit as he passed around him. Then, stopping, he drew in a thick bolt of radiant white light and projecting it out through his heart region, weaved it into a grid and then projected this against him. In response, Ryushin lost control of his being and was thrown back into his physical body with such force that he toppled off the boulder and into the water. Up until now he had been able to move freely through the higher realms, but this experience had completely shaken him. He had heard of mystics from Tibet who had such power, but until now he had never come across any. His confidence had been severely challenged and disturbed. He was no longer alone or in control in these realms and could no longer take his invisibility for granted.

Chapter 43

After successfully driving back Tadayoshi's forces at Mikawa, the combined forces of Kusunoki and Yoshisada marched forward en-masse towards Ashigara pass in the Hakone mountains. The victory at Mikawa should have been an obvious sign to the two leaders that the slight resistance they had encountered was by no means an indication of the overall strength of Takauji's forces, but each had their own agenda for reaching Kamakura.

The forward scouts they had sent ahead had returned, reporting that the pass was deserted and that there was no sign of Takauji's forces. But Kusunoki was still weary, he had never trusted this man and his feelings had been proven correct when Takauji hadn't returned from Kamakura after taking it on behalf of Go-Daigo.

However, there was no quick way around without adding another two days to the journey. As they proceeded up the steep hill to the summit, Kusunoki was distracted by the clear sight of Mt Fuji to the east, its snow capped peak shining in the afternoon sun like a beacon of the gods. Next to him Yoshisada scanned the area for any sign of danger and although there was nothing out of the ordinary, he felt a slight uneasiness come over him.

"It is best if one of us goes ahead, Kusunoki san, this way if there is any opposition or attack the other can provide re-enforcements," Yoshisada said, trying to conceal his nervousness.

But Kusunoki was not comfortable with this suggestion. Yoshisada had already taken it upon himself to advance to Kamakura without the approval of Go-Daigo, so he was suspicious of his motives for doing so. If he went ahead he could make it there before him and in the process trigger Takauji into harming or even killing Go-Daigo. On the other hand, if Kusunoki went first and met opposition, Yoshisada could take another route while he was preoccupied.

"No, I think it would be best if we made the journey together," Kusunoki insisted.

Yoshisada was not about to question Kusunoki; he knew better. But deep down he was hurting, knowing that his family's lands were fast disappearing into the hands of his enemies. Little did he know, this was a lure Takauji knew he could not resist.

They slowly descended the pass and as a sign of respect, Yoshisada let Kusunoki lead the way. This was a steep part of the track, narrow enough for only single file. The forest was getting thick around them and closed in the route like a set of hands squeezing the options out of them. As *Samurai* they were uncomfortable with such environs, being more accustomed to wide open spaces where one could see their adversary and engage in more of a fair contest. But Kusunoki also knew that to some extent they were safe from attack from forces loyal to Takauji.

He knew this was the domain of mythical creatures such as *Tengu*-the half man, half crow creatures that inhabited the mountains and reportedly guarded such places; however, he was not about to succumb to such superstition or let it deter him from finding his master. He had been this route many times and knew that once they cleared the Hakone Mountains the land flattened out. This was the point to be weary of and was perfect for an attack; here he suspected Takauji would be waiting with his army. The force they had encountered earlier was nowhere near the size that Takauji was capable of assembling, but Kusunoki knew he had to push through if the challenge arose. At least he had his best men by his side, but he was also aware that they would need to operate separately from Yoshisada's to be totally effective. As he looked back he could see a mix of both factions, so he decided that as soon as they were clear of the pass he would regroup and discuss how best to move forward. However, the issue was still how the two parties were both aiming to arrive at Kamakura first.

Kusunoki veered off to the right of the large clearing they had just entered and his men followed. Taking his lead, Yoshisada moved off to the left; his men followed. Looking back, Kusunoki could see that hardly half of all their men had made it through the narrow opening of the pass.

Suddenly something whistled by his head and embedded itself in the man behind. As he suspected it was a well targeted arrow, and it was followed by a hail of them whistling though the air. This was exactly the scenario Kusunoki feared, being caught unprepared and therefore vulnerable. As suddenly as the arrows started, they stopped and there was silence, apart from the groans of his men who had been wounded.

Then from the path on the far side of the clearing Kusunoki saw the unmistakable figure of Ashikaga Takauji, dressed in full battle *Yoroi,* indicating that he was prepared for a fight.

"Halt your fire," Kusunoki ordered to his archers loosely assembled in front of them, as Takauji advanced flanked by several of his commanders.

In the middle of the clearing he stopped, and in response Kusunoki and Yoshisada rode out to meet him. Both sides were following the unwritten code of *Bushido* by meeting and allowing the dialogue for the reason of the confrontation to take place.

Once both parties were satisfied they were at the appropriate distance they stopped and scanned each other's armies.

Takauji bowed, signalling he was going to speak first.

"Go-Daigo sends both of his greatest warriors to retake Kamakura: I should feel honoured for that. Even more so that he believes I am too much for either of you," Takauji said, smiling arrogantly.

Kusunoki found this comment strange, as if Takauji didn't know that Go-Daigo had been captured. However, he knew this could be a ruse to see what response he would get.

"Honour is something far from you, Takauji. Go-Daigo sent you to Kamakura to represent him, not double cross him," Takauji responded angrily. "And so he is- represented that is, or should I say was, by his son."

Takauji turned back to one of his men behind him and in response he cantered up. In his free hand he was carrying a large box. He stopped beside Takauji and removed the lid, allowing his master to reach inside. He lifted out an unmistakable object. It was a head and as Kusunoki and Yoshisada stared, they identified it as that of Prince Morinaga. Casually Takauji brushed back the matted hair from its face, holding it in front of him as if to admire it like some sort of trophy.

Rage swept over the two men, just as Takauji had hoped. But of even more concern now was the fate of Go-Daigo, who Kusunoki believed was also held captive under Takauji at Kamakura.

"What have you done with the Emperor?" Kusunoki asked, unable to restrain himself.

Yoshisada looked across at Kusunoki, surprised by his fellow warrior's question.

"I do not know what you mean, Kusunoki," he responded as he returned the head to its box.

"Where is he?" Yoshisada interjected, aiming his question at both men.

"He is safe and under my protection for now," Takauji responded, tapping the lid of the box.

"However, if you cannot protect him, Kusunoki, then someone else has to," he added antagonistically.

This riled Kusunoki, his horse stirred as it felt the discomfort of its rider.

Turning back to his men, some still filing down through the pass, Kusunoki shouted the command "Prepare to attack!"

318

Takauji laughed out loud, intentionally insulting his rivals and their attempt to seize control. Then the smile on his face turned to an angry sneer and as he turned he drew his *Katana* and raised it high in the air. In response the trees and hills behind them came alive as men came forward from their hiding positions; rows upon rows assembled filling the empty space. But Kusunoki's and Yoshisada's men were far from organised for battle as they were still filing out of the narrow pass.

Takauji turned and cantered back to his front line, followed by his commanders, giving the customary courtesy to his adversaries to prepare for battle.

In response, Kusunoki and Yoshisada did the same. As they rode, Kusunoki shouted to him "You take your men and drive forward, try to push them to the left. I will assemble mine and try to flank him from the right behind you.

Although Yoshisada was not happy with this strategy, he had little time or choice, but to do what Kusunoki suggested.

"My men, wait here!" he shouted as he made his way back up the pass alongside the descending stream of men.

"Halt your advance and move right into the trees on my command!" he continued as he rode up the track.

The men near the back of the column were confused, unable to see what was before them or the fact that they were about to go into battle.

"What about us?" one of Yoshisada's men called out.

"Continue down the track, your commander will give you your orders."

Suddenly Kusunoki's horse slipped on the track and lost its footing, sending it sliding backwards and off into the trees. Kusunoki leapt off to avoid being crushed beneath it, but the momentum projected him sideways into a large tree. He struck it with his knee full force, dislocating it in the process.

Immediately he tried to get up, but his leg gave way, causing him to slump back down at the base of the tree. What was more, he had only made it half way up the pass and informed a little more than half of him men of the plan. Several of them jumped off to his aide, but it was obvious he wasn't going to move anywhere in a hurry, let alone lead his men into battle.

It wasn't long before Kusunoki heard the call to retreat from Yoshisada. He had only just managed to get back on his horse with his injury when one of Yoshisada's commanders found him up the track.

"Yoshisada has called for us to retreat, Kusunoki san," he said in urgency.

"We have been outnumbered 10 to 1 and Takauji has managed to outflank us," he continued.

Kusunoki tried to direct his horse down the track in the direction of Kamakura, but the flow of men, some wounded steered him in the opposite direction and back up the hill. He had little option but to join them. The best they could do would be to run and attempt to regroup.

"Tell Yoshisada that we will regroup at Suruga," Kusunoki yelled over the chaos.

"I will make sure he understands, Master," he said, and began shouting out the order to everyone that he saw. Kusunoki could hear it being passed up and down the line as he kicked his horse into a canter, trying to ignore the pain in his knee as he rode. He felt angry that he hadn't had the opportunity to meet Takauji's forces head on, but also knew that if the tables had been turned he would have done the same thing.

-* -

At Enryaku-Ji Yamakiri had assembled a group of the top *Sohei* and was sitting with them in a small circle eating dinner. He needed them to accept a new way of training that was more offensive than in the role of just defending the temple. This was something he hadn't wanted to do as he aspired to leave the aspects of physical combat behind, having seen the destruction and sorrow it caused. But he also knew that this was the quickest way to peace, even if it did mean fighting for it. However, his main focus at the moment was finding out where Go-Daigo was and rescuing him-if it was not too late, that was.

He noticed the absence of Kasagi and Dharma from the group and was about to send someone to look for them when they appeared from around one of the buildings. The circle spread out as the two men joined the group. Dharma had a big smile on his face, although he always seemed to look that way.

"I have some news, Yamakiri, which could change things," Kasagi said, looking back at Dharma.

"It seems that Ryushin has not taken the Emperor to Kamakura as we had been told," he said confidently.

Yamakiri purposely avoided looking directly at Seiko, who stirred, as if uncomfortable with what she had told them about the Emperor.

"Are you sure, Kasagi?" Yamakiri asked.

"Yes. My friend here tells me that he is actually in Kyoto," Kasagi answered, looking back at Dharma.

"Do we know exactly where in Kyoto?" Yamakiri asked, looking back at Kasagi.

Dharma whispered something to Kasagi.

"No," Dharma uttered, followed by several other things.

"He says he would need to go there to get a stronger sense of exactly where he is-it seems that Ryushin is using some form of magic to conceal his exact whereabouts."

By this stage dusk was overcoming the day. Yamakiri looked back towards the setting sun. Dharma turned to Kasagi again and said something. Kasagi translated this "He says best to go there at first light, when the energy is clearer."

"I will go," Watanabe said, volunteering first.

Dharma looked at him and shook his head. Then he pointed to Seiko, followed by Kito and Yamakiri, counting crudely as he progressed.

"He says he would like these people to accompany him," Kasagi responded as Watanabe sat back.

Chapter 44

Kusunoki and Yoshisada had hastily retreated back to Suruga, some 16 hours ride to the south. They hoped to hide and rest when they arrived to try to re-gather their forces and prepare a defensive strategy. But they were on the back foot and no sooner had they arrived than Takauji had caught up and had launched another attack. He had followed them like a wild animal stalking its prey.

The pain in Kusunoki's knee was a distraction he didn't need at this point and he found it hard to even ride normally, let alone engage in battle. What was more frustrating was that he was pushed further away from Kamakura and any attempt to rescue Go-Daigo; little did he know fate was actually pushing him the right direction.

Takauji's assault was relentless. What was more, unlike Kusunoki's men, his own men had prepared themselves not only to do battle, but to push forward and had the logistical support to back them up. Their goal was further afield and with both men and their armies out of the way, it was his next major conquest.

The situation became dire as both commanders watched their armies decimated under the attack. Finally Yoshisada could take no more and called for his men to retreat and disperse. Kusunoki looked on in shock as he watched Yoshisada flee into the hills with his men behind him, leaving Kusunoki totally exposed and vulnerable. With Yoshisada fleeing, he had little choice but to do the same. His heart sank as he admitted defeat and quietly he apologised to his master Go-Daigo. 'I am very sorry Master, I will do my best to rescue you as soon as I can.'

Signalling for his men to do the same, he turned and cantered his horse down the road towards Kyoto, battling exhaustion. As he departed he heard the faint sound of Takauji's horns calling his men back to regroup. Takauji was in control and knew that as he had decimated most of the available forces from the south, his chances of over-running the capitol were greatly increased. He smiled to himself as he watched Kusunoki and his battle scarred men fleeing off down the dusty road. Time and the gods had been on his side. As far as he was concerned it was a foregone conclusion that not only would he take control of Kyoto, but with Go-Daigo in custody, the *Shogunate* would also be his.

-* -

Yamakiri had drifted off to sleep and as his body sank into complete rest his spirit became more active. He found himself standing in the courtyard of the temple, when before him the figure of a man appeared. He was darkly clothed with a cloth wrapped around his head to conceal his face. Yamakiri could see the handle of his sword strapped across his back

Yamakiri was unsure who it was or why he needed to confront this person, so was also unsure how to prepare. But the man's advance was direct and with purpose. Suddenly he flicked his wrist, sending a *Shuriken* whistling through the air towards Yamakiri's face. He twisted his body as it sped past and tumbled to the ground far behind him, sending up a cloud of dust. The intent was obvious.

Yamakiri checked himself for weapons and followed a cord over his shoulder, feeling the *Tsuka* of his own sword on his back. Again the masked man dispatched another s*huriken*-this time Yamakiri responded by ducking down and drawing his weapon over his head, a sharp twang rang out as it made contact with the metal of the throwing star, stopping its motion and dropping it to the ground. Yamakiri scooped it up as he cart wheeled to the side to give him distance from his attacker. Coming up, he turned and using the momentum threw the *Shuriken* back at his attacker. In response, he raised his arm and blocked it, the sound of it hitting his chain-mail under suit was unmistakable.

Yamakiri knew better than to attack, he needed to ascertain what he was up against and more importantly, recognise who his opponent was and why was he being attacked.

As he approached he drew his sword and placed it by his side.

Yamakiri was conscious of when he would enter striking distance, at least three feet away. Suddenly there was a brilliant flash of light as sunlight was reflected into his eyes. Momentarily blinded, he failed to see him pull an egg out of his jacket, crush it and disperse its powdery contents into his face. Yamakiri just had time to close his eyes as the rank smell of the concoction filled his nostrils and enveloped him. However, rather than being consumed by the tactic of trying to take his sight, he knew that this was also an opportunity to disappear behind its veil. He heard the sound of a blade slicing through the air from above his head and to the right. Instinctively he ducked down and to the right also, hoping his assessment was correct to avoid the diagonal cut. It wisped past, missing its target. Evading the cut gave him time to move, placing him on the outside flank of his attacker. He rolled forward through the setting powder and came to his feet behind him. At this point he had two options; he could escape and run, or he could counter-attack. If he engaged he ran the risk of losing. If he ran, he escaped with his life. He decided the latter and was about to run, but found he couldn't, as if something had frozen him in space.

Helpless and vulnerable, his attacker turned and faced him, then walked around him like an artist admiring his work.

"You are all out of physical techniques, Yamakiri," the man behind the mask said as he continued walking.

"These will only get you so far against others of the like. Now you must move to the next level, into the realms of the gods and exercise more control over those who seek to destroy you," the man continued.

Yamakiri thought he recognised the voice as someone familiar, even through the thick face mask. Suddenly the mask vanished and as he suspected he saw the face of his uncle and teacher, Saito Yamada.

With that he was free to move and in response stepped back, not knowing what to expect next.

"I am not going to hurt you, Yamakiri, but now it is time to continue your training into the higher *Ninja* art of *Ninpo*," he said, stepping back also.

"Why me?" Yamakiri asked.

"Because you were chosen a long time ago to carry on the lineage handed down to you. It is your destiny."

With that he waved his hand and suddenly people began appearing behind him. Some were carrying weapons, others unarmed, some old and others not so old.

"These are our predecessors, yours and mine. They have sacrificed much to bring these arts to you and to keep the traditions alive. You, we, must honour them," he said looking back at the large assembly of souls. Then the crowd parted and from the back walked someone Yamakiri had not seen since the night before he went missing. It was his father, Yoshiakai.

Saito stepped aside, allowing Yamakiri to advance in response to his father's open arms. Yamakiri ran to him and threw his arms around him.

"Father, I have missed you so much," he said as tears streamed down his face. He tightened his embrace.

"I know son, and I have too," he responded.

"I am sorry I had to leave you and your mother, but it was meant to be," he continued.

"You-you sent him to his death," Yamakiri said, looking across at his uncle and stepping back from his father.

"No, no, son, that is not true. Your uncle was just following orders, none of that was his fault," he interjected.

"I tried to tell you, I knew nothing of the bigger plan, Yamakiri," Saito responded.

"Yes, that is right, son, and what happened was beyond any of our control. That is the way," Yoshiakai said, staring back at him.

"Please do not be bitter or seek revenge. What happened did so for reasons we as mere men will never understand. It was the divine plan of the gods."

Yamakiri felt a hand on his shoulder and turned around to see his mother standing behind him. She had a big smile on her face.

"Mother!" he called out in surprise.

"Kansai, my beautiful son," she responded, reaching out and pulling him into her arms.

Yamakiri had only been called by his given name a few times since leaving his village, but this was different. The love that he felt and the warmth only a mother could give was unique and unlike anything else. Yamakiri felt relieved, as if a heavy weight had been lifted off his shoulders. He had been searching for so many answers to questions that had haunted and consumed him for the past few years and had suddenly realised these had trapped him from truly moving on.

As he felt his mother's embrace tighten around him, he looked over her shoulder and saw another familiar face. Standing by herself, was a young girl dressed in a beautiful *Kimono*-it was Saigo, Sakamura's five year old daughter. Since that fateful day, he had experienced the same painful nightmare nearly every night where he would find himself dancing with her and suddenly it would turn into a nightmare, ending with her being killed by a stray arrow as she had that day.

His mother pushed him back and held his hand.

"Go Kansai, please," she said, urging him forward.

Yamakiri was reluctant to move forward. He had experienced so many nightmares in a similar scenario and it always ended the same, with him enveloped in a swathe of emotion and grief.

But this time something was different. Unlike the past, he seemed to have a choice of whether to go forward or not. He had come this far and with the support of his family, he knew there was only one way forward. He walked towards her and stopped, dropping to his knees and bowing his head.

"I am very sorry," he said quietly.

He felt a tiny hand touch him on the head.

"There is nothing to be sorry for. It was not your fault," she said in an innocent voice, lifting his head up to look at her.

Yamakiri stared into her eyes; they sparkled like the brightest stars in the night's sky.

"Please," she continued, taking hold of his hands and urging him to his feet.

Music filled the air and she began to pull him around in a circle, just like in the nightmares. As he looked into her eyes he felt a strong connection, as if with her very soul. As they danced he felt something strange; it was usually at this point that everything turned dark and she would collapse, impaled by an arrow, but not this time. Spinning around he felt something fill his body, a feeling of something he had lost, seemingly a lifetime ago. Turning faster and faster, he felt his anticipation of the usual terrible outcome disappear and was completely overwhelmed with not only joy, but something far more precious: the innocence he had lost that day.

He woke from his dream, his body flooded with a new found energy. It was still dark outside and as he closed his eyes to go back to sleep, a big smile lit up his face as he bathed in the feeling of absolute liberation-he was finally free.

Chapter 45

Yamakiri's peaceful sleep was interrupted by Kito shaking him on the shoulder. Looking up through his sleepy eyes, he could see through the open doorway, the rest of the group standing behind him.

"Come on Yamakiri, time to go," Kito said quietly.

Walking outside everything looked very different; even though it was still dark, objects seemed to have a luminous glow to them. Looking at the small group, the glow was quite prominent and as he looked to Dharma he responded by shaking his head, as if Dharma could see what he now could see. Without a word they mounted their horses and set off through the gates and down the narrow track towards Kyoto to the morning song of the waking birds.

For some time no-one said a word and although they were on horseback, it was as if they needed to navigate the sometimes steep track themselves. Only when they reached the base of the mountain and daylight had overcome the night did someone dare to speak.

"Where to from here?" Yamakiri asked Kasagi as they paused at the crossroads.

"One moment please," Kasagi responded, turning back to the Tibetan.

With that Dharma dismounted and walked into the centre of the roadway. Then closing his eyes and extending his arms, he rocked backwards and forwards and then to the sides, as if completely letting go of himself and surrendering to some higher force.

Suddenly he opened his eyes and pointed to the road to their right. "This way, this way," he said to Kasagi nodding as he remounted his horse.

With that he trotted off in the direction of the road, this Yamakiri knew skirted around the large town, the rest of the group following close behind. As he rode along, Dharma seemed to be talking to someone as if in conversation, often nodding as if in agreement. Suddenly he stopped, turned, and said something to Kasagi.

"He knows we are coming," Kasagi said, relaying Dharma's words.

"Alright, so we progress with caution, especially as we get closer?" Yamakiri asked.

Dharma looked back at Yamakiri and shook his head. Then he said something else to Kasagi.

"Ah, there is a problem with that, Yamakiri. Dharma says that it is too dangerous to progress. It seems that Yakushimaru has disappeared," Kasagi responded cautiously.

"Yes, well, we know that," Kito said from the back of the group.

"No, I do not think you understand, Kito san-he is highly skilled in *Ninpo* and has used this to conceal himself and everyone around him, including the Emperor," Kasagi responded.

"I understand what he is saying," Seiko said, having kept silent until now.

"Best we follow what Dharma tells us. You saw how easily he defeated the *Sohei* and took control of Kito. He is someone who needs to be carefully approached, with a high degree of caution," Seiko said nervously.

Yamakiri had been thinking about finding Ryushin and Go-Daigo and had felt that they were getting closer to him. Something inside him was indicating his direction; then just before Dharma had called off the search, he had felt a distinct change as well, like a cold feeling, a subtle breeze. Then it was gone.

Kasagi turned his horse around and led the group back towards the track that had taken them there. Everyone was silent as they made their way back up the mountain.

-* -

On the outskirts of Kyoto at Kazanin palace, Ryushin had been woken earlier by a sense of someone projecting their intention to find him. He had been trained to a high level in the skill of *Haragei*-being able to sense danger. For most practitioners, they had only what he had come to understand as a short-distance sense of danger, but for Ryushin, there was no distinction in range and he was well-attuned to these subtle energies.

On the other side of this was a person's own projection or as it were, inability to conceal their intent. He was aware that Go-Daigo's concern for his life had created such a projection and that if it persisted someone with similar skills would be able to hone in on this. To that extent, he had set about shielding this projection from the outside world, but was not surprised that the monk he had encountered in the higher realms the night before was leading the search. He had had the luxury of operating virtually alone at this level, but not anymore, and now had to be extra vigilant. He reminded himself that there was no more room for complacency.

-* -

The group arrived back at Enryaku-Ji. Nothing had been said along the way and in some ways, nothing needed to be. As they rode through the gates the group separated. Yamakiri and Kito were greeted by Kazuki who was having breakfast with several of the *Sohei*.

As they saw the arrival of the group, they hurriedly finished their meal in anticipation of more training. Yamakiri rode over to Kazuki.

"We need to assemble the *Sohei* for training," Yamakiri said. Kazuki nodded.

Immediately he stood up and announced to the monks that training would commence right away, then trotted briskly around the temple announcing the same thing to everyone else.

Within a few minutes, a large group of *Sohei* had loosely assembled in the middle of the courtyard.

"Please, everyone stand still!" Yamakiri shouted.

For a moment he stood there as he cast his eye over the crowd and then began walking towards them, separating them into groups as he went. The ones directly in front he moved to one side, followed by those in the middle and then the remainder, until he had four separate groups. Taking a few steps back he admired his work, then he stepped in, made some adjustments and again moved back. Kito and Kazuki looked on, intrigued.

"Ah," Kito said, raising his finger as if something clicked.

"I don't understand," Kazuki said to Kito quietly.

Yamakiri turned back and said to Kazuki "*Chi, sui, ka, fu.*" Kazuki knew these to mean Earth, water, wind and fire.

"Look at their feet," he said to Kazuki.

Kazuki cast his eyes over the group, focussing on their feet; he stared but couldn't see anything significant.

"Ok, look at the direction their toes are pointing," Yamakiri said, helping him along.

Kazuki thought he saw what Yamakiri was alluding to now. Some of them were facing them directly to the front, others were off to the side and others different again, but the significant thing was that everyone in each group was pretty much standing the same way as the others.

"This is how we must train, if we are to take on Yakushimaru at his own strategy," Yamakiri said to Kito and Kazuki.

He turned to the groups of separated monks and addressed them.

"This is where we are strongest as individuals-*chi, sui, ka, fu*!" he called out, pointing at the different groups.

For some, it was a revelation and for others, there was a look of confusion. They had spent the last few years coming together to operate as a defensive unit for the temple, but now they were being split apart. However, the reality was that their fellow monks had been defeated by someone who obviously knew more about strategy that they did, so a change of approach was required.

"Yes, I agree. I will take this group," Kito responded, pointing at the small group in front of him.

"Of course," Yamakiri said, nodding in agreement.

"What about me?" Kazuki said, looking down at his feet.

Watanabe looked him up and down, then said, "You need to go with them," pointing to the larger group to his left.

Until now, Kito had always believed that it was better to operate as a group, but he could see the logic in what Yamakiri had done. He had assessed each person's strongest potential based on their elemental makeup and divided them accordingly. Now it was time to put this into practice.

Although separate, each group trained for most of the day under the guidance of Dharma and Yamakiri, having few breaks in between. As they practiced various skills and techniques Dharma would stop and adjust them, like a seamstress adjusting a newly made outfit on its model.

At mid-afternoon and during one of the breaks, Dharma walked with Kasagi over to where Kito and Yamakiri were sitting in the shade of the high compound wall.

Dharma smiled as he said something to Kasagi.

"He says he is very happy with the progress today and believes that is enough."

Looking across at the monks, Yamakiri noticed that as the day went on, the groups became more distinct and separate.

"For the training, it is important that these groups stay together, so we will need to rearrange the sleeping quarters accordingly," Kasagi added.

"Ok, Kazuki, did you want to help with that?" Kasagi asked.

"Oh yes, no problem," he answered, standing and walking off in the direction of the groups.

"There is a lot of work to do, but we need to develop this carefully and slowly. If we are to rescue Go-Daigo, it is not just a matter defeating Yakushimaru, but to ensure we work in harmony with the gods. If not, we risk being punished," Kasagi warned, looking back at Dharma. Dharma nodded, "Yes, yes," he said in his Tibetan accent.

Chapter 46

Kusunoki and the remnants of his defeated army had been riding all night and for the most part were exhausted. He had considered that Takauji, being the strategist he was, would not just be satisfied with defeating Yoshisada and himself, but that he would use the momentum of their retreat to take Kyoto, appreciating that Kusunoki would have little or no time to regroup. In fact he was correct; Takauji used the strategy of moving his forces up in a leap frog fashion, resting one while the other advanced. This also had the advantage of assuring re-enforcements were not far away if needed. This was a mistake that Kusunoki and Yoshisada had made, with each wanting to reach Kamakura first to satisfy their own agendas.

As Kusunoki reached the crossroads near Otsu on the northern side of Mt Hiei, he stopped and considered his options. If Kyoto was Takauji's goal, then he was best to digress from his path and provide some respite for his men in Otsu. He was determined not to play into Takauji's hands this time by doing what he anticipated. He advised his commander to take the men and set up camp on the shores of Lake Biwa. He would take a small contingent and continue on the road. He paused as he watched his exhausted men file past him; if Takauji was expecting some resistance at Kyoto, then he would be in for a surprise. If Takauji launched a full scale attack on Kyoto he could potentially exhaust his forces, which would provide an opportune time to attack.

He pulled hard on the reigns of his horse and headed down the road; his next stop, Enryaku-Ji.

The sun was just rising over the hills as Kusunoki approached the fortress gates. He saw a small head bob over the top of the rampart, followed by the gates swinging open. As he looked inside he could see the courtyard full of several groups of *Sohei*, engaged in various exercises and combat drills. What was strange was that they were not dressed in their usual white clothes, but seemed to be grouped by the colours they were wearing.

Seeing Kusunoki arrive, Yamakiri made his way to greet him with the news.

"Master, it is good to see you. It looks as if you encountered some heavy resistance?" Yamakiri said, referring to the blood on him and his men.

Kusunoki dismounted his horse without saying anything, carefully supporting himself on one leg and trying to endure the pain of his dislocation in his knee; this had been exacerbated by the long ride from Ashigara Pass.

"You are injured, Master," Yamakiri said, turning and waving for help to assist him.

Kazuki and Kito came running to assist. As soon as Kusunoki recognised Kito he drew his *Katana*.

"Why is he here? If he comes near me I will kill him," Kusunoki said, pointing his sword in Kito's direction.

Yamakiri looked back at Kito, who, having no recollection of what had transpired, looked confused.

Yamakiri didn't know what to say or how to explain what had happened. It was obvious that Kusunoki was in no mood to listen to any explanation at this point in time.

"Please Kito, we can sort this. Continue with the training," he said, ushering him back. At first Kito stood there and didn't move, but as Yamakiri asked him again, he bowed his head. "As you wish," he said, turning around and walking back to the group he had come from.

"Master, Yakushimaru is a very cunning adversary with knowledge and skills far above any of us, but now is not the time to explain. He is holding Go-Daigo somewhere in Kyoto and we need to find him," Yamakiri said.

"Kyoto? This cannot be right," Kusunoki responded angrily.

"We have reliable information," he responded and as if on cue, Dharma Rinpoche arrived.

Ignoring the formalities, he bowed and crouched down, placing his hands over Kusunoki's knee joint, at the same time, letting out a hissing sound.

Kusunoki looked down.

"Who is this?" he demanded.

But before anyone could answer, Dharma stood up and took Kusunoki under his armpit. "Please, please," he said.

Yamakiri cringed as Dharma ignored all of the protocols and began man-handling the *Samurai* leader.

He pulled Kusunoki's supporting hand from his horse and laid him down on the ground. Kusunoki looked bewildered as this stranger took control of him.

Immediately Dharma went to work. He placed his hand on Kusunoki's forehead and the other on his solar plexus, mumbling something to himself, seemingly oblivious to any respect Kusunoki expected of him. Each time he tried to lift his head, Dharma would push it back down.

Then he prompted Yamakiri to take up position at the top of Kusunoki, placing his hands on his shoulders and Kazuki to hold his leg.

Once the two men were in position, he moved to the injured knee and placing his hands over the area, uttered something and traced a series of figures in the air with his two fingers. Then he turned to Kazuki and waving his hand said "Ok, ok," ushering him to pull his leg. Yamakiri expected Kusunoki to yell out in pain as his leg was lifted off the ground, but he said nothing.

Dharma manipulated his knee as Kazuki pulled, suddenly there was a loud pop, as it returned to its place. Dharma ushered everyone to stand back and lifted Kusunoki to his feet. To everyone's surprise he stood up and steadied himself before walking around in a circle; he was obviously happy to be mobile again, but even happier not to be in any pain.

He turned to Dharma and bowing several times, thanked him. Dharma acknowledged his gratitude and bowed in return.

"You said you believe Go-Daigo is in Kyoto?" Kusunoki asked Yamakiri again.

"We are very sure, but we have yet to find where, Master," Yamakiri responded.

"Yes, Kyoto," Dharma added, pointing in the direction of the city.

"Dharma insists he is there, but because of Yakushimaru's cunning we are unsure exactly where – he is concealing his exact location."

Kusunoki thought for a moment. This confirmed his suspicions about the reason for Takauji's advance.

"Alright, then we have a problem," Kusunoki said, the concern obvious on his face.

"We need to find him and buy some time. Takauji and a large force are heading towards Kyoto and we must try to halt his advance," Kusunoki said in urgency. "I may have a plan. Come, we have no time to waste."

As he was mounting his horse Kito walked over again, still oblivious to what he had done to Kusunoki days before. Kusunoki stared back at him as he approached.

"What is he doing here?" he asked Yamakiri angrily.

Kito halted his advance, as if Kusunoki's words had struck him.

"Master, he has no memory of what happened or what he did," Yamakiri responded, defending his friend.

"Well, keep him away from me," Kusunoki said.

Kito looked back at Yamakiri.

"You stay here, Kito. I will explain to him what happened. We need to continue training the *Sohei*," Yamakiri said, whispering back to him.

"Very well," Kito responded, turning and walking back to the monks.

"Yamakiri, find a horse and come with me," he ordered.

As they made their way back down the narrow track, Kusunoki turned to Yamakiri.

"Harada san actually has no recollection of what he did to me?" Kusunoki asked Yamakiri.

"I am afraid not, Master," Yamakiri responded. "Yakushimaru is very skilled in *Ninpo*."

"*Ninpo*? What is that?" Kusunoki asked, intrigued.

"This is the higher order of *Ninjutsu*, this is how he can control people and take over their minds," Yamakiri said.

Kusunoki shrugged his shoulders, as if to discount what Yamakiri had just said. He didn't believe in any other form of fighting than that of one to one. Such use of spiritual advantage went against the ethos of his training, even though the plan he was about to employ involved disrupting the spirit of his opponent.

They reached the crossroads at the bottom of the mountain and turned right towards Kyoto. At one point the road narrowed onto a bridge across the Katsura River. On the other side was a big meadow overlooking the river and the road.

"There," he said pointing to the meadow as they crossed the river.

He turned off the road and rode up onto the hill overlooking the bridge and the road in the distance. Then he turned to his men and gave them instructions on what he wanted them to do. Happy they understood his plan, he turned to Yamakiri.

"Come, we need to get to Kyoto. We don't have much time, but hopefully this will get us more."

Yamakiri nodded as he was led in the direction of Kyoto, unsure of what Kusunoki had in mind.

Yamakiri wasn't sure how he could warn Kusunoki of the extent of Yakushimaru's skill, but knew that he would sense their presence in Kyoto and would be on guard. What he didn't know, was that the wheels were already in motion and Yakushimaru was already making his way out of his hiding place and in the direction of their approach.

-* -

Meanwhile, the first contingent of Takauji's army had just passed the crossroads to Otsu. One of his commanders suggested he send a contingent in that direction to search for Kusunoki and his men, but Takauji was more insistent on reaching Kyoto; his intention was to capture the town and setup his base there. However he did leave a small contingent of 50 men at the crossroads with the orders to ensure they were not to let anyone past, especially Kusunoki or his men.

Moving forward, they had passed the crossroads to the track to Enryaku-Ji when they saw a contingent of *Samurai* on the hill overlooking the narrow bridge crossing the river. Although it was misty he could easily define at least 100 or more men poised and waiting to attack. Takauji halted his men just before the bridge. Although he knew he had far more men than anyone from Go-Daigo's military could muster he was nevertheless weary, especially as this was the only crossing for many miles. Takauji felt uncomfortable at his predicament, however, he was not prepared to retreat. He decided to engage Kusunoki's men and push through regardless. He proceeded forward, leading the charge across the bridge. However, just as a he rode onto the bridge, there was a loud rumble from the cliffs above. As he looked up, he saw numerous large boulders careening at speed towards them.

"Quick, move!" he commanded, kicking his horse violently to escape the onslaught.

As he and only a few of his men crossed the bridge safely, he looked back to see several more succumb to the bombardment. The initial landslide had triggered a larger rock fall, leaving a large pile of debris and dead *Samurai* blocking the road. Around 50 men had made it, but the rest were left stranded on the other side of the rock fall. No sooner had he taken stock than a rain of arrows descended on them, striking several of his men and knocking some of them from their horses. Looking up on the hill, he noticed that none of the *Samurai* had moved: they were in fact dummies. They had worked well, achieving their strategic purpose to distract Takauji enough to break his rhythm and fragment his advance. Now with far fewer numbers, he would be more of a manageable threat. As the road was also blocked and the only other route would take days to reach Kyoto, Kusunoki had brought the valuable time he needed to find his master. But with Yakushimaru to contend with, this would still be an uneasy task.

Chapter 47

Kusunoki rode through the narrow streets of Kyoto, followed by a small contingent of men. They made their way to Arashiyama palace in the town centre. As soon as he rounded the corner and he was recognised by the guard on the gate, who ordered them to be opened. As quickly as they were swung open, they were instantly shut again behind them. As one of the commanders approached Kusunoki, he was halted by one of his men.

"Please, Kusunoki needs some time alone," he ordered, as Kusunoki dismounted and made his way quickly inside.

"Stay vigilant, we could be attacked at any moment," he added, smiling before turning and following Go-Daigo inside.

It was only a few minutes later that one of the guards called out again-"Someone is approaching from the south."

"Who is it?" the commander shouted back.

There was a short silence as the guard stared back down the road.

He looked back in disbelief "It is Kusunoki, Master," he said, seemingly repeating the observation he had made not that long ago.

"That's impossible!" he said looking back at the doorway he had seen Kusunoki pass through just before.

He quickly scaled the ladder to the parapet to see for himself.

Turning onto the short lane approaching the castle gate, he could easily make out the two men; one Kusunoki and the other he recognised as Yamakiri.

"Commander Hyashi, please let us in," Kusunoki said looking up.

No sooner had he heard the command than the unmistakable whistling sound of an arrow pierced the air. It embedded itself in his sternum, sending him toppling uncontrollably over the wall and into the deep moat below.

Instinctively Kusunoki drew his sword, his horse stirred as if his change in attitude had also triggered a battle readiness in the creature. Then from the rooftops adjacent to the gates, several men stood up, bows at the ready and aimed at the two men. The spot where Hyashi had just stood was suddenly filled by another figure, dressed in nearly identical clothing as Kusunoki. Yamakiri was the first to see beyond the disguise and recognise him as Ryushin Yakushimaru.

"Best you stay where you are Kusunoki, my men have you surrounded," he shouted down from the wall.

Kusunoki's horse stirred, as it sensed the anger in its rider.

"What do you want?" he shouted back, knowing that if Ryushin had wanted him dead, he would have killed him by now.

Ryushin leapt from the wall onto the bridge below just in front of Kusunoki's horse, startling it.

"Put your sword away, Kusunoki. I only want to talk, not fight and judging by your company you are in no way prepared to either," he said, referring to the lack of support.

"Where is the Emperor?" Kusunoki asked, looking down at Ryushin.

"He is safe. For now," Ryushin responded.

"What do you mean 'For now'?" Kusunoki asked.

"I am sure you are aware that Takauji is approaching Kyoto with the intention to take over the city. When he arrives I have been asked to hand over Go-Daigo to him," he replied.

"Why are you telling me this?" Kusunoki questioned him.

"I am well aware of your loyalty towards him. I find this quality admirable, and in some ways, oddly intriguing," Ryushin said, smiling.

"I imagine you would, considering your loyalty is bought Yakushimaru," Kusunoki replied angrily, referring to his mercenary status.

"You still have not explained your reasons for telling me such things," Kusunoki said.

"Let me just say that every man has his price and once Go-Daigo is handed over to Takauji, I cannot guarantee his safety or the stability of this country," Ryushin said in a concerned manner.

Kusunoki was a man of principle and from what Ryushin was saying, he believed he was suggesting that if Kusunoki paid him he would hand the Emperor over to him.

Suddenly one of his archers moaned and fell from the rooftop onto the street below, followed by a second, then a third.

Ryushin looked over in confusion as the last man fell to the ground. Yamakiri looked up to see Kito leap from one of the rooftops and realising what was going on, kicked Kusunoki's horse, sending it into a canter away from the castle. Then he leapt off his horse and confronted Ryushin, who appeared to be unarmed.

Ryushin sneered as Yamakiri confronted him.

"You think you are better than the great *Samurai* Kusunoki?" Ryushin said, goading him.

Yamakiri said nothing in response; he wasn't going to be lured into a fight. His intention was to give Kusunoki enough time to escape. Above him he heard the tell-tale sound of another arrow and looked up to see another of Ryushin's men fall forward. Looking back, he saw Kito and several *Sohei* armed with bows engaged in combat with his men.

Seizing the opportunity of the distraction, Ryushin kicked out, striking Yamakiri in the stomach and causing him to reel forward. Ryushin took hold of his shoulders and head butted him in the face; Yamakiri staggered backwards and fell to see Kito launch himself over his body. He launched in with a flying kick, hitting him in the chest and throwing him back against the large castle doors, hitting them with such a force that they shook violently.

Yamakiri rolled onto his stomach and pushed himself onto his knees. Seizing the opportunity, Ryushin counter attacked, shoulder charging Kito and causing him to fall backwards over Yamakiri. Following through, he drove Kito into the ground with a thumb to the throat, at the same time executing a forward roll and coming back onto his feet. Kito lay there with the wind knocked out of him as Yamakiri struggled to stand up.

"This is not your fight, so why make it so?" Ryushin asked Yamakiri, looking around at him.

"Because I believe in justice," Yamakiri responded.

"Justice, for who? Who determines what is right? Only the gods can determine such things," Ryushin responded, walking towards Kito.

"My men have you surrounded, I wouldn't try anything," Yamakiri said confidently.

"And so have mine. The only difference is you cannot see them. I will let you go this time, but next time I may not be so lenient," Ryushin said, walking around the injured men to the castle doors. These swung open before he reached them and he casually walked inside.

Yamakiri staggered over to Kito and lifted him to his feet.

"Come, we need to get back to Hieizan. Kyoto is no longer safe," he said, helping Kito onto his horse.

Ryushin watched as they left, satisfied that he had control of the situation. He had never planned to capture Kusunoki, at least not in a physical sense. His training had taught him that to capture the mind was a far more effective strategy.

-* -

Meanwhile, Takauji and his men had made their way into Kyoto. As they passed through the streets people shut their doors and windows and hid. His reputation was well known around Kyoto and rightly so; his appearance struck fear in those not loyal to him. They arrived at Arashiyama palace not expecting too warm of a welcome, especially seeing someone floating in the moat face down. However, as Ryushin had received word of his arrival, he was standing at the open gate to greet them as they rode onto the bridge.

"Greetings, Master," Ryushin said, bowing as they drew near.

Takauji looked surprised at the welcome.

"You have just missed your rival Kusunoki and his men. They left in a hurry," he said, smiling.

"Left? Why didn't you detain him, Yakushimaru? Or even better, kill him?" Takauji said angrily.

"He poses no real threat to you, does he?" Ryushin asked sarcastically.

Takauji paused before answering. He knew where Ryushin would go with this, in effect asking for more payment for capturing someone of such notoriety and value. However, he wasn't going to fall into that trap.

"Where is the Emperor?" Takauji asked nervously.

"He is safe and comfortable," Ryushin responded.

'Is he inside? I would like to see him."

"No, he is not here."

Takauji was becoming annoyed at the amount of control Ryushin had over the situation. He didn't like bowing down to anyone and knew that to completely secure Kyoto, he would need to have Go-Daigo in custody.

"The arrangement was that once you deliver him to me, then you will be paid," Takauji said.

"Alright, I will take you to him," Ryushin responded.

"Very well, let us talk inside."

With that he kicked his horse and waved his men inside.

From a hidden vantage point across the way, Yamakiri and Kito watched on.

"We must catch up to Kusunoki and inform him of Takauji's arrival," Yamakiri said, preparing to leave.

-* -

At the Katsura River, Takauji's men had already over-powered what was left of Kusunoki's resistance force and had regrouped on the Kyoto side of the bridge. Having been totally outnumbered, Kusunoki's men had no option but to flee into the mountains. This retreat had opened the doors to enable Takauji's troops to flood through, bolstered by the second wave of reinforcements. More than 10,000 men headed for the town, a much greater force than Kusunoki's men could defend it against. Not only did Kyoto look like it was about to fall, but it was possibly also a metaphor for Go-Daigo's short reign of power.

Chapter 48

Later that morning Kusunoki arrived back at Enryaku-Ji, followed not long after by Yamakiri and Kito.

"Master, we have some disturbing news. Takauji is at Arashiyama palace and it looks like that is where Go-Daigo is also being held," Yamakiri said to Kusunoki as they sat down to eat.

"Hmmm, this is not good. As long as they have Go-Daigo, there is little chance of any order in this country, especially with Takauji in power. This could potentially cause a power vacuum that could draw in even more ruthless contenders. We have to rescue Go-Daigo-and quickly." he concluded.

"Master, Yakushimaru has proved to be a formidable opponent and as long as he is serving Takauji, we have very little chance of an effective rescue," Yamakiri said.

"Well, a little chance is better than none at all. How is the training of the *Sohei* progressing?"

He looked over at the groups of warriors busy training. What he saw did not resemble any form of Martial Arts he was familiar with. Some were standing in a circle leaping higher and higher and shouting something. On another side of the compound there was a totally different scene; they were standing in pairs, one side trying to push the others as Dharma supervised.

"Dharma Rinpoche is assisting with some special training."

"So I see, Yamakiri," Kusunoki responded sceptically.

"This is the best chance we have to rescue Go-Daigo. Dharma has trained many this way and is confident it will work."

"We have very little time to prepare. With Takauji now in Kyoto and seeing what he did to Prince Morinaga, I have grave concerns for the fate of the Emperor."

Yamakiri was unaware of what Kusunoki was referring to in regards to Morinaga. The last he had heard was that the Prince had betrayed his father and had sided with Takauji.

"He has been put to death," Kusunoki said, seeing Yamakiri's look of confusion.

Yamakiri felt his heart sink. If only he could have been there to protect the Prince as he had been asked.

"Please excuse me," Yamakiri said standing up and walking across to where Dharma was training a group of monks.

Dharma stopped what he was doing. Sensing Yamakiri behind him, he turned and smiled.

"Kasagi san, we need to move quickly. How is Dharma going with the training?"

Kasagi turned and asked him in Tibetan.

"Yes, yes," he said, smiling back and nodding continually.

Yamakiri was unsure he had asked the appropriate question, but Dharma, taking his cue, took a hold of the nearest monk and placed him in front of Yamakiri.

"Please?" he asked Yamakiri, handing him a wooden *Bokken*.

Yamakiri looked back at Kasagi.

"Try to attack him," he said.

Yamakiri looked at the frail monk before him. He was well aware that strength was not everything in defending yourself, but as these monks had only a few days training with Dharma he was not sure what to expect.

He stepped back and raised his weapon high above his head. The monk stood still, as if the threat was insignificant to him, and closed his eyes.

Yamakiri looked back at Kasagi and Dharma.

"Yes-go, any time, please," Kasagi urged him.

As he looked at the monk he thought he saw a yellow hue around his head, accentuated by the deep green of the mountain trees behind him.

He moved forward and struck at the top of his head. A wave of shock rushed through him, seeing the monk still stationary as he struck down. He feared the worst; that his blow would make contact and do serious damage to the man.

However, he felt no contact; his *Bokken* glanced off something and struck the ground, sending him off balance.

At first Yamakiri thought the monk had somehow blocked the strike, but as he stood up again he saw that he had not moved and was still standing there with his eyes shut. He looked across at the two men, the confusion obvious on his face.

"Again," Kasagi urged.

Obliging, Yamakiri stepped back, this time into *RyuSui* – a low sword posture with the sword facing backwards.

Again he lunged forward and attempted to strike the monk on the side of his body. Once again, his cut was deflected, this time upwards. Again the monk appeared unaffected.

"How did he do that?" he asked, turning back to Kasagi.

"This is *Fu-no Kata*," he responded.

Yamakiri recognised this as the wind form, he had been taught the same series of *Kata* by his uncle during the years that they trained together. One thing he always reminded him was that there were many levels to this, and not all of them physical.

He looked across at another group, where they were in pairs with one trying unsuccessfully to push the other over.

"*Chi*-Earth?" he asked.

"Yes," Dharma responded.

Pointing to the other groups he said, "*Sui*-water and *Ka*-fire."

"You see, Dharma has identified the strengths in each person and trained them accordingly. In a strategic sense, we can use each for different purposes based on their inherent skills-this is how Yakushimaru has been so successful," he said, smiling.

"That is all very well, but what will give us an advantage if we are both using the same tactics?" Yamakiri asked.

Kasagi paused for a moment before answering.

"The gods-the gods are on our side," he responded.

These words reverberated within Yamakiri's psyche. He was unsure how to respond or even if there was a response to this. Sensing his confusion, Dharma took him by the arm and urged him to crouch down. He brushed a small patch of dirt smooth as if to create a blank canvas and then drew a character in the soft dirt with his finger.

"*Kokoro*," he said, after drawing it in the dirt.

Then he patted his own heart several times.

Yamakiri knew this as the symbol for 'Heart'.

"Good, good," he said, nodding.

Then he drew another character above it.

"*Yaiba*, - blade," he said affirmatively.

Yamakiri knew this as the *Kanji* for *Shinobi*. His uncle had explained once that a good heart wields a good blade and as the blade is a symbol of truth, the truer the heart, the more truth it could cut through.

However, he was making the sign of a cut across the heart and said "Bad!"

Yamakiri looked at Kasagi for a translation of what he was implying. Dharma tapped him on the arm and said "Yakushimaru," then drew several cuts in the air.

"He is saying that this is the difference between us and Yakushimaru-both are *Ninja* with similar backgrounds, but with two opposite intentions," Kasagi said.

"I see," Yamakiri said nodding.

"Yes-as long as the heart is pure the blade will cut through all evil," Kasagi said.

Dharma stood up and walked across to another group and began showing them something.

After Dharma's explanation Yamakiri searched his heart, making sure it was clear and free of any bad intention.

-* -

In Kyoto, Ryushin had taken Takauji and his men to Kazanin palace to see his captive Go-Daigo. He opened the small panel on the door so that Takauji could see the Emperor. He could see him sitting on his bed, looking back at the door. Quickly he slid the panel back and turned to Ryushin.

"You have done well, Yakushimaru. I will take him from here," he said, about to open the latch.

Ryushin pushed his hand away.

"He is not yours until I receive my payment," Ryushin protested, staring back at Takauji.

"Yes, of course," Takauji replied, reaching into his shirt and pulling out a scroll tied by a red silk ribbon.

Ryushin pulled it off and unravelled the scroll, reading it as he did so.

"What is this?" he demanded, looking up.

"It is your payment as you asked, Yakushimaru," Takauji responded insistently.

It was the title to a large area of land. However, it was not in the north as he had asked for, instead it was to the south in the Iga province.

"This is not what we agreed, Takauji," Ryushin said angrily.

"You asked for land, you didn't say where," Takauji responded.

He was correct, Ryushin had never stipulated exactly where he wanted this land. It was obvious that Takauji had given him this to ensure that he remained loyal, and with having Go-Daigo under arrest all of the mainland would now be under his control.

Ryushin knew it was futile to argue with Takauji. He had worked hard to ensure things went his way and was not about make more work for himself.

Takauji pulled another scroll from his shirt.

"This is from the new *Shogun,* decreeing your right to this land. You will have no argument with my name at the bottom of this," he said, pointing to it.

Yamakiri scoffed to himself at the sheer arrogance of this man. He was only in the position he was in with his help.

"Very well, he is yours now," Ryushin said, opening the latch on the door and moving to the side.

Takauji pushed the door open and marched into the small room. The look on Go-Daigo's face was one of shock and surprise. He knew who Ryushin had been working for and why he was there, but the reality struck at the sight of this man.

"You are not so powerful now are you, Go-Daigo?" Takauji said angrily.

Go-Daigo said nothing.

"Well?" he asked, prompting for an answer.

As he looked up Takauji punched him in the side of the face, sending him sliding off his bed and onto the floor.

Seeing this from the door, Ryushin leapt into the room.

"What are you doing? You said he would not be harmed," Ryushin said, protesting.

Takauji lashed out with his arm, sending Ryushin backwards into his guards, who restrained him.

"What I do with him is my business, Yakushimaru. I have a debt to settle that does not concern you, he said, lunging forward and kicking Go-Daigo in the stomach. He moaned as the kick sunk deep into his midriff.

"Best you leave now-you have your payment. See him out," he said to his guards.

They pulled him out through the narrow doorway and into the courtyard. His men had also been grouped together and were being held at bay by Takauji's *Samurai*. The line parted as Ryushin was pushed into his men.

He turned around to see Takauji standing in the doorway.

"Go, before I have my men arrest you as well."

"Come," Ryushin whispered to his men. "This is not the time to fight," he turned and led them out of the main gates.

His thoughts turned to Go-Daigo. He felt betrayed by Takauji and didn't trust him with the Emperor. He was angry at himself for not seeing Takauji's true intention and was unsure how far this man would go. He sensed the feeling of power had consumed him and even though Go-Daigo posed a threat to Takauji's bid for control, he was beginning to have doubts that his assistance in this plan may not have been the best move. For now he needed time to collect his thoughts. Turning to his men, he instructed them to head north and back to Kamakura, while Ryushin turned and headed up into the mountains.

Chapter 49

Kusunoki had observed from a distance the demonstration by one of the *Sohei*. Although he had employed the *Ninja* before, he was not convinced that this was the best way to overcome his opponent. However, this was a very different situation.

He had already witnessed Ryushin's methods and painfully conceded that this was a warrior who understood more than just how to fight; he knew how people thought. What was even more disturbing was the control he could exercise over people's minds. As he looked at Kito Harada, he found it hard to accept that he had no recollection of the past and what he had done.

His thoughts were interrupted by the appearance of Dharma and Kasagi.

"Master Kusunoki, Dharma has a question for you," Kasagi said, looking back at the Tibetan.

"Ask your question," he said.

"Dharma wants to know if you believe in the afterlife," Kasagi asked carefully.

Kusunoki thought for a moment before answering. He was unsure why he was being asked such a question.

"Yes, why do you ask?"

Dharma spoke to Kasagi for some time before Kasagi responded, as if explaining something to him based on Kusunoki's response.

"Well, it appears that Ryushin is not alone in his work. He has some assistance from an entity that harbours a grudge against you," Kasagi said.

Kusunoki was taken aback by what Kasagi had said. He wasn't completely sure his answer was as honest as it could be; he was aware of the existence of spirits, but these were more in the form of the *Shinto* gods, not ghosts, as it were.

"This entity, what is the nature of it?" he asked sceptically.

"Apparently it is someone who died as a result of your actions," Kasagi responded.

"You will be asked to go into battle in the near future, but Dharma strongly advises against it."

Kusunoki didn't want to hear any more. He had been responsible for the deaths of hundreds of adversaries over the years and understood the *Karma* in interfering with someone's life. He had resigned himself to the fact that whatever he did, he would be judged for it at the end of his life.

"Enough!" he said, "Please leave me to eat in peace." He returned to his food and purposefully ignored the men. He looked up as they walked away, feeling uncomfortable with the warning he had just been given.

Several hours had passed as the training continued. Kusunoki had retired to his hut, when there was a call from the guard on the gate. "Someone is approaching!"

"Who is it?" Yamakiri called back.

There was a pause as the guard waited to get a better opportunity to identify the person.

"It appears to be Ryushin Yakushimaru," he said tentatively.

Yamakiri looked back at Kito and the *Sohei*. "Take your positions-prepare for attack!" he shouted.

The men positioned themselves around the perimeter, but instead of their usual defensive positions most of them hid themselves, following the training from Dharma that it was more difficult for a combatant to engage his enemy if he couldn't see them.

Yamakiri and Kito scaled the ladder to the rampart to see a solitary figure standing outside the gate. Yamakiri scanned the surrounding trees for signs of his men, keeping his head low in case he was fired upon.

"I come alone!" Ryushin shouted up to the men.

For a moment there was silence. After the last assault on the fortress with Go-Daigo being kidnapped, they were not about to drop their guard.

"What do you think, Kito?" he said, turning to his friend.

"I am not sure," he responded.

"Why do you come here?" Yamakiri shouted over the wall.

By this stage Kusunoki had heard the commotion and had made his way to the gate.

"What is going on?" he asked Kito from below.

"It is Yakushimaru, Master, he is outside the gate," Kito whispered.

"I want to speak with Kusunoki," Ryushin replied.

"How do we know this is not one of your tricks, Yakushimaru?" Yamakiri shouted back nervously.

Ryushin jumped off his horse and removed his jacket.

"Look, I am unarmed and alone," he said, waving his hands behind him.

"Please, I need to talk to Kusunoki; it is about the Emperor Go-Daigo."

"He asks to speak with you about Go-Daigo, Master," Yamakiri relayed his request.

Kusunoki believed he knew what Ryushin wanted; to discuss some form of ransom with him to get the Emperor back.

"Alright, let him in, but make sure he is secured first," Kusunoki said to Yamakiri.

With that, Yamakiri waved several of the *Sohei* up into position behind the gate, organising them in a semi-circle.

"Keep an eye on him," he said to the men on the parapet that now had their bows trained on him.

Yamakiri jumped down off the wall, followed by Kito. As Dharma and Kasagi approached he waved them over.

"Kasagi, ask Dharma if he can sense any danger before we open the gates," Yamakiri said. Kasagi nodded and turned to Dharma to explain Yamakiri's request. In response Dharma closed his eyes and weaved his fingers together in a *Kuji-in* posture, uttering several incantations.

"Ok," he said, opening his eyes wide.

"Is he sure?" Kusunoki asked.

"Yes, yes," Dharma responded.

Yamakiri looked back at Kusunoki for approval.

"Alright, but I still want him secured; I do not trust him at all."

With that, Yamakiri slowly pried the gate open just enough for him and Kito to squeeze through. They crouched down as they moved outside, ready to react at any sign of an attack. As Yamakiri moved out, he looked up to ensure the archers still had Ryushin in their aim.

"That is not necessary," Ryushin said, showing his open palms as a sign of openness and submission.

Immediately both men leapt in and secured each of his arms, pushing him face first into the ground. At the same time keeping an eye on the trees for anything unusual. Kito removed a piece of rope from his jacket and bound Ryushin's wrists together and then lifted him onto his feet, leading him and his horse towards the now open gate.

Ryushin said nothing as he was led inside where he was immediately surrounded by armed *Sohei*. Kito pushed him down onto his knees.

Kusunoki stepped forward through the circle to confront him.

"What do you want? What is this about Go-Daigo?" he asked angrily.

"Go-Daigo is in grave danger," he responded.

This comment did not surprise Kusunoki, he knew that Takauji would not want him around if he wanted complete control.

"And you were the one who put him there!" Yamakiri said from behind Kusunoki.

"I was promised by Takauji that he would not be harmed after I handed him over, but I have seen that that was a lie. Takauji betrayed me," Ryushin said wearily.

"Betrayed you? You have betrayed the Emperor and the *Shogunate*!" Kusunoki responded, his anger growing.

"Wait please, this is not making sense," Kito interjected. "What is more, if Go-Daigo is in danger as he says, then we do not have time to stand here arguing."

Yamakiri turned and ushered Dharma to come forward.

"Ask him to find out if he is telling the truth," he said to Kasagi.

After Kasagi spoke to him, he moved forward and placed his hand on his forehead.

"Yes, yes, much danger," he said, turning to Kusunoki.

"He is telling the truth, Yamakiri," Kasagi said.

"You have still not answered my question about why you are here," Kusunoki asked.

"I need your help to rescue Go-Daigo," he said remorsefully.

"What, you are asking for our help?"

"I cannot do it alone. I sent all of my men back to Kamakura."

There was a stirring on the parapet above the gate.

" Master, someone else is approaching; it is an old lady."

Yamakiri turned and made his way to the gate. "Open it up," he ordered the guards.

As he stepped outside he saw an elderly woman run towards him. She appeared exhausted, as if she had run up the mountain.

"Please, please, I need to speak with Master Kusunoki, "she said between breaths, nearly collapsing at his feet.

Supporting her, Yamakiri assisted her inside to where Kusunoki was still standing over Ryushin.

"Master, please excuse me," she said, bowing in respect.

"I have heard a terrible thing. The tyrant Takauji has captured Emperor Go-Daigo and has declared that he is going to put him to death tomorrow morning at first light," she said collapsing on the ground.

"How do you know this?" Kusunoki asked.

"Takauji paraded him through the streets pulling him behind his horse like a captured animal. He announced that his execution would take place in the square outside Arashiyama Palace and that everyone had to be there to witness it," she continued, as the tears ran down her face.

"See what you have done!" Kusunoki said, angrily lunging at Ryushin. Yamakiri stepped in and restrained him.

"Please, Master, we will need his help," he said respectfully.

"Do you know where he was taken?" Kito asked.

"To the palace, I followed them there," she said.

"Most of my men are in Otsu, it would take more than a day to assemble them and have them battle ready," Kusunoki said.

"With all respect, Master, I believe with Yakushimaru's help we can rescue the Emperor," Yamakiri said, looking down at Ryushin.

Kusunoki was obviously angry at the insinuation that his troops would not be good enough to rescue Go-Daigo, but he was well aware that if Takauji was put under pressure he would not hesitate to kill him prematurely.

"Very well, do what you have to. I will send a messenger to have my men prepare and start making their way to Kyoto," he said, walking away.

Ryushin looked up at his captors as a tear ran down his face.

"I am sorry for this," he said remorsefully.

"So am I," Yamakiri responded angrily, crouching down and reluctantly untying Ryushin.

-* -

At Arashiyama Palace Takauji handed Go-Daigo a tray with food on it. The battered man looked up, his face swollen from the series of beatings he had received at the hands of Takauji.

"Best you eat this and enjoy your last day as Emperor," Takauji said, smiling.

Go-Daigo refused to respond to anything Takauji threw at him. However, he knew that Takauji had made a mistake parading him around the town and announcing his imminent execution. He had the love and support of many people there and knew that word would get back to those who could rescue him.

Frustrated by Go-Daigo's lack of response, he reached into the box he had brought into the room and pulled out an old looking scroll.

"All I need is this to prove my position as *Shogun*," he said, unravelling the document.

It was part of the three treasures of the imperial house and had been handed down to Go-Daigo by his ancestors and predecessors, or so Takauji thought. However, he was unaware that these were fake and worthless.

Knowing this, Go-Daigo smiled to himself. If he was successfully put to death, at least he was confident that the illegitimate rule of Takauji could be held into question and when challenged, he would have nothing to substantiate it.

Chapter 50

Ryushin Yakushimaru knew he had a lot to answer for and so proceeded with a great deal of trepidation. Kito had assembled the large force of *Sohei* together and stood at the front with Kito, Yamakiri, and Ryushin.

"Some of you will know this man and I am sure you seek revenge for what he has done, but at present we have more pressing concerns. Go-Daigo will be executed tomorrow morning if we do not rescue him. Furthermore the lineage of the imperial family will be decimated, leaving this country without a representative of god. We must not let this happen!" Yamakiri shouted.

"You have been training for such a mission and I am confident with Ryushin's assistance we can be successful," he continued, looking across at him.

"I am responsible for this mess and I need to fix it," Ryushin said remorsefully. "Now is not the time to pass judgment on me: I will stand before my god for that, as we all do. Now is the time to act and to put things right. My plan is to infiltrate the town tonight and be in place ready for tomorrow morning. I need to speak with each of the group's commanders and run through my plan, the rest of you need to ensure you have eaten well and are fit. We will assemble at dusk to depart for Kyoto," Ryushin said, looking back at Kusunoki, who was waiting to the side.

As they disassembled, Seiko stopped Ryushin, taking hold of his arm. She had been silent until now; observing and seemingly ignoring him.

"I cannot believe you had the audacity to come here and ask for help after everything that you have done," she said angrily.

"Why do you find it so hard to believe? No man or woman is devoid of a conscience and I am well aware that my actions have caused pain and suffering. Do you not think it would only be right to try and make amends for these?" he asked.

Seiko shook her head.

"Well, I hope your plan to rescue Go-Daigo works, if it doesn't the entire landscape of this country will be changed forever. What is more, I am sure there will be many a man who will hold you to account for it, myself included," she said.

"This is not the time for threats. I am well aware of my responsibilities," he said, walking off and joining the small group of monks assembled with Kusunoki behind them.

"Chi, Sui, Ka, Fu he said pointing to the respective group commanders," each nodding as he pointed to them.

"We will infiltrate the crowd and ensure a presence in the square, also enlisting as many of the townsfolk as we can for their assistance. As soon as we see Go-Daigo, we need to act, but only on my signal. Timing here is essential."

"He will be heavily guarded," Kito interjected.

"Yes, of course he will, but only by *Samurai,"* Ryushin responded, looking across at Kusunoki, who was busy briefing the messenger he was about to send to Otsu.

"As you are probably aware, their greatest weakness is that most of them seek power through capturing the fear of the people, hence the decision to carry out a public execution. So here is my plan," Ryushin added, running through the detail of the mission to each of the *Sohei* commanders. After he finished a series of orders and diagrams on the ground, he excused himself.

"Now please, I would like some time to pray to my ancestors for help. We can meet here again at dusk," he said, turning and walking towards the largest temple in the complex.

He was well aware that his mother, Chigusa-hime, had made a pilgrimage to this very temple to pray to Yakushi Buddha to assist in his conception. As a result of this success, he was given his name after the Buddha and *'Maru'* was added to mean 'something precious'. In some way he saw this as symbolic of his re-birth and believed that fate had led him to this point. Lighting the incense, he closed his eyes and joined his ancestors.

"How do we really know we can trust this man?" Kusunoki asked Yamakiri and Kito.

"I do not see we have any option, Master," Yamakiri responded.

"I believe he is sincere in his remorse," Kito replied.

"Well, I remain wary. I have met his type before."

"His type, you mean *Ninja?*" Yamakiri asked.

"It was not that long ago that you employed the same type of people to overthrow Sakamura, the Daimyo of Iga," Yamakiri reminded him. "I know how guilt can eat away at you, making you a slave to its power."

Kusunoki thought back to the last time he had seen Yamakiri. He was a lot younger then and had been deeply affected by the accident at Ueno, he knew exactly what he had been referring to. Then he looked at Kito and recalled how he had changed under Yakushimaru's spell. 'Who can you really trust?' he thought to himself.

As the sun slipped behind the mountains above Kyoto, everyone assembled in the large courtyard.

"Is everyone absolutely sure of what they are to do?" Yamakiri asked, looking back at Ryushin.

"*Hai!*" came the response en-masse.

"Good, it is time for the first group to move then," he said, ushering Yamakiri and his men towards the gate.

Kusunoki stood on the steps of his hut and watched them depart, acknowledging Yamakiri as he ran past with his men close behind. Although there were around 20 men, he couldn't hear a sound as they passed by, as if they were floating on air.

Watanabe's group were close behind them. Their role was to establish a forward position in which they could conceal everyone until the appropriate time. As intended they were to wait at the bottom of the mountain path, concealed in the trees and undergrowth for the signal from Yamakiri to advance.

At the same time Kito's group would take another route down the mountain to assemble on the outskirts of the town, the shortest distance from the square. There they would wait until the morning, again until the appropriate time.

Finally Ryushin and his group would follow Watanabe's and lay in wait until early morning, for them it was critical to get to the front of the crowd, as they would be spearheading the rescue.

Yamakiri and his men moved through the near deserted streets, staggering their advance and breaking anything that could be discerned as a logical rhythm. Some walked casually, as if taking a stroll, while shadowing others, who would advance upon a pre-decided signal to the next shadow or hiding position. Like the tentacles of large octopus, they made their way into the depths of the town. Their goal was a large house that was owned by Kusunoki and which was presently vacant. Once Yamakiri had entered, he signalled back through the line for Watanabe and his group to advance. Again they staggered their approach, awaiting the signals to advance from Yamakiri's men.

Once the last person was safely inside the house Yamakiri moved into the second phase of his mission, this time to secure a route deeper into the town and nearer the square for Ryushin's group. This part of the mission would be more difficult as Takauji had stationed most of his men around the palace where Go-Daigo was being held.

However Ryushin was a master of invisibility and as he made his approach, he glided effortlessly through the streets and over the rooftops. Where possible he instructed his men to replace Takauji's guards with his own, well aware that the further they were from Go-Daigo, the less significant their skills and familiarity with their commander. It had been planned that half of the group would assume the disguise of *Samurai* and the rest of common folk. So the rest dropped silently into yards and pulled clothing drying off lines, disappearing back into the darkness to conceal themselves until the signal was given.

Once enough time had passed, Watanabe moved out with his group. His was the largest with around 45 men. They would need to be some of the last to arrive in the morning and needed to stage themselves around the southern side of the square.

After several hours, everyone was in place. The town remained relatively quiet, a good sign that their positions had not been compromised. The preparation had been well rehearsed and with Ryushin's input and experience, was exactly as they had planned. Now it was a matter of waiting for the right moment to swing into action.

-* -

Meanwhile, inside Arashiyama Palace Go-Daigo was alone in his room. As he looked around he admired the artwork he had once commissioned from one of the region's top painters. It was a scene depicting a battle several centuries earlier; the flickering of candle light seemed to bring the painting alive, as if the characters had somehow materialised into the physical realm.

His room was high above the courtyard, with a small window which overlooked the town and on a good day framed Mt Hiei. Takauji had the palace well-guarded and knew Go-Daigo had no chance of escape. Go-Daigo believed his fate was sealed; Takauji had taken great pleasure in announcing his execution the next morning. As Go-Daigo turned to look out the open window, a shadow concealed the stars and lights beyond it as a black mass poured through it, like thick molasses onto the floor. He leered back as the mass transformed into a human form, illuminated by the soft candle light.

"Shhh, please," came a quiet whisper.

"Who are you?" Go-Daigo whispered back.

The figure took of his hood and revealed himself, it was Ryushin.

"Please, I don't have much time. We are preparing to rescue you from Takauji tomorrow and need your co-operation."

Go-Daigo was shocked at Ryushin's suggestion and struggled to comprehend what he was saying.

"Please, just follow my directions as I give them and you will be safe, do you understand?" he asked.

But before he could respond, there was a rattling on the other side of the door as the heavy latch was unbolted. Go-Daigo turned to see who it was and then looked back to warn Ryushin, but where he had been there was now empty space; he had disappeared back into the darkness.

As the door swung open, he saw the Takauji standing there.

"How does it feel to know this is your last night on earth, Go-Daigo?" he asked arrogantly.

Go-Daigo knew that the only reason for this visit was to torment him before his execution, but he was not going to be goaded into responding. He was well aware of the skills Ryushin Yakushimaru had, even though he was confused about how he had decided to change roles and affect a rescue.

"It will feel good to be out of your company Takauji," he finally responded, intentionally alluding to his acceptance of his fate, but knowing better.

Chapter 51

The distinct sound of a solitary crow broke the early morning silence in the streets of Kyoto. This was followed by a crescendo of responses from other parts of the town, slicing through the briskness of a soon-to-be new day.

In the large courtyard, Yamakiri watched as his men prepared for the mission; some were talking away to themselves, others in prayer.

As he climbed up the ladder to the rooftop, he saw the tip of the sun rise over the mountain and also observed the unmistakable group of Ryushin's men begin their advance, purposely keeping their distance from one another. Their goal was the front row of the platform where Go-Daigo would be executed.

Already many of the townspeople had risen and were making their way into the square. Not out of some macabre fascination to see their Emperor executed, but out of fear of becoming victims themselves, should they not attend. After all, this was something that Takauji wanted as many people as possible to witness and he wanted to send out a signal that there would be no turning back once he had assumed control.

The next part of the plan was for Watanabe to move his men into position. They would position themselves at the back of the crowd and provide not only a barrier for any pursuing *Samurai,* but also to channel them right to Kito's waiting group.

Finally Yamakiri's group was to provide support for the escape of Go-Daigo; they were the last to move out into the street and into position.

In the middle of the square there was a specially built platform for Takauji to carry out the execution. The crowd was thick as expected, it seemed as if everyone in the town was in attendance. They didn't have to wait long before the gates to the palace

opened, revealing a large group with Takauji at the front, flanked
by his men. As they walked across the bridge, Yamakiri could
see Go-Daigo, guarded by several ranks of *Naginata* and *Yari
Samurai*. Arriving at the platform the *Samurai* spread out across
the base as Takauji led Go-Daigo up the small flight of steps,
adding to his humiliation by leading him like a dog on a leash.

Several of Ryushin's men were standing facing outwards
disguised as *Samurai* supposedly guarding the platform. Directly
in front were more of his men, with Ryushin in the centre.
Yamakiri looked back to find Watanabe. At first he was hard to
make out, then Yamakiri realised the large woman about five
rows behind him was in fact his cousin. Watanabe nodded to
acknowledge his readiness.

Yamakiri made eye contact with Ryushin as he turned, signalling
his own readiness with a nod. As they watched Takauji, they
waited for the moment where he was in position and had
commenced his speech.

As soon as he opened his mouth everyone swung into action.
Ryushin leapt onto the platform, followed by his men, while
Yamakiri's men formed two lines to facilitate Go-Daigo's escape
by opening up a corridor for his extraction. At the same time,
Watanabe and his men formed a human wall around the crowd
to contain them.

As Ryushin ran at Takauji he jumped up and kicked him in the
chest, sending him flying backwards and onto the ground as one
of his men threw a *Naginata* to him. Swiftly Ryushin cut the rope
securing Go-Daigo and shouted to him – "Go, go!"

Without hesitation he led Go-Daigo off the platform past
Yamakiri and along the narrow corridor of men, which quickly
closed as they passed. Meanwhile, Ryushin's men were engaged
with Takauji's guards in a violent confrontation, their goal was to
give Yamakiri and Go-Daigo time to escape.

Takauji had risen to his feet and as he saw the Emperor disappearing into the street, ordered for his men to follow. Ryushin had retreated into the crowd and made his way through the confusion to the back, where Watanabe was still blocking people from escaping.

As Yamakiri passed by a doorway he ducked in, pulling the Emperor with him. At the same time Kito, who was dressed in similar clothes, pulled Go-Daigo's robe off him and gave it to the large monk beside him. Appearing as the two escaping men, she purposely moved him in sight of Takauji, who was scanning the crowd.

"There!" he shouted. "Don't let them escape!"

His men responded, jumping off the platform and in the direction of the fleeing Kito and decoy as expected, ruthlessly cutting down anyone in their way in the process.

"Get my horse!" Takauji shouted to one of the guards behind him.

Yamakiri looked out into the street and saw that Watanabe now had it blocked. He led Go-Daigo to one of his men and waiting horses.

"Come Master, we must go south as quickly as possible."

"South-would we not be better to head into the mountains?"

"No, that would be far too obvious. We have organised a safe haven for you in Yoshino," Yamakiri responded.

Go-Daigo was not about to question what Yamakiri was saying, he was just grateful that he had been rescued.

Behind them, Kito had successfully led Takauji's pursuing men in the opposite direction of the real Emperor and towards the mountain pass to Enryaku-Ji. However, as they crossed the last bridge before the pass arrows rained down on them from all directions, the ploy to ambush them a complete success. Some of the archers jumped onto the road wearing *Tengu* masks designed to scare the *Samurai*. Many of Takauji's men surrendered after realising it had been a trap, others retreated, frightened off by the half man-half bird grotesque figures.

As Takauji caught up to some of the retreating men, he yelled "What are you doing!"

The look of fear on their faces was enough to dissuade him from advancing, no sooner had he stopped than he heard the loud rumble of approaching horses. Turning to his left he saw a wall of stampeding *Samurai* led by Masashige Kusunoki. Unprepared for battle, he ordered his men back to the palace. When they arrived the gates were shut. The *Sohei* had stormed the palace and taken it over-he had no option but to continue his retreat out of the town.

On the outskirts of the town, Yamakiri waited for the arrival of Ryushin and Watanabe. Together they would provide an escort for Go-Daigo to Yoshino.

As they waited, Go-Daigo looked across to Yamakiri and said "Thank you-you saved my life."

Yamakiri acknowledged his gratitude by bowing and then turned to look at the two horsemen approaching.

"Ryushin is the one you need to thank, Master. It was his plan to rescue you."

As they caught up, Ryushin smiled.

"Come Master, we have to keep moving," he said, slapping his *Naginata* on the flank of his horse and leading them down the road towards Osaka.

Chapter 52

Ryushin led the group along the deserted road towards Osaka. Coming to a fork, they turned and made their way up the steep incline towards Kuragari pass, the shortest route over the mountains to Iga province.

After riding for just over an hour and rounding a sharp bend near the summit, they were suddenly confronted by a blockade of *Samurai*. At the front was Tadayoshi Ashikaga. He had been alerted to Go-Daigo's escape and suspected that he may try to make it to Iga and the protection of the mountain locked valley.

"Ah-what a surprise it is to see you Ryushin, and the company you are now keeping!" he called from across the space.

"You didn't think you could get away that easily, did you?"

"Get out of our way and none of you shall come to any harm!" Ryushin called back confidently.

Tadayoshi laughed loudly, mocking the small group as it opposed his much larger force.

"I have ten thousand men behind me and you have, what, four? Should I be worried?"

Yamakiri stirred in his saddle and made his way to Ryushin.

"What are we going to do?" he whispered out of the side of his mouth.

"We cannot let them get to the Emperor," He responded quietly.

"Your brother is presently on the run from Kusunoki and might like some company!" Ryushin shouted back.

Before Tadayoshi had time to respond, Ryushin rode closer, leapt off his horse and strode up to his adversary. Yamakiri followed him, Watanabe turned and said to Go-Daigo, "Stay behind us, Master," and also rode forward, dismounting.

Tadayoshi shook his head. "You fools-attack them!" he shouted, urging his men forward.

Ryushin spun his *Naginata,* blocking and delivering several well targeted counter-attacks to Tadayoshi's men as they advanced. In the meantime, Yamakiri and Watanabe did the same with their swords, cutting down each advancing man's horse and causing a pile up in the middle of the narrow track. Knowing the area well, Ryushin had chosen the route for this very reason. Behind Tadayoshi there was no other way through as the pass snaked through a deep ravine, so as long as he dealt with each immediate threat, he knew they could only advance in threes at best. As one of the *Samurai* attacked him and he attempted to block the cut, he lost the blade of his weapon, leaving him with only a *Bo* staff. Moving backwards and breathing deeply, he presented the *Ishizuka,* the butt of the weapon, to his attackers and began tracing various figures in the air at the same time uttering a series of incantations. Instantly Tadayoshi's forces halted their attack, as if frozen on the spot. Go-Daigo and the others looked on in disbelief as Ryushin single handedly held back the attack with nothing more than his magic.

Tadayoshi issued the order to advance, but to no avail. Furthermore, as Ryushin walked forward over and around the dead and injured, he started pushing Tadayoshi and his men back down the mountain path towards Iga.

"Come, follow me!" he called to the men behind.

As he continued his advance, several of Tadayoshi's men were pushed off a high bluff, toppling both men and horses end over end to their deaths.

"I will give you two choices-retreat or die!" he shouted to Tadayoshi.

Seeing his forces in disarray, Tadayoshi had no option but to sound the retreat.

Ryushin halted and watched the chaos as Tadayoshi and his men turned around and slowly made their way back down the treacherous pass.

Go-Daigo caught up to Ryushin.

"What was that? What did you do?"

"A technique passed on in my family-it is the secret art of Kuji," he responded.

After a brief wait they cautiously made their way down the mountain. Nearing the bottom they heard the battle horns of an approaching force from the south. It was reinforcements from Yoshino. This hurried Tadayoshi's defeat, sending them hastily retreating to the north.

As they reached the bottom of the pass, the reinforcements caught up with them.

Seeing the last of Tadayoshi's military disappear over the hill, the commander looked at the men, and recognising Go-Daigo, leapt off his horse, followed by the rest of his men.

"Please, these are the men you should be respecting-they saved my life," he said, smiling back at them.

"Yes of course, Master," the commander said, looking up.

"We are here to provide a safe escort to Yoshino for you," he added.

"These are all the men I need to be safe," he said tapping Ryushin and Yamakiri on the shoulders.

However, Yamakiri had other plans.

"If it is all the same master-I would like to take leave and return back to my village, my cousin and I have much to catch up on," Yamakiri said bowing and looking back at Watanabe.

Watanabe was taken aback by this comment, but knew that he had his family waiting for him back in Aoyama.

"Ah yes, if that is ok with you master?" Watanabe asked, excusing himself as well.

"Hmm-well I suppose I still have the security of Ryushin and these men. Yes, do as you must," he said nodding in approval.

"Thank you master," they both said in unison bowing.

Yamakiri pulled his horses reins and looked back at Watanabe- he did the same and together they rode off in the direction of the mountains and home, sending a cloud of dust bellowing out behind them.

The commander and his men mounted their horses-"shall we go master?" he asked, as Go-Daigo watched Yamakiri and Watanabe disappear over the hill on the road.

"Yes of course-lead on," Go-Daigo said, as his horse stirred.

The commander lead off the procession followed closely behind by Ryushin and Go-Daigo.

However, as he followed, he noticed that there was something strange about the way in which the so-called commander was riding. His style was not that of someone who had been schooled in the military ways of horsemanship-something just didn't seem right.

As if sensing his identity was in question, the commander suddenly turned around to face him. To Ryushin's surprise, he saw not a human face, but the grotesque features of something he had never seen before-the commander had a scaly face with an elongated nose and slits for eyes. Ryushin reached for his *Katana,* but seeing this, the commander's eyes lit up, the slits emitting an iridescent red light followed by an invisible force that struck Ryushin hard in the chest sending him flying backwards off his horse and pinning him to the ground.

Go-Daigo stared in shock at what had just happened and looking up the commander saw the same face that had surprised Ryushin only seconds before. Suddenly he felt his arms being seized and looked around to see a man at each side holding them tight.

"What is this?" he protested.

"You are now my prisoner Go-Daigo," the commander said as his face changed back to that of a human.

"As for you-I suggest you don't try to follow me or attempt any of your *Ninjutsu* on me-you would need far more than that to rescue the emperor. Oh-and thank you for delivering him to me, for that I will spare your life," he said, pulling his horse away in the opposite direction and urging his men to follow.

Ryushin knew better than to try to follow him-the power and nature of this person was far more than anything he had ever encountered. He would need to buy his time and prepare himself first.

Meanwhile as Yamakiri and Watanabe headed back towards the mountains and home, they couldn't but help notice a change in the sky above them-as if a storm was forming. Little did they know that this was a sign that things were about to change for the worst.

Epilogue

After being captured Go-Daigo established the Southern court from Yoshino, with Takauji ruling the northern court from Kyoto-this became the period known as the Nanboku-chō period.

However, it was obvious to some that he was not acting alone or of his own volition, the situation orchestrated by those disinterested in ruling or making peace-their mission was much more indulgent.

In hearing of the advance of Takauji , Go-Daigo ordered Kusunoki and Yoshisada to engage him in battle at Minotogawa, although Kusunoki protested against this, believing they would surely be defeated; instead recommending that they let Takauji back into Kyoto, using the Sohei from Mt Hiei to destroy him-however Go-Daigo was insistent that he confront him. Epitomising his loyalty to his master, Kusunoki proceeded under orders – as predicted , Kusunoki and Yoshisada were defeated at Minotogawa and as a result, Kusunoki committed *Sepukku*.

Yamakiri returned to his village of Aoyama, with his cousin Watanabe, to pursue his goal of becoming a Yamabushi. However, as they were to discover, there were forces that had driven the balance of power in a direction that was threaten the balance between good and evil.

After helping drive Takauji out of Kyoto, Kito Harada returned to Enryaku-Ji and then made his way back to his hillside retreat near Ueno. However, as he was to find, peace was not long lived and he would once again find himself caught up in the chaos of war.

Ryushin Yakushimaru retreated to the mountains and trained hard to develop the *Kukishinden Ryu*-the Nine Demon Gods School. From his encounter with Go-Daigo's capturer he realised that he needed more than physical technique to defeat such an opponent.

Character List

Name	Description	Comment
Yamakiri	Main character	Was Kansai Tokugawa
Kito Harada	Old friend of Yamakiri	Helped to liberate Iga
Go-Daigo	Emperor	Based in Kyoto
Masashige Kusunoki	Go-Daigo's Samurai Leader	Loyal to Go-Daigo
Takauji Ashikaga	Minamoto Samurai Leader	Based in Kamakura
Tadayoshi Ashikaga	Minamoto Samurai Leader	Takauji's brother
Prince Morinaga	Go-Daigo's Son	Abbot of Hieizan Temple
Nitta Yoshisada	Go-Daigo's Samurai	One of Go-Daigo's top Samurai
Ryushin Yakushimaru	Ninja	Hired by Takauji Ashikaga
Seiko	Kunoichi (Female Ninja)	Was married to Kito Harada
Watanabe Yamada	Yamakiri's cousin	From Aoyama Village
Mariko Yamada	Watanabe's wife	From Aoyama Village

Glossary

Term	Meaning	Term	Meaning
Bo	Staff	Karma	Cause and Effect
Bokken	Wooden Sword	Kata	Set of techniques
Budo	Way of the warrior	Kiai	Shout
Bujutsu	Art of the warrior	Kimono	Woman's dress
Bushido	Code of the warrior	Kokoro	Heart
chi, sui, ka, fu	Earth, Water, Fire, Wind	Kuji	Magic
Chi-mon	Geography	Kunai	Digging tool
Chitsumushi	Concealed Spy	Kunoichi	Female Ninja
Chunin	Middle Ninja Rank	Mantra	Incantation
Daimyo	Lord	Menkyo Kaiden	Masters license
Dojo	Martial Arts training place	Menpou	Face Mask
Fudo Myoo	The immovable god	Mikkyo	Magic from Tibet
Futon	Japanese bed	Miso	Soup
Gambatte	Keep going	Misogi	Water purification
Genin	Ninja foot soldier	Mu	Empty
Hai	Yes	Nagare	Flow
Hakama	Samurai Pants	Naginata	Samurai Halberd
Haragei	Sixth Sense	Nichiyobi	Day of the Sun
Henka	Change	Ninjutsu	Art of Ninja
Hojo	Regent	Ninpo	Higher form of Ninjutsu
Iga	Province in Japan	Ohiroma	Audience Room
Ishizuka	Blunt end of a halberd	Ronin	Masterless Samurai

Term	Meaning	Term	Meaning
Kami	Spirit	Sutemi	Sacrifice
Kanji	Japanese Writing Style	Tamagotchi	Omelet
Kappa	Mythical Water creature	Tanto	Knife
Seppuku	Suicide	Tempura	Battered food
Shakujo	Yamabushi Staff	Tengai	Hat
Shinken	Sharp Sword	Tengu	Mythical Winged Man
Shinobi	Another name for Ninja	Tesson	Fan
Shinto	Japanese Religion	Tori	Gate
Shogun	Head of Government	Tsuka	Sword Guard
Shogunate	Government	Tsuki	Weakness
Shugendo	Yamabushi Ritual Practices	Sensei	Teacher
Shuriken	Throwing Star	Yamate	Stop
Shuto	Knife Hand Strike	Yari	Spear
Sionara	Goodbye	Yoroi	Armor
Sohei	Warrior Monk	Yaiba	Blade
Soke	Grand Master	Yamabushi	Mountain Asce